The

Hadassah

THE

Hadassah

Covenant

TOMMY TENNEY
and Mark Andrew Olsen

BETHANYHOUSE
MINNEAPOLIS, MINNESOTA

Published by Bethany House Publishers
11400 Hampshire Avenue South
Bloomington, Minnesota 55438

Bethany House Publishers is a division of
Baker Publishing Group, Grand Rapids, Michigan.

Printed in the United States of America

ISBN 0-7642-2736-X (Hardcover)
ISBN 0-7642-0103-4 (Large Print)
ISBN 0-7642-0119-0 (Audio CD)
ISBN 0-7642-0101-8 (Audio Cassette)
ISBN 0-7642-0102-6 (International Trade Paper)

Library of Congress Cataloging-in-Publication Data

Tenney, Tommy, 1956–
     The Hadassah covenant / Tommy Tenney & Mark Andrew Olsen.
          p.   cm.
     Summary: "This sequel to Hadassah parallels the lives of Hadassah and Queen Esther in modern-day Israel and the Persian kingdom. Each woman must remain strong as she fights for her people"—Provided by publisher.
     ISBN 0-7642-2736-X (hardback (not large print) : alk. paper) — ISBN 0-7642-0103-4 (large-print pbk.) 1. Women—Israel—Fiction. 2. Women—Iran—Fiction. 3. Israel—Fiction. 4. Iran—Fiction. I. Olsen, Mark Andrew. II. Title.
     PS3620.E56H326   2005
     813'.54—dc22
                                                                              2005022542

Dedications

Without fail I have always dedicated my books to my family or perhaps the surrogate family of my staff. After nearly a decade of being a published writer, I have come to realize something: I have an even larger family, the readers who have chosen to allow me into their homes and lives. It is to them I dedicate this book. The mere fact that this novel is a sequel is a testimony to my "adoptive" family's acceptance.

I have observed you, my readers, from an anonymous distance reading my musings. For that I am thankful. To be published is one thing; to be read is another.

Tommy Tenney

I would like to dedicate my efforts on this book to Dr. Leroy Patterson, beloved father to my wife Connie, Gran-Gran to our children, and the most consistent example a man could ever wish for in a father-in-law. Leroy served God faithfully for forty-eight years, and followed Him without waver for far longer. He was called home within weeks of his retirement. I hope I am as prepared when that call comes for me.

Mark Andrew Olsen

Acknowledgments

After a decade of being a published writer, I have come to the realization that the production of a book is the work of a team, not a solitary writer.

Tom Winters, whose legal skills and agent's expertise have protected me from the beginning.

Carol Johnson, with her fine eye and red pen, who helped hone the dull blade of an idea into a story.

Mark Olsen, whose patience and literary skills have turned my private musings into a published novel.

It is to a team like this I extend grateful acknowledgment.

Tommy Tenney

Cast of Characters

Modern

Hadassah ben Yuda — First Lady of Israel, wife to Prime Minister Jacob ben Yuda, daughter of David Kesselman.

Jacob ben Yuda — Prime Minister of Israel, husband to Hadassah and champion of Middle East peace.

David Kesselman — "Poppa" to Hadassah, survivor of Nazi occupation and Holocaust escapee.

Ari al-Khalid — aka Ari Meyer, aka Dr. Clive Osborn—British-born antiquities expert, adviser to the coalition campaign to save Iraqi artifacts, and possessor of several more covert identities.

Anek al-Khalid — London-based, Iraqi-born businessman and champion of exiled Jewish causes.

Ancient

Leah — beautiful, young, royal-blooded Jewish resident of Persia's royal harem, a queen's candidate. Recipient of Queen Esther's original journals (see *Hadassah: One Night With the King*).

Hadassah — Queen Regent of Persia, the former Queen Esther, widow of Xerxes and de facto mother of new King Artaxerxes.

Mordecai — Hadassah's cousin and adoptive "Poppa," Master of the Audiences to the king, second most powerful and beloved man in the empire.

Hathach/Jesse — the king's chamberlain, master of the harem. Hadassah's first love until he was taken to the palace and made a eunuch.

Artaxerxes — king of the Persian Empire following the assassination of his father, Xerxes.

Ezra — Jewish priest in exile, revivor of the Torah, and leader of the restoration of Jerusalem.

Nehemiah — royal cupbearer and leader of the rebuilding of Jerusalem.

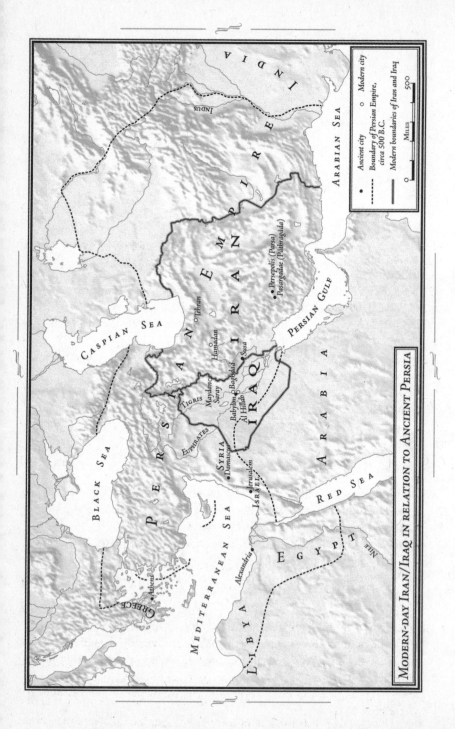

MODERN-DAY IRAN/IRAQ IN RELATION TO ANCIENT PERSIA

Chapter One

My Dearest Sister in Spirit Leah,

I write you in some anxiousness tonight. I even waited until after the sun had set and the shadows here in the harem had grown long, my candle had burned low, and the halls fell quiet. You may consider me overcautious, for even though my position in Persia as Queen Regent is an exalted one, no position is safe from danger right now. So I take up stylus in reply to the intriguing yet potentially dangerous information in your recent letter.

The rumors are true.

That is why, as much as I long to see you again and give you the warm embrace of a sister, it is too dangerous at the moment to see you in person. So I must write you from my quarters, even though we find ourselves behind the same palace walls.

Queen Mother Amestris, who as you know recently resurfaced as my palace nemesis, has posted her spies everywhere, and now even many of the guard have turned against me. There is so much rumor and so many threats spoken and unspoken. Most of what circulates about Commander Megabyzos, I am sorry to say, is true. Far from being a loyalist general, he is actually a hidden leader of the rebellion.

What's worse, I fear some of what they have said about my beloved Xerxes is true. I'm sure you also heard some of this gossip in ensuing years, but you never heard it from me—until now. How I wish he were here to explain his actions! All those lingering questions only compound the pain of my loneliness.

Nehemiah, along with our Jewish people's success with the return to Jerusalem and the rebuilding of the walls, has set everyone and everything in Persia on edge. As a result, I fear that even your painful predicament with the King and your politically motivated rejection have become guarded knowledge at court. Even passion must sometimes submit to politics, I fear. And the result is unrequited love. I know personally how much that hurts.

On top of all this, King Artaxerxes is in mortal peril, and as goes his fate, so will that of all the Jews. Do you recall your first letter to me, not so long ago? You began it with the words, "My dear friend, I am in trouble." Well tonight, my dear friend, I fear we are *all* in trouble.

Thinking of all of this, I feel an invisible band tighten about my heart. It almost feels like a return of the dark days I once wrote you about, the times of my own great dangers and sorrow. I feel that I risk my life every time I pass a cordon of the royal guardians, the Immortals, or even ordinary soldiers. My heart beats faster within me and I avert my gaze from theirs. For years I only felt security and comfort within the walls of the palace. Now I imagine that every time I venture into the innermost halls of the court I may well again stumble upon a headless body sprawled across a dais or a bodyguard holding a bloody scimitar. I try to consciously soften my breathing and unbolden my gaze, to make myself less recognized. Most of all, to conceal my inner defiance. But I saw far too much during those murderous days, and I can feel the fear return like a stench in the air.

As a result I now live under a self-imposed house arrest and dare not come to speak with you directly about this matter. That is why I asked Onesi to carry this to you herself. She is utterly trustworthy, I think you would agree, and knows all the back ways of the palace. I pray that she reaches you without being accosted or arousing suspicion.

Leah, you and I are very blessed to be able to communicate in this way—most unusual for women, as you know. My beloved Poppa certainly was going against tradition when he taught me to read and write as I was growing up. And your more recent tutelage has been most fortuitous, particularly now when it is dangerous for us to meet in person. You yourself must be so careful, even more so than your new confidant, my adopted father Mordecai, would urge. I'm afraid that as prudent as he has always been, even he is becoming bolder and less cautious of late than I would wish.

While protocol dictates that I sign this in my official capacity, our common blood covenant makes me long to close this simply as your sister, Hadassah. Sending this under the seal of Queen Regent may offer some small protection of respect were this letter to fall into the wrong hands.

I must go—please be careful and strong and obedient to G-d.

Your friend Esther, Queen Regent of Persia

Chapter Two

AL HILLAH, IRAQ—PRESENT DAY,
TWO IN THE MORNING, IRAQI TIME

The commandos struck precisely three minutes after the moon had melted across the desert horizon and plunged Al Hillah into a darkness nearly as sudden as the flicking of a switch.

Hours had passed since the day's last, fading echo of small-arms fire. Despite the late hour, Basra Street had only begun to cool, for even in autumn the Euphrates Valley remained a blistering cauldron—day or night. A stray dog pawed through gutter trash beneath the glow of a lone streetlamp. The scrawny beast was the only living thing along a sidewalk barren of all but two dented Mercedes and a dozen withered palm stumps.

The shadow of a nearby wall rippled across a row of camouflage-shirted chests and a row of tightly clasped guns. One of the faces, features smeared with black, leaned forward to glance up at a second-story window.

Nearly hidden by a parted curtain hovered the striking face of a young girl. Flawless light brown skin set off luminous green eyes, which searched the sidewalk until they finally met the commando leader's stare.

She started and her eyes widened. She gave an exaggerated nod and pointed almost shyly toward the other side of the street—

—toward a large white villa, shrouded in palm trees and thick bushes and encircled by a thick stucco wall.

The lovely face disappeared from the window. Leaning back, the commando leader pointed his thumb toward the villa and straightened a wire microphone around to his mouth. His barked order crackled in a dozen hidden earpieces.

"Sciopero!"

The dog cocked its head toward the sky and uttered a soft whine.

Less than a quarter mile away, a whir of rotor blades rose above the desert wind, and an A129 "Little Bird" Mongoose helicopter nudged its canopy over a jagged rooftop silhouette. The chopper's bubble window swiveled sideways, its pilot scanning the streetscape through twin, side-mounted infrared scopes.

The quiet of the street was shattered by the groan and a metallic shriek of a heavily chained gate crashing inward. The noise drew a shout from the home's balcony and the trademark staccato of a guard's Kalashnikov shooting on full automatic. From the opposite shadows, a single flash responded along with the *click* of a silenced gunshot. A low groan floated out—the guard's bulk flopped over the railing and plunged into deep bushes.

Shouts and a high wail rose from inside the sprawling Mediterranean-style villa. A light flicked on in an upstairs window while rumbles of falling furniture filled the air.

Then came a deafening crack. A battering ram had shattered the front door.

The camouflaged commandos holding Beretta semi-automatics raced in a crouch toward the open door's glare. Called *Viper 5*, they were the Italian Carabinieri's elite commando artifacts-recovery team—and they had breached their evening's target twelve seconds ahead of schedule.

At once the Mongoose shot up from its protective hover and was over Basra Street with a roar. The dog ran away, its howls muted by the descending thunder. Everything now seemed to happen with a stunning suddenness—the runners touched ground, men leaped from open doors, one of them in civilian garb, and the aircraft lifted away.

Another explosion, louder and heavier, lashed forward.

And the helicopter thrashed into pieces amidst a white-hot cloud of fire.

Flames billowed across the roadway. The chopper's metal carcass plummeted to earth, struck pavement, and flattened in a blinding spray of sparks and secondary detonations.

There were more screams, now rending the air in Italian, not Arabic. New splatters of automatic fire lit up corners of the property—a pinpoint counterattack, triggered by the rocket strike.

The civilian ducked away from the heat and launched himself across the trunk of the nearest parked sedan. The smoke and stench of burning fuel felt as though it was scorching his lungs. The air was so roasting hot he feared he would incinerate—flames pursued him over the barrier and licked at the back of his head as he landed hard and twisted his ankle in the opposite gutter. Panting heavily, he swerved around to a new fear—he had now exposed himself to sniper fire from the open driveway. With a single leap, he lunged toward the shelter of the wall and huddled against its pitted plaster.

A long barrage of automatic fire pummeled his ears. The fighting was growing more fierce. All around him, ricocheting bullets whined and whistled—a scream of agony from somewhere at his left sent a fierce shiver up his spine. A dying groan drifted up from the other side of the wall where he crouched. Fighting to catch his breath, he found himself reeling from combat frenzy and shook his head in disbelief. *This scene is flying apart!* There had been resistance before— the men who stole and smuggled ancient artifacts rarely failed to guard them. *But this?* They were fighting as though . . . as though something far more important than money was at stake.

He glanced across the street to a window where the wide-eyed young girl had made her brave appearance. Her face flashed there once more, aglow with morbid fascination. *How out of place she looks*, the man thought, *with those porcelain features and dark piercing eyes*. He had a flashback, in one of those odd, inappropriate thoughts people conjure up in moments of great stress, and noted that her haunting look reminded him of that famous *National Geographic* cover of the young Afghani girl with the striking eyes.

Surely her father, a former guard who had led the Italians here, would prevail over her curiosity and whisk her out of danger, far from the scene. But no—there she was, stealing another glance at the chaos unfolding below her. *Get out of there!* he found himself yelling inwardly.

"Run," he shouted, out loud now, as if she could hear him. "Get as far away as you can!"

He whirled back to his surroundings. Finally, a pause. The man breathed out and willed his balled muscles to relax, although he knew from the pit of his stomach that this was the most dangerous moment—the lull when incautious types tended to let their guard down and stand.

And earn themselves a bullet through the head.

No, even though his thighs burned from the unaccustomed crouch, he resolved to stay in his safe hideaway and make certain. A full minute or more passed. One lone shot rang out just as he started to rise. He cringed and sank down again but no more followed. At last he heard shouts in Italian and stood, grimacing from the sudden circulation to his cramped muscles.

The counterattack was over, suppressed by the commandos' overwhelming firepower.

He jogged briskly toward the home's driveway, crossing the dead guard's blood trail with a hop and turning away from the sullen stare of another dead insurgent on the patch of dirt that passed for a front lawn.

I'm not here to imbibe the local ambiance, he reminded himself with an inner shudder. He was here in the guise of a scholar on patrol— Dr. Clive Osborn, British-born antiquities expert, bearer of all the requisite credentials, volunteer rescuer of rare *objets d'histoire* from the crosshairs of modern warfare.

He wasn't even supposed to be at these raids, he reminded himself with a shrug. His official, approved role came into play at base, when all was secure and the ancient contraband carted back in for a type of "antique triage."

Yet he had learned the hard way that it was best to be there on site, while evaluations were still being made and priceless bits of archaeology could still be saved from being overlooked—or, worse yet, crunched under errant army boots. *You never know what's really important unless you're there to see it!* At least, that's what he'd shouted at his Italian liaison only two nights before.

He hurried into a narrow hallway choked with a cloud of plaster dust. Even without maps, he rarely found it difficult to find his destination after these raids—*simple, really: you just follow the lights and the sounds of clunking combat boots.*

He turned left into a large, cluttered room whose interior contents, in the glare of a makeshift spotlight, struck him as instantly and tragically familiar. Even without craning his neck, he saw stacks of Persian pottery, a shard of Babylonian *bas relief*, the statue of a small horse complete with a thin Greek saddle. Easy enough, he assured himself. Large and easily identified, these items were in no great danger. In rooms like these, his eyes always strayed toward the corners—the low, dimly lit places lying shrouded in layers of ancient grime. That's where his real objectives usually awaited him.

He saw only a pile of old rifles and a scattering of dusty ammo bandoliers, still full. A stack of thin, barkless kindling. A broken chair, sized for a child. And—

—*a pile of documents.* Leather bindings, thick, torn pages, engraved spines, a few scrolls.

He was standing over the stack without even knowing how he'd reached it, bending down, carefully picking up the first piece. Realizing that the parchment might be brittle, he silently reminded himself to proceed cautiously. It was a lone scroll, missing its center dowel, frayed about the edges. He slowly unrolled it and strained his eyes. He blew hard, the clichéd reflex of the archaeologist. He squinted against the thick dust he'd aroused.

His heart gave a small jump. He read for a moment. Then he frowned, took a long breath, and caught himself. He needed to be discreet. Yet he could hardly believe it. After a quick glance to each side, he carefully slid the lone document inside a plastic bag, which he zipped tightly shut. It not only needed protection, he told himself, but would make a perfect examination sample.

He picked up the first of the remaining bound papers, read it briefly, shook his head again, and laid it down on the stack with the others.

He exhaled slowly, carefully.

Hebrew.

And more, so much more.

The signature percussive throb announced the arrival of a new helicopter. He looked around him and stepped out of the room. For a moment, he fought an impulse to rush back to headquarters as fast as his lungs and legs would allow. His work in this place had just begun.

He breathed in deeply. The hours ahead would bring him endless heavy lifting, careful digging, and constant maintaining of appearances. *Cleaning up and moving out*, he'd heard one master sergeant call it. He looked around him and forced his face to relax.

Go. Work. And try to act like your world hasn't just been turned on its head.

Chapter Three

AL-SAYED IMPORT-EXPORT
COMPANY, BAGHDAD—FIVE HOURS LATER

T*he man known to* the Italian army as Dr. Clive Osborn briskly
entered the front office of the Al-Sayed Import-Export Company, pulling behind him a small wheeled cart loaded with canvas
bags. Once inside, he glanced briefly around the vestibule and, like a
familiar vendor making a scheduled delivery, shrugged and walked
past the front counter to disappear behind a curtain.

At the end of a narrow hallway, a lanky young man with cropped
brown hair stared at the newcomer and his load, his hand jerking
reflexively in the direction of a telltale lump beneath untucked shirt-
tails. His gaze softened immediately in recognition, and he nodded
his welcome.

Osborn turned sideways to pass the sentry and shouldered his way
through a nondescript doorway, painted green to match the walls.

He emerged in a large room brightly lit from overhead xenon
lights, its ceiling vaulted to the building's entire two-story height.
Automatic weapons and handguns of a dozen varieties overhung
countertops strewn with electronics. In one corner, four video monitors lay stacked, each flickering a different black-and-white angle of
the street traffic outside and the passageways through which he had
just emerged.

A young man wearing a small machine pistol tucked into his belt looked up quickly from his work, eyes flashing alarm. At the sight of Osborn, he nodded amiably, his expression transformed just like the other man's, and he turned back to his task.

Osborn hiked himself up onto a work stool and ran his fingers through dusty hair. He reached down, unbuttoned a side pocket, and pulled out a *yarmulke*, a thin black skullcap that he quickly flipped onto the top of his head with an almost rebellious flair. *Let the Imams come*, he told himself, narrowing his eyes fiercely. *If they kill me, at least it will be for the right reasons.*

"Osborn" had already put in four hours at the Italian base across town, evaluating thousands of fairly ordinary artifacts recovered in the raid and making a complete copy of the Hebrew documents, facsimiles that he now carried with him concealed under the usual pieces. But in this room, completely unknown to the Italians, he relaxed and allowed his true identity to wash back over him—Ari Meyer, British-born yet actually an Israeli citizen. Less loyal to "Osborn's" Manchester University than to the *ha-Mossad le-Modiin ule-Tafkidim Meyuhadim*, the Institute for Information and Special Operations—or simply as the world called it, the Mossad. Israel's feared and revered international police force.

The Al-Sayed Import-Export Company was actually Mossad's main Iraqi safehouse.

Meyer's liaison cover with the Italian army was not entirely dishonest, he reminded himself. He truly *was* intent on the safe recovery of stolen and smuggled artifacts. Except his interest in Gentile specimens was academic at best, feigned at worst. It was documents of the Jewish variety he was truly interested in. Meyer was actually in Iraq as part of a vast Mossad operation to save the last remaining Jews in the country, a number officially hovering around forty, as well as to intercept and save Jewish artifacts before they could be destroyed or held for ransom on world markets. Throughout the country at that moment, his fellow *katza*s, as Mossad operatives were called, combed warehouses and black-market alleys for Torahs, Menorahs, and other precious antiques stolen from Iraq's once-prominent Jewish population. Once found, they would be bought at market price, ransomed, or if the situation required it, confiscated by force.

Exhaling loudly, he turned to the man at the other workstation. "I may need the SAT phone to call Tel Aviv," he said in a weary voice. "The one with the level five encryption."

"Yeah, I know the one," interrupted the other, sounding slightly irritated.

"This could really be something."

Meyer said it with no expectation of a reply from his colleague. Idle conversation was rare in this place. Everyone performed two or three jobs in the Iraqi war zone, and tensions were part of the ambiance of the place. Right outside the walls lived five million people who would eagerly tear them limb from limb if they ever discovered Al-Sayed's true function.

Without turning, the younger man reached over to a shelf, grabbed the phone, and offered it behind him with a deft, one-handed flip of the wrist.

Meyer snatched the device and laid it on the table, leaned from his stool to heave the bags to the counter, and slit the topmost open with a box cutter. Pulling out the first bound document, he sighed and began a thorough examination.

Five minutes later, sweat broke out across his brow. If his colleague had looked, he would have seen eyes narrowed into a worried, somber gaze. Ari let his fingers wander and grip the metallic edge of the secure Iridium satellite telephone lying beside him. The phone was a flip-top resembling a common cellular design, yet far thicker and crowned by a wide antenna nearly a foot long. He slipped off the stool and walked over to a nearby skylight, brought the phone to his ear, and flicked on the power. Frowning, he glanced up to check his position. It irritated him that despite all their customized technology, even the Mossad's satellite phones still required a scrap of open sky in order to secure their connection. He found it a strange vulnerability—not being able to communicate with headquarters without searching out a patch of the outdoors.

"Tel Aviv," he said in a low, strong voice.

Meyer did not worry about anyone eavesdropping, for the satellite phone and the surrounding building were completely secure, protected by spy-proof construction materials. The phone's proprietary signal was scrambled and further safeguarded by incredibly dense computer encryption programmed by the *yahalomin*—Mossad teams tasked with establishing secure communications among the agency's network of safehouses. The young *katza* working across the room was one of those.

He waited for five seconds, then spoke again.

"It's Ari. *Shalom*. Listen, I struck pay dirt, but the news is not good." He took a deep breath. "Well, I found the Battaween genealogy."

He exhaled slowly.

"Yes. *The* one. And it looks to be complete. It must have been hidden well, because if it had been discovered before now, there wouldn't be a Jew left. It's just like they said. The document lists every family that ever went underground, along with its lineage. And that's not all. I found traces of duplicate lists. The men who stole the list apparently made copies. That means each and every Jewish family that ever assimilated into Iraqi society is known to the government, subject to being leaked who knows where. They're all in mortal danger. Understand what I'm saying? There's going to be a bloodbath. Not *if*—but *when*."

He held out the phone and peered at it with a puzzled look—his party had hung up. He chuckled wryly, for he understood why. The lack of courtesy wasn't meant as a slight, merely a sign of how urgently his news had been received. Folks in the Mossad didn't stand on ceremony. And given the bombshell he had just dropped, false tact was even less in order than usual.

He sighed, laid down the phone, and retrieved a small glass wand scanner from a corner of the room. For the next thirty minutes, he painstakingly scanned every page of the genealogy into a nearby laptop. Then, after burning a disc of his results, he reached into his pocket to stow it away and came across the single unbound document he had stashed away for personal inspection.

Reaching precariously to his left, he picked up a large black rifle and unscrewed its ornate infrared scope. Then he held it to his eye, aimed the far end downward, and bent over the document. For nearly an hour he leaned over the table, peering through the lens and translating the fragment from ancient Hebrew, pausing only to wipe his brow in the uncooled Iraqi swelter.

The young man left. The light grew long and dim. The late-afternoon heat subsided. The cool of the evening crept into the room.

Completely motionless, he sat at the desk and, nearly unblinking, worked through to the translation of the signature.

He leaned back, engrossed in his reading. His breathing stopped for a long moment, as air from his lungs whistled past tense lips like a quickly deflating tire.

Chapter Four

PERSEPOLIS, THE EIGHTEENTH
YEAR OF KING ARTAXERXES' REIGN

Dear Esther,

My dear friend, I am in trouble, and I desperately need your counsel.

I hope that despite your being so far away, and the many months since you left for the Promised Land, that you have not forgotten me, your little Leah of the Susa harem. For my part, I miss you dearly— in fact, hardly an hour goes by that your name and your wonderful instructions to me do not cross my mind. I wanted to write you because I miss you, but also, I must admit, for a more immediate reason.

Esther, my night with the King has come and gone. And I do not think you would have yet learned of its outcome from Mordecai. You see, the most shocking and unexpected thing has happened. In fact, I must admit the truth I have sought to conceal from all others. My heart is broken. I have not stopped weeping for days. I have not slept, I have not eaten. I do not know if I can bear this strain much longer. And while I know your reply will not arrive for a very long time, just knowing that I have reached out to you already has eased my suffering.

You see, when I entered the bedchamber of King Artaxerxes, I held out only faint hope for a favorable outcome and, at the same time, braced myself for the harsh reality of palace politics. I really did not want to be there, and felt as though I was sucked into a whirlpool beyond my control. Truth be told, the King was simply hunting for a bride, and I was easy prey.

I use those words because I was fully prepared to have nothing of lasting significance occur, no extraordinary bond develop, and to be rejected as queen. That is a natural outcome, which I would have understood.

That is most definitely *not* what has taken place.

Esther, knowing that you went through the same exact process with King Artaxerxes' father, your beloved Xerxes, I followed your advice to the letter, and much happened because I did. I will attempt to take my emotions in my hand and give you this full account of what took place that evening. A description certainly more complete than I have accorded anyone else.

During the final weeks leading up to that day, I found parts of your admonitions easy enough to carry out. Indeed, I felt that my whole year of preparation was a wonderful time of growing, both in body and spirit. For instance, paying special heed to the wisdom in the counsel of the King's chamberlain was hardly difficult, as he is Jesse, better known around the palace as Hathach, your lifelong friend and my new one as well. As I will describe, I found your advice about focusing on the King's preferences rather than my own to be a revelation, one which definitely set me apart from the other candidates as markedly as it distinguished you.

And of course dear Mordecai, as you know him even better than I, provided both wise counsel and encouragement during that year. The private meetings I shared with you and Mordecai kept the spirit of my Jewish heritage alive and abated my loneliness. From our first meeting, I had always felt a little awed in his presence, for he is, of course, the second most famous man in the empire, the Prime Minister and the King's Master of the Audiences, a figure with enormous royal favor and public adulation. Truly, both of your names have been on the lips of my family and community since the day I was born. As I'm sure I've told you, tales of your mutual courage during our people's near-annihilation flowed throughout my childhood.

Yet from my arrival, I had discovered you to be less intimidating than I would have expected—perhaps because you had so kindly sought me out. I will never forget the long letter and its account of your life that you wrote to me. During that year of preparation following your departure for Jerusalem, I clung to your words like a drowning man to a floating log! I intend to keep it with me forever.

However, it could have been the simple fact that you are also a woman. And that Mordecai seemed to act a bit aloof toward me at first. But for whatever reason, I still found your uncle a bit formidable until he and Jesse began to coach me in earnest. Then, as he was called upon to display his incredible knowledge of the palace and all that lay ahead for me, Mordecai quickly became a warm, witty, and wise counselor. He made me laugh as I seldom have in my life; certainly since being taken to the palace. As Exilarch and leader of the Jews in exile, he knew my family well, especially given its royal lineage, and spoke of them often to me, always raising my spirits in the process. Although I still missed my family terribly and spent many of my nights weeping for all I had lost, I was comforted by a growing sense that a new, improbable family was growing up around me, consisting of no less than the King's prime minister and chief chamberlain—two of the empire's most powerful men.

After you left for Jerusalem, this family-of-sorts always seemed to be missing a member, and your name was often spoken in wistful, even sad tones. But even with that absence forever before us, I began to see Mordecai in a whole new light: beyond his incredible power and renown and simply as a sometimes lonely, yet always fascinating and endearing, man. His lightheartedness makes him seem far younger than he is. I cannot imagine how many Jewish girls pursued him in his youth, yet he never married. He would have presented quite a catch, I am sure.

But the disappointment of that year was your absence. I had always expected that when the preparation began, you would stand beside me every step of the way, giving me even more of your wonderful advice.

On the day Jesse appeared at my door in all his palace finery, that smile of anticipation playing upon his lips, I felt calm, prepared, and within the bounds of divine providence, in spite of your being so far away.

Thanks to you, my friend. To you and the new family you brought into my life.

My approach to the palace was surely less visually enthralling than the one you described in your earlier letter. That is mainly due to the harem's placement this season here at Persepolis—instead of a long march through each of Susa's majestic inner courtyards, my new harem room lay deep inside the palace complex, requiring only a short walk across the courtyard to a corridor leading into the palace of Artaxerxes.

Yet I'm sure my emotions soared and dipped just as wildly as yours did. I had never ventured to the other side of the courtyard opposite my room; Jesse had most emphatically announced that the opposite doors sheltered the palaces of the King himself and were to be given a wide, fearful berth. Once my fellow harem-dwellers and I saw the gleaming lances and sword-edges of the Immortals guarding His Majesty, we had no trouble heeding the warnings.

Mine was perhaps a cooler day, especially as we are in the mountains of northern Persia instead of Susa of the southern deserts. In fact, the palace walls towered so high around me that they blocked direct sunlight. All I could see, framed between the stone rooftops, was a patch of deep blue afternoon sky. I remember drawing a breath as my foot struck its first step of courtyard marble and feeling a rush of excitement flood my veins. It truly did feel as though I was being ushered to the core of all that is splendid and opulent on this earth.

And, Esther, how beautiful I felt—my feet shod in gold-threaded sandals, my hair woven with rare purple lilies, my gown of iridescent red silk, my face intricately painted with Egyptian hues, my body seeming to travel within its own fragrant cloud of myrrh and incense. I'm sure I floated across that courtyard and in through the King's massive gold-leafed doors, although the truth is, I hardly remember the walk at all.

What a relief it was to be met at the door by none other than Mordecai, rather than some unfamiliar and perhaps unsympathetic Master of Audiences. And an additional solace to realize that King Artaxerxes is an altogether different man than his father, Xerxes, when you first met him. The son is young, less world-weary, and, forgive me, appears to be more like a sympathetic figure than the Xerxes of old. I expected him to be a good man simply because I know the woman who largely raised him.

I'll never forget the creak of those huge doors opening and that eternal walk across the marble floor to his bedchamber. He stared at me the whole time with an appraising smile upon his face. I worked very hard to meet that gaze and experience the joy of presenting him with the most precious gift I could give—that of myself.

I stood him before him, and his smile was so broad and infectious I simply stood in its warmth for a long moment.

"You're very beautiful . . . Leah, I believe your name is," he said. And then, almost catching himself, he added, "I do not say this to every woman who enters my chamber. In fact, I may have never uttered this before."

I did not know whether or not to believe him. "Thank you, Your Majesty," I said with a small bow. "You are quite . . . thrilling to behold yourself."

This reply seemed to please him, for he smiled wider, even chuckled a bit. "Oh, really? Am I? Now, would you have said this if I had been a sixty-year-old hunchback, as some of my ancestors who shall remain nameless?"

I thought for a moment. "Your Majesty, I hope I would have found some diplomatic way to frame an honest reply."

His eyebrows rose at that. "Ah. Wisdom and intelligence mixed with *beauty*. Leah may prove a formidable candidate for queen," he added, as if addressing an unseen throng.

"I do not believe in attempting anything halfway."

"So, determined as well. It is a rare quality in one so young."

"I am twenty years old, Your Majesty. But I am old enough to know that His Majesty would not be served by a spineless and silent queen."

"Oh, you are, are you?" he said with a raised eyebrow and a chuckle. "And what harem gossips have passed on these insights to you?"

I felt my face grow warm and looked down to search for an appropriate reply. "I know there are older women in the harem," I replied at last. "But I have received wise counsel since I arrived there, and I have listened closely."

"Have you become a favorite of my chamberlain, Hathach?"

"I count him as a friend, Your Majesty. As I do Her Highness, Queen Esther."

"You mean Queen-Regent *Hadassah?*" he queried with a knowing nod. "Surely you know of her retaking her childhood name."

"Yes, I do. I also know that she is an astute observer of the ways between kings and queens."

"Or kings and queen-*candidates?* You have not won yet, you know, Leah."

"No, but I place myself at your service," I said with another small bow.

He took a deep, portentous breath and met my gaze with a glint of awe in his look. He took two bold steps and embraced me.

Having never been with a man before, I was quite shocked at the sensations that swept over me. A flood tide of emotions I had held in check for years came rushing forth and simply overwhelmed my senses.

One part of me was thrilled to be plunging headlong into the tumbling well of passion that can grow between a man and a woman.

Another part of me felt guilt, having repressed these feelings for so long. I know that as Mordecai had taught me, I was not to accept any pangs of guilt. I really had no choice. Refusing this fate would have meant immediate death for me and my family alike. Just as I was taken forcefully into the palace, so was I taken to the King's bed. My mind understands that if I had no choice, I should feel no shame. Yet my heart struggled with mixed emotions over the pleasurable sensations now overwhelming my body.

Esther, it was almost as if I were a spectator, observing all that happened, attempting to pass judgment over right and wrong.

Thankfully, I need not elaborate for you what happened next, except to say that it was as wonderful, as frightening, and as pleasurable as you had led me to believe. And since I have heard of alternate outcomes from older concubines, I am very grateful for this fact: thanks to your advice, I must have pleased him, although I have nothing against which to compare that belief.

Several times during that night, Artaxerxes gave me looks of astonishment and even wonder. At one time during my upbringing I might have believed that behavior of this sort was a sign of wantonness or low character, but thanks to you and Mordecai, I was able to dismiss such perspectives in my current situation.

When our passion was expended, I thought I had slain him, or at least wounded him in some dreadful way. But after lying motionless for a terrifying moment, he opened his eyes, smiled at me, and raised himself to lean against the pillows. Upon seeing the fright on my face, he caressed my cheek and proceeded to reassure me that his stillness was actually due to a state of ecstasy, not of injury. In fact, rather than causing his demise, I had created delight.

That moment of brief repose was one item of sexual knowledge you failed to impart to me, my friend.

And then he and I gazed into each other's eyes for a very long time, longer than I can estimate, as a veil of incredible ease, warmth, and conversation seemed to float down upon us. He genuinely seemed as intrigued about my life as he was about my body. I opened my heart to him, although, because of Mordecai's warnings, I remained coy about my Jewish heritage.

On the surface I felt incredibly happy, even thrilled at all the things I felt coursing through my senses and my heart. Yet deeper down I continued to struggle with feelings of shame and remorse. As I have told you, I knew that I had no choice in the matter, and that my lack of choice absolved me from ultimate guilt. But something about how much I enjoyed this night ignited continued turmoil within me.

Finally, he spoke with the question that nearly became my undoing.

"Leah, what is so special about you? What sort of spell are you weaving about me?"

I laughed at those words and flashed him a meaningful glance through the corners of my eyes.

"Come here," he said, raising up one arm. So I snuggled in beside him, marveling at the intimacy of his whole skin upon mine, and laid my head upon his shoulder.

And we fell asleep.

I woke up to the sight of his face, shrouded in shadow, raised up and close to mine. Watching me with both passion and tenderness.

"Hello, Leah," he said in a low voice.

Momentarily startled, I replied. "Hello, Your Majesty."

He shook his head. "No, please, call me Artaxerxes."

And that is when the most extraordinary part of the evening began. The King began to talk without prodding, this time about his own history, and when I stopped him with thoughtful questions and observations, he began to open up even further. I learned more about the kingdom of Persia during that brief conversation than anyone could possibly imagine. Esther, your advice in this area of conversation proved more valuable than all my months of training. I became privy to things I really wish I did not know. His voice hardly rose above a whisper, and I couldn't tell if it was from some abiding fear of being overheard or an inbred caution. But his tone helped create a sense of intimacy around the words we shared. He spoke about being raised by strangers, believing that his mother was dead of natural causes, and then being told during his adolescence that she had been ordered murdered by his *own father*. He described the layers of jealousy and intrigue that existed between him and his brothers, most notably Darius II, the eldest and first in line to the throne, who had hoped to rule like his namesake grandfather.

Upon mentioning that name, he began to weep. And that is when I made my mistake.

I reached out to comfort him, stroked his face, and whispered, "It was not your fault. It was not your fault."

At once his eyes opened, the tears stopped, and he stared at me.

"What do you mean, not my fault?" he asked suspiciously.

And that is when I realized that I had betrayed knowledge of things unknown to anyone but you and Mordecai. Few in the world knew the truth about Darius' death.

Inside, my thoughts careened into an avalanche of desperate invention.

"I only meant, Your Majesty—I mean, Artaxerxes—only to soothe your grief. To reassure you that just because you ascended to the throne as a result of blood shed that night, it does not mean you wished it upon anyone."

My words tumbled over each other and he seemed satisfied, for his expression resumed its previous languid state and his taut muscles relaxed once more. I took note of this heightened sensitivity and realized its danger. Artaxerxes could be like the sea: calm and placid on the surface, but like any other sea, concealing treacherous rocks and shoals. The subjects of ascending to the throne and retaining rulership were clearly dangerous.

I breathed deeply again myself as he began to talk about the frustration of watching long-lost relatives resurface upon his ascension to vie for influence and complicate his life.

Throughout our conversation your name arose often and with great favor. Artaxerxes clearly does think of you as his truest and first mother. I guess you, of all people, would know how to treat an adopted child as a true and loving parent would.

He confessed the awesome strain of satisfying, placating, and defending himself against so many various factions within Persia. The threats to his throne.

At one point he stopped and looked into my eyes again.

"I never thought I would ever share these things with anyone," he said. "If candor is a result of love, then, Leah, I believe I am falling in love with you."

I smiled outwardly and trembled inwardly, for I could not forget stories of commoners perishing for their knowledge of such palace intrigues and secrets.

"And I with you, my dear Artaxerxes," I replied, displaying outward calm in spite of my fears.

Again I experienced that divided, spectatorlike sensation. Was this common? Did Artaxerxes the King say these things to all the concubines? Were these mere words meant to accompany another meaningless night of royal passion?

Despite these misgivings, what frightened me most of all was the growing certainty, deep within me, that his words of affection for me were true!

Yet even that inner spark could not convince me to believe the whispered affirmations. I could live with anything except a broken heart, I knew. I could bear the isolation of the women's quarters, tolerate the gossip and political backbiting. But to *believe* I was truly loved and then be ignored—that frightened me. Inwardly I began to harden myself against that possibility, even as outwardly I became more tender. The specter of rejection began to haunt my mind.

We kissed, long and warmly, after which he asked me more about myself. And I told him what was acceptable to tell—of my warm, comfortable upbringing in Susa, my loving parents and one brother. I did not tell him, of course, anything of my Hebrew heritage. Or of the fact that my great-great-grandfather was Jeconiah, the Jewish king and first leader of the Exile, carried as a captive here to this region. Nor of the terror that ransacked my senses when the soldiers seized me by force and whisked me into the palace. Of all the things I withheld from him, the one I felt most keenly at that moment was my familiarity with all things royal because of you, Esther.

Halfway through, I mercifully heard a light snore and allowed myself to fall asleep for a second time.

And then I awoke, as you had described from your own experience, to the slamming open of doors and the whole array of royal aides pouring into the room, oblivious to my presence. I am so glad you told me of this, for without your forewarning, I would have been just as appalled and confused as you were at the sudden end to our intimate tryst.

Furthermore, thanks to your descriptions, I was prepared for the letdown of being escorted back across those huge terraces and returned to the harem. Of course, Jesse and Mordecai awaited me with discreet and respectful inquiries about my evening.

I'm sure I looked as embarrassed as I felt as I hinted to them I might be their next queen. The two deflected glances to each other and shrugged to pass off the comment. Yet I felt my fear suddenly leave me; I knew the truth of what had transpired that night with the King. He loved me, of this I was certain. While my head did fear, my heart felt the truth of what had transpired that night.

So, my beloved Esther, we come to the one thing for which your cherished letter did not prepare me—nor could it have. The arrival of Mordecai on the fourth morning after my night with the King, a stricken and unhealthy pall upon his face. He sat beside me and informed me, in a level and grave voice, that I had been summarily rejected as queen.

The chill of my fear returned like a vengeful flood. I really have no idea what to do, which is why I await your response, my dear Queen Esther...

MOSSAD HEADQUARTERS,
BAGHDAD—LATER THAT AFTERNOON

Meyer backed up abruptly and knocked over his stool with a clatter.

For a long moment, he simply stood and stared at the last two words of his translation, then back at the Hebrew letters signifying the name and title.

Queen Esther!

His mind began to connect the dots. To run across the name *Esther*, a derivative of the Mesopotamian goddess *Ishtar*, could be coincidental, even within the Royal Records. But *Queen* Esther?

Without moving his gaze from the manuscript, he reached over to the desk's edge and fumbled for the phone amidst the jumble of papers and personal effects.

He should have seen it coming. Hints at the royal personage to whom the letter was addressed lay scattered throughout the document. But to find these comments, along with references to the Exilarch, ruler of the Jews in exile, on the same page together—it took his breath away.

He tried to calm the heaving of his chest and slow the frantic darting of his eyes but found his shock simply too powerful to suppress. He had to get out of there, he told himself, but without arousing suspicion. He knew that cameras and monitoring devices were everywhere—far more than what was needed to merely protect him. And the multitude of cameras he could detect were only a fraction of the total.

He made himself look away from the two documents on the desk and glanced around him again, as though someone might have sneaked in behind him during the preceding seconds. Frowning, he picked up the phone as casually as he could, yanked off his skullcap, and exited the room through a back door. He returned a moment later carrying a case, into which he slid the documents with a studied casualness, then left for good.

The only observer of his exit was an old street beggar who had taken up permanent residence in the alley. The rag-swathed body did not budge from its grimy crossed-legged position on the ground, but its oddly young eyes locked on to Ari's immediately, far more alert than an old man's drunken gaze should have been.

Ari nodded and, after a moment's flicker of recognition, so did the "beggar." Ari turned away from the safehouse's outermost and most cunningly disguised security layer, then launched himself into the street.

A wild blend of car horns, racing engines, and human shouts engulfed him at once. Without expression, the bearded "Osborn" elbowed his way through the Arab crowd to his car, a carefully disheveled Toyota truck, placed the case on the seat, started the engine with a long crank of the key, slammed it into gear, and sped into the streets of southern Baghdad like the proverbial drunken sheikh.

Through the crowded, claustrophobic lanes of the southern Aalam district he raced, crazily fighting a combination of shock, relief, and panic. He weaved and ducked into a side street, peering anxiously into his rearview mirror to make sure he was not being followed, finally south onto the broad lanes of Yafa Street, then into the lawns of Zawra Park, Baghdad's largest greenbelt.

There, barely twenty yards out of the cloverleaf that marked the park's entrance, he saw what he needed. He swerved over and brought the truck to a screeching halt. In a second the door slammed and locked, and he was out, crossing the grass with long strides and holding the phone back up to his ear. He looked around him, saw no one paying any attention, and took a deep breath.

Finally, a place he knew to be safe from electronic eavesdropping—from either side.

He dialed and spoke one word into the phone, low but strong.

For a minute, Osborn's eyes danced along with the cadence of the beeps and whistles rushing past his ear. Then he began to speak in a breathless rant.

"No, Father—I'm in Baghdad. Everything's fine. Except—and this is why I'm calling you—I've found something big. No, not even that. It's bigger, it's the motherlode, a two in one. Both of the pieces we've been searching for, praying for, in a single haul."

He waited while a deep, ponderous voice spoke quickly through the earpiece.

"Yes. You guessed it. I think it's authentic. It'll take the lab in Jerusalem to confirm it for certain, and maybe a comparison. All I had was a quick pass with my makeshift infrared."

He paused and turned around to make sure he was still far from the nearest park stroller.

"That's right. Hadassah, and the Exilarch bloodline, together. Our guesses could be validated. The Exilarch *did* start long before Alexander the Great." He laughed, then sobered quickly. "I *told* you it was the motherlode. I'm nearly one hundred percent sure. But I'll have to go to her, to validate them. The time has come. And then you'll be able to go public, except . . . well, you've already gone public. But wait. There's also a bad side to this. Some very bad news, I'm afraid."

◆ ◆ ◆ ◆ ◆ ◆ ◆ ◆ ◆ ◆ ◆ ◆ ◆

Chapter Five

The Wall Street Journal Europe
Monday, June 30, 2003, p. A1

For 1,500 years, from the era of Alexander the Great to the late 13th century, a high Mesopotamian priest in Babylon ruled as the supreme leader of Eastern Jewry. Known as the Exilarch, he settled all disputes brought before him by Jews living as far away as India and Spain. The Exilarch's authority ended only when Mongol hordes sacked Babylon, for centuries the city with the world's largest Jewish community.

—"EXILE SEEKS REPARATIONS FOR JEWS
FROM IRAQ IN FIRST STAGE OF PLAN"

COALITION HEADQUARTERS, THE GREEN
ZONE, BAGHDAD—THE FOLLOWING MORNING

With a loud slap, the leather-bound sheath of ancient documents struck the briefing room table and slid sideways. The short, thickly muscled United States Army officer who had slammed it down stood, exhaled loudly, and glared around at the four men sitting before him in the canvas-filtered light of the divisional briefing room.

It was a careless way to treat objects this sensitive, but Colonel John McIntosh also knew that he didn't care. Tiptoeing around ancient artifacts was just the kind of time-wasting frivolity he hated most about his job. Precisely the sort of politically correct goose chase that resulted in soldiers getting killed for no useful purpose. Such as the case at hand—classic example of bureaucrats messing with the mission profile and getting good men zipped into body bags.

For his opening salvo, the colonel fixed a disdainful scowl at the bearded Brit, Osborn, the personification of all this nonsense.

"So—you really think *this* is what those men fought and died for? Took out a chopper and a dozen men?"

"I do, sir."

Good. Ari "Osborn" was relieved he had been able to deliver the response flat and unmoved.

"Must have been real antique lovers." The colonel rolled his eyes at the others, military men all, and elicited a few cheap, sympathetic chuckles.

"Sir," Osborn continued, the first lilt of a defensive pitch unavoidably stealing into his voice, "the documents were likely stolen from the Battaween Synagogue in Baghdad when it was looted several months ago on orders from the highest ranks of the insurgency—maybe by al-Zarqawi himself. You know how sensitive the subject of Jews and Judaism is in this country. This whole region, for that matter. So you begin with the fact that truly ancient Jewish artifacts are extremely rare. To the rarity, you can add the anti-Semitism, which adds to their attraction. Then add any possible intelligence value they might hold."

"Well, that's fine, but I have neither the time nor the patience to front this little turf war. However, for the sake of clarity, let me state my sympathies right up front. We're here to conquer terrorism, not start a museum. So who's gonna end up signing for these things and baby-sitting them until we can get on to serious matters?"

The colonel's pugnacious demeanor was so stereotypical, Ari almost smiled.

The Italian colonel stood up and said in careful English, "As you said, Viper 5 lost twelve of our best men and friends to secure this material. Our mission is to protect or reclaim stolen antiquities. And we paid a very high price to carry it out. These items must be returned to the Antiquities Protectorate."

"Sir," began an American intelligence officer sitting beside him, "I've had a look at one of them since Dr. Osborn brought them in. And from what I could tell, it was still in pretty good shape. Hardly an antiquity."

"What is it, then?"

Another American in the corner mumbled, "It's a hot potato."

"You have no idea," Osborn put in with a nod at the comment. "I asked a friend from Israel to read—"

"You *what?*" The colonel leaned forward on his fists.

"I asked an Israeli friend to read the parchment."

Osborn was carrying off the ruse on orders. Headquarters in Jerusalem had instructed him to signal the American that Israel would soon know—without destroying his own cover. Osborn consciously relaxed his shoulders, his breathing, and fixed the American with strong eye contact. He was skilled in making these things work—only with expert training and a good deal of luck would the colonel know the truth. "There was no other way. I read Latin, Greek, and a smattering of Persian. But Hebrew—"

"An *Israeli?*" The colonel's face had turned bright red, and he leaned even further to stare into Osborn's face.

"Sir, there's not a single Hebrew interpreter anywhere in the theater, at least officially. We just never anticipated Jewish documents being trafficked. In order to assess these items properly, I had to move quickly and get expert help."

The colonel sighed deeply, stood to his full five foot seven, and swept the group with glowering eyes. "And what did your Israeli friend say?"

"He said the other documents were lists of family names. Genealogies."

"Harmless, no?" offered the Italian colonel hopefully.

"Well, I thought so at first. But then my friend explained further. It turns out quite the contrary. They're explosive. See, there are only a few dozen Jews left in Iraq. But there used to be an enormous population here. Hundreds of thousands in Baghdad alone. They were not only influential, but in many cases, enormously wealthy. They owned or controlled many of the organs of industry. Over the years, many of them escaped the occasional outbreak of persecution by moving away to more friendly countries. This exodus started centuries ago, but it picked up steam as time went on." Osborn paused a moment, but when no one spoke he continued. "And then, when Israel was formed in 1948, the Iraqi authorities cranked up the persecution to an all-time high. Finally, the government struck a deal with Israel. If the Jews would renounce their Iraqi citizenship and abandon their holdings, they'd be allowed to leave with a single suit-case and the equivalent of fifty dollars in cash. So for the next few months, Israel started flying out Jewish refugees in an airlift called Operations Ezra and Nehemiah. By the time they were done, only a few thousand Jews were left in the whole country. Ironically, Iraq was supposed to accept a sizable number of Palestinian refugees from the West Bank in exchange, but they reneged on that part of the deal."

"But, sir, what does this have to do with genealogies?" asked the Italian, shrugging expressively.

"Yeah," chimed in the colonel as he sat down again. "What's your point?"

"Well, when the anti-Jewish pogroms first started in Iraq, many of the Jews who remained started slipping away from their commu-nities and just melting into the population. Assimilating. Changed their names, their language, everything. They tried to erase every possible sign of their heritage. Not out of cowardice but genuine fear. Fear for their lives and for their children."

"And the documents . . ."

"They're the last reliable records of who all these assimilated Jews really were."

A long, knowing pause fell upon the group.

"See," Osborn's tutorial continued, "it was a tradition among these people to make their children memorize their genealogies going back twenty or more generations. So there was no written rec-ord—but in case they ever found themselves on free soil and were asked to prove their Jewishness, it was all in their heads. These other, written synagogue genealogies were kept as a sort of ultimate backup record and were very carefully hidden. But they could quickly become death warrants for every one of these people and their descendants if they ever fell into the wrong hands."

"Which they did."

"Yes, they did. In fact, there was something worse still."

The air suddenly filled with the colonel's expletives.

"We found fragments of translated copies. Into Arabic."

The colonel frowned and shook his head. "You mean—?"

"Yes, sir. The records were copied. These names were written down and moved elsewhere."

Now the colonel thrust his fingers across his face and up through his short blond hair. "Of course." His sarcasm was returning; his face bore the expression of one weary of living. "So these . . . death warrants, as you call them, may have been freely distributed into the ranks of Islamic insurgents."

Osborn replied, "To the thousands of Jews who'd gone underground, living like Iraqis, these documents are without a doubt roadmaps to their own assassinations."

The diminutive but powerful man looked upward, as though imploring G-d for help. "Now, is there any chance that your Jewish interpreter friend has no ties whatsoever to the Israeli government?"

Ari Osborn was silent for a moment. He fought back a wry smile as he thoughtfully stroked his full beard. "Little chance, sir. He works for the . . . Israeli National Library."

McIntosh's exhaled breath made every one of them jump.

Another officer spoke up from the center of the table. "Sir, the State Department will probably have to be notified."

"Of *course* I know State will have to be notified!" the colonel shouted.

"I don't understand," Ari said in his best lame-question voice.

"Really! You mean geopolitics isn't your specialty?" McIntosh was in full fury now. "Well, you may have heard that Israel has stayed as far from this war as it possibly could. At least officially, that is. Their Mossad is everywhere; we know that. But it's all as far undercover as possible. Best for both sides."

Osborn monitored every muscle in his body and even held his breath. The smallest inhalation, if taken too quickly, could give him away. For that matter, his own pupils could betray him—but he could hardly control that.

"If word ever reaches Jerusalem that some of their own people have been exposed to terrorists and are in grave danger," McIntosh continued his tutorial, "well, you know Israel has always taken the initiative. The *military* initiative. And the least involvement from Israel could destroy the Coalition. Radicalize the Iraqi Parliament. Maybe destabilize the whole region. Heck, who knows—maybe even fuel a real war. Is that serious enough for you? You sure fired up a storm with your little museum pieces!"

There was a pause. Finally, Ari spoke up in a low, measured voice. "You can assume that Jerusalem already knows."

"Why?"

Osborn shrugged.

"Why?" This time, McIntosh's voice had risen to a shout.

Osborn fixed the American with a dead-level stare. "Because my friend was, shall we say, highly agitated after I was finished with him. His credentials are from the Ministry of Religion in Jerusalem. And who knows, he could be . . ."

"Great. Mossad." The colonel's voice was flat. The histrionics were over. "These documents are property of CIA, all right? Forget the archaeological side ever existed. And Craig, fire up the Black Hawk. I'm going to have to see the general right away."

"Which one?"

"*The* general. Do I make myself clear? This is big problems. Things are about to hit the fan. Anonymous Jews are about to start dying all over the place."

As if to add its own exclamation point, the distant yet too-close crackle and thump of an exploding car bomb launched the normally unruffled men to the edge of their seats. Embarrassed chuckles filled the room.

But no one stayed behind to continue the discussion.

In the outer parking area, far removed from any American watchers, Osborn jumped into his car, sighed deeply to release the tension wracking his body, and slowly lowered his forehead to the steering wheel.

So far, so good, he told himself. He was nearly certain he had pulled off the deception with his cover intact. Not a meeting for the faint of heart.

Without even glancing aside, he fumbled between his front seats and tightly grasped a plastic bag wedged there. He sighed again in relief.

Thank goodness, he had made copies of everything, and withheld many of the originals for himself. . . .

Almost to reassure himself that he was in control of the unfolding events, he opened the bag, removed the first scroll, and carefully unrolled it. He chuckled to think of the sanitary environment in which a document like this would normally be handled.

Then, right there in the daylight, he pulled out the infrared scope again and began to read the second part of Leah's desperate letter— a plea that now threatened to shake a world three thousand years removed.

. . . Esther, I elaborated to you on my own night with the King to let you see why the events that followed came as such a shock, and also to spare myself the ordeal of trying to describe my emotional state in the minutes after Mordecai informed me of my rejection.

To have the most remarkable thing seemingly happen, to see the King actually fall in love with me before my very eyes, and then to have my instincts confirmed by—dare I say it?—awed and overwhelmed words from his very own lips, not only that but to feel myself fall in love with him, and *then be rejected,* with no knowledge of why. . . .

I have no words to convey my feelings. These have been the darkest days of my life. To have given away what is most precious to a woman, and then be spurned. Had I simply fooled myself? All I could think was that I finally had come to resemble my biblical namesake, Leah, the wife of Jacob, who was rejected by her husband after her long-ago wedding night.

I had left the King's bedchamber that morning feeling as though I was riding on the wind. So to have the dream-come-true dashed only three nights later, when Mordecai came in to tell me the King wished no further contact with me—no, not even as a concubine, much less as queen—well, again words fail me. Mordecai himself appeared shocked.

Self-doubt took up residence at my door. *Had I been wrong? Was I that deceived? Was I that unprepared? Had all my lessons from Jesse, the lessons of Mordecai, and your own intimate tutoring all gone to waste? Was I that poor a student?*

And then came the ultimate self-condemnation. . . . *Was I that unattractive?*

I struggle to fully describe to you my feelings, for fear of appearing selfish or naïve. But I will try, for I have always found you to be a wise and loving listener. And I am confident that, in time, you will understand my heart.

You see, I am of two minds. On one hand, I am quite content to offer my life—my hopes and aspirations, my love, even my innocence—in the service of our people. If the loss of my love will help relieve some of the tensions within the palace, and help in any way to ensure the rebuilding of Jerusalem, then please believe me, I am glad to endure it.

Esther, I have never forgotten your heroic undertakings when the entire palace had been turned against us, swayed into ordering the extermination of every Jew in the empire. Nor do I overlook the fact that even though I was only a child at the time, I and my family especially would have been numbered among the victims. You risked instant beheading to go before the King, reveal your sworn secret, and plead our cause. I have never heard of a braver thing in my life—except for maybe what Mordecai did, refusing to bow before the vile Haman even if it cost him his life.

Yes, you were willing to risk certain death, and I think I am no different. If I can play a part in ensuring the ongoing safety of our people and the rebuilding of Jerusalem, I am honored to do so. Even if the cost is a lifetime of boredom, humiliation, and loneliness, I will pay it. But what did this rejection have to do with that "price"? It seems without purpose, senseless.

However, now that the price is paid, I look ahead to the long, long years stretching before me, and can hardly believe I am now a relic of more worthwhile times, awaiting death and some hope of happiness in paradise. Is this lingering twilight all I can possibly hope for? Is it right to pray for something more? Is it selfish to wish for some sort of betterment of my lot in this long period of aftermath, of solitude?

Because, my friend, the harshest truth is this: When I see my reflection in those polished bronze serving dishes of ours, I see a young woman of twenty, and it nearly rips my breath away to think that at my age, life is already over, that I will never love again, never bear children, never even leave the palace grounds. The sheer outrageousness, the seeming unfairness, of the thought leaves me gasping

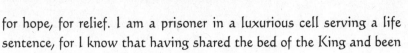

for hope, for relief. I am a prisoner in a luxurious cell serving a life sentence, for I know that having shared the bed of the King and been rejected, I will never be released from the harem.

I understand the realities of life. I also concede the advantages of my rather pampered surroundings here in the harem. Surely many women harried by the demands of family and children at least occasionally would long for a life of luxury and leisure within a royal palace. But for me, it is torture.

If all I have left is to wait, to count the weary moments until my earthly existence is over, then why not invite death? Why not take my life, as several of my sisters-in-bondage have done since I was moved to the harem?

Please forgive the selfishness and petulance, even the wickedness, of my words, dear Esther. I do not mean to turn the focus onto myself. In fact, I am equally concerned about the future of our people. In my foolish moments of premature triumph, I had pictured myself as queen, granting royal patronage to my parents in their old age, working to enshrine Mordecai's new position of Exilarch as some kind of permanent royal post in the empire, perhaps even in time adding the influence of my own royal Jewish blood to bolster the proposition. Knowing that the Exilarchy is not universally accepted among all the segments of Jewish society, especially the priesthood in Jerusalem, I imagined myself working alongside Mordecai to champion its cause, and that of our people, at a time when they are being hated as never before.

How glad I am that I never shared these presumptuous thoughts with Mordecai or Jesse before they were forced to come to me and deliver the terrible news!

As I count you such a trusted friend, I know you are the only one with whom I can share my tormenting and mortifying experiences. But here is the question I must ask you, and to which I desperately hope you can identify.

Esther, do you ever feel that your life is over? That you already have played the significant role you were born to play, and you have spent your life's purpose? Or possibly that you mismanaged life's cues and missed further opportunities for your life to have meaning? That since things did not turn out the way you had believed they would, others have taken the stage and now you're simply waiting in the wings for your turn to die?

That, my dear confidante Esther, is exactly how I feel.

I desperately need to know if you have ever felt the same. And if so, how you have managed to endure it. My only hope to retain the last shred of my sanity is that you indeed have endured some of this pain and have some secret that will help me survive.

Would to G-d I had never let my fantasies deceive me that night!

I await your reply, my cherished friend, with every breath left in me.

Leah

Osborn started his vehicle quickly and sped into the Baghdad night—not due to any appointment or deadline, but his knowledge that merely sitting alone in a vehicle for so long could turn him into a target of random terrorism. Not to mention the explosive information the ratty little truck now harbored.

His mind sped just as quickly over the passage he had just translated. Even the abbreviated symbols referring to "G-d" confirmed the authenticity of the document. His heart pounded with jubilation—and fear.

Chapter Six

The Jerusalem Center for
the Performing Arts—three days later

*I*n the minutes before* it happened, Jerusalem had seemed to be in a celebratory mood, as hope for a long-awaited peace settlement hovered in the air. The night-shrouded capital fairly throbbed with the prospect of a just-negotiated land-for-security agreement between its leader and the new Palestinian prime minister—unaware that a few hundred kilometers away, unfolding events would hurl fresh challenges at the long-harbored dream.

In Jerusalem's cultural district, triumphant Prime Minister Jacob ben Yuda was oblivious to the threat—even in the mood for a night out. His bride of several years, the one-time Hadassah Kesselman, had even chosen the occasion to invite her dearly loved Poppa to share it with them.

After that evening, Israel's First Lady would remember only a few of the evening's preliminaries. What she would somehow remember best and most vividly was the moment the dogs began to bark.

She would recall an odd collection of other jumbled moments leading up to the barking. She would recollect key lines of dialogue from the premiere performance of the play she, her husband, and her father had just attended—a taut thriller about a deeply conflicted housewife and her homicidal lover. She would recall the words her father had just muttered in her ear about the lead actor's mediocre performance. And the sly grin of agreement she had flashed him, just out of reporters' sight—grateful that Poppa had, for once, remembered to keep his voice down. She could feel again her hunger, not having eaten since a meager breakfast that morning. And, complacently accustomed to standing just one crosshair away from the Prime Minister's spotlight, she would recall precisely where her husband had stood—or to whom he had been waving—at the critical moment.

Yet the memory that somehow stuck in her mind was the instant the bomb-sniffing dogs flew into full alarm.

She would forever recall the suddenness and savagery of the noise. How viciously the growls engulfed the marble lobby and drowned out the *glitterati*'s murmur, the reporters' shouts. She would remember its odd quality—more fierce and rapid than any barking she had ever heard from any large dog, and at such an anguished, unnaturally high pitch. As though the German shepherds were being choked by the brightly colored climbing-rope leashes along which her husband's bodyguards held them fast.

She would remember turning away from her father and frowning toward the chaos, seeing the animals lunge across the crowded vestibule in exaggerated frenzy. She had recoiled at the sight of the dogs at full alarm, their bodies straining so hard against their straps that their heads stood as high as their handlers'. And the sight of fangs snapping in the light of the chandeliers, saliva slinging away from open jaws onto nearby ball gowns.

All this from animals usually so gentle she had gone months without even noting their presence.

Somehow she would remember these details far more clearly than the attacker's face. Of that, she would only recall the slightest details, yet those details were enough. A split second of fear pouring from dark eyes. Neck tendons strained and flexing. A lean visage twisted with hate so powerful that as brief as it was, the sight sent a shiver freezing down her whole body.

Then the bellow of a *Galil* sniper rifle, fired at short range.

And the running man jerking back, recoiling against the blow.

Then seeing him recover. Regain his footing. Refocus that vicious expression onto them—onto *her*? Oddly thinking, *It's only because I'm standing next to my husband. The Prime Minister.* Hearing shouts reach her ears, or perhaps her awareness, about a vest. *The man was wearing a bulletproof vest!*

Then came another strange sound—the clatter of several thousand dress shoes and high heels racing in unison across polished marble. Out of the corner of an eye she saw the scuffed bottoms of her husband's loafers and realized he was being dragged away to safety as well.

Without her.

More shots rang out. The room filled with echoes of ratcheted thunder—she recognized machine-gun fire. This time the man running toward them was knocked off his feet. The noise stopped and she glimpsed him being buried under the hurtling bodies of more bodyguards.

Someone pushed her back, and she realized that her father was shoving her down with all the strength left in an old man's limbs. Her own high heels slipped and she felt herself fall to the floor. Land *hard*. A dark shape filled her vision—her father . . . on top of her. And as feeble as he was, she knew he had not tripped out of weakness or instability.

Poppa had thrown himself. Two other large, dark shapes leaped on top of him, crushing her. *Bodyguards.*

A male voice screamed—

And a new explosion shredded her world apart!

Its shock wave slammed into her body.

White light seared her retinas.

Roaring flooded her ears.

Flame scorched her exposed skin.

Her body and those of the men on top of her, joined for a moment by gravity, jerked apart with unimaginable savagery. She saw an arm fly away, and a hand, in a strange slow motion. She curled like a child against the burning and clutched her abdomen. Her ears felt attacked by an awful *something*, a rumble that was more vibration than sound.

A strange person unleashed a long, anguished cry. Eerily, she recognized her own disembodied voice.

Then the blast was spent, replaced by a mist of dust upon her face. And darkness—a lack of light through her closed eyelids. The chandeliers had blown out. For an awful second, she heard nothing but a distant ringing sound. Then came a whimper, and she again realized that it had come from her mouth. And that she was sobbing.

Her eyelashes were clotted shut, so she spent a moment wiping them clean. Dreading what she would see, she opened her eyes. She glanced at her hands—they gleamed red with blood. Silhouetted by spotlights outside the lobby's clear glass walls, she could see her husband teeter to his feet and, with an authority more characteristic of a husband than a prime minister, yank himself away from the grasps of two bodyguards. He stumbled to her side and dropped to his knees.

"Honey, are you . . . are you all right?" As she read his lips, her ears still ringing from the thunder of the explosion, an eerie quiet reigned over her world.

"Yes . . . yes," she heard herself answer in a voice higher and more breathy than her own. "But Poppa?"

Her husband did not answer, only tightened his grip around her shoulders. She pushed against him. The hold grew tighter still. She rebelled.

"Poppa!" She felt panic rise up, fierce enough to bury her alive. Then she felt defiant again. She *would* see him. "Poppa!"

She tore herself from her husband and fell away to one side. Her eyes took in the horrible sight of three lumps lying motionless in a thick layer of debris. Then two onlookers moved aside and unknowingly let another shaft of outside light shine upon the floor.

And she saw.

The two bodyguards who had flung themselves upon her lay motionless, steeped in crimson. Poppa was lying on his back, his chest and the floor around him covered with shards of glass from the shattered windows and chandelier. She could not see the state of his torso very clearly, other than a faintly wet gleam. And the strange absence of a limb at his left shoulder socket.

Her lungs heaved themselves into runaway train mode. She could not catch her breath. She threw herself at what remained of . . .

. . . *everything*. The man who had crafted her entire person. Who had changed her diapers. Who had taught her to read. Who had made her who she was. The influence that had shaped every day of her childhood. The imposing figure who had first taught her that a truly strong man was more than capable of showing tenderness and affection. Who had, beyond that, taught her what a man even *was*. Who had shaped her entire perspective of the world, then launched her into its uncaring chaos with the confidence of a young woman who knew that no matter what, she was the apple of her Poppa's eye, and that she *mattered* immensely to at least one good man, one very good man. . . .

It all streamed through her frantic mind in one awful moment.

Hadassah struggled to regain control of her breathing, then became aware that she was uttering loud, hoarse gasps. The sound of someone in hypoxia—deprived of air.

She bent down into his face, desperate for a familiar look at him. For just one reassuring familiar aspect. She felt a hand tremble up to the back of her neck and realized that it was his right. He was feebly pulling her forward. Closer toward him.

He was gasping as well, only not as loudly. "Hadassah," he groaned, hardly audible.

"No, no!" She couldn't be sure whether she was revolting against the situation, against what was happening, or merely pleading with him not to speak. But she kept repeating the word. *"No!!"*

"Hadassah, I have to tell you—"

"No, Poppa. I love you. I love you, and you have to stay quiet. You have to let them—"

"You too, darling . . . please listen . . ."

The word *listen* was almost pure breath.

"No! I won't. You'll stay still, and they'll take care of you, and you'll be fine."

"I am dying." Strangely, there was more steel in his voice now. "Listen."

She said nothing but gritted her teeth and pressed her lips into his bloody cheek. She brought her ears closer.

"She did not perish. You must find her."

The hand slipped from her neck and struck marble with a small slap. The cheek fell away from her lips.

She slumped backward and screamed into the shredded ceiling until her breath gave out, until more hands surrounded her and she heard her husband's voice and was lifted to her feet without having to make the effort.

◆ ◆ ◆ ◆ ◆ ◆ ◆ ◆ ◆ ◆ ◆ ◆ ◆

Chapter Seven

THE PRIME MINISTER'S RESIDENCE—
REHAVIA, JERUSALEM—TWO WEEKS LATER

He *stood before her* again—Poppa's wrinkled, beloved face just two feet away, still caked white with dust, streaked with trails of dried blood, his sparse gray hairs still on end from the explosion. He was leaning gently in the doorway just as she had seen him do when she was a child, on those many long afternoons when he returned from work. But now he wore a sheepish, almost embarrassed, grin. As if to say, *Pardon my appearance, dear. I know it's a bit alarming, but then, as you know—I am dead. . . .*

Even in her sleep, she could feel her head jerk back and her heart race, her insides recoil with a complex blend of love, revulsion, self-reproach, and longing. She felt her arms strain forward. *Poppa, I don't mean to shudder. I don't mean to pull back. It's just that I'm grieving for you, and now to see you here, looking like this . . .*

And then he would speak those words again. The cryptic utterance would leave his mouth with an echo that seemed to physically travel across space to her ears, invading her senses with an unrelenting cadence.

"She did not perish. You must find her."

In the dream she always looked around her. Perhaps she did so to detect any eavesdroppers, perhaps to give herself a moment for processing once again the strange words' meaning. But then when she turned back, he was gone. Only the words, with their mysterious challenge, remained.

And yet, as disturbing as was his appearance, she immediately longed for its return. His presence, however illusory, felt like a wisp of warmth in an arctic winter.

Now its departure once more caused an ache inside her and the extinguishing of her last hope.

She cried out piteously and struck her pillows with a groan. But she was losing the fight. The more resolutely Hadassah tried to resist waking, the more the effort itself revived her.

I simply cannot wake up, she told herself. Not to the ordeal of another day. Another fourteen hours of fog, one more dawn-to-dusk living with despair, of groping through a thick, cottony haze, fighting for the strength to carry out any of the things she once loved.

Before *it* happened. Before life had become a living nightmare. Before the doctors had walked in to tell her that her father had slipped away, and then, less than twenty-four hours later, to be told that one of the three shrapnel bits in her abdomen had pierced her uterus and put in doubt any chance she had ever entertained of becoming a mother.

That final realization caused her to lose the fight against waking, and again her senses converged to a razor point. Whisked to the here-and-now, she found herself lying fetal-style in the soft four-poster bed of the Prime Minister's master bedroom.

Alone.

On a Sunday morning. The first day of the Jewish week.

Much later in the day than ordinary—respectable—people ever slept.

Yes, she was definitely awake, she noted with a wince, distraught that the sleeping pills had only worked for a few hours. She momentarily contemplated taking a handful more. . . . A permanently pain-free state beckoned just beyond conscious thought. Then, as if to remind herself that her namesake, the ancient Hadassah, would not have retreated so easily, her awareness slipped away from the confines of her half-dormant self to probe her surroundings. Her eyes remained shut, but her ears noted a high, oppressive silence. The kind of late-in-the-day stillness she remembered from better times, when she had merely overslept on a carefree weekend and couldn't wait to jump out of bed and redeem what was left of the morning. The only sound was a faint nuisance from the ticking bedside alarm clock. A nagging reminder that *time is passing. You're wasting your life. . . .*

She gritted her teeth. Her failure to stay asleep now thrust her into a whole new gauntlet of challenges. She reluctantly opened her eyes. There was light, way too much and far too bright. High above her floated the bedroom's pale white ceiling, distant and ethereal. She groaned again, for her husband had left the bedside lamp on. She knew it was his own subtle challenge to her—*Get up. Do something. Overcome this.*

It was his only way. He was a good man, but he possessed no other skills with which to address what she was suffering. No words to soothe her pain or to frame his helplessness. Only symbolic gestures.

She rolled over, extended her arm, wincing at the pain of still-healing stitches across her abdomen, and flicked the light off. Under her arm, still open, lay the only book that meant anything to her now: the journals of Queen Esther, recopied from scrolls in the Israel State Museum, the Shrine of the Book. These had been bound and given to her as a wedding gift from her Poppa. This most precious scroll actually belonged to her family but was on permanent loan to the museum for safekeeping. It traced her family's genealogy back for nearly three thousand years—not to Queen Esther, but to her young friend Leah. It enshrined the memory of her mother, who had added her signature only three days before marrying Hadassah's father. This treasure left to her by her family was such a cherished heirloom that, for generations, her ancestors had kept it a secret until a young woman's marriage. She had read them for the umpteenth time throughout the previous day, five minutes at a time as her strength allowed. It was the only sense of connection left to her—a link of words and dimly recollected emotions reaching several millennium into the past. *That's how far back I have to go,* she lamented. *Thousands of years to find someone who means anything to me now. . . .*

She rolled back over into her pillows with a sigh torn from the depths of her being. *You have to do it,* she whispered into the cotton, gritting her teeth. *Force yourself. Get out of bed, make yourself up for the day. Eat something. Read the newspaper. . . .*

Especially *that,* she remembered. She had once loved her morning papers, thrilled to the sense of being connected to the day's great events, the thrilling bustle of modern existence, the unpredictably of news. In Israel—especially for a modern woman with a master's degree and a nearly finished doctorate, a learned, opinionated prime minister's wife—there was always a Big Story—or two, or a half dozen. Complete with vociferous differences of opinion from countless vocal factions. Endless analysis. Commentary *ad nauseam.* And in Israel, the stakes were always high. Armageddon always seemed just a minor crisis or two away. Once, the very sight of those half dozen newspaper rolls lying against her front doorstep in the dawn's half-light filled her with a throb of anticipation.

The Jerusalem Post, Ha'aretz, Yedioth Ahronoth, Globes, Maariv, even the *International Edition of The New York Times*—once she had devoured them like the avid knowledge-hound she used to be. Now they lay there like an intrusion of horror into her life. Now *she* was the news, or at least a key element of the Big Story, and it didn't feel so thrilling. An assassination attempt on the Prime Minister, even an unsuccessful one, offered fodder enough for several months' worth of media frenzy, so the Israeli press had been handed a rare double handful. Not to mention that the close call had occurred hard on the heels of Jerusalem's initiating the most serious and promising Palestinian peace talks in half a century—the very real prospect of a lasting solution hanging in the balance. That angle had infused the story with a screaming sense of urgency. *The very embryo of peace,* headlines shouted, seemingly aborted by a failed attack that should have been anticipated by the Prime Minister's myriad security forces. Or something to that effect. Never before had suicide bombers been so desperate and gotten so close. And never at a worse time. It was the story of the decade.

Could it be that the death of one warlike Palestinian leader and the surrender of Gaza had opened the door to peace, only for it to slam shut with the permanent silencing of his conciliatory Israeli counterpart? There was much speculation that any replacement for her husband might not be as inclined to nurture the climate for peace. Especially now. . . . The bombing had given fresh fuel to the Knesset's opposition party.

Every second of her ordeal had been parsed to shreds by a hundred commentators and a thousand more assorted pundits. Four different television cameras had captured the tragic image of her cradling her father's body, the blood from their wounds mingled, and mercilessly replayed it, frame by frame, for global television.

An entire nation had grieved with her—but she had never felt more alone.

And when she had failed to publicly demonstrate that she was back to normal at the end of the traditional seven-day mourning period, the papers had started to sniff a new story. Perhaps the formidable Mrs. ben Yuda was weaker, more vulnerable, than previously thought. A tad self-indulgent. *"Is Seven Days of Shiva Not Long Enough?"* asked one trashy paper with allegiances to the opposing political party. Even sympathetic coverage began to acquire a condescending, patronizing edge. *"Hadassah's overwhelming grief seems to have compromised her public duties. . . ."* For all the details they knew, they appeared still unaware of her medical condition, of the surgical removal of a small piece of shrapnel from her side. Maybe if they knew . . .

Hadassah groaned and shook her head.

Now it had become a vigil. This very minute, she could—if she had the energy—walk over to her window, nudge open the curtains, and look down upon a television crew camped out beside the barricade and the IDF guards, there to chronicle her husband's shock and her ongoing seclusion. Despite the intruders' best wishes, she felt herself well up with resentment at the thought of them.

Just imagining it made her want to curl back up in her sheets and never leave them again. She could only think of two words to embody the inchoate desperation and despondency smothering her.

Oh G-d . . . She tried it aloud, picturing the word as translated in her book, but the sound was no more than a whisper.

She uttered the words as a lament, a senseless expression of misery. But hearing them resonate in her thoughts, she felt the words expand somehow, acquire a rooted meaning of their own.

She thought them again, but now as a salutation of sorts. A greeting.

"*Oh G-d . . .*"

She sighed. Personal prayer had never been her thing. Was it really possible to just form thoughts and have them ascend to the Creator of the universe? *Really* possible? She lived in a region where the certainty of such things was considered as sure as the land under one's feet. And yet she had never truly believed it. It had never seemed likely—at least as sure as the love of her father, the solidity of her own abilities, the spark of her own reliable intelligence.

"Oh G-d . . ."

She took a breath, then another. She felt stupid—to simply release words into the air? Talk into the emptiness. But then . . .

". . . *help me. Please.* I don't know how to talk to you. Or whether I even *am* talking to you. But I need help. I'm in trouble. And I have no way, no strength, nothing to dig myself out with. I've never felt this helpless before. Or this broken inside. But if you're there and in the business of rescuing people, then here I am. I could use your help. I need . . ."

She shook her head. She had never put it into words before, even to herself.

". . . *a reason to live.*"

The last words faded into a plaintive whisper. She closed her eyes, lay down again, and let herself go into a blank, wordless place.

Then she opened her eyes, as though it were the equivalent of hanging up the phone on an abruptly ended divine call. She took a deep breath and looked around her, trying to ascertain whether the world felt any different, the light brighter, her emotions lifted at all.

If she felt anything, it was hardly noticed. A spark, perhaps. Hard to quantify. She shrugged—at least she had tried it. Couldn't hurt . . .

What now?

She turned some inward corner and felt a new conviction well up within her.

She had to speak with her husband.

Desperately. Not here, in the context of her weakness, but in a room where things, and people, were taken seriously. She had to get up, get out. She needed a real conversation with him.

And she had some questions demanding answers.

Hadassah forced her forearm muscle to flex and raise her hand to flip back the sheet. She sat up, protecting her stomach wounds with her hands, then willed her leg muscles to swing over and allow her feet to nudge the floor. She summoned up the determination to stand, then remained still for a moment and waited for a swooning sensation to drain from her head.

It's a start, she told herself with a grim pursing of her lips.

She dressed and readied herself with the resolve of someone preparing for battle, slowly but resolutely choosing a navy business suit. She walked over to her vanity—its mirror still shrouded with a black mourning drape she had not removed after the end of Shiva—and slowly pulled back one corner. She shook her head and pulled down the rest of the fabric. She sat down before it and began applying makeup for the first time in a fortnight. She called for and ate her favorite light breakfast of eggs and fruit.

The housekeeper had brought the tray up herself, clucked over Madam's obvious intent to go out, then voiced her obligatory cautions about surgery recovery and healing time. Hadassah attempted a smile, nodded agreement, and waved her away.

Finally, Hadassah could feel a measure of fortitude seep back in. She picked up the telephone and dialed.

"Mora, could you have a car prepared immediately? I'd like to go visit my husband."

Hearing the reply, she closed her eyes wearily.

"I know how much notice they need. But I don't care. I need to see my husband. Now. If you can't help me, I'll either take a cab or hitchhike."

She started to breathe heavily as her assistant argued on the other end. Her cheeks turned a quick shade darker.

"Look, I know it's raining. I don't care about the weather. And I know the security risks. Just tell them I assume all risks myself and absolve them of all responsibility."

Then she *did* hang up. She would see her husband.

She had to.

Chapter Eight

WorldNetDaily.com
June 27, 2001

Anthony C. LoBaido, *"Rescuing scrolls from Saddam's Iraq—Israeli intelligence smuggles out Torah documents"*

NICOSIA, Cyprus—As new Prime Minister Ariel Sharon takes power in Israel, a half-century-old intelligence operation may be nearing completion, one which seeks to bring a sense of closure to the biblical Babylonian captivity, after Israel's Mossad spy agency smuggled out a few dozen Torah scrolls from Iraq.

It is an operation that deals with both treasured manuscripts and something far more valuable—Jewish believers still trapped in Iraq by Saddam Hussein's police apparatus.

Hussein wanted to destroy the Torah scrolls—some of which are hundreds of years old—but was unable to complete that task.

The existence of the 30-some scrolls was made known last year when the chief rabbi of Israel used one of the smuggled scrolls in a religious festival in the city of Afula.

Ashkenazi Chief Rabbi Yisrael Meir Lau explained to the Israeli media that "one branch" of the Israeli intelligence apparatus—either Shin Bet (akin to the U.S. FBI) or the Mossad (Israel's version of the CIA) carried out the smuggling operation.

—HTTP://WND.COM/NEWS/
ARTICLE.ASP?ARTICLE_ID=21647

ISRAELI PRIME MINISTER'S OFFICE, CABINET ROOM

The large oak doors flew open: the four waiting men stood in respect as Jacob ben Yuda strode in at a brisk pace for his morning intelligence briefing, still reading from an open folder. The

Prime Minister of Israel looked them over, acknowledged the groups with a warm nod, and sat briskly at the head of the table.

"Mr. Prime Minister," said Mossad director Joseph Libyon, motioning to a man on his left, "this is Ari Meyer, one of our longest-functioning undercover operatives, currently on assignment in Iraq. He is back for consultations, and we'd like him to brief you."

Ben Yuda leaned forward and shook the man's hand.

"Welcome back home, Ari," Jacob said, noting that the man's full beard did not fit the common image of a Mossad agent.

"It's my pleasure, Mr. Prime Minister."

"As you know, sir," continued Libyon, "we don't usually ask our agents to attend a cabinet meeting, however crucial it may be. In this case, however, we thought it would be essential that Agent Meyer, known to the Italians as the British 'Clive Osborn,' brief you himself, as he is not only an agent but an educated scholar of ancient history and languages. His specialty and his cover, both."

"Ah," remarked Jacob with a grin, "a Renaissance Mossad man."

"Merely a professional student, sir," Meyer demurred.

"Well, in this case," said Libyon, "the studies have given a great service to Eretz Yisroel. But I wish it portended good news, sir. You know, of course, how long and intensely Mossad has been working to retrieve Jewish survivors and all precious Hebrew artifacts in Iraq. Agent Meyer has been a vital part of that initiative for years. In his undercover work as a liaison with the Italian artifacts recovery squad, he now has discovered some highly disquieting documents."

"At first," Meyer said, picking up the report, "it appeared to simply be an old genealogy stolen last year from Baghdad's Battaween Synagogue. Had that been true, the loss would have been harmless, since, as you know, most Jews were removed from Iraq during Operations Ezra and Nehemiah. They would have carried great sentimental interest for the surviving families who now live in Israel, but little more."

Meyer handed the Prime Minister a thick, stapled pad of photocopied sheets.

"On further inspection, however, none of the names matched the Ezra and Nehemiah manifests of 1948 through 1949. I'll cut to the chase, sir. They were the names of Jewish families who years ago went into deep hiding throughout Iraq. Because of the continuing unstable conditions and the new leadership in Iraq, most if not all of them are still afraid of revealing themselves. In fact, they even changed their names, and have been living as Iraqis for, in some cases, over fifty years."

"Are some quarters going to consider them cowards for going underground like this?"

"They would have no reason to, sir. These measures not only helped many families hold on to their assets, but are actually in perfect accordance with Hebrew tradition. For centuries, Jews in peril have freely tolerated name changes to escape danger, including Babylon's Hananiah, Mishael, and Azariah, better known to posterity as Shadrach, Meshach, and Abednego."

"Then I don't understand," said ben Yuda with a frown. "Isn't this a fortunate discovery? If we once had no way to find these families, doesn't this present us with an opportunity to make contact?"

"You're absolutely right, sir," Meyer said. "Except for one thing. Prior to these documents being intercepted, it appears they were copied by the men who stole them. We hoped this might be a meaningless occurrence, that the thieves would not realize what they had. That is, until we began to see this."

Meyer glanced at Libyon, who took the cue to slide a large black-and-white photograph over to the Prime Minister. Ben Yuda picked it up. His eyes widened and his face lost its color.

The photo depicted a pile of rubble with a large Star of David spray-painted onto the largest piece of intact slab. A small leg and foot, the size of a child's, protruded from the nearest edge of the pile.

"In the last six days," Meyer continued, "four civilian homes have been destroyed in various parts of Iraq. They all have certain things in common. First, neither the authorities or the Western military command had any warning of the raids, or why they might have been committed. Second, every one was considered a normal civilian Iraqi family. Third, the raids were designed to ensure that every member of the family died. And last, every one had a Star of David posthumously marked somewhere on the ruins. What initially appeared to be a random car bombing was actually carefully researched and planned."

"You're forgetting one last thing," Libyon prompted.

"From our end—after the fact—each family name has been linked with this genealogy."

The Defense Minister on the left of the Prime Minister swore viciously under his breath.

"You mean. . . ?" began ben Yuda.

"Yes, sir. The hidden Jews of Iraq are being targeted for elimination. It's a modern repeat of Haman's 'ultimate solution,' on the very same piece of ground."

The Prime Minister leaned downward and massaged his eyes for a long moment. Then he looked up, his expression grim. "No! I cannot authorize covert action in Iraq. I gave the Americans my word. Not to mention, it's simply too dangerous. Everything could blow up, literally and figuratively, if we were discovered. It's bad enough now. But if we take unilateral action—"

"Sir, the Americans know about this situation already," Meyer offered.

"How is *that*?"

"Well, my cover is as a British scholar, liaison to the Italians. My initial discovery came after a raid on a large artifacts cache in which numerous casualties were sustained. The Americans were called in for a briefing."

"Besides, sir," Libyon inserted, "we at headquarters instructed Meyer to tell the Americans he had accidentally leaked this to an Israeli. We did it to give him cover and an opening for dialogue on the subject. It was hardly a surprising disclosure to them, although its repercussions alarmed them. After all, as you said, they know of our presence in Iraq."

"So, Joseph, do you think they're expecting to hear from me?"

"I would say so. At least an ambassador-level contact, if not higher. They know how aggressively we protect our own, so they must be prepared for some kind of contact from us and have a response ready."

"What do you think they're prepared to do?"

"Well, certainly not to allow us in. I think they expect us to *do* something. You see, the Americans have a dilemma. They know that most of the factions in Iraq are violently anti-Semitic, even the ones they publicly support. And the thugs carrying out these attacks know that we recovered the original list in the raid. So any direct action to punish or prevent this genocide will be detected and its motives known immediately. If the Americans are involved, then Washington will be accused of carrying out Israel's wishes and being a Zionist puppet. Iraqi officials will feel obligated to denounce the American action in order to maintain public support, even if they privately sympathize. U.S.–Iraqi relations will be weakened at the most vulnerable time, when the new Iraq is just beginning to take control. The whole Middle East house of cards could collapse."

"So you think the U.S. will do nothing to stop these killings?"

"Sir, I believe that at best, they will debate and vacillate and play turf wars between the Pentagon and the State Department for so long that by the time they reach consensus, the last Jews in Iraq will be dead."

"So you're recommending we bluff them and take action anyway?"

"It depends on how much these surviving Iraqis mean to you," Joseph answered, looking the Prime Minister directly in the eye. "A pragmatic case could be made that it's hardly worth risking the lives of every Israeli in a regional war for the sake of who-knows-how-many families."

"Certainly," ben Yuda agreed with a scowl. "But as we all know, that's never been the policy of the State of Israel. We go after our own. Tell me this: can we reach these Jews ourselves, simply based on the lists in that genealogy?"

"It would take a great deal of Mossad manpower, sir—at a time when our resources are stretched very thin. But yes, it can be done," the Defense Minister finished, his tone wary.

"I'm not asking yet to pull the trigger on an operation, Joseph," ben Yuda said, standing abruptly. "But if I decide to do just that, I want the information ready. If I choose to go in, we need to know where to find them. Right away. Is everyone in agreement?"

The men around the table nodded somberly. The Prime Minister's recommendation had hardly been reckless. The real debate over options would begin as soon as the meeting ended and the entire cabinet came in.

"Mr. Prime Minister?" Meyer asked quietly as the others began to leave. "I have a small additional request. It's of a quasi-private nature." His voice had dropped to barely above a whisper.

"Oh, really?"

"Well, when I examined the parchments under improvised infrared in the field, I discovered another document along with the genealogy. One which possesses, shall we say, more historical than military value. Although that value is considerable."

"I'm not following you."

"Sir, this document's authorship is not properly attributed. But from its text, it would appear to be written by—well, by Queen Esther herself. I couriered them back to Jerusalem, where our new infrared technology confirmed its age but not its authenticity. To our knowledge, there is only one place where we can do that, one extant text against which to compare it. It is, as you know, privately controlled by your wife's family. And I know this is a sensitive time, yet I would deeply appreciate if she could be asked for her permission to examine it."

Jacob ben Yuda nodded, now intrigued in spite of himself. He laid a hand on Meyer's shoulder. "I will speak to my wife. I have one question, though. Why is a Mossad agent concerning himself with such a thing? Why not the antiquities people?"

The agent shrugged inscrutably, nodded his farewell, and took his leave.

MOSSAD HEADQUARTERS, JERUSALEM—MIDNIGHT

The intruder entered the highly protected perimeter like someone who knew the place—which he did. First, shrouded in the late-night shadows, he pulled out an invisible panel from the wall, reached in, and switched on an emergency override, which instantly disabled all alarm systems.

Then he slipped inside, holding a gun at the ready inside his jacket pocket, and made his way swiftly and guardedly into the central workroom.

There the Battaween documents awaited him.

Eagerly, with just enough pause to sweep his gaze around the room and check for camera lights, he held up the next document into a shaft of moonlight streaming in from a skylight above.

Then, like an addicted booklover unwilling to end his day's reading, he began to devour the words before him.

He *had* to know what happened next.

Chapter Nine

My Dear Leah,

I just finished your letter, and have only now sufficiently recovered my breath to sit down and write back to you.

I can hardly believe what you have told me.

I am sitting here in a simple chair right outside my tent, not even two paces away from where the Damascus courier just handed me your scroll. You might be shocked to see the outward humility of my current abode, and I must admit that compared to my former quarters in the royal palace, a tent on the rocky soil of Jerusalem could seem like a vast step down. Yet you would hardly believe what freedom I feel here! What utter liberation from the stifling sense of being guarded and watched every second of my life! It has been bliss—at least until now.

Artaxerxes has not been King even two decades, and already threats to his reign may cause me to leave on the next caravan for home. In fact, I may return hard on the heels of the very reply you are holding.

But I digress, for reasons you probably understand. You see, when I grasped the scroll from his fingers and read your name beside the seal, I exclaimed out loud in delight, so overjoyed I was to be receiving news from you. But when I began to read and realized the import of your message, I could not help but gasp aloud, followed by frantic, anguished breathing, and finally sobbing tears. All in the space of merely a few moments. A sallow-faced little girl who dwells two doors down and has always been frightened of me turned with wide eyes, fled indoors, and summoned her mother, who stood at their threshold carefully watching me through dark eyes. I wiped my face and attempted a smile to assure both that I was in control of my faculties, but she has returned to the doorway several more times to check on me.

Oh, how my heart aches for you! To cautiously open your heart, to have it intimately examined, and then to have it summarily rejected is the cruelest of all agonies. My mind is racing as I try to find a place to start answering your question. For I certainly intend to.

But, my dear, the question you posed has been the central anguish of my life for the past few years. And not only mine, but that of the people dearest to me. Now including you.

Is my life, at least for any meaningful purpose, over? Has G-d's plan for me been fulfilled?

My dear, Leah, I will certainly answer this question, if it takes all I have. Even if it requires me leaving my beloved Jerusalem and returning to Persia.

This is why I am praying that G-d will remove the wound of Artaxerxes' rejection from your heart. That He will deaden your mind to the memories that evening seared into your deepest being. Having said that, remember, "Memories do not die. Memories must simply be replaced—with new memories." You may never fully understand why you were not chosen.

But first, let me begin with what I know this moment. I will tell you about a conversation I shared with Mordecai on the very day I left for this place. The words of it came flooding back into my mind even as I read your letter.

As you probably have been told, Nehemiah's caravan was delayed beside the Ahava River for several days. But on the morning our final go-ahead was signaled, Mordecai stood beside me, arms crossed, as I packed my final few items. I could tell something was burrowing deep within him.

"Well, my little Hadassah," he finally said with a faintly bitter note in his voice, "I certainly hope you find the adventure you seek."

"What do you mean?" I replied, not bothering to mask my defensive reaction. "You speak as if I am some youth off on a foolhardy jaunt."

"I do not mean that. I only mean that you have had such a rich life. And yet you act as though experiencing even more is some kind of birthright."

"Poppa!" I exclaimed in surprise, my voice raised higher than I intended. "We have talked about this so many times over the last few years. You know what I have lived through. You know what it was like to walk away from being Queen."

"Yes, and you survived it. Just like millions of people before you have outlasted disappointment and loneliness."

Just then I realized, from the deep pain in his eyes, that my beloved Mordecai was speaking of himself. I reached out to touch his hand.

"I'm sorry," I said, my voice now softer. "I haven't thought of you. I wasn't thinking of . . ."

He covered my hand with his remaining palm and shook his head slowly. "You don't know how much joy and fulfillment it has given me to raise you. To see what G-d has done with your life. But at the same time, today, I find myself wishing, looking around me . . ." His voice drifted off, and he looked into the sun, which he always seemed to do at times of great anguish, as though to burn away what they might reveal. When he spoke again, his voice had changed completely. "I was just thinking of life without you. Without anyone." He glanced away, and the pain in his face seemed to mirror the loneliness he would soon experience. He had never married, for I had always been his world. While young, I had innocently believed that to be sufficient. Yet just then I realized the truth: Mordecai was lonely.

And I realized something else. He was being specific. By "looking around me" he meant that there was an ache in his heart—and it had a face, and a name.

"Tell me. Where have you been looking? Who?"

He shook his head most resolutely now. "No. I will not speak her name. There is no chance. It is not a possibility."

"*What* is not a possibility? Love? Marriage? Why not? The wish for happiness and acceptance are also legitimate desires. G-d himself placed these hungers inside of us. You taught me that yourself, Poppa."

He looked at me with the saddest expression I had ever seen him wear. "I am an old man far beyond the prime of his youth and the fullness of his vitality. I am not a man who attracts a single look from a woman."

"You're wrong. I have seen many women look at you."

"That is only because of my station. My position in the empire."

"Maybe, but that's part of your appeal! You have every right to rely on your position and fame as Exilarch to woo a woman. Even though it's only a part of who you are. You are so much more. You are kind and wise and the godliest man I will ever know. And you also happen to be the most beloved and famous man in all of Persia, second only to the King. Each of those things can be legitimately attractive."

"Please, Hadassah," he said, shaking his head emphatically, "let us speak of this no more. I am sorry to have brought it up."

"Just tell me one thing," I pleaded. "You are speaking of one woman in particular? There is one you long for?"

He inhaled deeply and stared up at the sky, and from that, knowing Mordecai, I knew the truth.

"She sees me as the King's advisor," he murmured. "A father image more than anything else. She esteems me, but not . . ." His voice trailed off. "And besides. She is absolutely unapproachable."

"Poppa, I am a woman, and I can tell you that nothing is as simple as that. Perhaps she only pictures you that way because she sees the resignation on your face. Or maybe G-d has yet to open her eyes. Maybe she has more of life's road to travel before she is ready for you."

He waved his hand. "It is not important, Hadassah. Please. These are trivial matters compared to the work G-d has given me."

"No!" I said, almost shouting again. "That is where I disagree with you the most. You may be a godly man, but you do not know how He intends to accomplish His purposes in this world. How do you know that we only serve G-d through positions of power and influence?"

He sighed, looked at me, and chuckled. "Hadassah, as usual, you leave me without words."

"You don't need words with me. But let me end with this. You know this is the whole reason I am leaving for the Promised Land. I feel YHWH calling me there, even though I have no idea how I can possibly be of help. But I'm willing to trust what He put in my heart. And if He put love for a woman in yours, then you must explore that with Him."

And, my dear Leah, you must explore that question with Him, too. To complete my reply to you, I now ask you to embark with me on yet another journey back into my life—this time into events and emotions more recent than our last correspondence.

The good news? I do, in fact, have an answer for you. And it is an encouraging answer. A heart-lifting, joyful affirmation. You will be glad to hear what I have to say.

The bad news? As your question is deeply felt, my reply might seem lengthy. But to have a peaceful answer to your question, I must tell you of some events that I mercifully withheld from you. They comprise some of the darkest and most agonizing low points of my life.

I have been where you are. And I know that if . . .

◆ ◆ ◆ ◆ ◆ ◆ ◆ ◆ ◆ ◆ ◆ ◆ ◆ ◆ ◆

Chapter Ten

THE PRIME MINISTER'S LIMOUSINE—DOWNTOWN
JERUSALEM—MINUTES AFTER HADASSAH MADE HER CALL

In the gloom of the Residence garage beyond her limousine window, Hadassah's two escorts from Shin Beth, Israel's domestic counter-intelligence and protective service, struggled to ready their motor-cycles. Like her, they had not ventured beyond the walls of the Res-idence in weeks, and lacking the proper lead time, her right "wingman," as she had always mischievously called him, could not electrically start his motor. She could see him glance back at her with irritation as he rose and fell in his seat, futilely trying to stomp down on his starter pedal.

Clearly, both he and his partner were agitated by the abruptness of her departure, her apparent flaunting of observed procedure. She knew that in these days following the attempt on her husband's life, security measures would be at their strongest. She could remember, from her briefings upon entering the Prime Minister's Residence, that even sched-uled outings could provoke a flurry of covert communications among a small army of sentries, reconnaissance assets, and even undercover oper-atives.

Yet today the whole apparatus would have to wait. If she had to, she would walk to Jacob's office. She felt the certainty of this meeting like a tiny pebble gathering mass and hardness deep inside her heart, and she clung to its solidity as if her life depended on it.

To calm herself she leaned back into the leather headrest and savored the feeling of once more being dressed, out of her bedroom, and sitting upright.

She had not even sat in a vehicle seat since returning from her father's *Yiskor* service, which she had attended with husband on one side, doctor on the other, each taking anxious glimpses of her face as she stared ahead without acknowledging either. Only three days after surgery to remove the shrapnel inside her, her pain extended beyond inner shock and grief.

At least all the media hype had resulted in one bittersweet by-product. The circumstances of his death had made her father's memorial a state event. Broadcast over live television, attended by thousands. She pictured the sea of anguished faces stretched before her in Jerusalem's Great Synagogue, reserved mainly for state events—"*The Great Synagogue!*" he would have exclaimed, eyes wide, his voice making that hoarse rasp it used to convey amazement—"*For me?*"

The thought was definitely a source of comfort, for Poppa had been a simple, modest man, completely unknown beyond family and friends until his little girl had married the head of state. He would have been shocked and overwhelmed to know he was mourned by an entire nation. *His* entire nation. *If only he could have seen it*, she thought with her first hint of a smile. *If only . . .*

With the deaths of her elderly aunts in the last few years, she had become sadly familiar with the Yizkor, the "Memorial Prayers" service. Yet she had not been prepared for the sight of Israel's whole cabinet and assembled Knesset leadership sitting behind her in a show of solidarity, wearing stricken expressions.

Nor had she been ready for the words of the Yizkor Father's Version, read with sonorous dignity by Israel's Chief Rabbi: "May the Lord remember the soul of my father, my teacher, David Kesselman, who has gone on to his eternal rest. . . ." And when the cantor, the most famous in the Jewish world, had begun to sing the classic lament *E-l Malei Rachamim*—"G-d, Full of Mercy"—his plaintive voice filling the synagogue's vaulted heights with aching notes of loss, she had lost her composure and wept openly.

And she hadn't been weeping only for her father. Every one of her relatives who had attended her wedding only five years before were now gone. Aunt Rose, who had surprised her by flying in early from America for her wedding, had been the first. *Stroke.* Grandma Grossman had died in her sleep, peacefully, from an aneurysm. Aunt Connie had died just four months ago of pneumonia in a Tel Aviv hospital.

Now, with the loss of her father, an entire generation that had once nurtured and upheld her had vanished within just a few short years. They had survived the Holocaust, but they could not survive time.

Now, without brother or sister, she found herself utterly alone. With both hands, she had clutched her husband's arm, for he was now all she had left.

With a feeling of nostalgia so keen that it twisted cruelly in her still-healing abdomen, Hadassah tried to picture the world her relatives had known. The tumult they had outlived. The thought of it only plunged her into a swirl of pride, grief, and resentment. But she willed herself to continue, to remember and reminisce. As painful as it was, comfort accompanied the memories.

She tried to picture her father growing up in the rural Hungary of the early twentieth century—a place of occasional persecution for Jews, yet idyllic nevertheless. How he and five other relatives had survived the Holocaust by tracing a harrowing walk to the port of Trieste, where they had bribed their way aboard a ship to London and to distant, previously emigrated relatives. How a sister, two uncles and their families who had declined to make the trip perished in Nazi death camps. She strained to remember the stories he had told her about being a cold and terrified teenager, trekking through forests at night, avoiding German patrols and the shotguns of suspicious locals.

A growl from the long-delayed motorcycle start jerked her back to the present. The garage door tilted upward, greeting her eyes with the slate gray of a rainy midday, and the limousine was off at last. She moved her eyes away from the Residence driveway, the gates sliding open, traffic on Balfour Street braking suddenly to make way for the motorcade. But she could not shift her thoughts.

What a blessing this place, the reborn State of Israel, must have been to her beleaguered relatives, those first few years after war's end! It was more than the rebirth of their homeland—it was an actual open invitation to a place they had only heard spoken of in hushed, emotional tones over Seder and Passover.

Still a bit light-headed from her prolonged bed rest, she yawned, refocused her gaze on the pedestrians lining the elegant sidewalks of Rehavia, Jerusalem's most gracious residential neighborhood, and squinted to banish the ache inside her. But the sight of curious onlookers only reminded her of the crowds that had lined this same street on the morning of Poppa's funeral. She could not forget the gratitude that had accompanied her first glimpse of eerie candle glow flickering up into all those tearstained, sympathetic faces. For hours they had stood that night outside her residence.

And once again the thought of missing loved ones whisked forward all the memories, and the treasured people who housed them . . . now gone forever. No one to call and be greeted in a thick Yiddish accent, the lilt of pleasant surprise, the sound of those stories retold from a living mouth. No one to meet her for breakfast in the King David Hotel lobby and chat about the odd trials of being married to a head of state. No one to call and confess, as she would have if she could, *"I'm depressed, Poppa. I'm so terribly depressed that I can hardly function; it's the biggest challenge just getting out of bed. . . ."*

She shook her head, determined to rouse her emotions from the depths of grief. Glancing up beyond the front windshield, she saw Paris Square approaching—the busy interchange where not only would she turn left onto one of West Jerusalem's busiest thoroughfares, but where large, vocal anti-Israeli protests often gathered.

A high wall caught the sun, casting its glare into her eyes—

—and she remembered. How could she have forgotten? The Great Synagogue, site of her father's service, was hardly a block away, up King George Street.

A quick intake of breath and she quickly leaned forward from her position inside as—

—the long body of the Prime Minister's armored limousine trembled between the crosshairs of anti-reflective binoculars protruding from the front drape of a large *kaffiyeh*, the ubiquitous Palestinian headdress, in the shadow of a quiet Rehavia rooftop.

The scout, a young Arab—ironically, not a Palestinian but an

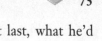

Iraqi—breathed more quickly at the sight. Here, at last, what he'd waited for, all these long days. *The Jew she-dog was at last making her appearance.* He reached out with his free hand and picked up his cell phone.

He held his thumb over the speed dial button of a preprogrammed phone number.

Through his binoculars, the limousine prepared to turn onto Ramban Street. A disguised Red Cross van awaited them, parked innocuously along a busy sidewalk but loaded with fourteen thousand pounds of ammonium nitrate and a recipient cell phone whose ringer was wired to complete an electrical circuit. A tiny spark would trigger an explosion even the infidel Americans' armored plating would not withstand.

His thumb minutely began a downward plunge as he saw the tires begin their swerve, and the oddly out-of-place Cadillac began to turn—

—and Hadassah called out to her driver, "Bernard, I'm so sorry, but could we go straight instead, please? I'd like to drive past the Great Synagogue. Just a small detour. It would mean so much to me. . . ."

Bernard took a deep breath, gritted his teeth, and gave a light warning honk to the motorcycle escorts, whom he knew would soon despise him. Then he muttered a warning into his radio headpiece, corrected the wheel, and began to abort his turn. He did so broadly, giving the inside motorcycle room to not only heed his verbal warning but compensate for the change in direction and avoid being clipped.

The escort expertly evaded the limousine's front bumper with an abrupt turn of his front wheel—almost jack-knifing on the wet pavement, the kind of impulsive maneuver a new rider might make under less challenging circumstances.

Back on the nearby rooftop veranda, the spotter's mouth fell open, his hand still tight upon his cell phone digit. He tried to calculate whether there was still time, whether the turning vehicle was still within range of his blast perimeter. But he hesitated, and within a second and a half, it was too late. The limousine had vanished into the distance of King George Street.

He swore softly and threw down the binoculars with a loud clatter. For the second time, the target had escaped by mere feet. His brief moment in the spotlight had been delayed—not denied, mind you—for he would still make certain that her assassination would be recorded to his credit.

Chapter Eleven

A quarter-mile away, Hadassah Kesselman finally ended her Shiva mourning period—eight days later than mandated by Jewish tradition.

She glanced up at the Great Synagogue passing her window, whispered a strangled good-bye to her Poppa, then buried her face in her hands, sobbing more loudly than she had in years—perhaps her whole life. She wept for her vanished family, her heritage now consigned to the realm of memory and written word. Most of all, she wept for her own ruptured connection to the world. With the rain falling, it seemed that the whole world was weeping with her.

She could not stop her tears for two miles, while her motorcade traced a detour back to Ramban Street and proceeded toward the Valley of the Cross. By the time they passed the southern end of the templelike Knesset building and turned onto Kaplan Street, home to the Prime Minister's office, she had regained control of her breathing and was holding up a mirrored compact to repair her smudged makeup. *How ironic*, she thought, looking at her face. *All these drivers' efforts to keep me dry and perfect, yet here I am, still managing to look like I just ran through the rain. . . .*

The emotional eruption left her heaving and weak, yet it also served a helpful purpose—it seemed to have swept away the depression, at least for a time, and left a whole new inner weather pattern in its place. She felt the limo nose down into the office building's parking garage, took a deep breath, and knew she was ready.

Darkness returned around her; ahead was only motorcycle brake lights and the tug of sharp turns upon her torso. Finally, they stopped. She didn't wait: she flung open her door, muttered "Thank you, guys" to the escorts, and walked into the brightly lit elevator entrance with the stride of one who would not be deterred.

Her personal security guard missed the elevator door and, with a disgusted sigh, turned for the stairs with a grim assessment of her destination etched upon his face.

Strangely, once the elevator door opened to the fifth floor, Hadassah hardly needed to remember her way. It seemed that a shock wave preceded her, parting the hallway's knots of bureaucrats and loiterers and forging a path of swerving feet and shocked faces for her to follow. She feigned a taciturn expression and steered straight ahead, noting nothing and acknowledging no one. Part of her felt guilty, for the eyes seeking hers bore mostly sympathy and affection. But she simply could not afford to make eye contact and risk losing her delicate composure. She attempted to keep her face from conveying anything worse than conviction, and walked on.

Finally the path ended before a twin set of dark oaken doors. Despite their thickness, she could still hear a wave of male voices arguing in Hebrew from inside. She understood, for she knew the sight well—the entrance into the Israeli Cabinet Chamber. A simple façade well known to any informed Jew, laden with history and a fractious heritage of debate and even occasional shouting and shoving.

She did not pause. With a forbidden thrill cascading across her back through her insides, she reached out her right hand and pushed straight through. A Shin Beth guard standing at post recognized her and, in a nod to protocol, began to step forward and hesitantly intervene; but she gave him her most imperious stare and inwardly defied him to stop her. She stepped forward and walked right up to the edge of the parquet floor.

Her husband's face was the first to enter her field of sight. He was in midsentence, gesturing indistinctly into midair, but his words failed and his eyes locked on hers. On every side of him sat bodies and faces well known to every Israeli with a television. The members of the Israeli Cabinet. Those with their backs to her swiveled abruptly backward, anticipating trouble. Within two seconds, every wide-eyed stare in the room was fixed most resolutely upon her.

"Jacob," she said, in her most wifely, intimate tone, ignoring the assembled group. "I must speak with you."

"Hadassah." He spoke the word more as a declaration than a greeting. "I am so glad to see you. I am so sorry to say this"—and then his features regained their solemn, official demeanor. He swept the air with a grand, apologetic gesture—"but I cannot talk with you until dinner tonight. I am so sorry, but I'm sure you realize these are critical times—"

"They certainly are, my dear. That's why I need to talk to you so urgently. . . . I need a favor."

"Hadassah, I literally have the chairman of the Palestinian Authority waiting on the phone." His eyes begged for her cooperation and understanding, but his tone was firm.

"Who better to wait on me than *him*." She did not try to conceal the bite in her voice.

Jacob couldn't help but chuckle at that fierce rejoinder. Even the cabinet would have to admit that it was true—having suffered the loss she had, no Israeli expected her to grant the political mouthpiece of her father's murderers any measure of respect.

"Mr. Prime Minister," offered his chief deputy in a rising, tentative voice, "I'm sure Chairman Abboud would be willing to postpone for a half hour, given the circumstances."

She stood perfectly still, not moving a muscle, and watched her husband's eyes dart about in furious rumination—calculating the consequences. Finally, his eyes met hers again and narrowed, trying to gauge the determination in her face.

A split second of deep connection passed between them.

And she smiled.

Perhaps the smile was only a knee-jerk reaction to the errant memory that had just wandered into her mind—*Esther entering unannounced before the King!* At least she did not face the prospect of execution for daring to enter. . . .

Only he recognized it as brave and forced. But it did not matter to him. It was the first semblance of joy he had seen her display in weeks. The very effort of forming it opened her face, lightened her eyes, and filled him with an immediate surge of hope.

Before she knew it, he was nodding almost despite himself, as though his assent to her request was a reflex.

"All right." He spoke without breaking eye contact with her. "Convey my deepest apologies to the chairman, and tell him that my wife and I will harbor endless gratitude for his forbearance in a personal emergency. No, not emergency—"

"Lunch. It's called *lunch*," she announced.

A sympathetic chuckle swept through the cabinet members.

"All right," Jacob said, finally glancing about with a sheepish grin. "Let's call it a personal matter. That will have to do."

"The Ramallah headquarters have cable," muttered Moshe, the Defense Minister.

Hadassah hesitated, trying to grasp the man's meaning, then regretted having understood. *Your wife's predicament is a matter of national media,* he had meant. *Even in the West Bank, they know what is at hand. . . .*

Jacob stood, the decision clear in his face. "We'll adjourn until one-thirty, my friends. Thank you all."

And the Israeli Cabinet filed past her, each one fixing her with a moment's somber and sympathetic nod.

Finally, they were alone. He reached out his hand, inviting her to sit, yet uncomfortable with treating her like just another caller. Especially in this room. He stifled a chuckle, for without meaning to—yet with incredible portent—she had chosen the chair with a nameplate bearing the title *Secretary of Defense.*

How appropriate, he told himself with just the faintest hint of a grin as she stood behind the chair.

Finally Jacob rediscovered his wits and walked around to give her a soft kiss on the cheek. His hand grazed her forearm in an additional gesture of intimacy.

"Honey," he whispered, and both of them knew this tone of voice had never been used in that room before. "A surprise, of course, but I'm so glad to see you. Up. And about."

"Me too." She smiled at her own ambiguity. "Glad to see *me* 'up and about,' I mean. You have no trouble getting around."

"I'll call for lunch." He pulled out the chair for her, then went to the phone.

She had chosen to sit across from him—for despite their very personal relationship, she most definitely had a petition to bring.

He finished muttering the lunch order, hung up, sat down and faced her with a blank expression.

"So. Did you come here with a specific goal in mind? That is, beyond making a grand entrance and spooking my entire cabinet?"

She recoiled slightly at the directness of his words, and so did he. Clearly, he had not intended to start by chastising her. But a sentence that had begun as humor had somehow escalated.

She decided to respond in kind. Not mean, but not wilting, either.

"Yes, I had a goal. I came here to see if I had a marriage. Or just an official, state-approved bedroom partner."

He closed his eyes briefly and breathed out in frustration. "Please, Hadassah. I'm about to reinitiate peace talks that could affect the future of this country. And quite possibly the geopolitical balance of the entire world. Can I be forgiven for needing to focus?"

"I need you, Jacob."

She said it in a low, intimate, almost pleading tone. One which no man who loved his wife could possibly rebuff.

He sighed again. "I appreciate that, honey. And that means a great deal to me. But honestly, my people—*our* people—need me too, right now."

"They can wait through the most decisive thirty minutes of your marriage. As Moshe implied, everyone knows what happened. They all know I'm the national 'basket case.' They'll appreciate your husbandly commitment."

He sighed even more deeply, resolutely. Accepting her terms.

"What is it, Hadassah?"

She shook her head. "I want to talk to you. You're the only one left in the world I can have a heartfelt conversation with—do you know that? I used to have Poppa. Now it's you, or no one."

"How about G-d?" His eyes gazed at her from atop his steepled fingers. He had voiced the question softly, for he knew he was more religious than she.

"Please. You know what I'm talking about. G-d and I aren't exactly on speaking terms right now."

"Maybe you should work on that." But his voice held no rebuke.

"Maybe. But in the meantime, I don't want my emotional survival treated like some cabinet agenda item. I need to talk to you, not mark off a checklist."

He laughed out loud. "For such a vulnerable person, you're very much in my face right now, you know that?"

She laughed, too. It had struck her also that her pose of abject weakness was starting to wear thin. She had, in fact, come with a clear goal in mind. But she also knew that she would require several long minutes of thawing to coax it out.

Chapter Twelve

H er face sobered quickly.

"When we met," she said, "I had a life. A career, a trajectory, that was about as stratospheric as yours. At least, it seemed that way to me. For a while."

He nodded, his face softening at the memory of it. "No, you weren't fooling yourself. It seemed that way to me, too. In fact, I was intimidated by you. At first."

"So what happened?"

"I don't know." He shrugged. "Life. Political destiny." He paused and looked down at his folded hands. "I know I have failed to make you feel a part of my career the way I wanted to."

"No, that's not it. But you can't let yourself off that easy."

She spread her hands out flat on the table and stared at them as though they contained some exotic secret.

"I've lost my life, Jacob." She looked into his face a moment. "I've lost my meaning, my momentum, my reason for living. I don't know where it went. I mean, I didn't lose it like you misplace a wallet. And I can't really see why my father's death would have suddenly destroyed it. All I know is, I can't seem to grasp ahold of it anymore."

"What can I do?"

"You can listen," she replied hastily, emphatically. "A few years from now, you'll be out of office and living the comfortable, respected life of a national statesman. You'll have media appearances, speeches in faraway countries, books to write, protégés to counsel. And me, I'll just be one of the well-dressed ladies-who-lunch, shopping in the boutiques, with no children"—she rushed over the words—"whose greatest achievement is what she *used* to be—First Lady."

She stared at him for a sign of affirmation and received none.

"What happened to the young woman you met, who wanted to write the definitive history of the Holocaust, who wanted to be the best mother who ever lived, who wanted to run for the Knesset?"

He bent forward to rub his forehead, obviously realizing she intended to wait for his reply. His politician's mind quickly strung together her demands—to be young, to write, to be a mother, to be a politician in her own right. With an ability honed by years of negotiating, he mentally zeroed in on what might be the true source of her frustration.

He again ran his hand over his face, then stared at her as though he was seeing her for the first time. He briefly wondered if the small bit of shrapnel that had pierced her womb had also blown apart his marriage. The physical wound was healing quickly enough—yet the question of children festered, unanswered.

"What does Hadassah tell you about this?" he finally replied.

She frowned, misunderstanding. "*Me?*"

"No. The ancient one. The Hadassah who wrote in your family's journals."

Her eyes flashed with quick anger. "What about *her*?"

"G-d had a plan for her."

"Yes. She was one in a million. What I wonder, when I read those journals, is what about the young concubine to whom she wrote the letters? Leah? *She's* my ancestor, remember. Not Esther. What about *her*? Is it possible that her only reason for being on earth was to pass on that journal? Was that it? To spend years in some royal harem being essentially raped once every few months, year after year? Is that what a loving G-d had in mind for her life?"

"I don't know." Jacob shook his head slowly, wishing he had not brought up the subject.

"No. We don't. But here's what I came to ask you. See, I didn't want you to just listen. I have a request. Not from my husband, but from my Prime Minister. I need a favor."

"Name it."

"I'm a scholar. An investigator, at least in an academic sense. Let me help find out who came after you. The one who killed my Poppa."

"You don't think it's the usual suspects? Hamas, Hezbollah, Fatah . . ."

"No, honey. Jacob. I don't." She smiled wryly at the inadvertent endearment.

"Why not?"

"First of all, because if it had been, they'd be stumbling all over themselves to claim responsibility. And in over two weeks, there's been complete silence. Second, because I know you would have told me if the intelligence had come back with anything. And third . . ."

"Yes? Third?"

"Because of Poppa's last words." She automatically lowered her voice. "He wanted me to hear him so badly, he just refused to die until he'd gotten the words out. He said, *'She did not perish. You must find her.'*"

"Why didn't you tell me this? I didn't know he said anything!"

"Because I haven't been sure if it meant anything. But I've been thinking about it for the last two weeks, and now I'm convinced. Besides, I think you and your people haven't the first clue why that man attacked. And I think my father knew. Something."

For the first time all day, Prime Minister ben Yuda looked shocked. He stared ahead into space, searching for an answer in the thin air.

"Do you have an answer for me?" she asked.

Rather than speaking, he reached over to a dark green folder among the papers to his left. He pressed down on its surface and slid the cardboard toward her.

She made no move to open it.

"What does it say?" she asked.

"This top-secret report concludes that the bombing was not carried out by any known Palestinian group. And that it was probably not even directed at me. Who it was actually directed at may never be known, although the investigation continues. The document was presented to me twenty minutes before you arrived."

They both exhaled and let a long, tense pause flow between them.

"Hadassah, I suppose it makes sense for you to spend some time researching this. You might even be entitled. I'll open some doors for you, quietly. Try to improve your access to people and documents. But I have to warn you. First, you have to be careful. No playing secret agent. And second, this cannot come out. If the world discovered that the Israeli First Lady was conducting some kind of *ad hoc* personal investigation, I and my intelligence cadres would be humiliated. Do you understand? With the very first media report of this, it's over. Nonnegotiable."

"I agree. I'll be totally discreet."

There was a knock on the door. A steward entered, carrying two steaming lunches, set them down before each, then backed out, closing the door behind him.

Both of them looked wearily at the plates, then broke into laughter. The food had arrived just as they were through. And then a sudden pain in the still-healing muscle wall of her abdomen cut short her laugh. With a grimace, she reached for her belly.

"I'm sorry," he said. "I didn't mean to make you hurt yourself."

She shook her head forgivingly. "The doctor said it's healing fine. I'm lucky to have only had such a small wound."

"But in such a critical area," he said, his voice gentle. Then he leaned across the table and looked deeply into her face. "You have such extraordinary eyes, Hadassah. I've always . . ."

But he didn't know how to finish, and an awkward silence descended on them.

"I just had an idea," Jacob suddenly said with a forced energy. "It's not much, but . . . just this morning, I was given a strange briefing from the head of Mossad, about a matter that might possibly involve you. One of our top undercover men has just been rushed back from Iraq with some documents that, if they're authentic, could set off bombshells across the Middle East. In an odd twist, it looks like the

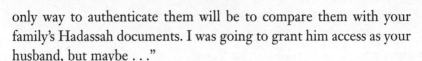

only way to authenticate them will be to compare them with your family's Hadassah documents. I was going to grant him access as your husband, but maybe . . ."

"Maybe I could help him myself?"

"Exactly. Might help you open some of your own back channels with intelligence. Make some connections that have nothing to do with me."

"That's exactly what I need. And I could take it from there."

"Just remember, my dear, I'm not sure I'm doing the right thing, letting you do this. I'm certainly not setting you loose because I think you won't come up with anything. Quite the opposite. And also, quite frankly, I'm afraid that if you truly get somewhere, I'm not sure I'll be able to protect you. Every Israeli can use a little help from the Mossad at some point or other."

"I understand. And thank you. Now where could I meet this man?"

"I'll arrange it. He wanted to see the Hadassah scroll, so—back to where it all started. The Shrine."

Chapter Thirteen

ISRAEL MUSEUM, SHRINE
OF THE BOOK—LATE THAT NIGHT

S*he had stepped onto* the floor beneath the Shrine of the Book's curved dome many times in her life—especially since learning right before her wedding day that the famous museum housed her own family's oldest and most cherished documents.

Yet she had never seen it at this hour—eleven o'clock at night—and never in these conditions. All lighting was turned off, and the only illumination in its curved roof line glowed from a pool of moonlight pouring in through the hole overhead. Banks of deep shadow only seemed to lengthen the stone floors and heighten its sensuous overhead lines. Its only sounds were the faint echo of her delegation's footsteps upon marble and her own breathing.

She paused for a second to take in the strange sight, causing her Shin Beth bodyguard—at least the only one she could see—to almost collide with her back. He stepped back with a cowed grunt of apology. *Surely only a handful of people have ever seen the room in this eerie atmosphere*, she noted silently. She fought back a shiver of privilege mixed with unease, feeling a bit like one of those reckless teenagers in the horror movies who inexplicably walk into a cemetery at midnight on a full moon.

Looking around, she remembered another reason she was liking the Shrine's unusual appearance—she appreciated the contrast with the bright, vivid tourist attraction she had visited with Poppa on that day barely five years before. The wonderful morning when he had brought her here and first informed her of her family's unique heritage.

Her museum escort, the same matronly woman who had introduced her to the Hadassah journals on that fateful visit, walked her across. A man waited, so upright and motionless that Hadassah did not even notice his presence until she was less than twenty feet away.

Fighting the weariness of a first, long day out, she peered closer for a better look. She had been wondering who this mystery man was ever since learning of this meeting. The first thing she noticed was the dim outline of a medium-built man wearing dark, nondescript street clothing. Close-cropped dark hair, a lean jawline concealed by a full beard. Wasn't exactly young. *Could be anybody*, she remarked to herself, and then realized that this was precisely the man's intention.

"Mrs. Prime Minister, Ari Meyer of the . . . Investigative Archaeology Committee," stammered the museum guide, likely set off kilter by the unusual time and august company.

He lowered his head in greeting and held out his hand, the dim light glinting off his aviator glasses.

"Ari Meyer." Then, as the matron stepped back, he whispered with a sly smile, "*Mossad*. I am very grateful for this meeting and for your being willing to grant me access." He had a low, confident voice with just a trace of a British accent.

"Pleased to meet you," Hadassah said as they shook hands. His was cool and dry, and he held her hand loosely, almost indifferently.

Now came an awkward pause. Trying not to stare at her mysterious greeter, Hadassah felt for a moment as though she had been transported into some obscure spy thriller. Finally Meyer raised a small handpiece to his mouth and muttered something to an unseen colleague. He lowered it and tilted his head.

"Shall we go in?"

The escort nodded, and Meyer turned to her bodyguard. "Would you care to remain here and secure the entrance? It's the only way down."

The Shin Beth operative glanced at Hadassah thoughtfully and nodded. Meyer tossed the man another handpiece from his pocket, murmured, "We're on channel four," and they left him behind.

Walking to the recessed staircase and descending again into the hidden passageway, she felt herself swept back once more, reluctantly, to that landmark day with her father. She could not help smiling faintly as she recalled how coy he had been with her on the way to the Shrine, wearing the mischievous smile she had only seen in his later years.

At first her father's refusal to explain their museum visit had irritated her. Her wedding was only a few days away and time far too short for idle distractions. Then he had inexplicably diverted them right past the museum's ticket counter and first-floor exhibits, even more thoroughly confusing her. But when he had unerringly steered them to the out-of-the-way stairs and nearly bounded down the steps as if he owned the place, she had found herself completely bewildered. And there at the end of an isolated corridor had stood an even greater oddity: her aunt Rose from America and nearly every living older woman in her family.

It was the repetition of a hidden ritual her family had observed for centuries. And now she was the only one left who even remembered it.

Hadassah narrowed her eyes for an instant and pictured the proud glow that had swept over her father's features. And then the way his facial muscles had constricted as a wave of emotion had overtaken him. It had been one of the most moving episodes in his life, he had told her later.

But the matrons' appearance had been far from the final mystery, Hadassah reminded herself as she followed the museum guide and the Mossad agent to a now-familiar reinforced-metal door. Where before her father had ploddingly extricated the paper with the entry codes from his pocket and deliberately poked in every digit, now the hostess keyed in the codes swiftly from memory. The thick barrier swung open with a *whoosh!*—such a specific and singular sound, it made Hadassah feel that no time had passed since she had last heard it.

Stepping into the sprawling, dimly lit room and glimpsing the rows of faintly glowing display tables, awash in the special lighting that allowed study but did not deteriorate the document, she now felt thoroughly immersed in two time periods at once. She turned, half expecting her father's warm, gruff presence to await behind her, only to find Meyer standing there.

But she kept turning toward him, for something about his body language caught her attention.

As still as he had stood before, now he seemed veritably carved of stone. The man, transfixed, stared at the documents lying before him. Even though she could not see his eyes, only the rows of ancient parchment eerily suspended in his lenses, intensity seemed to radiate from him in waves. After several seconds completely without motion, he bent down, removed the glasses, and whisked a viewing lens over one eye. He surely acted as though he was more in awe of parchment pages than a prime minister's wife!

She now had seen his eyes for the first time. She peered at him further. She could be wrong—the dim light could be fooling her—but his deep-set, expressive brown eyes seemed to be shining with tears. This man was somehow emotionally overwhelmed. This simply could not be a routine document check. She shook her head slightly and stepped back. *Who is this man?*

Finally his eyes veered over to her face, and Meyer seemed to remember himself. A professional veneer claimed his features, and he instantly was the taciturn operative of before.

"Well, let's see if we have a match," he said, glancing down to a leather satchel at his side. He unlatched the flap and carefully pulled out several inches of ancient-looking documents.

Yes, to the business at hand, she told herself, trying to shake off the strange impression. She turned and looked down at the spot where she had signed her own name to the end of the document. The signature linked her life to the long chain of women who had signed the ancient story of Queen Esther and this secret epistle to an unknown Jewish concubine named Leah—a young girl in a Persian court lost to history, who had nevertheless been her distant ancestor.

Just as on that first day, Hadassah felt a vast presence suck the present moment away with an almost palpable sensation. The enormity of time surrounded her, dwarfed her, caused her troubles to seem trivial, even insectlike. Emotion like a surge of violins in some aching minor key swept through her. And despite being bittersweet, the storm of feelings felt bracingly fresh to her now, a welcome renewal from the stupor of the last few weeks.

She stepped toward Meyer and glanced down at his samples.

"So I hear you may have a companion text," she offered.

He turned toward her as though surprised she knew that much. She sensed a complex personality—but a good one. A man of integrity.

"Yes," he answered. "I believe what I found was written in Esther's hand, but I had no other way to confirm it. Again, the Institute thanks you and your family for your . . . forbearance."

"You're quite welcome."

"And also," he said, as though once provoked he could not stop himself from talking, "you have my deepest sympathies in the loss of your father. He was a good man."

She shook her head, perplexed at the tone of his reference. "You . . . you knew of my father?"

He glanced away, and she had a distinct impression that she had caught him in some imprudent disclosure.

"Just from the media accounts. I was captivated by the story of how he and his family members survived the *Shoah*."

She nodded at that last word, the Jewish term for the Holocaust. Reminded of her Poppa's familiar tale of escaping the Holocaust by hiking through Eastern Europe, she felt a reassuring warmth spread over her and gave Meyer another appraising look. *Weird* . . . Even while he stared at one of the ancient documents through a thick magnifying loop, his expression appeared strangely wistful. And despite his obvious competence, he also seemed unable to hide his reaction— a fact that intrigued her as much as any other.

At the very least, an unusual Mossad agent—although she had to remind herself that she had no other frame of reference.

He bent closer and once again, stillness overtook him. Finally, he straightened and faced her and the museum hostess.

"Clearly this is what scholars would call a cursory examination. Yet from what I can tell, it's reasonably certain the two documents are a match. My parchments were most likely written by Queen Esther herself."

"Can you tell me to whom she wrote it?"

He shook his head. "We are most grateful, but I couldn't tell you more without severe consequences. Maybe someday, when the urgency has passed and the proper releases have been authorized . . ."

"I understand." She heard her voice and felt embarrassed at the tone of girlish disappointment it conveyed. "And yet, from what you say, it sounds like this comparison has some . . . national security repercussions to it. My husband said you were assigned to Iraq?"

He leaned in closer to her.

"We *are* grateful. Extremely grateful. Please convey the Institute's thanks to your family members."

"I'm the only one left," she heard herself say.

She sighed and remembered the vague promises her husband had made to her—that helping the Mossad agent might result in some helpful contacts toward her own covert quest.

Now was the time to act.

Chapter Fourteen

Hadassah *put a hand* to his shoulder, leaning in to whisper so as to avoid any prying attentions. He stiffened at her touch and warily glanced around for the hostess.

"Agent Meyer, might I have a . . . private word with you," she said softly. "You see," she continued, lowering her voice even further, "I'm engaged in a little fact-finding of my own. It concerns my father. Obviously, your confidentiality is assured. And of course my husband is aware of my curiosity."

She said this with a gleam that conveyed a sense of expectation—*Now you know something you didn't before, so it's your turn to tell me something I don't know. . . .* By helping her, he could acquire some political favor, was the implication.

She suddenly felt his eyes bore into hers with an intensity that shocked her.

"I ask"—she paused a moment to regroup—"I ask partly because you spoke of my father and his background. You see, without disclosing any privileged information on my part," she let another moment pass, realizing that her informational trump card was about to be played, "I can tell you that the attack which killed him has not yet been attributed to anyone. As unlikely as this may sound, it seems to have had nothing to do with my husband."

Meyer grew perfectly still for a second. Then she saw his head lower. He was moving to meet her exact eye level; she had definitely seized his attention.

"Is there any way," she asked more confidently, "through your associations, your briefing—that you could imagine my father being a valid target for assassination?"

His pupils darted around quickly. He could not resist the challenge; he was thinking hard. Finally, his eyes returned to her.

"Have you considered," he said, matching her hushed tones, "that the actual target might have been *you*?"

Like a sheet of ice water poured from a bucket, a cold bath of shock rushed over her head and through her being. The room's corners reeled slightly, tilting her vertigo.

Truly she had never considered the possibility—at least not consciously. As she quickly thought back over the last few weeks, she realized that the notion had floated somewhere around the periphery of her mind, always just out of sight, never close enough for her to deal with head-on.

Perhaps she had not faced the idea because she could not bear the thought of her father dying as a result of something directed at *her*. The obvious theory of a politically motivated attack on her husband was at least predictable. Yet how could she *not* have faced this other possibility? She felt stupid and naïve, like a schoolgirl trying to insinuate herself into the world of grown-ups.

Then, without warning, the faint hallway lights blinked out. One overhead light and the dim glow from the glass cabinets was the only illumination.

Meyer glanced up at the ceiling in a sudden movement that whisked her back to the present. "Now that I've mentioned that possibility," he muttered as he grabbed his handheld. "Perimeter one, status?" he whispered into the device.

He released the button and waited. Nothing came.

"Perimeter one? Perimeter two?"

She could sense his every muscle tighten in the ensuing pause. His scholarly demeanor had vanished—in its place came a coiled poise and an endless vigilance. The silent throb of alarm seemed to hover between them, awaiting his signal. The wait must have lasted only ten seconds, but it was still time enough for her mind to run through a thousand dire scenarios.

He gritted his teeth and muttered something under his breath. He swerved around to find their hostess.

"How secure is this room?"

"If I close this door, it's everything-proof," she answered quickly but sounding surprisingly calm. "We can wait inside indefinitely, but of course we can't get out, either. There's no other exit. And if power goes out, we may start running out of oxygen."

He shook his head. "We have to have an exit route," he said. "Are there any video monitors, hidden security?"

"In a room down the hall. Not here."

"How much radio interference and signal obstruction does this building put out?"

"Ultra-thick walls and insulated wiring, but we've always been able to radio out. . . ."

Meyer raised the handpiece and adjusted its settings.

"Dark Wing, Dark Wing, Lebev 12 here. I have a shattered eyeglass at the Shrine of the Book. Possible broken bones. And Ladybug is with me. Repeat Ladybug is in the mix. Please respond at once."

He exhaled tensely, reached to his waist, and pulled out a large, gleaming machine pistol which seemed to fill the room with import and menace. His other hand reached over to the gun's action and pulled it back with a ratchet sound that rang out in the quiet of the room. His eyes swept their surroundings, and for a moment, she caught a bit of the moment through his eyes—*No real cover, just a bunch of delicate, priceless antiquities—hardly a great place for a shootout. . . .*

"Ladies, please sit down over there," he whispered, pointing to the corner just inside the room's entrance. Hadassah saw his thinking—the narrow space behind the open metal door was a perfect place to take cover. She hurried over and crouched behind the thick wedge of steel, the other woman huddled behind her.

Wincing at the hardness of floor beneath her and the insult of rigid wall at her back, she was finally struck with the realization that here was the possibility of mortal danger. This excursion had never been considered high-risk and had therefore been unscheduled, executed with unmarked, inconspicuous vehicles and minimal protection. The one Shin Beth bodyguard inside, several more possibly outside. Now with an intruder possibly inside the Shrine and the bodyguard apparently bound—or worse, she thought with a shudder—only this Mossad agent stood between her and the threat.

She found she could hardly get enough air into her lungs. Her chest began to heave with deep gasps, her vision spinning with a new wave of vertigo.

Flattened against the wall on the doorway's other side, Meyer made a single rapid lunge, reached up, and flicked the light switch. Then he looked around and grimaced. The room's brightness level had hardly changed—clearly, overhead lighting was kept at minimum levels to protect its documents. Now the room's main light still came from the recessed purplish glow within the displays themselves.

"Can we turn *those* off?" he whispered to the hostess half-obscured behind the open door. The urgency was obvious—as long as light was giving them away, especially with so many reflecting glass tables, any attacker in the darkened hallway would have a good chance of spotting their hiding places.

Her eyes now wide with terror, the museum hostess could only reply by nodding emphatically toward a bank of controls behind him, at the end of the room's longest wall. The agent gripped his weapon harder and grimaced again—it was a spot completely exposed to the hallway.

Hadassah peeked around the corner to see if it was possible to help him. She could make an unexposed dogleg through some of the back tables to the control panel. But her lower body would still be visible and completely vulnerable under the tables' legs. And during that split second of reaching up to flip the lights off, she would be totally out in the open.

She looked in Meyer's direction for guidance and gulped back a scream.

A bright red laser sight-target was trembling across the wall, midway between his position and the controls. Furthermore, she could see that even though Meyer had spread himself flat against the wall, a two-foot span of mirrored glass table was about to reveal both Ari and the attacker to each other.

She held her breath. Meyer would be killed. Not only was Meyer seconds away from death, but if he went down, she and the other woman were also absolutely defenseless. The scroll—to be precise, the final span of display where all of the modern names were inscribed—was right in the target area and would be shredded in the crossfire.

Then *she* would be next.

She had to do it. Meyer's earlier radio distress call would certainly bring help, but from her experience, it wouldn't do so with the required speed.

Her peripheral vision still following the red dot, she crept out from behind the door's shelter, down the width of several tables, then cut across the third row.

The red dot jerked and waved wildly. *She must have been heard!* If it dipped down below the tables, indicating that he was looking low, she knew it would be all over.

Five seconds passed. She could hear her heart thump as though a stethoscope was glued to her ears. Her skin quivered like the head of an overtightened drum. Trying to hold her out-of-control breath, she inched down the row toward the far wall and the awaiting light switch.

The red dot moved slowly down along the wall, then dipped in her direction.

She stopped and pressed herself against the floor, bracing for a bullet's cruel smash into her body.

Another moment passed. She concentrated on calming her breath without letting any huffing sounds escape. Without even moving her head, she shifted her eyes under the table to catch a glimpse of Ari. There were his shoes, still flush against the wall, waiting like the rest of him.

Motion caught her eye—she looked up to see the dot leaving, moving back in Ari's direction. She moved stealthily down the rest of the row. The lighting controls were only five feet away now. Five long feet of brutally dangerous space. She turned and found that she could see Ari's face, constricted and reddened by stress. He was shaking his head *no* to her.

Don't do it!

She nodded back yes—she most definitely would. Then half to make her point and half to force herself into the act, she held up one hand and three fingers.

Counting, she lowered one . . .

. . . then another, as his headshaking grew more vigorous . . .

. . . the last one, as the dot seemed to quiver, undecided, and as she lunged for the switch, the gunman seemed to guess her intention at last because the laser swerved across the wall, found the center of her back at the split second she slammed her fist into the switch, plunging the room into complete blackness, and then fell to the carpet, once more sheltered by tables . . .

. . . and Ari stepped forward, his machine pistol in a perfect modified-Weaver stance, and filled the hallway with a thunderstorm of gunfire.

Hadassah rolled, and she would never remember precisely why—whether from some awareness that she was a second away from being shot, or utter shock at the barrage from Ari, or disorientation in the sudden darkness, she would never be able to distinguish.

What followed seemed to take place in slow motion.

First came mad, deep-throated shouting, so chaotic that when it rang out, Hadassah could not tell whom it was coming from. It was Ari, of course, pulling her to her feet and yelling at her to follow him, that if she wanted to live she had to hang on and keep moving. The persistent fury of his shouts reminded her of that archetypal footage she had seen as a little girl of U.S. President Ronald Reagan's attempted assassination—the way the Secret Service agents had started shouting *Go! Go! Go!* and not stopped their harangue until long after the president was out of view.

The now-familiar hallway streamed past her in an altered state: dark, slippery—for she almost tripped over a bleeding body on the way out—even creepy in its near-total darkness. Yet somewhere in the near-gloom of the museum stairs, she realized something amazing: she was alive. She had survived the attack and they were on their way out to safety, to open air and escape routes and freedom.

A hand gripped the back of her blouse. She turned abruptly and immediately recognized the hostess, frantic in her own right not to be left behind.

The dome room whizzed by, an exit door punched open and suddenly she was out in the cool, drafty night. Speeding SUVs with roof lights blazing were screeching into various parking angles in the lot, and dark-uniformed men rushed forward with their weapons held high.

A small clot of them surrounded her and began to pull her toward the closest vehicle. She broke free to look for Meyer, but he was nowhere among the faces swirling around her.

He had already disappeared into the night.

Chapter Fifteen

Even in her trauma and disorientation, Hadassah figured the Shin Beth wouldn't take her far, and she was right. The SUV door had slammed shut, the engine roared ahead, and with her eyes closed, she had endured a series of jars and hard bumps as her new protectors raced her through the late-night streets of Western Jerusalem.

It was less than a minute before she felt a sudden plunging sensation and knew down in her stomach, from memory, that they had just plummeted into the underground parking garage beneath her husband's offices. *My second trip here in a day*, she noted grimly.

And then she remembered one of the early security briefings she and Jacob had endured during his first few weeks in office. In case of an attempt on one of their lives, the most secure room available lay eighty-four feet below the basement of 3 Kaplan Street. Jacob might have been rushed here on the night of her father's murder, she realized, while she had lain in the hospital, under heavy sedation and with crowds of protectors hovering outside her door.

Her door flew open and four male hands reached in to help her step out. Trying to stand again, she realized that her head was still dizzy and her knees quite unsteady. She let the men's shoulders bear her up and half carry her wherever they intended. They entered an open elevator, but instead of pushing a normal button to go up, one of the men whisked an electronic key card from his breast pocket and waved it at an innocuous receiver on the elevator panel. Activated by that day's security code, the cab plunged downward. Almost thirty seconds later, the door opened onto a plushly carpeted, dimly lit vestibule.

Jacob stood there in the half-light, the expression on his face unfit for public view. He rushed forward, elbowed one of the men in the process, and grabbed her tighter than he ever had before. His chin burrowed down onto her breast and he muttered over and over, "I'm sorry, I'm so sorry . . ." while her hands reached beneath his underarms and fluttered helplessly somewhere below his shoulder blades.

They both stood there and wept while the surrounding bodyguards shifted on their feet and the elevator door beeped its slow, patient tone.

At last their tears ran out—or their sense of social embarrassment revived, she couldn't tell which—and Jacob took her hand, pulling her toward his personal office.

The door had hardly closed before she reached for his neck and held him close again.

"Jacob, the strangest thing happened."

He raised an upright index finger over his lips to shush her, then pulled her down onto his lap in a leather armchair.

"Honey," she insisted, trying to sit up to look into his face, "it wasn't just the attack. The strangest thing happened. Less than twenty seconds before everything fell apart, that Mossad agent had just gotten through suggesting that *I* was the target for the bombing. *Me.* And then, almost like it made him remember, he checked in on the radio loop, and no one was there. Like on cue."

He sighed deeply. "Well, then, honey, you won't believe this. I shouldn't give this to you right now. But . . . you deserve to know."

He reached over to the desk and lifted another manila folder, its name tab fringed in half a dozen different colors, delineating a specific security clearance.

Jacob handed it to her. She held it in midair, mentally and emotionally unprepared for the effort of reading. She knew he would summarize it for her.

"I received this only this afternoon. Your hunch, and his, may have been exactly right," Jacob said, his voice tense. "They scoured every inch of the Palestinian terrorist infrastructure and came up dry. Then they cast the net further. Even brought in the Americans for some help with satellite reconnaissance. It turns out that two weeks before the bombing, a single infrared signature was spotted in the middle of the Jordanian desert's most desolate plain. A keyhole satellite was tasked for a personal ID. They came up with this face."

He reached in and held up a grainy black-and-white photo of a face that made her stiffen abruptly in her husband's grasp.

She remembered that face, those eyes, rushing inexorably toward her on a real evening and in her every nightmare since then. She remembered those features laughing, snarling, screaming, falling backward under a wave of bodyguards.

"The face was easy to identify, even before the bombing. His name was Id-Abrahim Khazbar, and after being the Taliban's chief executioner in Kabul for almost four years, he migrated west and became the finest terrorist organizer in Iraq. That's where he had walked from, almost fourteen hundred miles, when he entered Jordan. Just strolled through one of the world's harshest deserts, alone, as if it were a stroll on the beach. His latest patron group is a secret cadre of former Iraqi Baath Party elites who call themselves *Death to the Exilarch*."

She frowned. That name sent a chill down to her toes, but she was too frazzled to examine why. And then the knowledge burst upon her whole. "Wait. *Exilarch*. Isn't that a term from my family scrolls? A reference to the ruler of the Jews in exile? You know—the Patriarchs of Israel, their counterparts among the Diaspora, the Exilarchs—"

"Yes," he was nodding. "It's the honorary title given to Mordecai after the whole Esther saga was over."

She frowned as she mentally connected the dots, almost wishing she could avoid the inevitable conclusion. "I'm not related to Mordecai but to Leah," she said slowly, "the woman to whom Esther gave the scrolls. But some people who know about them have gotten that point confused. If they were after descendents of the Exilarch, and I'm the most high-profile person associated with his story, then . . . I was probably the one to be bombed that night."

"It appears that way."

He let the pause that followed wash over them slowly.

"Honey," he said, "I'm so sorry I didn't have better oversight over this meeting. I never would have knowingly let you go there with so little security."

"I'm the one who cut back on the security detail at the last minute," she replied, her voice low.

"Why?"

"Because this was an ultra low-profile, informal event at a secure location. I thought I needed some flexibility, and I was sure it wouldn't cost me in this setting."

"Never again," he said quietly but with deep emotion. "You're a target. And you're my wife. I'm going to protect you."

She exhaled so deeply that it seemed she had been holding her breath all evening.

"Are you going to be all right?" he asked, tightening his hold around her, still seated in his lap.

"What? You mean, am I going to slip back into my depression? No. As frightening as tonight was, I feel more alive right now than I have in a long time. I have to keep going, Jacob. If this is really about me, then it's all the more reason I have to get to the bottom of it."

"Fine. Yes. But not on your own, and remember our agreement."

"I haven't forgotten. I will keep my end of the bargain." Her promise was underscored with a tender kiss. "And by the way, I still would like more time to talk with Meyer, the Mossad agent."

Her husband frowned and shook his head. "From the radio traffic I heard before you got here, he's being blamed for this situation getting out of hand. I'd bet he's on a plane back to Iraq as we speak. And he won't be allowed within a mile of you ever again."

"He saved my life, Jacob. It's not fair!" She climbed off his lap and stood before him, arms crossed.

"I'm sure it isn't, honey. But that's life in the security forces. Anyway, he got what he wanted. And in a way, so did you." Jacob stood and put an arm around her shoulders.

"I suppose. I just wish there was more to go with than *'She did not perish—you must find her.'*"

Chapter Sixteen

MANSOUR DISTRICT, BAGHDAD—DAWN

A *hazy sun was just* beginning to silhouette Baghdad's distant roof-tops and minarets, but the inhabitants of the well-kept home in the city's upscale Mansour District were still in their beds asleep.

A rumpled red pickup came down the street and cruised slowly by the home. Four white-robed men in the extended cab stared briefly but intently at the edifice and its surrounding neighbors. Not a soul was about on the block. The Americans weren't within a half mile. No movement from the house.

The pickup circled the block and returned.

On this pass, it stopped in front of the house and three of the men jumped out holding AK–47s at their midsections. The fourth hefted a missile launcher to his right shoulder. A shrill scream rang out, and the morning stillness turned into a nightmare.

First the missile whooshed into the home's front window and set off a blast that caused the entire structure to burst apart with a roar of fire and smoke. Then the automatics kicked in, spraying the ruin with a lethal matrix of ricocheting bullets and crisscrossing dust trails.

More screams arose—whether from aroused neighbors or dying

inhabitants was hard to tell. Barking dogs added to the cacophony of sounds. A robed woman appeared in a yard two houses away, waving her arms wildly.

The men jumped back in the vehicle and it raced away.

The enraged woman ran to the edge of the rubble and raised her fists to the sky.

"Why, O Allah, why!" she screamed in Arabic. "A good Shiite home! A good Iraqi family! What could they have done? What could they have *possibly* done?"

She turned away, her anger turned to tears as more neighbors began to emerge from their yards. An American Bradley Fighting Vehicle nudged its front bumper carefully around the far corner, its machine-gun barrel trained sideways along the street.

Not ten yards from where the neighbor stood lay the hidden answer to her anguished questions—the remnants of the home's inner doorpost. There, along the demolished right beam of the door-frame, lay a polished, highly ornamented strip of wood. The neigh-bor probably would never have recognized it had she been invited in, which she never had been, for although the family was respectable, they were also highly private people. She probably would not have guessed the truth even had she noticed, curling out from its inciner-ated edges, a strip of paper bearing nearly illegible lines in a language she would not have recognized. To be precise, they were Hebrew passages from the *Shema Yisroel*, more commonly known as the book of Deuteronomy.

Together, the cryptic shards formed the remains of a discreetly mounted *Mezuzah*, the sign of a conservative Torah-keeping family.

A Jewish family deep in hiding. Or so they had thought.

AL-SAYED IMPORT-EXPORT COMPANY, BAGHDAD—THAT EVENING

Barely an hour after the massacre of a hidden Jewish family three miles away in Mansour, the same dingy pickup pulled up in front of the unassuming storefront that housed the Mossad's secret Iraqi headquarters.

This time there was no leisurely reconnoiter. Along the busy street outside, the truck, traveling no faster than most, braked to a sudden halt. This time six men jumped out from the cab. They did not wait for the instant stampede of bystanders, sidewalk merchants, and loiterers to scramble away from the scene before starting their rampage.

This time two missiles shrieked into the building and detonated in a single, punctuated explosion, followed two seconds later by a fireball so vicious and huge that it crossed the street and rose high into the sky, not only turning over the hapless pickup onto its assassins, but also scorching innocent traffic, passersby snarled in the ambush and everything else in its path.

Before he died, the truck's driver praised Allah in a final strangled shout: "Praise him—we truly did strike the Zionist anthill. . . ."

Prime Minister's Residence—Rehavia, Jerusalem

The following morning Hadassah began her quest in earnest. Armed with nothing more than a mug of hot Earl Grey tea, a telephone, and a pad of paper, she installed herself in the small office provided for her in a corner of the Residence complex.

She sat down in her deepest chair, took a long sip of tea, and closed her eyes to think.

"She did not perish. . . ."

She knew to keep it simple. Start with the familiar, the logical. In what context had she most often heard the phrase's defining word "perish," uttered by her father during his life? And which of these contexts would be important enough to consume his final breath, his last words to her?

Perish . . . The word was almost Torahlike in its formality, its sentimentality. She thought back to her earliest Seder memories. His holding her on his knee, telling her stories from the Torah.

Hearing the Megillah read at Purim—Esther's most courageous words, *"If I perish, I perish. . . ."*

Then later, the word would punctuate stories from his own life. . . .

Perish . . . The word seemed to sink deeper into her memory. And then something burst into her mind. It was his voice, as clear and full of import as the day he had spoken the words. "My sister Rivke, my grandmother and grandfather, my uncle Likul, my own dear mother, they stayed behind when we escaped Hungary. And they *perished* in the camps. . . ." She had winced, because in his solemnity he had used the same intonation he affected when he read from Esther.

Of course, she told herself. He had never failed to use that verb when he had described the horrible fate of the relatives he had heart-breakingly left behind in Hungary.

Perhaps there *had* been a survivor. It made no immediate sense that she would not have been told of one. But if there had been some reason, some bizarre segregation for safety's sake, it certainly would justify his eagerness to disclose it to her as he lay dying.

She jotted down the names as best she could remember them, feeling as though she was recreating the family names upon the scroll back at the Shrine. Maybe there would be an obvious skip—a missing link. Who else could the "she" be?

She thought hard, picturing those names—*Rivke Kesselman. Isaac and Deborah Kesselman, Likul Kesselman, Pavel Kesselman*, she mentally recited.

She would start with the first. Rivke, his father's youngest sister. Hadassah had been told little of her, except that she was very beautiful and possessed of an enchanting wit. Poppa had sometimes looked at his Hadassah a certain way, murmuring that she reminded him "of Rivke. . . ."

She opened her laptop, loaded its Web browser, and marveling again at the ease of it all, typed in *http://www.yadvashem.org*—the address for Yad Vashem, Israel's Holocaust Martyrs' and Heroes' Remembrance Authority. And there it was, right on the home page, over a heartrending drawing of a smiling young girl.

"The Central Database of Shoah Victims' Names. Click here."

She typed the name, clicked, and to her surprise, two matches flashed onscreen. *Riveka Keselman*, from Ukraine, and *Ryvka Keselman* from Lithuania. Neither was the one. She felt a pang of sadness to think that so many women had died that even a specific name like Rivka could encompass three different women from three nations.

The Yad Vashem Web site warned that only half of the Shoah's total victims were loaded into its database, so she did not allow herself to feel discouragement. She continued on to the other family names and found their records without effort. Seeing them onscreen like that—disembodied in their glowing pixels, yet so real, the letters of the names so precisely formed—brought a flood of tears to her eyes. She had known none of them, of course, but she had felt their presence throughout her childhood and their loss in every year of her adulthood. And reading their names on a government Web site of this sort seemed to make the injustice of their murders fresh and raw again.

"I promise you, I will never forget," she whispered, her voice breaking as she touched the screen with a trembling finger. She felt as if she was joining the ranks of those from the past, the present, and the future as she said aloud, "And I will fight to the death to stop anything like that from happening again. . . ."

And then her phone rang. It was Jacob, fresh from an intelligence briefing. His voice was both professional and personal, she noted in a detached manner. It seemed Ari Meyer—the man who had saved her life and been sent back to the front for his troubles—had just perished in a horrific attack upon Mossad's Baghdad headquarters. Positive identification would not be completed for weeks, if ever, for the explosion of hidden weapons and ammunition had been so severe, it had exceeded the kilotonnage of a plane-dropped bomb.

Then barely able to say the words, he told her that Ari Meyer had been scheduled for his return briefing the very moment the missiles had struck.

Hadassah thanked her husband and hung up without her customary "I love you," trembling too hard to press the phone's OFF button.

She could not understand what was happening—only that whatever it was, she was beginning to feel as though she could be in the center of a giant, global bull's-eye.

And just at that moment, the panic returned full-force. She felt a vast, malevolent force, so hate-filled that it would not rest until its victim was destroyed. It encircled her, even here in her very own little office. It seemed to be stalking her, circling her body with the cold stare of a Bengal tiger, preparing to leap the final gap and devour her whole.

She gulped air in huge breaths, telling herself in one absurd moment that passing out from hyperventilation might be the most merciful conclusion to this moment.

She stood up, unable to tolerate the constriction of a sitting position upon her diaphragm. Glancing up at the ceiling to change her view, she found no solace. So she stared down at the floor. And there it was again, waiting for her.

She reached down. Jacob had ordered a bound copy of the Esther letter discovered by Meyer—she picked it up and opened to a random page.

Concubine.

Have you ever noticed, Leah, that I never speak that word out loud? I don't think it has left my lips for thirty years or more. I detest that word. As someone who had spent most of her adult life within the royal palace, I know better than anyone what it conjures up in people's minds. . . .

Sexual object. Plaything. Discarded at will. Used. Unwanted. Forgotten. Taken for granted.

Forgive me if even writing these words causes you more pain. But I write them now to strip them of their power, their illusion of truth. They not only fail to describe you but actually suggest the opposite of what you truly are.

Do you know what I see in you instead of these pathetic idiocies?

I see a tall Jewish beauty with piercing green eyes, dazzling black hair, and long, lean limbs, whose loveliness is amply matched by her wisdom and her godliness. A bright, resourceful young woman making the best of events not of her own making. Still in her prime, a woman entering some difficult times in her life—times that I understand well, for I have only begun to step away from similar trials myself.

You know, I said something like this to Jesse a while back, before I came to Jerusalem, for he too is given to such questions. I still refer to him by his Jewish name and not Hathach, as he is now known. And Mordecai too, for that matter.

Jesse and I were enjoying one of our frequent excursions to the Persepolis palace gardens—substituting them for the old familiar orchards from Susa, where we once stole away as young people so long ago—when he turned to me with a suddenly intense expression.

"Do you know that you and Mordecai are the only ones alive who remember me before I became a . . ."

Like me, he never speaks aloud the word *eunuch,* the word the outside world would use to describe him. Whenever the subject arises, he always allows the sentence to drift off in a tellingly deliberate way. And I always know what has remained unspoken.

"Jesse," I answered, suddenly grasping his hand, "do you know who I see when I look into your eyes?"

"Please, Hadassah. I do not want to hear that word."

"That word was the farthest thing from my mind."

I winced at my boldness, and for a moment wondered if my point would prove healing or merely painful. Yet I had launched into the topic, and I needed to carry it through.

"I see a man as magnificent today as he ever was. I see the man you really are—who you still are—during all the time I've known you since childhood. In that noble brow of yours, in the intelligence pouring from those deep-set eyes, in your glowing skin, I still see the Jesse I knew at fifteen. The same youth with those great broad shoulders, the thick hair, that irresistible, lightning-quick laugh. The boy who first taught me about"—and I turned suddenly shy, and the last word was barely a whisper—"love."

At that he turned and smiled at me, so bright and genuine that I vow I was pulled back to those very days. Yet I also looked deeper into his eyes and saw tears, and was poignantly reminded of what I often allowed myself to forget—that the love of so long ago had never died. Though it had ripened into a beautiful friendship, there also throbbed a vital, inner core that remained too hot to touch, to even approach without care.

"You're still there, Jesse," I continued as straightforward as I could manage, "the boy who led me on the most breathtaking adventure of my life. Do you remember? Running as fast as we could through the Royal Gates market and that impossible crush of hawkers and travelers and soldiers, then jumping onto the old palace's gryphon gates. You were so fast and you had such long legs, I despaired of ever catching up with you."

"Why are you telling me all this?" he asked, shaking his head. "Do you honestly think my memory needs refreshing?"

"Because you said that Mordecai and I were the only ones left who might remember your younger days. And I want to reassure you that I do. I remember all of it—the kind, handsome youth you once were—and every age of your life since then. Nor do I have to work hard to remember. It's all right there, in the man you are today." I took both of his hands and stared into his eyes. "Every wonderful quality you ever had seems to simply pour out of the man you've become."

His fingers tightened around mine, while his eyes remained fixed upon the distant columns of the Apadana. Although its only sign was a slight trembling of the shoulders, I knew Jesse well enough to realize that he was weeping.

"Nor have I forgotten my first kiss," I said in a voice now breathy and wistful. "I've never forgotten the sensation, the swoon, that came over me. It seemed to just separate my head from my shoulders. The soft feeling of strength that took hold of my whole body when our lips touched. Or the sense of you, an essence far more powerful than anything I'd ever felt before. . . ." My voice drifted to a close, and I stood searching his face.

He smiled a little self-consciously. I remember because I never see that smile except at the most gentle, close moments between us.

Then I heard a sob, and the sound of panting. And I realized that it was coming from me. Emotion had just launched itself out of my lungs. My legs weakened beneath me, my knees gave way, and I found myself sitting precipitously on a patch of bare earth.

"What is it, Hadassah?" Jesse asked, lowering himself into my line of sight.

I shook my head and merely tried to breathe, partly because I knew that any attempt at speech would only result in embarrassment, and partly because I knew I could never answer him. *Never.*

I could never answer him because I was weeping, despite all my kind words, over all the bittersweet years life had forced between that carefree, vibrant young man of fifteen I had loved with such intensity and the man he had become. I wept because my next memory was of how the virile young Jesse of my first kiss had only survived a short while after that golden afternoon. My anguish had yanked me back to the sound of pounding in the middle of the night, of his grandmother bursting in to tell Mordecai and me that he'd been taken. That the royal patrols had snatched him and several hundred other young men, then carried them away to suffer the most cruel disfigurement possible.

I think my dear friend instinctively knew the cause of my tears, for he did not ask further. He merely encircled my shoulders with his strong arms, pulled me to my feet, and led me, one slow step at a time, back to the harem.

But, dear Leah, I weep as bitterly for you on this day as I did for Jesse on that one, for just as his manhood was torn from him, your woman's heart has been torn apart and those beautiful emerald eyes of yours filled with a sadness which . . .

Prime Minister's Residence—the next morning

One good thing about being the Prime Minister's wife, Hadassah reminded herself, is getting better-than-average assistance from government bureaucrats. Thanks to the Internet and the help of a few overeager researchers, she was managing to conduct a respectable investigation from the privacy of her living quarters.

At ten o'clock the doorbell rang, and Hadassah let in a young case manager from the Interior Ministry, a very nervous and too-thin young blonde, who introduced herself as Isabelle as she paused over a thin file.

"Ma'am, there is no record of any Israeli citizen, Holocaust victim or survivor, or repatriated remains bearing the name of Rivke Kesselman, sister of David. I'm very sorry."

Hadassah sighed and sank to a chair. Perhaps the simplest interpretation of her father's words had not been the true one after all.

"The only thing I *did* find, however," the girl continued, pulling a large manila envelope out of her backpack, "I'm not sure if you'd be interested in. You see, it comes from London."

Hadassah sat upright. *London! Of course . . .* that's where the family had ended up!

"No, please go on," Hadassah replied, "I'm very interested."

"Well, there's a public record of a 1950 marriage between an Iraqi citizen named Anek al-Khalid and a young Hungarian émigrée listed as R. Kesselman. There're no relatives listed, though. It just says she was a war orphan. She died a few years later."

Hadassah felt as though the air around her was growing thick, like a flow of cooling lava. She stared hard at the floor, transported in thought. *Of course . . .*

"Of course what, ma'am. . . ? May I be of some assistance?"

"I've been so blind! If she *is* living, what other kind of record would there be? I've been trying to prove a negative. Tell me, Isabelle. Did you find any further records of this Mr. al-Khalid?"

The young girl pursed her lips and nodded emphatically. "Actually, it seems this Mr. al-Khalid has been making quite a public spectacle of himself lately."

Hadassah gasped. "You mean he's the al-Khalid who's stirred up so much trouble at the World Court?"

Isabelle nodded somberly. "One and the same."

"Oh, man," Hadassah sighed. "Here we go . . ."

JERUSALEM

In the next few days, an odd rumor began to trickle through the intricate layers of Jerusalem's social and political circles. It seemed the First Lady of the nation, so recently described in the press as homebound and depressed, had been sighted walking briskly through a variety of governmental offices and archives. Sometimes she had been spotted with a frustrated-looking bodyguard rushing to keep up with her, sometimes with a befuddled bureaucrat at her side, sometimes even alone.

Mindless of protocol, regulations, or accepted procedure, Mrs. ben Yuda had apparently charged into these various offices, blithely challenging their occupants to provide her with sensitive information not usually provided to anyone outside of the intelligence community.

Even more mysterious than the manner or location of these appearances, however, was Mrs. ben Yuda's personal demeanor. She was almost universally described as radiant with purpose and energy.

What the capital gossips could never have known—not to mention the First Lady's *Shin Beth* protectors—was that every one of her excursions had been relentlessly shadowed by a Palestinian man following her from an always discreet and concealed distance. The thin young man wore mirrored sunglasses and a bulky student's backpack, but a different change of clothes on nearly every occasion—one of a dozen reasons why his constant shadowing had not been detected.

Perhaps another is that when the First Lady came closest to him (that is, within even seventy yards), he always seemed to be listening intently to someone speaking through his cell phone. In a strange side-effect of cell phone use, his lack of focus on her presence, his gaze trained instead upon the ground during such moments, had seemed to render him almost invisible.

Perhaps Hadassah's greatest safeguard, unbeknownst to her, had been her haste. Her bristling determination to proceed quickly from one place to another had made her a veritable dervish through the various corridors and lobbies. Combined with her perimeter of red-faced bodyguards, her rapid pace had given the young terrorist the briefest reason to pause and hesitate on the four occasions when he had shifted forward on the balls of his feet and come within a split second of charging toward her, cell phone still in hand—its speed dial's explosive recipient now strapped heavily upon his back.

Chapter Seventeen

The Wall Street Journal
June 30, 2003, pp. A1, A6

... Last week at the United Nations, a new organization, Jews for Justice from Arab Countries, was established to seek reparations for Jewish refugees and for centuries of Muslim racism. Abraham Sofaer, himself an Iraqi Jew, states the claims of Iraqi Jews are legitimate: He notes that much of the real estate of Baghdad and central Iraq is really Jewish owned. The Israeli Ministry of Justice has set up the World Organization for Jews of Arab Countries (WOJAC) to collect reparations claims against all Arab countries: So far 25,000 forms have been filed. ...

In Baghdad, Muslims are becoming aware of the game that is afoot: One local newspaper, Al-Saah, has noted that "returning Jews" are trying to seize Baghdad real estate. A sign on a factory bulletin board in Baghdad warns Muslims to "resist the temptation to sell anything to the Jews [lest] the money they make be turned into bullets to be used against the Palestinians." Iraqis who endured Saddam's rule have contempt for the Jews and Kurds now clamoring for property after years of comfortable exile.

—"LONDONER CLAIMS ANCIENT JEWISH
TITLE AND A FORTUNE IN IRAQ"

PRIME MINISTER'S RESIDENCE—REHAVIA, JERUSALEM

That evening Hadassah borrowed a page from the ancient queen with whom she shared a name and prepared dinner for her husband. The official residence of course boasted a full complement of chefs and serving staff, but every so often she liked to slip back to her days as a gourmet cook and give the staff an unexpected night off.

While standing over poached whitefish and broiled asparagus in the nearby private kitchen, she thought through her strategy. And when the hour came and Jacob arrived home, she and the meal were more than ready. All that remained was the lighting of the candles upon the small table she had set up in their living quarters in front of a glowing fireplace.

He arrived the way he always did, a Burberry overcoat folded over his right forearm and his cell phone unfolded in the other as he attempted to finish up his last call.

"Well," he said with a smile as he snapped the cell phone shut and perused the table setting. "What have we here?"

"You're going to have to endure another intelligence briefing, I'm afraid. So I thought I'd make it go down easier by presenting it Queen Esther–style. With a little fish and soft candles."

"I think I can handle that," he answered with a chuckle and raised eyebrows.

His arms briefly encircled her waist as he brushed her cheek with a kiss and whispered, "I'm just glad to have *my* queen back."

"Then come and sit, please," she replied with an answering smile.

She came back from the kitchen with two plates of food. He smiled as she set them on the table, sat down and held his hand.

"This must be pretty important," he said with mock sincerity.

She nodded. "It certainly is. And I'll wager it's the most fruitful intel briefing you'll have all day."

"Oh, my dear, I hope not. My intel briefings have been growing all too fruitful, as you put it. As a matter of fact, I could use a lot more dull and boring ones at this point in my life."

"Sorry, sweetheart." She raised a fork to his lips. "Then taste the fish."

They were already halfway through the meal when she finally gathered up the courage to tell him.

"I've found my man," she said with forced casualness.

"What man?"

"Well, actually, my woman. I found the one who did not perish."

"You're kidding," he asked, serious at first, then grinning at her coyness.

"Not at all. In the last few days I've had to revert to my graduate student days, back when I was hustling to document my thesis by hook and by crook. It's taken every bit of cunning and resourceful-ness I ever had back then, and more. I may have even broken a law or two—who knows? But after scouring every public record between Yad Vashem and the Smithsonian, I think I found her."

"Well," he asked with an impatient drawing of breath, "are you going to tell me who she is?"

"She's my aunt Rivke. I'm sure of it. Now I just have to prove it. She was the one who supposedly died in the Holocaust. That was never true, all these years. Rivke actually made it to London with all the others and wound up marrying several years later. A man who, if old records and his own statements are correct, was from, of all places, Iraq."

"Why, then, did your family say she had died?"

"I have no idea. And you know, the more I think about it, it's possible I was told she had died and I just assumed it was in the Holocaust, given the times. But it's clear: she made it through and married. The groom seems to have come from an old Jewish family. There shouldn't have been a problem with the marriage."

"That's strange."

"Well, that's only mildly odd compared to what I'm about to tell you. See, Aunt Rivke did die eventually, in 1954. But her husband never remarried, and he's alive today. I ran his name through the Internet and received thousands of browser hits."

"Is he famous?"

"You might say that. He's extremely wealthy, and rather notori-ous. In fact, you may have heard of him. His name is Anek al-Khalid, and he's making a rather controversial claim in World Court of rep-arations for the wealth taken from Iraqi Jews over the years."

"I've certainly heard about that." Jacob stared at her over the goblet that had gone still in his hand.

"Well, there's more. According to an intelligence report I was able to coerce from someone on your staff who shall remain name-less"—she grinned and wrinkled her nose at him—"al-Khalid has another scheme in the works. He is quietly planning to revive the office of the Leader of Jews in Exile."

"You mean. . . ?"

"That's right. The Exilarch."

Jacob whistled in amazement. "You're right. This is the most interesting briefing I've had in some time."

She leaned forward, her eyes intense. "You do understand, don't you? Remember the word *Exilarch*? It was part of the name of the group that killed my father! This means there must be some connection between *that* terrorist and *this* man, apparently my uncle by marriage, whose existence my family disguised for decades!"

"Of course I understand." He reached over to clasp her chin. "What I don't understand is, why am I getting the impression you think you're going to London?"

"Of course I'm going. It's the next step." She moved back from his hand.

"Honey, I'm sorry to dictate to you, but you are *not* going. Not on your life. Literally. Hadassah, you don't know anything about this man. What if he's the one who had your father killed, out of some old personal vendetta? What if he's an Iraqi double agent? What if he's nuts? You already know he's making some very troublesome claims before the World Court. What if he's some kind of out-of-control crackpot?"

"Then at least I'll have my answer."

"Mossad will get the answers. I promise, I'll have this man fully investigated and a twenty-page report on my desk in twenty-four hours."

"I'll take the report," she replied with a knowing look. "And then I'll bring it with me to London. You promised me, Jacob."

"And you promised not to do anything unwise or unsafe. You were almost killed less than three days ago!"

"Yes! And do you know where *that* happened? Right here in West Jerusalem, less than a half mile from your office. Three-quarters of a mile from the *last* attack, at the synagogue. I seem to be in the greatest danger right here, going about my routine! Sitting right here in our quarters, coming or going in the limousine. Think about it: going to London may be the safest thing I can do right now."

He sighed deeply. "That's assuming you go there with adequate security."

"Fine. You provide me with your best and most unobtrusive detail, and we'll both be happy. But I'm going. You know I have nothing else to cling to, other than you." She briefly considered quoting Esther's *"If I perish, I perish,"* but decided it would take her proclamation over the top. Instead, she paused.

Neither one looked at each other for an interminable moment. Then Jacob met her gaze, and a smile began to toy with the ends of his mouth, to spread along his face. He caressed her hand and slowly, gradually, started to laugh. They both knew he'd be unable to resist her.

"I *would* like your help," she said with an intimate smile.

He reached again across the table and clasped both her hands in his. "Do you know what worries me?"

"Tell me."

"The death of Ari Meyer—who was, by the way, a British citizen—and the fact that he had a document just like yours. And it came from Iraq. As did the suicide bomber who tried to kill you."

"So you think his appearance was not a coincidence?"

He shook his head and his expression became even more sober. "I'm a head of state, honey. I'm not allowed to believe in coincidence."

Chapter Eighteen

THE SKIES OVER THE
MEDITERRANEAN SEA—THE NEXT DAY

T*he Gulfstream V jet*—crème de la crème of civil aviation, a business aircraft capable of flying nonstop from London to Beijing at 50,000 feet, Mach 8.5, only fifteen percent below the speed of sound, and in five-star luxury—took off without fanfare from Lod Airfield, the military side of David Ben Gurion Airport. The aircraft was secretly registered to the Israeli government and was usually employed in the "extraordinary rendition," the discreet transport of so-called extrajudicial prisoners for interrogation in countries unimpressed with niceties like human rights. On other occasions it carried upper diplomatic echelons on top-secret negotiations.

That morning, however, the plane was carrying one official passenger on a special mission: the First Lady of Israel and a half-dozen-strong security detail, on a trans-European flight to London.

Fifteen minutes before, two Israeli Defense Force F–16s had lifted off in close succession and now flew nearly a mile off the Gulfstream's wing, weapons racks thick with fully armed complements of air-to-air missiles.

And at that moment, five miles over the Mediterranean, a chubby AWACS surveillance-control plane lumbered in slow circles, monitoring every inch of airspace within seventy-five miles and relaying it in small electronic bursts to the Lod control tower, then from there to a military conference room deep within the Prime Minister's complex.

Jacob ben Yuda had held true to both his promises—he had allowed his wife to leave, and she was accompanied by the most complete security his nation could provide.

The only thing a casual observer would have noticed about the jet's takeoff was its unusually sharp rate of climb; indeed, the Gulfstream nearly assumed ballistic trajectory in its impatience to gain altitude. The tactic would have betrayed itself to a seasoned observer as a maneuver proprietary to military pilots, for it kept to an absolute minimum the first forty thousand feet of elevation—the space above terra firma when any flying craft was most vulnerable to small-arms fire and assorted ground-to-air attack.

Once approaching fifty thousand feet, far above the level of commercial airliners, the plane veered eastward and rocketed out over the Mediterranean Sea. Hadassah stared out her port with a calm that surprised her. The aircraft traced a largely seaborne route, avoiding the dry lands of Western Europe, out through the Strait of Gibraltar and then sharply north along the Spanish and French coasts, to the English Channel.

The F–16s, which unlike the private jet had required midair refueling during the journey, only peeled away when the Gulfstream approached British airspace two miles from Dover. Ten minutes later, a little over three hours after its departure, the jet landed at London's Luton Airport in a driving rain and taxied for three miles along a private lane usually reserved for the royal family. At the end, along the fringe of a dense British green forest the likes of which Hadassah ben Yuda had not seen in years, awaited a large hangar with its double doors yawning open.

They taxied inside, and the suspended door slowly lowered itself to the ground. Only with the enclosure finally complete did the staircase begin to unfold from the side of the plane.

Outside, high in the canopies of oak trees lining the forest's edge, snipers lowered their rifle barrels while below them, a van of Royal Fusillier commandos spilled out to take position.

From her leather chair at the center of it all, Hadassah now tried in vain to shake off a combination of awe and trepidation. If only her father had been here, to see all this hoopla. Of course, it had taken his death to provoke such extraordinary measures, but she chose not to dwell on that.

Instead, she fought to shake her thoughts from the one subject that had, strangely, occupied her mind for nearly the entire trip. Despite the excitement of the mission unfolding around her, her obsession had been a subject nearly three thousand years old—the life of Queen Esther as described in her family's documents. She had carried along with her the bound copy of the ancient scrolls, unable to part with it for the trip, and today, as Israel had slipped effortlessly behind her to a seaborne horizon and then out of sight, she felt something she never had before.

It was almost as though Esther, in writing to the faceless concubine Leah, had made a promise to all the women of her family who would read the letter in years to come. An unspoken contract of sorts.

If my life can count for something, if my existence has meaning to you after all these centuries, so can yours.

I vow to you who follow, significance, meaning, and a place in history.

There were holes in the notion, of course. Mainly the fact that Leah, the very girl to whom this was addressed, seemed herself to have slipped through history's cracks and fallen into total anonymity. If Leah, the recipient of this letter, had not escaped history's ash heap, then what promise could there be to women of lesser bonds, so many years removed?

And yet Hadassah could not shake the idea. At times, dozing off in the comfort of her chair, she had almost heard an audible voice say to her, *My dear, you are more than the wife of an important man. Follow your heart and you will make a difference. . . .*

Was this her existential ego trying to make sense of the whirlwind of recent events?

In fact, this trip was officially classified as so risky that Jacob had been prevented by government policy from accompanying her. But the issue had been rendered moot when he finally had been compelled to stay behind by a last-minute Mossad briefing about the Iraqi headquarter shootout.

Yet now, watching the ungainly stairway lurch down into place outside her window, she missed her Jacob tremendously. She had strained the boundaries of their marriage in coming here, she knew that. But despite how rash it seemed in the light of recent events, she knew deep down that she had not been bluffing. There was a path here, however reckless, which compelled her to follow. And it had ignited the only spark of life she had felt in months. Maybe longer . . .

At last the stairway's clasp announced itself with a thump, and one of the burly men with her looked out through the open cabin door. A damp, cold blast of fuel-scented air rushed in, reminding her of where she was.

She took a deep breath and rose from the Gulfstream's luxurious armchair. Nodding silently at the lead security man, she walked out of the plane and, seeing the vast hangar before her and the dozens of men arrayed to protect her, wondered what in the world she had set in motion.

Am I crazy to be doing this? Yet it's all I know to do. . . .

◆ ◆ ◆ ◆ ◆ ◆ ◆ ◆ ◆ ◆ ◆ ◆ ◆

Chapter Nineteen

KENSINGTON, LONDON—LATER THAT DAY

Anek al-Khalid, aged eighty-nine, shuffled through London's Israeli Embassy at its banquet entrance with a scowl upon his lips, an invitation in his fist, and the jaunty sway of a boxer about to dodge a Joe Louis bolo punch.

It was his traditional game-face, and he wore it well.

That is, until he glanced around him, closed his eyes, and felt himself transported.

It had been twelve long years since he had last stepped inside these halls, ever since he had announced his intention to press a highly controversial claim before the World Court. On behalf of his own and thousands of other Jewish Iraqi families in exile, he had filed a massive lawsuit demanding reparations for all the wealth stolen from them. The amount of money was awesome, numbering in the tens of billions of dollars, and the destabilization it could potentially cause was enormous. But his motives had been neither gain nor disruption. Anek al-Khalid, as anyone who knew him could attest, was very wealthy, carried neither debt nor abiding need for more money. But he did carry within him a huge burden of grief, regret, and even rage—and relieving himself of that burden was his real reason for taking such action.

As he had anticipated, the contentious action had caused an immediate chill in his relations with the Israeli establishment—not to mention a permanent stamp of *persona non grata* within some of the more squeamish circles of London's Jewish community. Add to that his Islamic-sounding last name, and he was a virtual exile in his adopted city.

Not that his quest did not boast many closet supporters. News of the legal claim seemed to have been kept purposely quiet by even the most raucous British tabloids. To put it succinctly, the concept of an Arab country paying reparations to Jews was far too fraught with issues for most folks to comprehend or accept. To the vast Jewish majority, it simply smelled like trouble. And for a twentieth-century European Jew, trouble was not something one provoked without extraordinary cause.

That's all right, he had always told himself. *You'll invite me to your parties again when I single-handedly win back thirty billion dollars stolen from your brothers and sisters. That is, should I live to see the day. . . .*

Besides, he remembered wryly, the lawsuit was only round one. If they only knew what he had planned next. . . .

Despite the fact that he held his first embassy invitation in years, he had almost decided to stay home and let the other invitees finish the Brie and Cristal on their own. Yet something about the wording of tonight's card, a slight nuance of tone within its text, had conveyed to him that the invitation was more than routine.

Mister al-Khalid, the pleasure of your company is most earnestly desired. . . .

One didn't often see "most earnestly desired" in this sort of communication. A curious itch had burrowed into his side and resisted his best efforts at extrication.

Now he was here, like it or not. As he breached the threshold, he breathed in the scent of burnished wood and brewing coffee, handed his coat and gloves to the butler, and peered around him with an even deeper scowl.

"I'm sorry, but you see I was sent this invitation here—I believed there was to be some sort of . . . function. A soirée."

"Ah yes, Mr. al-Khalid," the butler replied, pronouncing the last name so precisely that the old man immediately realized there had been a briefing about him, and not long ago, either. "There is to be a gathering tonight, and you are most certainly a guest of honor. Would you please come with me?"

The pair started down a long, carpeted hallway. Looking about him at the familiar walls wainscoted in marble and hand-scrubbed oak, the old man sighed wistfully and allowed his mind to travel back over half a century.

Israel had been a young country in 1952, still desperately fighting off her Arab enemies and threats of being pushed into the sea. The ink was barely dry on the U.N. Partition Resolution which had re-created the tiny nation when the Israeli Embassy in London first opened its doors. The very notion of a State of Israel still seemed so miraculous to the war's survivors that whole crowds of them had been content to just show up and stare at this physical embodiment of the miracle, their eyes welling up at the sight of an Israeli flag, a living, breathing Star of David in the breeze. And invariably stopping short before a gun-wielding guard, for no Jew of that generation would ever look upon a military uniform again without a reflexive, heart-stopping gasp. That is, until it sank in that these uniforms bore Hebrew markings—and then, as one, they would stand there, trans-fixed, and choke back sobs of raw, unalloyed emotion.

Now, all these decades later, al-Khalid coughed hard to give himself a chance to regather his composure. Then he blinked repeatedly and took another few halting steps, as his mind replayed more of the precious, luminous memories.

Those days now seemed like a long dawn after a decade of hellish night. And never more so than when he sat in some embassy ante-chamber on those mornings and looked out a window to watch the newcomers blink in the sunshine. Still just a few steps out of Kensington High Street's Underground station, they would traverse these cobblestoned, treelined streets, a mere block from Kensington Palace and its luscious gardens, and enter the complex in thick clusters. He closed his eyes briefly and pictured them. How splendid they had been, how blessed. Their gazes always so wide, their voices ever hushed like schoolchildren on holiday, and, thank G-d, those death stares nearly always washed from their eyes, at least for the moment.

Yes, he usually would have scorned the pilgrims from his perch of world-weary jadedness, as he did most awestruck tourists—except he had recently learned of the horrors from which many of them had come. He read the newspapers enough to know that most were fresh from the refugee camps of Central Europe, and before that, the ghettoes and death camps whose photographs were beginning to sear themselves onto the world's collective conscience.

These are not young people, he remembered telling himself, disregarding their youthful appearances. *Their souls are older than time itself.*

In those days he had not been one of the wide-eyed wanderers. No, his was a different tale of woe—no less heart-wrenching yet still in progress, its final chapter as yet unwritten. In those days he had been known as a "case," his identity forever linked with the persistent and volatile problem of his family's disposition. He had lived through this period under an abiding sense that he was enduring the torments of the bureaucratically damned, waiting like some condemned man in a Kafkaesque succession of embassy offices and antechambers for the next chapter of his life to begin.

And now, being back in that same building revived that emotion a thousandfold.

The old man stopped in midcorridor, glanced to his right through a windowed door, and raised a trembling hand to his mouth. The butler sensed his pause and turned with a puzzled look.

This is the room, al-Khalid told himself with a barely concealed surge of awe. The paint and the furnishings had changed, but some of the most indelible details had not—the peculiar arrangement of those fourteen-foot Renaissance windows, the intricate Restoration carving on the fireplace, the same gaudy, inaccessible chandelier. It was not the grandeur of the room that gave him pause. The rooms in his estates were far more opulent. No, it was the memories. This had been an office then, the domain of one of its most immovable, legalistic attachés, back before the embassy had grown large enough to separate its ceremonial from its administrative suites.

He stepped in, closed his eyes, and breathed in the past with deep draughts. *"You are not a Jew,"* he heard the British-accented voice roar in his ears once again, as clear and thunderous as if the words had been uttered an hour ago. *"You cannot be a Jew, do you understand, my boy? The moment anybody knows, your whole family may die! Their fate rests on your shoulders! Now leave here and don't come back until we call for you, or it will all be for naught!"*

He blinked away twin eyefuls of tears and sent the drops down his cheeks.

"Let's go, my man," he said in an age-crackled voice to the butler. "What on earth do you people want with me?"

At that, the butler turned swiftly on his heels, proceeded barely twenty feet farther, and turned the handle of a dark wooden door. Al-Khalid nodded his thanks and stepped into a thoroughly traditional British library, complete with massive granite fireplace and hardwood fire, high-slung wooden beams, and from somewhere, redolent in the air, the tiniest whiff of scotch. In fact, the only signs that this was Israel's embassy came from a wireframe Star of David over the fireplace and a large Israeli flag hanging from a pole in the corner.

Next he spotted the Israeli ambassador, a patrician dolt resplendent in his Savile Row pinstripe making his way across the intricately woven carpet. *The man at least deigns to offer a handshake*, al-Khalid noted as he took the proffered clasp with all the enthusiasm of a condemned man. In his mind, a competent ambassador was supposed to bring his native values to the country of his posting, not allow the new culture to transform *him*. And this man, once a decent Jewish *sabra* from Hebron, had scarcely set foot in London before promptly hardening into one long, crunchy bite of British upper crust. For his part, the ambassador merely considered al-Khalid a run-of-the-mill, loose-cannon crackpot. These opinions were hardly national secrets. The two men had leaked their mutual distaste to the London press, a rare show of Jewish disunity upon which the Fleet Street press had pounced with relish.

"Mr. al-Khalid, welcome to our embassy. Indeed, it has been too far long."

"Yes, it has," he replied with thinly veiled disdain. "Much as I would have expected. My pursuits have not been of the sort designed to win me friends in this place."

The ambassador wrinkled his nose and directed a small wave at him, as if to say, *Ah—what's a little global controversy between friends...?*

"Well, much as I enjoy standing here and mending fences with you, I'm confused," al-Khalid continued. "I received an invitation to what I thought would be a sort of official function. Yet you and I seem to be the only guests. Did I arrive too early? Too late? Or is this some sort of ... *briefing*?" He could not manage to erase the contempt from his voice at the sound of that word. His younger years had been afflicted with such inane appointments.

The ambassador let out an accommodating laugh and shook his head.

"No, sir. You have been invited here for a purpose. A most singular evening, I would imagine. Would you care for a seat? Some single malt, or tea perhaps?"

"Thank you, no. As long as we're taking our time ..."

He fell into a parlor chair and leaned his head back, as though he had just finished some kind of marathon. The ambassador leaned over to pat his arm familiarly.

"You will know more about this meeting soon enough, my good sir."

"Does that mean the security was for me?"

"What security?"

"Well, I detected helicopters above my car all the way from Notting Hill Gate, four camouflaged snipers above the front gate, at least another three along the courtyard, laser profiling and metal detection at the door."

"Yes, you are quite correct, but you are also not being honest with me. It is physically impossible to have detected all of those things from the inside of a limousine."

Al-Khalid smiled and nodded at the ambassador's recognition of his little deceit. "I have a little security of my own, sir, as you certainly know. My life requires safety as much as yours. And somebody has assembled an array that far exceeds the normal retinue of this embassy. What exactly is going on?"

"Actually, it has to do with your guest. But after you're finished with her, you'll probably want even more security for yourself."

"I don't understand."

"Perhaps the time has come for you to meet her."

"*Her?*"

"Oh, absolutely." The official raised his chin toward some unseen helper out in the hallway.

There was a small commotion at the door, and al-Khalid swerved around in his chair.

His face underwent a dramatic transformation, shedding its mask of scarcely concealed irritation so rapidly that those watching almost thought they saw the skin on his face physically drop. With all the huffing that accompanies old age, he began his typically prolonged struggle to stand.

With a minimum of fanfare, a petite, elegantly clad woman bearing the unmistakable features of the First Lady of Israel had quietly walked into the room. But the improbability of it . . .

He was standing now, shakily. Gaining his balance, he stood for a long moment, glaring at the newcomer, as though trying to choose between several reasons to be angry or impressed.

"I . . . I don't understand. This is not only highly inappropriate but cruel. This is an affront. Do you intend for me to stand for this? Ma'am, I make it a policy never to insult people I have never met before, yet I must also say that with all respect for your position, I have no intention to sit here and be politically ambushed by a member of—"

"The Kesselman family, Mr. al-Khalid? Or should I say . . ." Her voice lilted upward and nearly edged into a taunting tone but stopped just short.

". . . *Uncle?*"

Chapter Twenty

Al-Khalid snorted and grabbed his cane, eyeing the door. "That's it. I will not be mocked by anyone—"

"Please." Her tone was a bit above plaintive. "I mean absolutely no ambush, nor disrespect. I was never told. Please believe me. I was never told anything except that my aunt Rivke perished. I never knew of your existence until last week. I promise you. Would you *please* stay?"

He stopped in midstride, utterly taken aback by her words. He turned and stared long into her eyes, clearly trying to assess her sincerity. But, of course, there was no reason for her to lie. . . .

He relaxed, lowered his arm, and looked around him, exhaling deeply.

"I apologize for the manner in which this happened," she continued. "But I had no idea how to initiate contact with you. I believed that inviting you to Jerusalem was out of the question. Even security dictated that I not allow any pause between informing you of my intentions and our initial face-to-face meetings. You see, there are a great many urgent reasons for us to talk. More than you might imagine."

"Fine," he grumbled, "but if we talk, then all these functionaries must leave the room. There are private issues at hand."

Hadassah nodded her agreement and gave the ambassador an apologetic glance.

"My apologies, Mr. Ambassador," al-Khalid said, barely covering a gloating tone.

The ambassador nodded gravely and turned to leave with the rest.

"However," said Hadassah, "my bodyguards insist on staying."

"You mean you came halfway across a continent to locate a lost uncle, and then suspect that he might harm you?"

"No. It's merely the rules. You may have heard that I was nearly killed recently."

"Yes. Well, then I'm gone. If you can't trust me with your personal safety, we have no basis to discuss anything else. Really . . ."

He gathered up his cane once more.

Hadassah faced her lead bodyguard with a direct stare. The Mossad agent shrugged.

"All right," she said. "No bodyguards."

He sat down more emphatically than before, as if to punctuate the repetition of it. After all it was his second time to sit in the same chair within a quarter hour.

Hadassah sat in the opposite chair, looked around to a now-vacant room, sighed deeply, and took her first true, appraising look at the man.

"May I call you uncle? For I believe that you are . . ." She stopped to watch him stare at her, his eyes glimmering with tears, his lips moving silently in a vain attempt to form a reply.

"Yes, you may," he finally managed. "And what do I call you?"

"Hadassah would be wonderful. Just Hadassah."

"First of all," she began, "I truly wish to ask for forgiveness. I must tell you that I'm here on a fishing expedition, but a highly important one. It started the night when my father died. He whispered something which led me to an apparent family secret. One from which I was most definitely excluded. And that expedition has led me to you."

"Then, Hadassah, I must ask for your forgiveness as well. You see,

I cannot offer you my condolences upon your father's death."

She straightened awkwardly in her seat. "Why is that?"

"It is terrible to lose a father, as I learned myself at an all-too-young age. And I do not wish to insult your grief. However, your father was no friend of mine. No friend at all. I would say, actually, that he ruined my life."

Hadassah held absolutely still in her seat, genuine surprise engulfing her features. "I'm shocked. I did not know my father had any enemies."

"I was never his enemy, Hadassah. At least I have not been for a very long time. I wish him no harm. I have made my peace with the past. But as you learn more, perhaps you will understand."

"I hope so. Understanding is one of my objectives. Let me start at the beginning of this search. The only thing I was ever told of my aunt Rivke was that she perished. For many years, I could have sworn that I was explicitly told she had perished in the *Shoah*. But now I realize that her actual fate was never explained to me. I merely filled in the blanks. Incorrectly, as it turns out. The word *perished* was always used in reference to her fate. And that was a word my family never used except in a historical context. Usually, discussing our relatives murdered by the Nazis."

"I can assure you, she survived," he said with a faraway look. "She survived the Holocaust by several years."

"And this is what I do not understand. Neither my family nor my other relatives were given to falsehoods."

"I think I can explain," al-Khalid said flatly.

"What is it?"

"Your father meant that she had died not because she had ceased to physically exist, but because he had said Shiva over her. He declared her dead."

Hadassah shook her head in bewilderment. "I'm sorry—what in the world do you *mean*?"

"Maybe I should start at the beginning."

Al-Khalid shifted in his seat and took a deep breath. "Surely you're aware of your father's 1941 traverse across Hungary to Trieste with a group of his closest family members."

"Yes, I am. Or at least, I thought I was."

"Well, Rivke was with him on that journey. She used to spend hours describing the two months they spent sneaking along country roads at night, sleeping in haylofts and forest glens, living off the stores in their backpacks and whatever fruit or produce they could scrounge from the fields. When they reached Trieste, they stowed away aboard a ship with the help of one of David's childhood friends, who was a sailor aboard a cargo vessel."

"Yes, this much I've heard."

"Oh, well . . . then you probably know how they reached London and were given refuge by their second cousins, the Rosensweigs."

"Yes."

"Then I suppose, the new part of this story begins four years later. You know, I met Rivke not twenty yards away from where we sit right now. She and her brothers had come, like so many before them, to see what an Israeli embassy would look like. I spotted her in the crowd. She was . . . stunning. Especially on that day. Her hair was long and free, her eyes sparkled. She had the glowing skin of someone who has just regained her health after a long illness. She was with her brothers, teasing, bantering, beaming, laughing more freely and openly than she probably ever would again—simply from the sheer joy of seeing for herself that there really was a State of Israel. I'm sure it was the best day of her life."

He let out a sigh that ended in a sob.

"That is, until our eyes met."

He closed his eyes, seemingly fighting back tears, and fell silent. For several minutes Hadassah felt it would be sacrilege to urge him on.

Finally, she lightly touched his arm. "How did you meet her?"

His chuckle was wistful. "I was a confident young man back then. And I certainly cut a more dashing figure than I do today. But there was more. Something incredible passed between us in that moment our eyes locked onto each other. Her smile did not diminish one bit. Even though I was a stranger, she seemed to realize immediately that I was reveling in her smile, and everything it represented, as much as anyone with her. So my stare only added to her joy, and she just continued to ride the crest of her bliss and included me in its warmth. Just wrapped me up in that smile. Such generosity of spirit . . . And for the first time ever with a girl that beautiful, I did not wince, waver or glance away. So when the moment had passed, I simply walked up, offered my hand, and introduced myself. The instant our fingers touched, her brothers fell completely silent. By the time our hands parted, it was already clear that something remarkable was in the offing."

"But then you believe my father saw you as a threat."

"Of a sort. It was only natural—he had been her protector for so long now. They had learned the year before that their parents had died, so he acted in every way as her father."

"Yes, and now here you were, cutting a dashing figure, as you said. . . ."

"And I did what any dashing young man would do. I asked her, in my best calm voice, if I might take her to dinner. She glanced over at her brother—your father—ever so quickly, in a way that told me his assent would be required. And he fixed me with this piercing look and said in a flat voice I will never forget, 'How about you meet us for Shabbat tomorrow. What shul do you attend?' I looked at him and asked, 'Shul?' Because you see, I was not raised in the faith."

"You are not Jewish?" she exclaimed.

Al-Khalid shrugged, raising his eyebrows. *There's the question. . . .*

"Your father then shook his head in disgust and used the word he thought a lesser Jew might recognize. 'Synagogue. You've heard of a synagogue?' And I nodded my head yes, although I had never set foot in one of those, either."

"I'm sorry. I-I'm becoming very confused," she stammered.

He held up his hand with a look that said, *One more minute, please, and you'll understand.*

"And then I heard the voice I hated most in the world. The anglicized, un-Jewish, high-British voice of the same attaché who'd been making my life miserable the whole week prior. He marched up and interrupted me with these words I will never forget: 'I'm sorry, Mr. Kesselman. But as we both know, Shabbat services are only for Jews.' At that moment a look of such disdain filled your father David's eyes that I had to look away. I'm sure it wasn't that he hated all Gentiles. He simply thought I had been trying to deceive him and his sister."

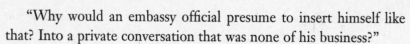

"Why would an embassy official presume to insert himself like that? Into a private conversation that was none of his business?"

"Because he considered it every bit his business. You see, I was under an Esther Edict. And he was the one who had placed it on me."

Chapter Twenty-one

"An *Esther Edict*? I've never heard of such a thing!" Hadassah exclaimed.

"They were quite common in those days. An absolute order not to divulge that one is Jewish. Its name is taken from Mordecai's admonition to Esther to hide her true identity."

"So you actually *were* Jewish? And the Israeli government asked you to do this? Why would they require that?"

Al-Khalid nodded sadly. "Another long story. For your purposes, it starts nine years before, when I arrived on a passenger ship from Kuwait. I grew up in Iraq—Baghdad, actually, where my family was one of the country's wealthiest and most influential business dynasties. My father once owned the largest, most successful textile plant in the Middle East, employing several thousand people. He advised the Iraqi prime minister. Supplied uniforms to the Iraqi Army. Sold most of the black silk used by Iraqi women in making *Abayahs*, the body-length veil worn by the most conservative Muslims. Women were not forced to wear them in those days, although many chose to do so. But life was good. Jews were known as *dhimmis* back then, a protected minority with guaranteed freedom of worship. Half the seats on Baghdad's municipal council were held by Jews. The *M'halat-el 'Yhud*, the Jewish quarter, occupied nearly a fourth of all Baghdad, and one hundred thirty-seven thousand people lived in it. But that all ended one summer night in 1941."

"The infamous *Shavuot* massacre."

He nodded with a faint smile. "You've been well taught, Madam. A pro-Nazi dictator seized power just days before, and, fascist syco-phant that he was, wasted no time trying to carry out his own version of the Third Reich. A huge government-sanctioned crowd swept into the Jewish district, bent on mayhem. Nine hundred Jews were killed during the next twelve hours in a particularly vicious *farhod*—Iraqi slang for what their European counterparts would have called a *pogrom*. I lost three cousins, an uncle, and my best friend that night. They were buried in a mass grave on the outskirts of town, uniden-tified."

"How old were you?"

"Seventeen. Even though the British army soon swooped in and reversed the coup, things only grew worse for the Jews from then on. Nearly every morning, another rabbi or patriarch would be found hanging in a Baghdad square. It was open season on Jewish girls out-side at night. Robbery and open looting of Jewish businesses became almost expected. The papers brazenly called for our extermination."

"And their readers obeyed, apparently."

"They tried their hardest. So my father engineered an intricate business maneuver. He made a big pretense of selling all his holdings to his Iraqi foreman for a relatively modest sum. He held a press conference, took out ads throughout the country. Our family was leaving Iraq, they said. El-Khalid Textile would now be a Muslim-owned enterprise."

He stopped and turned, for even through the embassy's thick walls they had both heard the sound of police sirens approaching. The wail crested, and with a flashing of bright lights against their ancient window, it turned away and began to diminish.

He shrugged, closed his eyes, and continued.

"Behind the scenes, however, my father had crafted an agreement whereby he would continue to receive half of all net profits for as long as he lived. We would enjoy a comfortable exile, living off of our dividend checks and working for the Zionist cause. And should my father ever return, which we anticipated would happen within a few years, his share would be returned for a simple refund of the purchase price."

"Did the plan work?"

Al-Khalid shook his head and sighed heavily. "For about two days. But my father's plan depended on one flimsy intangible, and that was the trust he was placing in his Sunni Muslim partner of over twenty years, a man whom he had plucked from direst poverty. His trust was sorely misplaced. This partner turned out to be a cunning animal with a keen eye on the political landscape. He betrayed my father's plan to the authorities and lodged a false charge of sedition to seal our doom. My whole family was arrested just before Haditha, right outside the Syrian border."

The old man closed his eyes and sank his head back onto the headrest of his Edwardian leather chaise. Hadassah could almost feel the past sweeping over him in waves, filling the room.

"I will never forget it," he continued, suddenly out of breath. "It was noon, and we were dead center in Iraq's Western Desert. As soon as we heard the police lorry's doors close behind us, my father turned to me in our lead car and whispered, 'Run. Run as fast as you can, my son,' he said in a voice so filled with emotion he sounded like he was trying to sing me a lullaby. I felt him press something hard into my hands, looked down, and saw the gold-filled lap belt he had worn under his robes."

With his eyes tilted up and wistful, and a voice that betrayed the number of times he had repeated these phrases by memory, al-Khalid quoted verbatim his father's last words.

"He said, 'Take this and find the Mizrahi Synagogue in London. Beg them to name an Exilarch. And to remember their brothers. Go!'"

Al-Khalid's reverie was interrupted by the loud throb of a helicopter flying low overhead and very fast. And then another just behind it. Al-Khalid scowled, shook his head in curiosity, and continued.

"I wrapped the belt around my arm and fell out into the blinding sunlight. I could scarcely see where I was going, so fierce was the sun, and so bitterly was I weeping. The sensation of my beloved dada's fingers digging into the flesh of my arm, shoving me with all his strength out into a world that wanted me dead . . . I can still feel it." He paused and looked away for a moment. "I scrambled to my feet and began to sprint. I remember the sound of my sobs following me through the dunes over the pop-pop of the police carbines and the fizz of bullets striking the sand around my ankles. But I was young, fast, and in fear of my life, and I ran like a rabbit on fire. I was so quick that I never saw my father again. Not even a look back."

Hadassah couldn't tell if the remorse in his voice stemmed from escaping without that final glimpse, or from escaping at all. "And so you came here."

"Over time, yes. I came here just as Operations Ezra and Nehemiah were in their planning stages. By then, most of my family members were imprisoned in Mosul, and there were plans under way to break them out."

"That explains the Esther Edict," Hadassah commented.

"Oh, of course. One word in the wrong circle and they would have all died horribly. And make no mistake; my silence was as important then as my Arab-sounding name had been in years past. It was the best protection I had."

"So you never mentioned it to anyone?"

"No one. The plans to free them were so sensitive and London so full of anti-Semitic spies that the embassy operatives refused to work with me unless I swore it. When the attaché cornered me, I had no choice. I had to lie about my identity or all efforts to save my family would have been suspended immediately. And that was more important to me than anything else in the world. Even more important than love."

Al-Khalid now seemed more like a patient on a psychiatrist's couch, speaking toward the ceiling, with his body more and more relaxed in the chair.

The spell was broken with more alarming noises from the hallway—shoes scuffling furiously, anxious voices, even a growl of warning. Sounds defiantly out of place within a well-protected embassy. Alarming sounds . . .

Hadassah jumped from her chair, her whole body rigid with concern. Al-Khalid struggled to rise. At once three men seemed to tumble from the hallway into the room, their faces red and their breaths panting audibly.

"Madam ben Yuda," said the nearest one, her lead Mossad bodyguard, "there's been . . . there's been a situation. Your husband has asked that we come for you."

She stifled a sound of panic from her throat. "Is he all right? Has there been an attack?"

The bodyguard shook his head no, swallowing to catch his breath. "No, ma'am. Nothing like that. But we've been ordered to bring you both with us to . . . view something."

A shout came from the hallway. A man's voice, strained and angry, echoed down to them. "I'm with *him*! I'm not here with you!"

And then it seemed as though the hallway launched the man into their midst, still glancing angrily behind him at the person to whom he had yelled.

Then he must have realized where he was, and he turned around.

Hadassah couldn't help her quick intake of breath.

He was not wearing the horn-rimmed glasses, or the nondescript black clothing he had worn at the Shrine of the Book. His full beard was gone.

But he was alive.

Their gazes met and his eyes dropped toward the floor.

Against all her instincts, she spoke. "He—this is a member of Mossad. I know him—" she began, pointing at him but speaking to the other men gathered around the room's entrance and glaring at the man.

"We know that, ma'am," said her lead bodyguard. "But he isn't with *us*."

"He's with *me*," said a voice from beside her. She turned in amazement to al-Khalid, whose mouth was still stretched wide, still forming that last amazing word.

"He's my son."

Chapter Twenty-two

At that point, Hadassah's grasp on the situation collapsed. She had a sense of wrinkling her forehead in bewilderment, stammering some opening syllables of an inane question, and being led out docilely by the arm, like someone struck over the head and slightly dazed.

Fortunately, the old man's disclosure seemed to dispel further hostile tension, and without further debate they were all now up and out, walking as fast as their numbers would allow down the narrow hallway. There was a turn, and a second, and a third, and soon she had lost all track of where they were. The group seemed to have burrowed much deeper into the building complex than its outer dimensions would have allowed.

At last they came to a dead end and a metallic panel, which in some urban high-tech loft might have indicated the door of a recessed stainless-steel refrigerator. Its outer panel slid open silently at their approach, revealing an elevator compartment as gleaming and solid as the inside of a safe.

Somehow they all crowded inside, and Hadassah must have been expecting an upward climb, for she felt distinctly jarred when they dropped swiftly downward. She turned and found herself nose to chin with Meyer—the awkward self-consciousness of a shared elevator aggravated by the amazement, and tinge of unreasonable anger, she felt at meeting him there.

"So, Agent Meyer. We seem to meet in all sorts of dire situations," she murmured, refusing to match the flippancy of her question with a forgiving look. "You disappeared right after our last meeting. And then I was told you were dead. I grieved, you know. Strange, because we'd known each other all of fifteen minutes. But they were, you know . . . rather *intense*."

"It was not of my choosing," he said in a low, sincere voice she had not previously heard from him. "And I was not in a position to reveal my having survived."

His reply did not seem to bear answering, which was good because they had reached bottom, and the doors hummed open.

They walked into a vast, coolly lit control room. Hadassah recognized it at once—more from eighties-vintage American military thrillers than from any personal experience.

The room's ambient light glowed from walls hung with oversized map-laden LCD screens and rows of glowing laptops stared at by men in uniforms of the Israeli Defense Force, the IDF. She knew the American President had a similar installation below the White House, and that it was called, at least colloquially, the *Situation Room*. Surely this one had some sort of similar name, but given her attempts at composure, she knew she would not risk asking the room's name.

An officer appeared from the shadows while she was glancing around. "Mrs. ben Yuda, I apologize for the interruption. And I do not wish to alarm you, but as you may have been told, the Prime Minister asked personally for you *and* your guest"—he paused, angling his head toward al-Khalid with a deliberate nod—"to receive personal briefings. We think you'll realize why momentarily. Unfortunately, I must warn you that what you're about to see is quite disturbing. Feel free to look away at any point, of course. You're not likely to misunderstand."

He turned and walked them over to the largest of the room's screens, all of which were cued up to the same Iraqi broadcast at once—twenty simultaneous faces of a winsome young teenaged girl in a horrific situation.

In normal circumstances one might only have noticed that she was a strikingly beautiful young girl. In particular, she possessed a set of piercing green eyes that seemed to shine with a radiant inner glow.

But now those eyes were nearly impossible to meet straight-on, for they blazed with a terror that few of even the room's most hardened warriors had ever seen before.

First of all, what appeared to be an oversized kitchen knife was held snugly against her throat.

Secondly, the rest of her face was twisted in a horrific expression which no young girl should ever have to wear, and no human being should ever have to watch. Hadassah learned in a moment that genuine terror is unforgettable enough, but the look of someone expecting to be horribly murdered within the following seconds is infinitely worse.

Thirdly, the tortured words tumbling from her lips froze Hadassah's blood within her veins.

"Please. My name is Ariana al-Feliz. I am Iraqi. And . . . and I am also Jewish. My whole family is about to die if you do not help me!" Her voice broke, and the pain and terror said as much as her words. "We have been apprehended by the Death to the Exilarch Committee, and we . . . we are about to become . . ." She looked up to listen to a voice from above her and repeated, ". . . sacrificial lambs of the modern Shi'ite fatwa." She stumbled over the last words.

Her image multiplied across the wall, she cried out and squinted. Hadassah was horrified to see the knife had pressed further into her tender neck. Blood oozed onto the blade and down to her clavicle.

"Their demands are these," the girl panted out the words. "The Jihad insists that all Zionist claims against the rightful property of the Iraqi people be . . . be ceased immediately and withdrawn from the international courts. Please, sir . . . my four-year-old sister is about to be slaughtered next if you do not show mercy. Please, Mr. al-Khalid? I beg you—"

The last was strangled, and the girl's voice drowned in a gurgling, liquid sound. Hadassah looked away just as the room began to rotate. Her eyes rolled upward into her head as four male arms appeared from either side and held her fast. From somewhere offscreen came the sound of wild, hysterical screaming. A gray pall descended over her vision. Her stomach heaved and her throat, all on its own, launched into the initial throes of retching. She clasped a hand to her mouth.

A frenzy of motion beside her caught her attention, and an adrenaline charge shocked her nausea under control as she turned just in time to see the old man fall backward. The glow of a single monitor illuminated a glimpse of his face—cheek and forehead muscles gripped by waves of merciless contractions.

In a single sweep of her head, she saw that Ari Meyer had not seen his father's collapse, but stood pointing at the screen, his finger shaking.

"I know her. I know that girl. I recognize those eyes—I saw them through a window just two weeks ago. She and her family—they were trigger sentries for the Al Hillah raid! She's not just a Jewish girl in hiding—she's a coalition collaborator!"

"What on earth do you mean?" Hadassah asked.

"The Viper 5 squad got reports of potential targets within a block or two. But often they need a local sympathizer to help them pinpoint an exact location to attack. This girl and her family had volunteered through some kind of local network. I don't even think we knew they were Jewish."

And then Ari glimpsed his father sagging into the arms of Hadassah's bodyguards, and his professional reserve shattered whole.

They were not able to speak again for another hour—a mind-numbing sixty minutes of shouted code words and chaotic but perpetual movement.

When the madness was over, Hadassah and Ari Meyer found themselves standing in an improvised medical suite somewhere in the same underground floor, next to a bed where Anek al-Khalid lay unconscious but stable. A doctor in civilian clothes stood watch beside a faintly beeping crash-cart from which snaked a dozen tubes and electrical contacts. Behind them, half visible through a door slightly ajar, lurked a dozen men in varying aspects of military and diplomatic attire.

"I don't have the equipment to say with complete certainty that he did not have a heart attack," the doctor said to Ari. "But from his blood analysis, I would give you a ninety-percent likelihood that he came as close to a myocardial infarction as it's possible to come without actually suffering one."

"That's quite understandable," Meyer said, his voice cracking. "He suffered an incredible shock. I still can't believe my colleagues were so—so callous as to rush him in there to witness that without some kind of preparation."

"For what it's worth, I'm truly sorry," Hadassah told Meyer, stepping forward. Then the sympathetic look was replaced with something else. "However, I have some questions—"

"Yes." He nodded grimly. "I'm sure you do."

"Your sudden appearance up there"—she waved vaguely toward the ceiling—"what was that all about?"

"I did not plan on being seen. If the emergency call had not come, you would never have known of my presence. However, please remember that my father and I were never told you were the reason for the invitation. Your arrival at the embassy was a complete surprise."

"Yes. Well, there are shocks on my side, too. The fact that you are alive, that you are here, and most of all, that you are my cousin." She paused to appraise him carefully. "I have so many questions, I hardly know where to begin."

Before he could answer, an aide stepped in and handed her a telephone.

"My dearest, did you see it? Did you see . . . see the footage?"

The voice was Jacob's, as clear as the next room, and he sounded tense. He rushed on, "I had no idea, no warning they would go through with it—"

"Yes, I'm afraid we did see the whole terrible thing—" Her voice caught before she added, "And Mr. al-Khalid suffered a near heart attack."

"Honey, I'm very sorry you had to go through that." Jacob's genuine regret was clear. "Like I said, I had no idea—but I do need to speak to him right away. I can't tell him to call off his lawsuit, of course, but I must talk with him."

"Did you understand me, Jacob? He almost died."

"Is he conscious?"

"I'm not . . . not sure. Semiconscious at best."

"Well, I'm going to have to ask you to find out." His tone was gentle but firm. "Look, this is the most volatile, dangerous, and tragic event I've ever seen. I've been on the phone with the President of the United States. His Secretary of State is right now on hold, waiting for my line to clear. As you can imagine, the sight of this young girl has grabbed the world's attention. It's not just the lead story, it's been the *only* story for the last two hours. And now her actual death—" He stopped to clear his throat. "And the only question on any Arab street is *Who is this Anek al-Khalid, and why is he so greedy that he'd rather steal food from starving Iraqi children than lift a finger to save a Jewish child from a horrible death?* And did you hear the terrorists claim earlier that the 2005 London bombings were actually a warning to him? A personal warning about which he was given prior warning, and did nothing to heed, let alone pass on to authorities?"

"Oh, Jacob, I can't believe that—"

"It gets worse. Iraq has exploded. There's fighting across the country. Gaza too. The Palestinian peace talks have been suspended out of pressure from Muslim states, even so-called moderates. In the last hour there've been riots outside twelve of our embassies around the world. Including the one you are at."

"I don't understand. There've been atrocities before—why would this one be so . . . so incendiary?"

"They've never taken a whole family hostage before or publicly murdered a child like this. And it's never been a Jewish family before. The dilemma has caused Muslim factions to actually declare war *against each other*! Some say the Koran forbids the killing of infidel children. Others insist it's a sacred duty. Six different mullahs on three continents have issued fatwas against the others for their opinions about the taking of this girl and her family. And that's not to mention the fatwas against Anek, like the one leveled years ago against Salman Rushdie. He is a marked man."

"I can't believe this—"

"And Hadassah, consider this. All this is without anyone knowing that the First Lady of Israel was personally meeting with Anek al-

Khalid when the girl was murdered! Not to mention that he happens to be her *uncle*! Do you realize what fuel that would add to the fire? I can hardly think about it! For the Arab World to realize al-Khalid is related to the Israeli Prime Minister!"

Her head was spinning. Forcing herself to stay in control, she asked, "All right . . . so what do I do now, Jacob?"

"Honey, crowds are gathered right outside the compound where you are. They've been held back only because London police can lock down the entire street, but it won't last long. Especially if they learn that al-Khalid is actually on the premises. You have to come home. *Now*. And you really ought to persuade him—your uncle—to come back with you. He cannot be kept safe anywhere but in Israel."

"Did you hear me, Jacob?" Hadassah demanded once more. "He's unconscious, and it's only with G-d's help he didn't die when he heard that girl speak his name. He's incapable of conversing with anybody, let alone a head of state." She paused to look around. "However, there is someone here you can speak with in his stead."

"Who in the world might that be?"

"You already know the man—in fact, you told me about him. In the Mossad, he goes by Ari Meyer. Actually, it's al-Khalid's son. My cousin, whom I never even knew existed."

The line went silent. He finally asked, "What in the world is going on, Hadassah? I thought your investigation was going in a different direction—"

"It *is* a strange story, honey. I had no idea how involved it would become."

"Or how bizarre. I am so worried, with all these strange convergences—saving exiled Jews, Esther Edicts, genocidal plots—I feel as though I'm reliving Esther myself, and Haman's evil plot is still under way!"

"I told you the old story was important."

"I never doubted it, honey," he said dryly. "Regardless, I want you and this Meyer on the plane back here within an hour. This time, my dear, it's an order. Be safe."

Chapter Twenty-three

Emunah America Magazine
2003

Although the Jewish community in Iraq dated back 2,700 years, by the time the most recent images of Iraq were being transmitted around the globe, nearly all of the Iraqi Jews were living elsewhere, mainly in Israel, some concentrated in the United States, Canada, and Europe. The vast majority of these Jews left Iraq without anything tangible.

The Iraqi Jews are split on the issue of their former homeland. Some retain warm reminiscences of the country, while others nothing more than bitterness. And others take a more financially oriented approach to the country, seeking to regain some of the of the property that was taken from them by the Iraqi government. An East Coast–based organization that calls itself the American Committee for the Rescue and Resettlement of Iraqi Jews is spearheading a drive to file a class-action lawsuit like the one filed against the Swiss Banks on behalf of Holocaust survivors.

—SHERYL KATZ ELIAS, "GOOOOD
MORNING, BAGHDAD!!!!" HTTP://
WWW.EMUNAH.ORG/MAGAZINE_
COMMENTS.PHP?ID=P175_0_4_0_C

LONDON—LATER THAT NIGHT

The *mob gathered* outside the security gate leading down Palace Green Street to the nearby Israeli Embassy had now grown into a sprawling, strident human mass—a single organism three hundred yards across, spilling all the way onto Kensington Road and heaving with oceanlike surges of rage and crescendos of shrill anti-Semitic chanting. Rioters from London's huge Islamic community along nearby Edgeware Road had now been joined by an even more volatile element: young, liberal bohemians from London's hipper neighborhoods like adjacent Notting Hill, drawn by the banking of choppers overhead and the irritating echoes of impending bedlam.

At the mob's outer edges stood the press, shooting spotlights and camera lenses into the melee, inevitable participants of any event this photogenic. In fact, Fleet Street's contribution to the chaos was even more obvious than usual, for several of the city's television stations had just announced the presence of Hadassah ben Yuda, First Lady of Israel, inside the embassy walls. The media's helicopters had begun their slow, circular dance in the sky.

Drunk with this knowledge, the mob was smelling and demanding blood.

The roar intensified when a phalanx of vehicles appeared from inside the embassy complex and edged to the outer gates. Swirling lights on two flanking police vans and a thick, armored limousine between them announced to the crowd that someone important urgently wanted to leave. Surely, this was ben Yuda attempting to flee—and that was all the provocation the mob needed.

The gates opened slowly, pressing back the crush, and the vehicles moved forward, slowly but inexorably. The human beast only pushed back harder. Bodies were crushed without mercy from behind against the vehicles' metallic surfaces. A hollow drumbeat of fists struck up against the motorcades' outer shells. A rock appeared in a hand and came down hard against a window. The glass splintered into a spiderweb array of cracks, but held. More rocks fell upon the limousine roof, causing visible dents but no rending of the body itself.

Barely twenty yards out of the gate, the trio of vehicles seemed to run aground against a beachhead of unmovable humanity. A fanfare of honks rang out over the bobbing heads. Commanding voices rang out through the metallic buzz of loudspeakers, ordering the crowd to disperse. And from the various corners of Kensington Palace Park, for the first time, came the shrill sirens of approaching London riot squads.

While the rioters concentrated their wrath upon the more obvious vehicles at the embassy's Kensington Road entrance, a much smaller service gate in the compound's rear alleyway swung inauspiciously open. Even had the enraged pedestrians known to stand watch at this spot, they likely would have overlooked the drab panel truck bearing the sign *Kensington Uniform Supply*. The lorry pulled out from beside the neighboring fire brigade building—an inauspicious delivery vehicle making its normal rounds, unremarkable except for a dark protrusion from its roof.

You would have needed a high perch to glimpse the black-clad figure sprawled on that roof—a brave SAS operative with an M800 assault rifle held tightly in his hands. Or the concealed forms of snipers watching from surrounding rooftops, peering through infrared scopes. And in all the surrounding noise of other helicopters, they surely would not have heard the sleek black two-man chopper, its nearly silent rotors plying the darkness in tight circles a mere three hundred yards above.

In all, this ordinary-looking departure featured twice the security measures of its more public counterpart on the other side of the embassy. The difference: these were deliberately and cunningly concealed.

Without even a single pair of hostile or curious eyes watching it, the van turned right, away from busy Kensington High Road to Kensington Church Street, then drove the long way to Notting Hill Gate and the A40 dual carriageway to M25.

Inside the darkened van, far more comfortably appointed than its exterior might have suggested, four people huddled around a hospital bed strapped to the floor. One of them held tightly to the hand of the immobilized patient.

Another, a woman, leaned forward to catch a view of the retreating masses through the back mirrored windows. She leaned toward him and whispered, "I think it's working."

Ari Meyer nodded seriously without taking his eyes from his father on the hospital bed.

"I was sure it would. It's a lot easier to fool a bunch of ticked-off crazies than a dedicated terrorist squad. We'll be all right."

"Call me Hadassah, by the way. After all, we're cousins."

"Can I wait until you're not angry with me anymore?"

She didn't answer but nodded. She wasn't quite ready yet to surrender her irritation.

"When all hell broke loose, your father was in the middle of telling me the whole story of our two families," she told him.

"You mean you don't know it?" he exclaimed with a small, incredulous laugh.

She shook her head. "Why don't you start by telling me what happened between your father and mine."

"My *mother* happened, that's what. She and my father started to see each other after meeting at the embassy."

"Even though he'd told her and everyone he wasn't a Jew?"

"Yes. He'd been forced to say that to protect his family still in Iraq. From what he's told me, their attraction was an incredible, impractical affection that flamed quickly and never wavered. It wasn't three months before everything exploded. Your father, David, struck the match, in fact."

"It feels like we're not talking about the same man. My father always seemed conciliatory, forgiving and open-minded."

"People have a way of mellowing with age," he agreed. "I know my father did. But at the time, Father fell hard and fast for Rivke Kesselman. It took only a week or two before he'd told her his secret—although he swore her to silence, including her promise never to tell the rest of her family. This of course placed her in a horrible dilemma. David Kesselman objected in the worst way to her seeing a Gentile, especially an Arab one who seemed to be passing himself off as a Jew. My dad even thinks David may have suspected him in some more sinister way—at least at first."

"What? Of being a spy?"

"Perhaps. The town was full of them—in fact, that's largely why the problem started in the first place. The Edict was placed on my father because of Arab spies."

Ari swayed backward on a sudden turn and caught himself against the van's wall, then reached out and straightened his father's stretcher. The vehicle now sped up considerably—they apparently had reached the M25.

"When it became clear this was a serious relationship, Rivke begged her brother David to trust her choice. She as much as told him there was a secret at the heart of it all, but he would not put any stock in her hints. He seemed to channel his grief at the destruction of their family into some newfound rigidity, an absolute unwillingness to bend the rules of their faith. He insisted that she not see him anymore, and forbade him from coming inside their house. When she would sneak out to see him, he threatened to kick her out, although he didn't follow through.

"Then your father learned that they had become betrothed. He completely lost it. He did throw her out then, and she had no choice but to move in with Dad. She had not been able to find work, as only the brothers had succeeded in finding very strenuous construction jobs. She found the arrangement shameful, but according to the old ways, betrothal is equivalent to marriage, so they treated it that way.

"When David learned they'd made a household together, he made one last overture. He came to their house one night and asked if Anek would be converting to Judaism. Now it was my father's turn to be caught in an unbearable dilemma. His answer was no, because of course he was already a Jew. Not an observant one, but he'd hoped to fix that also, as soon as possible. Yet he could say nothing of this to David. The only thing he thought of to say, which was halfway truthful, is what he swallowed hard and told him in a firm voice: 'She will follow me in my faith.' And that is what he told him. My dad was proud of himself; he had honestly answered the question without betraying the Esther Edict.

"But to David, it was the worst reply imaginable. He assumed Rivke would be converting to Islam, and he did the unthinkable. He returned home and said Shiva over Rivke, declaring that she was dead to him, to all of them. Forbade any member of the family from ever having contact with her again. Cut her out of the few pictures they'd taken with them. She had married out of the faith, and for members of his Jewish generation, that meant her 'death.'"

The van sped on at unusual speeds toward Gatwick Airport while inside, Ari's tale continued to deepen. . . .

Chapter Twenty-four

U*pon becoming betrothed* to Anek, Rivke Kesselman had hoped that soon her beloved's family would be whisked from Iraq," Ari continued as the fast-moving van swayed around corners on its way to the airport. "That evacuation could happen either through secret channels by the Mossad, or publicly through the Nehemiah Airlift. Anek's claims of a family fortune would soon be vindicated, allowing him to not only finally explain his Jewish identity to her family, but provide for them all in a way that would make her proud.

"But after hearing that her beloved brother had declared her 'dead,' Rivke was totally devastated. Desperate to reverse the family's verdict, she brought Anek to the family home late one Shabbat evening, when she knew that all the siblings and cousins would be in the apartment.

"Upon seeing her, David immediately started to shout at them. Then he realized that even asking who had allowed them to enter had inadvertently acknowledged her existence, so he turned his back and fixed his stony gaze upon a far wall. Rivke's sisters both burst into sobs and began begging David to reconsider.

"'Please, David. At least talk to her! She says she has something important to say!'"

"'David,'" Rivke added her own plea, "'what I have to tell you will change everything. I promise.'"

"Slowly, David had turned around, his own cheeks stained with tears.

"It was Anek who spoke next.

"'I *am* Jewish.'" He paused, allowing the words to sink in. "'I am Jewish, and the hardest thing I've ever done was to let you think otherwise. But you see, I had no choice. Part of my family is in prison back in Iraq, others in hiding unable to escape, and the Israeli government is desperately trying to negotiate for their release. But until things are resolved, I am under a firm Esther Edict imposed here by the embassy staff. I am prohibited from telling anyone the truth about my heritage. I risked everything even telling Rivke, and I'm risking even more telling this to you now. Do you remember, it was that attaché who told you I was Gentile, not me. Had I told you the truth in front of him, all efforts to save my family would have ceased immediately.'"

"David looked at Anek for a long moment, his face slack and his expression inscrutable.

"'I don't believe you,'" he said at last.

"The sisters' sobs sounded as one around the room.

"'Why not?'"

"'Because when I look at you, I don't see a Jew. All I see is a lonely young man madly in love with my sister and willing to do anything, say anything, to have her for himself. Tell me, if you're a Jew, have you been bar mitzvah'ed?'"

"'No, I'm afraid not. Hardly any boys have had bar mitzvah in Baghdad for the last ten years. It's just too risky. The last two ceremonies I heard of were attacked by mobs and the whole families slaughtered.'"

"'Do you read Hebrew? Speak it?'" David demanded.

"'No, I cannot. All yeshivas and Jewish schools of any kind have been closed for years.'"

"'Can you even tell me a word of it?'"

"'What? Like Shabbat? Seder? Pesach? Eretz Yisroel?'"

"'Stop this!'" shouted Rivke's sister Rachel at her brother David.

"Anek was now as angry as David. 'Would you like me to

remove my pants?'" he asked, lips curled.

"'*What?*'" David roared.

"'You know what I mean,'" Anek said, keeping his voice cool and level. "'Would you like to see it?'"

"'Shut your mouth! You have the gall, having already taken our sister from us, to come back here and insult the women of this house, on Shabbat, with this obscene proposal?'"

"'Come now, I am a decent man, David,'" Anek now said contritely. "'I've behaved toward your sister with complete honor and decency. I would never have revealed my circumcision without respectfully asking the ladies in the room to leave us for a moment.'"

"'It doesn't matter,'" David spat back. "'Even Muslims sometimes circumcise. It doesn't prove you're a Jew. Look—even if what you say is true, you're the most dishonorable Jew imaginable. At a time when millions of your people went to their deaths because they refused to hide, because they dared to wear the Yellow Star, you hid who you are. If some bureaucrat had told me to lie about my Judaism, I would strike him down.'"

"'Really? Even if it doomed the lives of your whole family?'"

"'I would strike anyone who questioned or undermined my Jewishness.'"

"'Oh, I see. Well, maybe I should, too.'"

"Anek stepped forward and shoved David hard across the chest. David reeled backward, caught his balance, and chuckled oddly toward the floor, as though ruefully conceding the validity of Anek's rebuttal.

"Then in a split second he was upon the younger man, both of them staggering under a flurry of blows that filled the air with fists and blood and the screams of the women and the hands of two male cousins trying to insert themselves and stop the fight. Anek was restrained first, from behind, and in the instant it took to pull David away, the older man landed a hard blow on the defenseless man's mouth, sending a spray of blood across the room to hit Rivke's face.

"Another round of screams erupted. David was pulled back to the other side of the room. Rivke reeled backward, and while wiping her cheek, she felt something die inside of her.

"Anek violently shrugged himself loose from the cousins' grasp, turned back, and took hold of Rivke's hand.

"'Now you know what kind of family you came from,'" he said to her in a tortured voice. "'Jewish or not . . .'"

——————— ⌐⌐ ———————

"Anek and Rivke walked out," Ari said wistfully to Hadassah over the whine of jet engines, glancing out the Gulfstream's oval window at the lights of London tilting away far below him. "They slammed the door behind them, and the family was ruptured forever."

He looked over at where his father lay wrapped on a fold-down bed, the embassy doctor keeping careful watch over him from a nearby seat.

"I grew up in a home without relatives," he continued, looking back at Hadassah. "My mother's Jewish family was a subject of great pain and anguish. My father's family no less so, because soon after they were married, he received word that the whole family had disappeared—bribed a guard to escape prison, but with no passport with which to leave the country they had probably assimilated into the general population, passing themselves off as Arabs. My father's hopes—his whole reason for living all the years since arriving alone in London—were shattered. Without the written records hidden in Iraq, he could not even prove that he was born Jewish. So even immigrating to Israel would be a nightmare. And things only grew worse when my mother exchanged letters with one of her sisters and learned about the Hadassah Scrolls—that her family privately owned an ancient letter written by none other than Queen Esther herself, addressed to a young Jewish exile named Leah, who happened to be their great-grandmother several dozen times back."

"I knew there was something strange about your reaction in the museum," Hadassah said, "the night you first saw them."

Ari nodded. "In all my years of intelligence work, I have never had such a hard time hiding my emotions. Thank G-d for the dim lighting. I know the shades looked absurd in that dark place, but at least they helped mask what I was feeling."

"Why didn't you reveal yourself to me? And why were the scrolls such an issue? Of all the things you've lost, I'd think people were far more significant than some old documents."

"You're right—it wasn't just the scrolls, although they were important. It was meeting *you*. The impact of seeing someone of my own family bloodline, for the first time in my life, caught me totally off guard. That, and the fact that you resemble old pictures of my mother. I never knew it from your press photographs, but you both have the same beautiful green eyes I was always told appear once in ten generations. I had no idea that seeing you would affect me as it did. As it *has*."

"So why did you ask to see the Hadassah journals? You can't tell me it's some sort of coincidence in your work."

"No. I needed to authenticate what I'd found, for both job-related and family reasons. See, I've crafted my whole Mossad career to dovetail with the mission drilled into me by my father ever since I was a boy. Which is to discover the documents that would prove who my father was, who I am. To find Iraq's Jewish genealogies and prove that we are Jewish. And to find the records of the Exilarch, fulfilling my grandfather's final request to my father."

"There's that word again. *Exilarch*."

"You know it?"

"I've heard it several times in the last few weeks. In the strangest of places."

"It is a word with ancient roots. It means the leader of the Jews in exile."

"Of course. Mordecai bore that title, at least if legend is true."

"I believe it is. *Exilarch* is a word familiar to all Iraqi Jews, because it comes from a much better time, a time when Jews were respected and even celebrated by the Islamic rulers of the country. The Exilarch sat on a throne opposite the caliph himself. Every Jew and Muslim alike had to stand and salute the Exilarch or face a hundred lashes."

"But the word seems doubly important to your family for some reason."

"It was. For the al-Khalids, the word and the office meant even more. Before he lost his fortune, when he still moved among Iraq's rich and mighty, my grandfather dreamed of reviving the office, even though it's been dormant for centuries. He thought it could be the solution to all the oppression against his people. He claimed that buried somewhere under the Battaween Synagogue in Iraq, and maybe hidden under the text of Jewish records elsewhere, were documents proving he was descended from the family of David and the hereditary office of the Exilarch. After they lost everything, it became an obsession. My grandfather would talk of it all the time, as if just mentioning it would somehow restore what had been stolen from us. His last words to my father were a plea that he return to save his family, and to always mention that he was descended from the Exilarch. When my father reached London but failed to prove that he and his family were Jewish, he vowed to keep searching for proof. He also vowed to find the Exilarch link, which could not only make him a Jew, but a powerful one as well. Now he's passed that quest on to me."

"But how did the Exilarch issue come to involve our two families? Or our scrolls, for that matter?"

"When my father learned of your family's Hadassah scrolls, he became even more enraged at David than ever before. Rivke tried to calm him by reminding him that their existence was a secret even within your own family—that traditionally, even Kesselman girls were not told about them until just before their wedding day."

"That's the way it was for me. Just a few days before," said Hadassah.

"Well, that meant nothing to him," Ari continued. "In his eyes, it was another important thing the Kesselmans had kept from him. Not the story of Esther, although that would have been a great blessing to my mother. But the names."

"The *names*?"

"The signatures at the end of the scroll. Surely you signed yours."

"Of course I did, but—"

"The names are a link proving an unbroken descent between Kesselman women and the ancient office of the Exilarch."

"But that's not true. They're a link to Leah, the girl to whom Esther wrote her letters and who was our ancestor. But that's all anyone knows. I know Mordecai has always been rumored to have been an Exilarch. At least the first *real* one. But that seems unlikely, because he wasn't of the line of David. And even then, it doesn't matter, because Leah was not related to him, so she had nothing to do with the Exilarchy."

"Maybe—but there's one possibility that could have erased all those problems *at once*. And that possibility is what I've been trying to confirm all these years. You see, in Jewish Iraqi legend, it was often rumored that Mordecai married late in his life, and fathered the ancestors of many of our people. According to legend, this wife was a young woman in the palace, a young Jewish girl from the royal line—"

"You mean. . . ?" Hadassah barely breathed the question.

"Why not? It's just a rumor, but a persistent and pervasive one. According to my father, there was hardly a Jewish woman in Iraq who wouldn't have repeated it to you with all the fervency of Torah truth. This is what I have been groomed to do my whole life, Hadassah. To reach a place where I could retrieve this knowledge kept from us, to vindicate our family and save our people."

"So—if Mordecai had married Leah," Hadassah continued, staring through her eyelashes like a schoolgirl struggling with long division, "then their offspring would have combined his political influence with her Davidic pedigree—"

"Making them the perfect source for the all the Exilarchs that followed. Which would mean that the Kesselman family would have a provable claim to the Exilarchy itself. And by joining the heritage of our two families, my father's son would have been a viable al-Khalid heir to the Exilarchy."

"That's you," she said in a voice breathy with astonishment.

"That's *me*. If I could prove that link, I could be a new Exilarch."

"But by denying your father any access or proof of the Hadassah scrolls, my father made all that impossible. No wonder you were so moved to see the scrolls in person. They mean everything to you. They're the key to saving all your lost relatives, to carrying out your grandfather's wish, restoring your family's fortune, vindicating your father's whole life, not to mention healing the breach between our families. . . ."

"But only if we can prove that Mordecai married Leah. If that's not true, or provable, then it's all for nothing."

"So that's why the documents you found mean so much. If they'd actually proven that the marriage took place, they could tie it all together."

"Yes, on the personal front. But on the global front, the genealogies I found with them also complicate things immensely. They have started the clock ticking, by identifying helpless Jewish families in their midst and facilitating their extermination. And putting you and your husband right in the path of a scandal related to the whole thing."

"Yes. And if the documents prove something else, then everything is lost."

The implications of that unfinished sentence shoved both back into their seats with a force greater than that of accelerating jet engines. Their minds traveled down identical "what if" pathways. And they both arrived at the same destination.

If Jews in hiding were being exterminated, in some revival of Haman's ancient hatred, then the nation of Israel would not stand idly by. And Israeli involvement in Iraq would drastically escalate the conflict.

Only a strong, untainted prime minister could take the action necessary to avoid a fresh war in the Middle East. And Jacob ben Yuda, with a wife recently linked to a provocateur in London whose purse strings were tightly wound around the whole affair, could hardly qualify.

The only person who could save the Jews of Iraq without drawing in Israel would be a leader they trusted, from their own midst, their own blood.

Only a new Exilarch could stop a new Middle East war. And if Mordecai and Leah had never married, there would be no new Exilarch.

Chapter Twenty-five

T *he Israeli jet had* left Ben Gurion Airport on a Tuesday night with Hadassah ben Yuda aboard and landed back on the same runway less than sixteen hours later. The journey had proven even more of a lightning trip than anyone had anticipated. Luckily, they had been able to sleep aboard the Gulfstream—all except for the embassy doctor and the pilots.

It was two-thirty in the morning, Jerusalem time, when an ambulance met the aircraft just inside the Lod Air Base side of the tarmac, without even waiting for it to finish taxiing. Within four minutes, the recovering Anek al-Khalid was leveraged out of the plane's door and stowed aboard the ambulance.

Another vehicle, a black SUV with mirrored windows, pulled up and accepted three passengers: Israel's First Lady, her bodyguard, and her newly discovered cousin, Ari. The GMC Suburban made the trip to Jerusalem in less than an hour, accompanied in front and back by identical vehicles with flashing red lights on their rooftops. Once in the Eternal City, the convoy was joined by a pair of Israeli helicopters, while the flanking SUVs lowered their windows to permit their infrared scopes and sniper rifles to do their work.

Alerted by a prearranged phone call that had roused him from a restless sleep, Jacob ben Yuda—looking less like the Prime Minister of Israel than a sleep-deprived husband—stood waiting in the shadows when the Suburban pulled up inside his office's underground parking complex.

Even as her SUV coasted to his side, Hadassah could see that her husband's gaze was cast downward in deep concentration. Hard to believe a man this preoccupied had nothing more serious on his agenda than meeting *her*.

But then—she reminded herself with an inner smile of satisfaction—this time, his serious matter had everything to do with her. This time, she stood at the very core of those white-hot "national affairs" that had once seemed to preempt her existence and hijack her husband's time and focus on nearly every other day of her marriage.

Whether or not the Mideast was once again a political cauldron, her husband's genuine care for her was part and parcel of the crisis.

Her door flew open and without even trying, she fell into her husband's arms. He embraced her more tightly than he ever had before; held her to his chest longer than he ever had in public. She frowned anxiously, for he seemed different somehow. Then she found that her eyes were filled with tears. *A short trip . . .* she reminded herself. *Short trip, indeed.*

He let her go, aimed a searching glance up and down her body, then once again grasped her to himself.

"Oh, sweetheart," he whispered hoarsely. "I've been so afraid for you. Things are moving so fast, so dangerously."

He pulled back again and caught Ari's eye. Silent for a moment, the two shook hands.

"We meet again, under different understanding."

"Yes. A *true* one, sir."

"Is your father doing any better?"

"Yes. He's stable, and sleeping quite stubbornly."

"Well, thank you for leaving his side to speak with me. I intend to make it worth your while. You too, Hadassah. Ari, are you able to come with us now?"

At Ari's nod, Jacob led at a brisk pace through the same hallways Hadassah had covered barely a week before—on her way to crashing the cabinet meeting. She found it almost eerie, seeing these spaces devoid of people and only lit by floor-mounted sconces. Jacob swept open the double doors to the cabinet room and ushered the two into his domain.

Jacob held a chair for his wife, nodded to one on the opposite side of the table for Ari, and sat down in his own. He leaned far forward and extended his palms flat on the table in an unusually casual pose. Hadassah noted with concern how tired Jacob looked, the circles under his eyes.

"So, Mr. Meyer. I understand that your work with Mossad included a good deal of research into ancient documents, and it turns out that this endeavor was of a rather personal nature."

Ari adopted a somber look and blinked several times.

"Before I answer that," he began slowly, "I need to know something. Am I speaking to you as my ultimate boss, the Prime Minister of the Nation of Israel, or as my cousin by marriage?"

Jacob shrugged. "Very good question. And the fact that you asked it leads me to believe that I can probably trust you in either capacity. The truth is, I'm not sure it matters."

"Well, what I meant was—should I be concerned about protecting myself against disciplinary action, or may I speak freely?"

"It depends. Have you broken any laws?"

"I don't think so. But I've certainly broken faith with the Mossad by operating in part with a private agenda. I've never let it compromise any of my work or the extent of my efforts. But I have, when it mattered, shared some of my findings with my father."

"Look, Jacob," Hadassah broke in, "I've learned so much about my family history in the last few hours. Things that were held from me all these years. I definitely understand that there's a lack of trust between Ari's side and the Kesselman side. A justifiable one. It wouldn't hurt to extend a little latitude here."

Jacob sighed. "All right. For the sake of this crisis, I, Jacob ben Yuda, Prime Minister of Israel, grant you functional immunity for your actions as a Mossad agent. However, this immunity does not extend to any act which might diminish or harm the security of the state of Israel to the least extent. Do you understand me?" He stared hard at Ari.

"Sure. But would you please put that in writing?"

"No. We're operating on trust here. The beginning of it, anyway."

The two men faced each other in a momentary standoff. Then Ari nodded once, extended his hand. The two men shook again.

"All right. So let's hear this great family saga, and figure out what role it's played in bringing this whole part of the world to the brink of war."

Hadassah then leaned forward, once more inserted herself into the conversation, and began relaying the story Anek al-Khalid had told her the night before. When she was through with her uncle's part of the tale, Ari jumped in—supplying the more recent, operational parts of the story.

When they were through, Jacob sat perfectly still, only his eyes darting rapidly between the two as he tried to process the mountain of pertinent facts.

"So . . ." he began, "you're part of the official Mossad operation to find, save, and protect the lost Jewish treasures of Iraq. But your true, ultimate objective was to discover documents that would help you find your lost relatives."

"Well, I would describe both objectives as true. They were parallel. And also to establish the bloodline of the Exilarch in a way that will validate its royal pedigree as well as my father's relation to the title."

"All right. And in the Hillah raid with the Italian commandos, you discovered a cache of Jewish documents that nearly accomplished both of those missions."

"Yes. They apparently were stolen from their hiding place at the Battaween Synagogue in Baghdad. I found a record of Iraq's hidden Jewish population, and hidden underneath, a letter written by the ancient Queen Esther. The first gives me hints of where my father's family hid after escaping from prison fifty years ago. And the second one lends great credibility to the ancient rumor that Mordecai produced an heir carrying the royal bloodline of Israel. This would legitimize the ancient bloodline of the Exilarch, and lead its genealogy straight to my father."

"And my wife."

A short nod was Ari's answer. Jacob had understood immediately.

"Would you have retrieved and analyzed these documents for your work even if you hadn't been privately looking for them?" Jacob asked.

"Absolutely. Even without my personal interest I would have treated these findings with great care and extensive study."

"And do you think your discovery could have triggered this wave of attacks against the hidden Jewish population?"

"It's impossible to say one way or another with complete certainty. But we do know that the names had been copied before we ever attacked. So some form of preparation to unveil their ancestry was already under way."

Jacob folded his hands behind his head and leaned back abruptly in his chair. "I'm just trying to establish whether this personal angle is actually to blame for the crisis, or merely a useful coincidence."

"Maybe a little of both," Hadassah commented.

"The reference to your father on that poor girl's broadcast was no one's fault, definitely not his," Jacob continued after a nod at Hadassah, almost speaking to himself. "It's just an effort to stir up anti-Semitism in Iraq. The Arab population has been agitated with tales about swarms of Jews coming in to reclaim all the city's wealth and real estate. Ultimately, it's all bait to force me into committing military action in Iraq. Which would, of course, force even less-militant Arabs into the fray and destroy the entire Iraqi Freedom coalition, along with everything the West has done to stabilize Iraq."

"There are so many angles, it's hard for me to keep up," Hadassah said. "For instance, who do you think is trying to kill me?"

"This group of former Hussein loyalists called Death to the Exilarch," Jacob said.

"Their name makes sense," said Ari. "They've heard the rumors that have swirled around Baghdad for years."

"Which rumors are you referring to?" asked Jacob, sitting forward once more.

"Rumors that someone in the expatriate community would someday seek to revive the office of the Exilarch," Ari replied, his eyes intense. "And would use it to consolidate and strengthen the reparation claims, not to mention the general influence, of exiled Jews. Are you aware of the accumulated value of the seized assets of the Jews of Baghdad? When they walked off and left their property behind in Operations Ezra and Nehemiah, the Iraqi Jews controlled most of the country's concentrations of finance, industry, and commerce. Today those holdings would be worth multiplied tens of billions of dollars. If the proper lineage truly did succeed in reviving the office of the Exilarch, that person could provide leadership and credibility to all the claims. And it would put the ownership of a large portion of the nation's economy back in Jewish hands. Until now, the exiled Jewish community has been too scattered and frightened to demand their return, although they've talked about it. For years they've clamored and agitated about naming a new Exilarch who would solve all their problems, champion their grievances, legitimize them in the eyes of the world. Just enough to make the Arabs paranoid about an imminent Jewish takeover of their economy—maybe their country."

"So why has no one ever followed through and named an Exilarch?"

"First of all, the man would have to be descended from the proper lineage—and the precise nature of that lineage has become the subject of huge debate. For one, the person would have to be descended from Mordecai, among many others. However, Mordecai was not of the bloodline of David, and there has been no known record of his having married or produced heirs. Only rumors. That's for starters."

"Sounds like a rabbinical, theological debate to me," Jacob said, shaking his head ruefully.

"You have no idea," Ari continued. "It gets more Talmudic the further you dig. See, there were two competing lines of authority in the exiled Jewish communities—the rabbinic, or clerical, and the civil leadership. It's a remnant of some of the oldest schisms in all of Judaism. Partly a feud between the Patriarchy and the Diaspora Jews. Partly between the faith tradition of the Temple and that of the synagogue, which developed just after these events. Partly between the rabbinical and the political side. Because no one has ever been able to prove that the Exilarch combined all of these competing factions, especially the royal line of David with the political heritage of Mordecai, Jerusalem has never recognized the Exilarch as a legitimate leader of the Jewish people. Not for two and a half thousand years."

"Can a person be found who fits this profile?" asked Jacob. "The only Jews left in Iraq are old and frightened. The Exilarchy ended . . . let's see . . . over four hundred years ago, leaving the bloodline hanging, unresolved. I can't imagine there being someone who could revive it."

"There is someone," Ari said.

Chapter Twenty-six

N ot a word was spoken for several minutes.

"And you mean. . . ?" Jacob added quietly.

There was another pause, and then Ari said just as quietly, "Me."

Hadassah, for her own part, could feel her heart pound in her ears. She could hardly keep from smiling, for Ari's bombshell seem to stitch together all the far-flung threads of this crisis. The motives had finally come into focus—both friends' and foes'. Now they possibly could make some progress.

But if Hadassah smiled, her husband was anything but smiling. She looked at his expression and said, "Jacob, it seems to me that our next question is simply—what's next? You've got things to decide as Prime Minister, and it could be that Ari and I have our part to play. . . ."

Jacob was still staring at the table, lost in contemplation. He spoke without breaking his absent gaze.

"Ari, did that letter you found in Iraq, supposedly written in Esther's hand, settle the question of the *Exilarch* bloodline?"

"No, I can't say it did. It seemed to encourage the belief that Mordecai might have entered into a relationship in his old age. It's a promising piece, but it didn't settle the question. In some ways, it may have sharpened the mystery."

"Are there any other documents that could close the gap?"

"It's possible. The old Iraqi Jews believe there are hundreds of precious documents still hidden around the country. We just have to find them. Some of them, by the way, were not stolen at all, but were held for safekeeping by secret Jews. With every such family murdered by Islamic insurgents, we not only lose lives, but also another chance at locating those pieces of history and possibly the documentation we need."

"Could you find them in a hurry?"

"There's only one person who could help us find the additional Esther documents in Jewish hands. That's the old Rabbi of Baghdad. Assuming he survives until we find him."

"Yes, good," Jacob said, brushing his hands together. "Find him, and those documents. They may hold the only key to saving our people and resolving this crisis without going to war. Your Mossad supervisor is leaving for Baghdad in three hours, hand-carrying a full translation and interpretation of your hidden-Jews list. He's going to meet with American generals and help coordinate a multi-pronged rescue operation that'll deploy across Iraq for the next twenty-four hours. I want you to keep your job. You go with him, and I want you to find your rabbi. While there's still time."

AL HILLAH, IRAQ—DAWN

The al-Feliz family's four-year-old daughter was even more beautiful than their eldest, the recently murdered Ariana. Her eyes seemed to radiate across the whole upper third of her face. Combined with a soft button-nose and an expressive mouth, they made her the perfect Jewish version of those wide-eyed pixie urchins painted by street artists the world over.

But right now the fairylike quality was dampened by a flood of tears, two-day-old dirt, and harsh electric glare from a cheap television spotlight. She turned to her mother, sitting beside her, and held on tightly to her arm.

After her mother, her favorite person in the world had been Ariana. The vibrant teenager's body had for hours lain crumpled in a crimson-splattered heap against the far corner of the room, just below the black wall hanging with the Arabic lettering stitched across it. The horror had stayed there until early the previous evening, when a surly group of terrorists had burst in, stuffed the body into a large sack, and stormed out of the room.

Little Hana did not look over there. Not then and not now. The very thought of that direction and the blood still staining the floor had been so horrendous that her emotions simply shut down and a terrible numbness had taken over. Her beautiful eyes were glazed with horror.

She stared at the little shiny glass disc in front of the scowling bad man, squinting against the bright light over his shoulders. That's what her mother was looking at, very hard.

"Please, I only ask for some hope for my remaining child," her mommy said in a strange voice Hana had only heard once before, right before the bad men had made Ariana scream. "I have one more—my two-year-old daughter." Her mother checked a sob and hurried on. "You know now how determined these warriors are. Please listen to what they ask. I beg you. Is it so outrageous? Is it impossible to heed? Is . . . is this money worth more than the lives of my little one? Please think about that when you tuck your own children into bed this night." She glanced down at a paper hidden in a trembling hand and said in a rush, "Please abandon these selfish claims against the people of Iraq and let us live in peace."

Al-Jazeera TV had never live-cast one of these appeals before. Until the previous day's broadcast of the teen Jewish girl's public murder, they had always insisted on the proper observances—the discreetly delivered videotape in the crisp manila envelope just inside the outer entrance to their unofficial Baghdad offices. The protocol fooled no one within a thousand miles, but it provided wonderful cover to the Western world, where liberal journalists defended Al-Jazeera's journalistic objectivity.

But the ground rules had changed. Call it a kidnapping, an unfriendly invitation, whatever—the trembling, sweat-covered man had appeared in their improvised newsroom and pulled a thick Glock pistol from his belt. He pointed the barrel straight at the temple of the first face he recognized—that of Mohammed Obeejan, the network's famous Baghdad correspondent.

"Move," the intruder had growled in Arabic, his voice cracking with his own terror as he waved his gun toward the door.

And that's how the Al-Jazeera team had found themselves first broadcasting the previous day's murder and now the hostage mother's torment through a set of wires to an unobtrusive white dish mounted on the windowsill. It was a cunning disguise, for the apartment building, like so many in the Arabic world, was studded with dozens of identical-looking satellite receivers. Even the poorest Iraqis loved their newfound freedom, with its hundred channels of television.

Only this was an uplink—broadcasting instead of receiving. Yet despite its concealment, the ruse still practically invited detection from the Americans' formidable signal-intelligence service, the NSA. The nervous man behind the camera wondered how long it would take a Predator drone to center them in its sights. Then he wondered if the recklessness was truly a result of stupidity, or some plan to deliberately incite a bloodbath.

Regardless of the insurgents' motives, he silently gave himself a nearly fifty-fifty chance of surviving the day. Then he began to pray.

BATTAWEEN QUARTER, BAGHDAD

The end overtook the old synagogue in one great rush—a rhythmic roar, a blur of rotors chopping apart the sun, bystanders running off screaming. Then came ropes, six of them, their uncoiled portions tossed from a great height to strike the plaza's cobblestones with a startling clatter. Finally came the men themselves from the hovering chaos overhead, zipping down the lengths of cord as swiftly as dropped stones. Their faces and uniforms were so black they seemed to be pools of absent light, fast-moving voids against the glare.

The old man saw all this happen through the last, smeared pane of intact glass on the first floor of the Battaween Synagogue, Baghdad's oldest and only remaining Jewish house of worship. Not knowing what lay ahead, he grasped his prayer shawl about his shoulders, straightened his yarmulke and began to pray, chanting and bobbing forward and back.

He knew the soldiers were coming for him.

Lithe bodies vaulted to the rim of the concrete wall erected just ten years before around the actual temple. The first man up produced a hand tool that made quick work of the concertina wire strewn there. The old man clasped trembling hands to his mouth, for those bright metal coils had defined his life for so long he did not know how to look at the wall without them. Less than two minutes later, three of the commandos had jumped gracefully to the inside.

A dark-featured face filled the space of his window.

"Rabbi Mehl, we're here for you," he said in perfect Hebrew. "I am here with the United States Army. On behalf of the State of Israel, I am here to escort you out and offer you Return. Will you please open the door?"

He stood without moving, half wishing his stillness would drive the intruders away. In one sense he hated his solitude, despised what it meant about the fate of his people. It had been years since the synagogue's last regularly scheduled service. The once-thriving religious life of the quarter had now dwindled to one or two conversations per week with elderly, frightened people who sneaked in for a few minutes of conversation, affirmation in their faith, and grim commiseration about *the state of things in general*—then sneaked out the back through a variety of hidden exits. All public Seder services and high holiday observances had been canceled because of the all-encompassing "security concerns," and he had long since assured the most faithful that G-d knew of their devotion and did not expect them to brave car bombings to worship Him.

And yet, despite the incredible sadness and nostalgia that permeated his solitude, he had lately come to appreciate the utter privacy of it. He had become one with his prison, at home with its intimate spaces. Perversely, the old man wished the soldiers gone.

And then again, there was that word *Return*, those syllables that detonated volcanic emotions inside him. The Right of Return was one of the things which set Israel apart from all other nations, which confirmed how remarkable in human history the Covenant truly was.

It meant, essentially, that any person of Hebrew blood could claim Israeli citizenship upon their return from wherever in the world the Diaspora—the exile sparked upon the destruction of Jerusalem millennia before—had flung them.

He cracked the door open, and with the shock of actual sunlight came a hand, then two, forcing the crack farther apart. The door flew wide and another man in civilian clothes stepped through.

It was the end, finally delivered to his doorstep.

Chapter Twenty-seven

The man faced him a moment, his eyes warm and shining, and extended his hand.

"Rebbe, my name is Ari Meyer, from—well, from the government of Israel. I regret the intrusion."

"I regret it, too," said the rabbi.

"Sir," the man continued without apology, "there's another farhod under way. You're likely old enough to remember 'forty-one? I'm sorry to be so blunt, but you'll be killed. We're gathering as many of your people as we can and taking them to safety. Will you please come with us? There is no other choice. As I'm sure you know, the Jews of Baghdad, both open and concealed, are being targeted. I imagine you're aware of the hostage situation with the al-Feliz family."

"Aware of it? Mr. Meyer, only three weeks ago I traveled to Al Hillah to conduct Ariana al-Feliz's secret Bas Mitzvah. I have known her since the night she was born. And her family for most of my life."

"I'm very sorry, sir. My colleagues and I are fully aware that your synagogue has been the discreet hub for what remains of Iraqi Jewry. Not to mention that you are the person at the core of it all."

"Then your apology is accepted. But don't assume again that just because we're isolated and endangered, we're not a community and very aware of each other's concerns."

"Agreed. But, Rabbi, there is not much time. I must ask you. Are you ready to make your Return?"

"No, I am not. If I had been inclined to turn tail for Israel, I would have done so decades ago."

"I understand, Rabbi. But the final hour has arrived. There's no more time, no refuge left. This is it."

"Then I would rather stay here and die with my people."

Ari nodded understandingly and glanced briefly out the door, where sunshine blazed in the courtyard.

"But, Rabbi, what if you could save them?" he asked, looking directly at the rabbi. "What if you could help me find those who remain, those others who are in peril?"

"Do not patronize me, young man. The survival of my people— it is all I live for. What is your name again?"

"Actually, Meyer is only an operational surname. My true last name is al-Khalid."

"You mean . . . of the Iraq, Baghdad, al-Khalids?"

Ari nodded solemnly.

"I always wondered what happened to your family," said the rabbi slowly.

"Yes. I was hoping you could shed some light on that for me."

"My son, so many have disappeared into thin air over the last thirty years. I am afraid your family was among them, although they were certainly one of the most powerful and well known. You are the son of Anek?"

"Yes, Rebbe. And I aspire to something else. Something I hope you can support."

The rabbi waved dismissively. "I'm afraid I no longer have any authority or approval to confer on anyone."

"You are the living heart of Iraqi Jewry. And I, G-d willing, would be its new Exilarch."

The old man stared at him through the shadows, his face slack with amazement.

"Do you carry the bloodline?"

"Yes."

"Can you prove it?"

"Not quite. The final evidence I was hoping you could help me find. This is one of my objectives. I am also here to protect the remnant and find out what happened to my own."

The rabbi sighed forcefully, then gave the younger man a fierce look.

"Then I suppose we'd better get on with it."

Ari held out his hand, and they stepped through the door, free of the Battaween Synagogue, into the harsh glare of noonday.

It all made Rabbi Mehl want to weep, for in many ways, this was the final gasp of a population that had lived in these streets and alleys for over twenty-five hundred years. He himself had witnessed only its most eventful final half century. He had survived the pogroms of the forties and fifties. Stayed behind after the heady days of the Ezra and Nehemiah Airlifts. Outlasted the long madness of Hussein's regime, with its alternating periods of tolerance, murderous brutality, and eventual indifference. He had seen the wall go up around the synagogue's perimeter. And then the wire on top of that.

And now, to see it all come to an end with his being escorted away without time for even a backward glance. He was striding across the small plaza as he had not done in years, being rushed through a cordon of soldiers, who shouldered their rifles out toward the surrounding buildings, sighting on the cowering citizens who had themselves made him cower for so very long. For the smallest glint of a second, he felt the bittersweet comeuppance of it all rise like a bitter surge of bile.

And then he was inside the infernal machine, the army helicopter, with a great door slamming and men shouting gruffly and a sudden lifting sensation pressed against his limbs. He looked out the glass and saw the building, whose preservation had consumed his entire life, tilt and shrink into the puzzle grid of greater Baghdad.

"How much fuel does this awful thing carry?" he asked Ari over the roar of the propellers. "There may not be much time, but if you have maps, I can help you find some documents and save some of our brothers and sisters—at one time. . . ."

Chapter Twenty-eight

Abadi, *the youngest son,* saw it first, coming fast and low across the valley below him.

Kicking his soccer ball out on the mountain farm's only flat patch of ground, he stiffened, distractedly letting the ball strike his shin and bounce away down the slope. This sort of mistake on most days meant an hour-long descent to correct—but Abadi wasn't concerned. He'd always found the ball before. After all, he was the only boy this side of Maydan Saray, and who else would risk life and limb astride a thousand-foot clifftop for an inflated piece of leather?

At that moment, the eight-year-old didn't care about the ball, anyway. He was too preoccupied with the object flying toward him along the twenty-five-mile-long Zagros Mountain valley. The high cleft in the range separating eastern Iraq from Iran was his home— where his family eked out a meager living, yet experienced a relatively safe existence, as high-altitude sheep farmers.

It was late afternoon, Abadi's favorite time to get outside and escape Momma's constant vigilance. At that hour in early fall, their home site's merciless winds usually subsided to a cool kiss upon the forehead, while the dwindling sun filled their valley with infinite hues of burnt orange and turquoise and a thousand gradations of alpine detail.

Abadi knew the panorama well enough to realize that the growing speck with the flat glide path was no eagle. He could also tell it was not native to his part of the world.

Despite ever-present drop-offs and assorted mountain perils, living here was far less frightening than his old neighborhood far away in Baghdad. Back then, every single vehicle driving down their tiny street, every car horn's echo, was grounds for an anxious pause or a sweeping glance out the window. He had grown up in fear of the sniper and the car bomb, learning from his youngest years to slam windows shut and stay indoors.

Living out here in the country wasn't perfect. There was still need for some vigilance; over in the next valley, local Kurds had once exchanged small-arms fire with Hussein's Republican Guard, back before the coming of the Americans. Today, the Sunni insurgency still persisted, and they had few friends down in the closest town of Maydan Saray. And now, since the overthrow of Saddam, there were the sonic booms, the high bomber contrails and the Predator drones cruising past on their way to Iran.

But that was nothing. At least that's what Poppa always said. *That is the price of freedom.* In Baghdad, Abadi never once played outside the front door. It had never even occurred to him.

So now he called out, in the best alarm voice his older brother had taught him. A wordless cry, simply meant to echo as loudly and as far as possible.

Owwwweeeeeeeeeeeweeee!

He had never let one go that loud and bold before—he hoped he didn't get spanked. But the black shape was growing larger, more quickly than he'd ever seen. Even in his nightmares.

Suddenly an arm encircled his waist and yanked him back into the house. It was Momma, of course, but suddenly Poppa's face and shoulders filled the doorway, and his older brother, Jalaal's, behind him. They were panting heavily. The two couldn't have heard his warning and arrived here so quickly from the upper pastures, the boy calculated. They must have seen the thing for themselves and run like an ibex.

"What is it?" Abadi shouted.

Poppa ignored him, barking the old orders to huddle in the corners and stay quiet. His father hopped in the air and in one quick swipe, grabbed their old rifle from over the kitchen cabinet. Cracking the gun open to check its ammo, he snapped it shut and took up his position beside the doorframe, holding just the tip of the barrel out into open air.

The chopping sound grew ever closer, deafening now. Its vibration became more of a throb in their bodies than a sound in their ears. Atop the room's small kitchen table, plates and glasses began to rattle and shake.

Abadi turned back to his family. Momma was crying again, by herself in a corner. Poppa had once told him that when she was a little girl, his mother had seen her own momma and poppa shot dead in front of her eyes, and that as a result she did not have the inner hardness to keep quiet. Abadi had no such handicap. He tightened his lips and willed himself not to cry as a huge shadow descended over the house. A roaring wind hurled dirt and bits of grass through the doorway, threatening to blow Poppa back into the far wall.

Poppa winced, frowned, and turned to Momma with a question twisting his face, an overly puzzled look oddly akin to the one he parodied every year on the night of *Pesach Seder*, when Abadi asked him the *Mah Nishtanah*, the first of the Four Questions: "Why is this night different from all other nights?"

He shouted at her, over the noise of the rotors, "They're American!"

Now Abadi could no longer contain his curiosity. He edged his toe into the mortar crack below the front windowsill and, as he always did for a view, scrambled up on the edge. And there it was—now so close that it obscured the mountains behind it. A military helicopter complete with bristling gun barrels, mist curling under its rotor wash, and a pilot's smoked-glass bubble reflecting their house at an odd, cockeyed angle.

It was landing right in front of them.

Then Abadi saw brand-new things, quite different from the Arabic markings and symbols he'd always seen on military equipment.

He saw, painted along the nose, a flag with red and white stripes and a blue corner scattered with stars.

Then motion caught his eye from the helicopter's flank; a door flew open and a tall man in long green coveralls was running toward them with his head bent, holding the arm of a stooped man in a long black coat whose gray beard flapped sideways in the wind.

Abadi and his brother recognized the second, older man at once.

He looked over at the front door—the rifle was leaning against the wall, and Poppa was already out the door, running toward the old man with his arms open.

Behind the approaching pair, an American commando in full combat gear, brandishing an automatic rifle nearly as long as he was, hopped down and, without even pausing for a look around, sprinted out to the edge of the slope. Another, then another, and a third followed him. All four threw themselves on the ground in succession, propped their weapons from their elbows and began lensing the surrounding mountainside and valley below with wide sweeps of their targeting scopes.

His father paid no attention to them. He was throwing a strong embrace around the Rabbi of Baghdad, the same beloved septuagenarian who, three years before, had driven to their apartment home in the middle of the afternoon with a truck and a driver to move them out to safety. To take them here, out of harm's way.

That long, long horrible day had begun with a massive explosion knocking out their windows and jarring them from their dawn slumber—*a car bomb, right there on their street, not three doors from their own!* Then had come a day-long procession of police and ambulances and morgue trucks and well-wishers and idle bystanders gawking at the bloodstains running down the cracks in the street.

The morning had turned into an unbearable afternoon until the rabbi, the very same man now in front of their house—the last rebbe in the country, if rumor was true—entered their apartment all out of breath and full of warnings about further violence and emergency plans.

They had not seen him since late that afternoon, so long ago, when he had walked away from their loaded truck, waving three fingers of his right hand as sole acknowledgment of their shouted *thank-you's.* As though saving whole families from murder was a feat akin to retrieving a lost puppy.

And now here he was, having emerged from an American helicopter like some geriatric paratrooper. The strangeness of it certainly didn't trouble Poppa, who still held the old man locked in a fervent hug.

Finally, the rotors began to slow, and the inferno of noise abated. The two men backed apart. Rabbi Mehl pointed to the man next to him.

"Ebrahim, this is Ari. He is a special emissary from our brothers and sisters in Israel. On a very important mission. My friend, I fear another crisis has overtaken us."

"And after all this time. . . ."

"It seems there is another killing campaign under way. Another farhod."

"Yes. We heard about the al-Feliz girl over the satellite. It is a horrible escalation, is it not?"

"It is indeed. And now you must move. Fast. We have reason to believe they aim to kill or kidnap every remaining Jew in the country."

Abadi's father breathed in deeply and slowly so that his chest seemed to hold the air eternally before exhaling again. He took a long look at the mountain landscape before him, as though already bidding it farewell. This had been a difficult, forbidding spot to take his family, but it had proven a successful refuge as well. It had kept them alive. The shine in his eyes betrayed a sudden realization that he had come to love the place more than he had known.

The rabbi put a hand on his shoulder. "Some of the records stolen from our hiding cache several years ago have surfaced in the wrong hands. They know who you are, where you are, where you live. It is only a matter of divine intervention that you have not been attacked already. I am sorry to be so abrupt, as I was with you so many years ago. But we have to move quickly."

"I understand, Rebbe. And I am very grateful. I will gather my family now."

"We'll need to hurry," Ari spoke up, "because it's entirely possible you're being watched right now. And if so, our arrival in this big helicopter would likely trigger an attack."

"Oh, and another thing, Ebrahim," said the rabbi. "Do you remember the three cases of old records I sent with you? We'd like to take a look at them right away. First. Even before we leave."

Ebrahim nodded to his right, toward a flimsy barbed wire fence strung thirty yards away to keep precocious young mountain climbers from straying too close.

"I buried it over here," he said and walked over toward the enclosure.

Just then, the soldier in the middle held up an arm and barked something. The two men flanking him adjusted their sights—

—a flat, sharp sound drifted up to them on the wind—

—and just as he reached the fence line, Abadi's father jerked backward so sharply it seemed he'd been slammed by an invisible battering ram. A fine red spray filled the air beyond him and he fell to the ground with a moan.

◆ ◆ ◆ ◆ ◆ ◆ ◆ ◆ ◆ ◆ ◆ ◆ ◆ ◆

Chapter Twenty-nine

A badi's mother screamed.

The boy yelled for his father as loud as his lungs would allow him. He started to run for him, but his older brother leaped on top of the boy and drove him to the ground. "Abadi! They'll kill you!" he shouted into the younger boy's ear. "Let the soldiers!"

The Americans rose to a kneeling position, shouldered their weapons, and all at once their rifle barrels filled the valley with the roar of gunfire, glints of ejected cartridges, and ribbons of bitter white smoke.

Abadi heard a metallic popping sound, saw the rotors start to move, and realized that the helicopter had also been struck on its side.

Then came a thump and a *whoosh!* as a rocket-propelled grenade shot away from one of the commando's shoulders, trailing a thin line of smoke. Across the valley, where a smaller peak met the flatness of his father's grazing pasture, a tongue of fire and smoke shot upward. A moment later, the sound of an explosion popped in his ears.

Taking advantage of the rocket's diversion, two of the commandos rushed over to Abadi's father, picked him up, and began to carry his prone form toward the chopper. All around them, incoming bullets lofted tufts of grass and dirt.

The rotors were rapidly picking up speed. The American officer stood and pulled Abadi to his feet.

"We have to go! Now!" the officer shouted to Ari and Rabbi Mehl.

Ari turned and shook his head.

"I'm not going without those documents!"

"What about you, Rabbi?"

Unable to shout over the noise of the now-spinning rotors, the older man merely grasped his friend's shoulders, as if to say, *I'm staying, too. But thank you. . . .*

The American looked over at Ari and shook his head in dismay. "Just how much do you folks want these papers, anyway?"

"They're as important a part of this extraction as the family! Maybe more. . . !" Ari shouted over his shoulder as he ran a jagged line toward the place where Abadi's father had fallen. With the intensity of a man under fire, he began to scoop up large handfuls of dirt, glancing back with a scowl.

And that's when Abadi felt a mad idea burst into his head, and he did something more rash, and more manly, than anything he had ever done before.

He fixed the Israeli with a stare, willed his legs into action, and began to sprint across the open ground toward the bent form. Above the drumming of his own heart and the pants of his breathing, he heard the whistle of incoming bullets, and in that instant knew they were coming for him. Hundreds of yards away, grown men were holding his silhouette in their sights and trying to shoot him just for crossing his front yard. The brief thought made him clench his teeth, seethe with rage, and run more fluidly and swiftly than he ever had in his life. He heard, even felt, the rounds striking the earth—once, just off his right foot, so he swerved this way and that, and when another impact just missed his left ankle, he feinted, changed course, imagining himself Maradona, dribbling the soccer ball through the German defense in the closing seconds of the World Cup, with the roar around him merely chants from his fans instead of automatic gunfire.

And before he knew it, he was upon Meyer's position.

He practically threw himself upon the older man. Then he heard commotion behind and turned to see his older brother Jalaal weaving a jagged course along the same route he had just taken. Trying to catch his breath, Abadi winced at first to see his brother diminishing what he had done, stealing away his solo glory. Then he realized that for the first time in his memory, he had seen his brother imitate *him*. Abadi had set the standard. He swelled with pride and turned back to the task at hand. At once all three were tearing so furiously into the soil that it became impossible to distinguish one digger's hands from the other.

Abadi forced himself to concentrate on the task and ignore everything else taking place around him—the chopper, now at lift-off rotation, flinging a stiff wind across everything in its path, the roar of large-caliber bullets bursting from the soldiers' machine guns, the whining ricochets of incoming fire, his mother's screams. Most of all, the thought of his strong, capable father being carried away bloodied, as helpless as a child.

He told himself *I don't hear any of it*, and made himself concentrate on clawing out as much as possible with each pull of his arms. But then a bullet whizzed past his ear so close that he could almost hear the projectile's rotation, like an insanely rapid twirling sound. Another bullet struck dirt and sent clods into both of his eyes. Jalaal's shirt sleeve seemed to jerk forward of its own accord, and Abadi realized his brother's arm had been nicked. Somehow, the snipers had them sighted in.

Meyer reached up and yanked the boys as hard as he could down into the small depression they had just dug. He turned back toward the American squad leader and shouted.

"We need air support! They've zeroed us in!"

The American officer nodded emphatically and turned back to the helicopter.

"*FAC! FAC!*" he yelled into the cabin over the noise of the rotors, summoning someone out with frantic waves of his hand. An instant later two more soldiers wearing black berets and loaded with thick backpacks leaped from the chopper and ran over to the spot where the others had been sighting the enemy positions. One now swiftly removed a laptop computer from the bag and laid it next to his right elbow as he aimed the binocular straight at their enemies. The other removed a set of thin headphones from his backpack and threaded them around his head.

Back at their location, Abadi felt a sharp pain across his right shoulder and realized that he was bleeding. He had no idea how it had happened—a devastating weight of helplessness and terror engulfed him.

"Ari, are they going to kill us?" he asked, his eyes welling with tears. "Am I going to die?"

Ari pointed to the two men in black berets.

"Abadi, you see those men?"

Abadi nodded fiercely through his tears.

"Those are what they call 'Forward Air Controllers,' son. Air Force enlisted men, part of a special group nicknamed 'Death on Call.' And a few seconds from now, they're going to make those men pay."

"Tell me." Abadi's order, awash in a childlike hopefulness, was nearly irresistible.

"Well, first of all, that's no regular set of binoculars the first guy's holding. It's a laser-guided range finder. And right now, it's using a laser beam to fix the exact geographic coordinates of those shooting at us, then feeding that data into the laptop, which has a GPS unit installed in it along with a software program that has mapped out an exact picture of the whole combat area around us. And then"—Ari looked around to see if any of the army men were close enough to hear his rather imprudent disclosure—"they beam these coordinates through a powerful radio on the second guy's back, up to a couple of fighter planes flying what we call 'tactical air support' in the skies not far from us."

"And they're going to get the men who shot my father? Who are trying to kill me?"

Ari smiled, noted the tears shining in the boy's eyes, and gripped him by the shoulder. "Let's finish digging. You'll see."

Despite the seeming casualness of his descriptions, Ari Meyer was being modest. As a member of the Israeli defense and a former officer in its Air Force, he knew a great deal about the operation of the F–16 Falcon.

As such, it would not have surprised him to know that only two miles behind them, a pair of Air National Guard F–16s was racing toward them on full afterburner, at an inbound, final approach altitude of twenty thousand feet. Or that at that moment, the lead pilot had in fact just received a signal bounced to him from the two air controllers via a "gateway" computer programmed to resolve incompatibilities between his network and that of the active duty Air Force—little more than a laptop mounted in the galley of an American AWACS plane circling discretely in the distance.

The signal's arrival had caused a small red triangle to appear on the jet's HUD, its "heads-up display," a holographic recreation of the craft's control data projected against the inside of its cockpit's glass bubble.

The pilot reached out and "selected" the triangle with the tip of his finger from the center of his Situational Awareness Data Link. Instantly the GPS coordinates uploaded into the innards of the F–16's internal computer, as well as the guidance kit of a five-hundred-pound bomb slung under its wing. This brand-new state-of-the-art ordnance, pride of Air Force tech squads, had cut the weight of previous bombs by three-quarters, thereby allowing the jets to carry more munitions, save on fuel, and reduce collateral damage.

The target area doomed to encounter this menace was flowing swiftly into sight. A long, straight mountain valley, anchored by a large mountaintop fringed in smoke.

"Tiger One FAC, can you confirm target package?" the pilot mumbled.

"This is Tiger One" came the muffled reply. "Viper Driver, you are cleared hot for target package Alpha-six. Repeat, *cleared hot*."

Nearly invisibly in his helmet, the pilot nodded. His target was certified. No friendlies would be in the line of fire.

"Roger, Tiger One. Stand by. . . ."

Chapter Thirty

A ri Meyer glanced at his watch, then back up. . . .

Just in time for Abadi to hear a roar rip the sky apart and spot the elegant nose of the sleek lead fighter pierce the air above him with its wingman nestled close behind and to its left.

Right above the house, the warplanes left their course and dove southward with a precision so deft and beautiful that it formed a knot of awe in Abadi's chest.

"Now watch, son!" Ari shouted.

Normally, an F–16 would have delivered its bombs from a high-altitude, level angle. But because of the steep mountain profile of its target, the lead pilot was in for a thrill. At precisely fifteen thousand feet, he reached his intended diving delivery angle of thirty degrees. At that exact second, his thumb pressed down on the "pickle button" of his stick, detonating two shotgun-shell-sized cartridges that propelled the bomb well clear of the wing for a safe separation.

Watching from his front yard, Abadi had barely enough time to focus his eyes on the small dark shape falling from the diving aircraft.

Nor could he see the flurry of invisible electronic signals that knitted the skies between the bomb and GPS satellites above them in outer space.

As the planes raced away from him, two overwhelming noises engulfed Abadi: the thunder of two military-size turbines on full afterburner, their flames quivering orange just before him, and then, only seconds later—the fighters already dots in the eastern sky—twin detonations so savage and merciless that he would never forget the sensation.

He felt them like a double-punch to his solar plexus, a sonic frying pan striking him in the ears and twin tsunamis of air pounding him across the torso.

It was the detonation shockwave of the five-hundred-pound laser-guided bomb striking its target, its FMU–113 nose-mounted fuse detonating at exactly fifteen feet above the ground to shoot its force outward and pulverize everything within a three-thousand-foot radius. Effectively vaporizing his father's sheep pasture—approximately twenty-one acres of alpine Middle Eastern grazing meadow—into airborne particles of dusty mushroom cloud.

The clouds drifted off with an almost insolent nonchalance, the F–16 engines throbbed away into the distant horizon, and the guns fell silent.

And that is when it occurred to Abadi that the coward who had confidently stalked his father and brother and then ambushed the rescue, shooting his Poppa from a perch they had thought impregnable, and targeting an eight-year-old boy for death, had just become charred scraps strewn across a half mile of mountainside.

Despite his relief, the thought of it also made him want to vomit.

Instead he looked over, saw that his brother and the Israeli officer had resumed their digging, and threw himself into the fray with them. One minute later they struck canvas. In one swift move the officer had pulled out a thick, flat wrapping stained with mildew and dirt. With hardly an acknowledgment, he scrambled to his feet, grabbed the two boys by the wrists, and shouted, "It's time to go! Into the chopper!"

JERUSALEM, IDF COMMAND
CENTER, MINISTRY OF DEFENSE

Four hours and twenty-eight minutes after American bombs fell
above Maydan Saray, a fax machine began to hum in the half-light of
a military command center eight hundred miles away in Jerusalem.

Its heading read, "*Spot Translation of Rescued Battaween Documents—Arabic to English*. For Classified Raven 5–290 use only."

Over a dozen officers from across the spectrum of Israel's intelligence and military establishment stood waiting in the shadows to
receive, assess, and respond to the information contained in the fresh
translation.

But the first fingers on the first sheet, yanking it away to read
before anyone else could, belonged to the nation's First Lady, Hadassah Kesselman.

She sat next to the machine—better to establish her territorial
claim over all subsequent pages that would emerge—and began to
read as if her life, and the life of everyone in that room, depended on
the content of its words.

Chapter Thirty-one

THE ROYAL BEDCHAMBER, SUSA—
TEN YEARS INTO THE REIGN OF XERXES

That night with Xerxes, the nightmare started as it always does.
With darkness broken by veils of shadow, by gently waving ribbons
of alternating gray and black . . .

. . . and my awareness, through the fog of sleep, that something,
someone, is approaching.

It might only be a faint change in the temperature, betraying an
opened door or a window's shutter now left ajar. It might be the
slightest flex in the floor beneath me. Or some foreign shape inching
past the light somehow at variance with the pattern drifting across
my face. Or the sound of a muffled step approaching *oh-so* carefully
across the floor.

But it always ends the same way. My eyes fly open to glints of
moonlight framing the upraised curve of a scimitar. My ears fill with
chilling sounds of murder, my nostrils with the odor of freshly spilled
blood. My world ends with the plunge of that blade down across my
mother's neck to sever flesh with that awful sound I have never been
able to forget. The face I have loved more than any other, falling from
its shoulders and striking the floor not five inches from my own. To
see her loving eyes frozen open, staring at me but not seeing me. The

mouth that kissed me good night gushing forth blood down her cheek and across the floor to within an inch of my own trembling lips . . .

And then I usually awake, unable to bear again what I actually *did* endure all those years ago.

Very few people know how horribly this memory has plagued my nights ever since childhood. Ever since it took place. The night of my seventh birthday, when I awoke in the midst of my entire family being slaughtered by a gang of Agagite marauders. I survived only because there had been no bed for me, there at my uncle's house, so I was sleeping on a pallet on the floor.

On this night, though—the actual evening of which I write, my warning did not consist of the usual cues. *It came as sound.*

It was a barely audible scraping accompanied by rapid breathing under desperate control. Some aspect of it—its timbre, its strength— told me at once that it was that of a man. Or maybe several. All of a sudden my mind, my entire body, clenched with a sense of impending danger, a throbbing sense of alarm.

Then came a disorienting uncertainty. Was this the old nightmare returning, or something real intruding through the clouds of my slumber? Or a third possibility—was this a routine confusion I encountered every single night and promptly forgot every time? Did my nightmare always arrive after a period of wondering if some real-life murderer actually *was* sneaking toward my bed?

You see, I knew one thing for certain—I wasn't awake. I lay suspended somewhere between true sleep and consciousness, but I was not a fully wakeful person at that moment. And yet something was objectively not right. Even within the routine of my perennial nightmare, this seemed jarringly out of the ordinary.

I sensed motion, lightning fast and graceful. And movement just next to me, yet nearly silent. Not enough provocation to truly awaken me. Was Xerxes having his own restless dream?

Until . . . a *groan.* A man's voice, not in the throes of a nightmare. It was a groan of mortal agony forced into some form of restraint.

Thank G-d I did not allow my eyes to fly open as swiftly and emphatically as my mind did. Yet in the tiniest instant I was truly alert, aware only of my heart hammering away in my chest. I parted my eyelids, but only by the slightest margin.

And, Leah, I cannot—nor do I wish to try—describe to you the full weight of terror that crushed down upon my entire body, soul, and mind at that moment.

For it hung there—quivering in the gloom of a real night. A long, polished sword, poised barely a cubit above me.

As on that earlier night, my shock and fear kept me silent far more than my actual poise. My limbs were paralyzed. The air within me seemed frozen still. I could not have moved even the tiniest bit if flight had been my only hope.

But now confusion, mixed with an implacable dread, descended upon me. Every sensory cue I had told me that I was now awake, in the real, present world. Yet how could I be once again in the center of a midnight murder? How could I awaken twice in one lifetime to the reflection of moonlight on sharpened steel? This was not a coincidence, or a fate, I could bear to live through again. One such night was enough.

I parted my eyelids again and rolled my shoulders slightly, feigning sleep-induced motion. Now I could glimpse a ways beyond my immediate surroundings. And not ten cubits beyond, I saw my Xerxes in all his bulging nakedness, struggling with every muscle he had against the grip of two men with giant arms holding him from behind. A cloth covered his mouth, pulled as tightly as seemed possible.

Another man stood before him, holding a sword in that two-fisted, downward-facing hold of an executioner about to make his thrust.

And then I gained my true bearings about the situation. I had been asleep next to Xerxes in the royal retiring chamber, for I often spent the night with him in those days, and plotters had chosen this of all nights on which to strike. Something inside me shattered into pieces. My husband was going to be killed, and any attempt to help him would mean we would both be dead within moments of each other. My only hope for survival lay in continuing to feign sleep and give his killers no reason to fear me. If I even twitched, the sword quivering above me would surely plunge down and eliminate my witness along with my husband's.

I did the only thing I knew: I shut my eyelids again and concentrated on imitating the languid rhythm of deep sleep. But from Xerxes I now heard an emphatic *thump!* and a long exhale, and I realized my husband was dead. Only the terror of my closest brush with death was keeping my throat closed against the cry of a heart rent in two. The killer watching me had to make his final, crucial determination of whether or not to let me survive. I poured every ounce of my will into continuing the breaths without interruption, pause, or acceleration.

A moment passed—the most terrible and endless of my life. I was not sure I could bear another instant without succumbing to the ice bath of terror and heartbreaking sorrow pumping throughout my body. Yet I knew: the tiniest mistake, the slightest miscalculation, and the next thing I felt would be a blade cleaving my own chest.

The moment passed. I heard a whispered cry and footsteps in the foreground, felt the air move about me, and heard more running, closer. I parted my eyelids again and saw only the distant, ornate ceiling.

The massive doors shut with a slapping sound.

The murderers were gone.

I practically fell off the bed to crawl over toward Xerxes' prone shape. I cradled his body, bent down toward him, and felt the whole vastness of emotion I had trapped within me now escape in one violent, inner heave—then a shrill scream flung up in the air. I know it was imprudent to raise such a cry, for I did not know how far evil had fled. But now it was not a matter of choice.

There was never even a moment of conceding his death—I had felt it was coming, almost as a matter of fact, since catching sight of that sharpened sword. But now his terrible death felt like a vast, threatening fact into which I plunged whole. Inside my chest, I felt again the sensation of something coming apart.

Still lying upon the cold marble, I bent backward and gave my screaming full vent. As though I were trying to fill the cavernous room with my grief. I emptied my lungs, gulped for air, and started again. And again. I'm not sure the sounds that poured from my throat sounded sane, or even human. But I could not have stopped them to save my life.

Leah, you know as much as anyone how much I loved the King. Anyone else would be forgiven for suspecting that I loved being Queen more than I loved Xerxes himself.

But the truth turns out, as it so often does, to be far more complex and interesting than shallow conjecture. Xerxes and I had carved a special affection out of an insane and impossible existence. He loved me because I gave myself to him like no other woman he had ever known, or even imagined. And I loved him because he had opened himself to me in ways no King ever had with anyone, ways that made me feel incredibly close and needed.

He was a deeply flawed man, to an extent I am only now learning. I'm entirely unsure whether history will record him kindly. And I offer no defense for the many errant deeds attributed to him. But even though this sounds like the rationale of a foolish teenager, I have to insist that when he was with me, Xerxes was a different person. Often when we were together, nearby courtiers would turn around and stare, not sure if the man laughing so heartily and speaking in such a relaxed voice was the King they knew. They had simply never heard him laugh that freely, or speak with such a tone.

He was such a virile personality that I felt his presence like a stamp on nearly every memory of my adult life. And that is why the life drained from my veins when I realized he was gone from my world. I had never contemplated a future without him.

Finally, the strain of my screams drained the final measure of strength from me, and the world around me simply blinked away.

Chapter Thirty-two

I am unsure how long I lay like that. All I remember is snapping back upright at the sound of the doors being punched open and dozens of feet running in. Deep growling shouts rang out, even screams.

I looked up and saw that the five soldiers wore the gilded finery of the Immortals, the elite royal bodyguards. Their faces were wracked by anguish. And well they might, for rumor had it that if a king was murdered, the Immortals on the watch would be impaled within the hour.

I felt hands about my shoulders, bearing me up gently. And then I saw Mordecai's face, and never have I been more relieved and grateful to see anyone. Although, for some reason, the sight of his anxious expression seemed to trigger even greater emotion. Sobs wracked my body, and in between the same phrase, over and over, burst through my lips from my soul. *"He's gone, Poppa. They killed him. . . ."*

How helpless and hopeless I felt at that moment! I repeated those words countless times before Mordecai found a pause in which to ask me if I was hurt. I shook my head through my sobs, and I remember feeling at that point, for just a moment, that I wish the killers had taken me with him.

Mordecai helped me to my shaky feet. With gravity beneath me, I felt like an old woman shuffling along in a century-old body. I know I moved like one.

"I'll try to remember one of the attackers," I told him hoarsely. "I might recall the man who held the sword." And Mordecai, always on his "palace guard," hushed me quickly, causing me to recall that on a night like this, one never knows who the plotters were. The soldiers around me could have been the killers, only feigning grief and shock. Anyone within earshot could be a conspirator who might interpret the least wayward utterance as a pretext for more murder.

And it was true. I could almost smell the madness in the air. There was a feeling about that all was unhinged, that bloodlust, like that ominous hint of sulfur in the nostrils, could explode at any moment.

We heard more loud voices, shouts of alarm, from the hallway outside. My blood went cold, for I remembered that the assassination of a king was often the occasion for whole strings of secondary murders, like the cascading aftershocks of an earthquake.

Finally, my feet rediscovered their rhythm and we emerged through the doorway. Guards and servants were running as one down the corridor, away from us.

"Who is it?" Mordecai cried at the top of his voice.

A palace servant, running past, glanced at him and yelled over his shoulder, "It's Darius, sir! Darius!"

I remember stopping cold in the hall, surrounded by bleary-eyed, panicked palace staff, and feeling a new wave of vertigo overwhelm me, unaware whether the sensation came from events in the chamber behind me or the shock of what I had just heard.

Darius—of course. The crown prince, Xerxes' oldest and most beloved son, namesake of Darius the Great. He would be next.

No . . . I heard myself groaning over and over, and then holding on to Mordecai's hand, I too began to run and watch the hallway flow fitfully past me. In my haze of residual stupor and caustic grief, I could not remember the direction of Darius' quarters. I looked around me, fought a cresting surge of nausea, and then realized the imbecilic truth—the best source was there right beside me: Mordecai, faithful, unquestioning, supportive. And he knew exactly where to go.

Three turns, two more hallways, and one covered veranda later, we rounded the final corner and rushed upon a scene that left me even more faint and closer to retching.

Sprawled in the open doorway to his own personal quarters lay the body of a broad-shouldered young man whose wristbands, headband, and boots were trimmed in gold. I could not see his face, which lay pressed into a puddle of blood, but I knew at once it was Prince Darius, once the future King of Persia. Less than five cubits away lay three more bodies clad in the attire of the Palace Guard.

I remember the gray look on Mordecai's lined, hard-breathing face when he whirled around to look at me.

"What about Artaxerxes?" he asked in a voice I had never heard issued from his mouth before. I remember asking myself whether he had asked me a question or issued me a warning, for his tone was equal parts foreboding and outright fear.

Despite my haze, I realized instantly how correct he was. Artaxerxes was the next in line to the throne. He was also one member of the extended royal family whom I knew better than any other. In fact, few remember it now, but he was practically my adoptive son.

All at once my body remembered its old energy and speed. I leaped from the hallway, it seemed, with Mordecai in close pursuit, and we ran without hesitation to an apartment not far away. I began pounding on the door.

"Go away!" came a feeble shout from inside. It was that of Artaxerxes—tense and weak, but his.

I nearly fainted from relief at the mere sound of his voice, yet I persisted. "It's me! Esther! You must open this door!"

A moment later the door swung open and the two of us swept into the room. Artaxerxes was fully dressed, alone in the light of a single candle. He had started walking back to his bed but suddenly turned, slumped against the entry wall and slid down to the ground. He looked so small and defenseless that it was only then I remembered the prince was merely sixteen years old. A strong, tall lad, but hardly a man—yet. Much older for one of his station than most; indeed, many of his forefathers had taken the throne at much younger ages. And yet, he was so young, and he looked so lost.

We closed the doors and huddled around him like conspirators of some sort.

"He did it!" Artaxerxes mumbled. "He was the one!"

"Who?" I asked.

"Darius. He killed our father because he was impatient to become King. Everyone knows how contemptuous he is of our father's mistakes. And, of course, there's—well, you know. He believed that Father seduced Princess Artaynte. His own wife; it was a terrible thing to believe, of course. Thank the gods, Artabanus and the rest of the palace guards came in to tell me and warn me of Darius' plans to kill me next."

"*Artabanus* told you that?" asked Mordecai.

"Yes, and I will be eternally grateful," Artaxerxes replied.

"Do not be too hasty in that judgment. And what did you do on that information?"

"I bid Artabanus and his men to go stop Darius at once, detain him, and imprison him for trial."

Then Artaxerxes saw our faces, and his own expression changed in an instant.

"What? What did he do?" I remember how he took Mordecai by the shoulders and shook him. He allowed Poppa's whole upper body to sway in his hands, so loathe was Mordecai to tell him the truth. "What did he *do*?" Artaxerxes finally screamed.

"Darius is dead, and three palace guards beside him," he said in a low, grim voice. "And, Artaxerxes, tell no one else what you just told us. At least for now. Just remember this, however. You were tricked. I would daresay that Artabanus was your father's killer, not your brother. And in having enraged you within a fear of your life, he has arranged for you to look like the conspirator. Be very, very careful, Your Highness. Artabanus is your enemy. Never doubt it. He has made you the murderer of your brother, rather than the avenger of your father. You had better move fast against him."

Artaxerxes' face flattened into a mask of cold determination, and he stood to his full height.

"I will."

So much happened during the ensuing forty-eight hours. Things grew maddeningly chaotic indeed. And young Artaxerxes definitely took things in hand for one so young.

Unwilling to return to the site of my husband's murder, I spent the rest of the night in Mordecai's quarters, not sleeping but pacing and listening for the various palace sounds around me. Sometime around dawn, more profoundly exhausted than perhaps ever before in my life, I fell asleep curled up on the floor next to the . . .

Chapter Thirty-three

H*adassah ben Yuda's eyes* were still fixed on the last words of Hadassah's night of horror when the voice of an Israeli army general broke the silence.

"Forget it, everybody. I just reached the end. What we're looking for isn't there."

"How did you finish so quickly?" Hadassah demanded.

The tall, middle-aged officer smiled gamely. "Occupational hazard, ma'am. Years of military reports. Speed reading becomes a survival mechanism."

"And reading that quickly, you're sure of what you saw?"

He nodded. "There's fascinating stuff in there about Persian history and the lives of the principals—I'm sure scholars will have a field day. It's clearly weighted toward Hadassah's initial response to a plea from this Leah person. But nothing regarding a Mordecai bloodline or even an indication that he ever fathered a child."

"I find that hard to believe," she said slowly. "Granted, I haven't read as far as you have, but the previous documents had all this talk about Mordecai's love for someone, and Hadassah urging him to find a mate—"

"Sorry, ma'am. I read those, too, yet this new fragment doesn't come any closer to giving us the actual outcome. It may hold clues about where to find the next installment, as it were. But it's almost as if someone knew what we were looking for and decided to play games with us."

"Great," she sighed. "We're going to have to find more scrolls."

"Or think of a more conventional resolution to the crisis," the general noted, looking at her from under lowered brows.

Taking that as a personal rebuke, she glared at the general, gathered her papers, and strode out of the room, her exasperation clear to all.

PRIME MINISTER'S RESIDENCE—LATER THAT NIGHT

Hadassah bolted upright from her covers, her eyes wide and her heart pounding rhythmically in her chest. She glanced around wildly but saw only the room before her swimming in its usual midnight palette of shadow and gloom. Everything seemed normal. Her husband snored lightly on the far side of the bed. From opposing nightstands, their respective clock radios glowed 2:34 A.M. Light from Rehavia Street shone faintly through the shuttered window, then splintered into pale shards beyond the ceiling fan's spinning blades.

Nevertheless, something was wrong. As she examined her senses, she understood it was not an external threat—some frightening noise or shift in light. Whatever had woken her lay *inside* her. As soon as she realized this, she knew it was far worse than an external enemy. This distress lay poised to engulf her. She could feel that it was powerful and complex but was about to tell nothing else. She found this ignorance even more terrifying.

She breathed in and found that the very act of inhaling filled her with a claustrophobic terror. Not only could she not catch her breath, but she could not shake the sensation that there would be no satisfying her lungs.

She felt drained of all meaning, purpose, direction. Not as she had described to her husband at their surprise conference at his office, not in some abstract, intellectual sense, but in a loss more direct and gut-wrenching than anything she had ever experienced. As though hope and substance had been some sort of fluid, a liquid, and someone had drained it from her as cleanly and completely as the opening of a valve.

What is happening to me? The question whirled unchecked through her frantic mind. Was this a cruel mutation of the depression she had struggled against in the time since her father's death? A byproduct of her unspoken fear that she had unwittingly caused her husband's political demise? That her very identity was providing fodder for not only Jacob's downfall as Prime Minister but also the unraveling of a year's worth of intricate negotiations with the Palestinian leadership? Or was it the fact that she was now alone in the world, that her once-rich collection of relatives and friends had either died off or dwindled away in the face of her new fame and notoriety? Or even more basic—a growing awareness that she was a pathetic reduction of her younger self, that celebrity and power had failed to compensate for the barren person she had become. She could feel the new burden of childlessness gnawing at the corners of her heart like a festering reproach. *You will never be a mother, and what else are you?*

The lack of an answer left her with a hopelessness more desperate than the wildest hunger.

She stepped out of bed, in the odd hope that the mere motion of her limbs on the hardness of the floor beneath her feet might jar the despair loose, or at least distract her for a moment.

It didn't help, and the knowledge deepened her panic. What would she do now? She glanced around for stronger distractions. Should she quietly go to the living room bar for a stiff drink? She shook her head slowly, for she certainly knew that was no solution. She could turn on the television for distraction, but she did not want to wake her husband and doubted that the early-morning lineup, heavy on news recaps—which meant reports of her husband's political travails—would do anything to ease her anxiety.

She glanced around her. In younger days she would have gone out for a midnight run of five miles or more. She had once been a highly conditioned athlete in the days before her marriage and its attendant security precautions. She could feel her old muscles crying out for release, but tonight, on the spur of the moment, physical renewal would have to wait.

Something thick and shiny on her makeup table caught her eye. It was the cover of the Battaween Translations, the ancient documents unearthed, deciphered, and faxed to Jerusalem the day before. She still had only read the earliest pages—interrupted by the general's sudden pronouncement that nothing further would be gained.

Of course. Esther. Maybe you have nothing to offer the generals, or even Jacob. But horrific as your account is, you might bring me through the next few minutes. . . . Even a distraction has appeal.

She walked over, picked up the pages of the document, and took a seat against the wall. The glow from an outer window just behind proved barely enough to read by. She turned to the first new page, looked upward in a silent plea for relief, and began where she had left off.

Something spiritual began soothing her the minute she picked up the ancient words.

"I remember awakening . . ."

Chapter Thirty-four

———————— ~ ————————

I remember awakening late from that blood-drenched night to the sounds of men shouting outside the window. I grimaced, for it was not the sound of mourning. Or of a funeral, though many were in the offing on that day. Fearing some sort of large-scale palace coup, I stole to the curtain and peered outside.

It took me several moments to see what was actually taking place in the early-morning light. But soon I made out a large assembly of soldiers at attention, in full uniform, upon the innermost terrace. Artabanus stood in the front row with his five surviving commanders of the top regiment of palace guards. Before them stood a figure in full battle armor, which I soon recognized as Artaxerxes himself. I could not help my gasp of concern, for despite his height he seemed like such a boy, standing alone before the murderous intentions of such grown, battle-hardened men. Yet behind him, in full armor and holding one of the largest swords I have ever seen a man grasp, I recognized Megabyzos, the famous general of his father's and even grandfather's wars against the Greeks. The silver glint on the sword matched the color of his hair and beard.

I remember thinking to myself, *There before Artaxerxes stands* assembled probably the whole gang of conspirators who murdered his father. And then it struck me—that surely was no coincidence. Artaxerxes had assembled them there for a purpose. I whispered a quick prayer of gratitude that Mordecai and I had been able to give him that information.

Gripped by curiosity now, I knelt and continued to watch from my hidden place in the shadow of the curtain. Artaxerxes barked out several orders which I could not make out, clearly intending to review the troops. Was he merely asserting his impending kingship over the army? I hoped there was more to his scheme. Clearly, shouts and martial trappings would not be sufficient to quell the conspiracy.

Then the loud voices ceased. Artaxerxes stepped up to Artabanus and inclined his head, speaking softly. I would later learn that the prince was making an odd request of the man who supposedly managed a great deal of his personal safety—he was complaining of his own armor being too small and asking to exchange his with the older man's. How I wish I had been there, standing over the prince's shoulder, to see the proud captain's expression upon being asked to disrobe before most of the Royal Palace!

And yet Artabanus, anxious to continue his guise of amiable friend to the prince, could not refuse such a command from a royal—not publicly, not today. So, reluctantly, he began to do the unthinkable—right there in the front row of the military review—the arduous process of removing his armor plates, one by one. Of course, the Palace Guard, like their more elite colleagues the Immortals, are quite fastidious about their battle dress, festooning their armor with all sorts of capes, feathers, and gold adornments. I nearly laughed out loud at seeing the captain's pink, very unwarriorlike flesh revealed to the light of day.

Finally Artabanus stood almost nude in only his inner short tunic before the prince who—I suddenly noticed—had not removed any armor of his own.

There was a charged, confused pause in which Artabanus seemed to scowl, apparently unaware of what he should do next. Making all sorts of uncertain nods and shrugs, he grasped his helmet and attempted a ceremonious gesture of handing it to Artaxerxes. Which, of course, looked all the more ridiculous because of the giver's laughable state. Imagine an almost-naked man bowing forward, holding a helmet nearly large and decorated enough to cover his entire midsection, with five hundred fully-armed soldiers standing at attention behind him! I strained my ears for the sound of laughter, of even snickering. Amazingly, I heard none. The guards' discipline was amazing.

Artaxerxes did not move a muscle to accept the captain's proffered headpiece.

With a swiftness and a ferocity that took my breath away, he grasped his sword, withdrew its blade, wheeled and plunged it straight through the captain's pale belly.

I heard a sound, whether my own or that of the combined soldiers, I would never be sure. For Artabanus fell to his knees, a bright red fount gushing from the wound, as the prince withdrew his sword with a grimace and the body fell heavily sideways.

Then everything seemed to happen at once. Never having witnessed actual battle firsthand before, I was struck by the chaotic and frenzied pace of its motion. But the front row of Artabanus' commanders unsheathed their weapons and, with a single shout, moved upon Artaxerxes. The prince had the advantage, with not only an already drawn sword but the charge of bloodlust upon him, and then an even better fortune still—for Megabyzos sprang into action, waving his massive blade about him like a madman. I saw at least one head fly off its shoulders, and severed limbs tossed about like branches in a windstorm.

I wanted to turn away and vomit, but I could not wrench my eyes from the scene.

For a moment I found it impossible to gauge who had won the advantage, so furious was the grappling and massing of combatants. But the scene quickly grew even more difficult to watch, for the terrace's fine gray marble now shone a bright, slick crimson, and screams of terror and agony now drowned out bellows of challenge and triumph.

Behind the frontmost rows, the greater number of soldiers had abandoned their formation and seemed to mill about in confusion, unsure whether to take the side of their captain or their king.

But their uncertainty did not last long.

From a side walkway came the unmistakable sound of countless leather boots and another shout, so loud and strong that I realized at once it came from the throats of a hundred men at full battle charge.

I recognized the uniforms at once—the Immortals.

Of course! The Immortals' commander was Otanes, one of the empire's most celebrated war heroes and noblemen. And, as it happened, he was also the father of Vashti, Xerxes' disgraced Queen and Artaxerxes' mother. But this also made Otanes Artaxerxes' grandfather. In three straight columns the vaunted warriors fell upon the scene of carnage—not so much to massacre as to quell the confusion, I soon realized. At top speed and with an intensity of purpose that filled me with awe, one column inserted itself between the bewildered troops and the actual fighting. Another jumped heedlessly into the fray, pulling apart combatants both wounded and whole.

The third column seemed to concentrate itself on the surviving sons of Artabanus, who once pulled from the carnage were quickly deprived of their heads.

Just as quickly, the battle was over.

But my eyes could not discern the state of Artaxerxes—

—until, with my heart in my throat, I saw him being pulled to one side by a pair of Immortals. He seemed to be thrashing in pain, his armor stained with blood. Just beside him, Megabyzos was being attended, too, seemingly in even greater injury.

I had just seen an historic display of bravery and cunning. But I also realized that someone I loved was in danger of his life, for the second time in less than a day.

And perhaps my own survival lay in the balance. As Queen I was inextricably linked with Xerxes and his family. Any change in the dynasty would likely mean my own head.

The time for watching from a high perch was over. If I was to be in danger, I would at least be at the side of my surrogate son, the young man I had loved like my own since he was a mere baby—for I did truly love him.

I rushed out of my quarters and ran at my best speed through the palace, threading my path through a labyrinth of pale and frightened faces, down long corridors and the grand staircase to the terrace doors. I burst out and found my momentum slowed first by the brightness of the day, and then by a cordon of Immortals who had now surrounded the battleground. In fact, I actually rushed into the arms of one hapless soldier, who made to restrain me until he heard me call out my name and recognized my face. Bewildered, he lowered his arms and allowed me through.

A moment later I almost wished he had held me back.

I literally felt myself skating on a sheen of blood as I rushed toward Artaxerxes' side. I did not find him by spotting him directly, but rather the thick cordon of Immortals and two grieving women— his weeping sisters Amytis and Rhodogyne.

Friend to both of them, but not as close as to their brother, I shouldered my way through to see what I could of my beloved prince. I dare not call him *son* precisely, because I did not give birth to him. Nevertheless, ever since his mother Vashti's disappearance and presumed murder (at a time when she was widely rumored to be with child) followed by his strange arrival—a sleeping baby carried into the palace on the arm of a warrior and left there with only a note stating his name—I had acted much as a mother would have.

And that is why, when I first looked down and beheld his condition, my grief was so much more intense than that of a subject toward her new king. Although he was pale, and his eyes seemed to be half trained elsewhere, the state of his wounds allowed me to roughly estimate that he would live.

He focused his eyes on mine and smiled grimly. And though weak in body, he muttered to me with as much finality and authority as he could muster, "Tell Mordecai I heeded his warning. I took care of my enemy."

I nodded and squeezed his hand. In that moment, kneeling before him, I realized that the Persian Empire had a new King.

My next thought was, *I am no longer Queen.* The knowledge dawned within me like the sudden quenching of a precious light.

But true to my training, I kissed his bloody hand before rising, then whispered my acknowledgment to him.

"Let me be the first to say to you, my son, 'Live long and live well, O King of Persia.'"

That is all I remember of that scene. The rest is a hazy dream of hurrying forms and shouted orders. I must have gone weak in the knees, for I do recall being carried by courtiers into my private Queen's chambers. I think it was my arrival there that brought the full emotional onslaught surging into my bosom.

Xerxes is dead. My husband is gone. I am no longer Queen of Persia. These would no longer be my living quarters.

And yet, I lamented, why should I worry about where I live, when I'm not sure I *want* to live without him? I vacillated between extreme grief and overwhelming anxiety. And to make matters worse, I knew full well the utterly dangerous place the palace had just become.

Chapter Thirty-five

NAQSHI-I-RUSTAM, SOUTH OF PERSEPOLIS, BURIAL DAY

I will always remember the funeral procession to Naqshi-i-Rustam, Xerxes' burial place. Despite being pressed mercilessly for decisions from every level of palace leadership, Mordecai had set aside his urgent Prime Minister's duties long enough to ride with me and Jesse *cum* Hathach at the head of the stadias-long mourners' procession. I was endlessly grateful for his compassion, for I feared I would not have endured the trip without both of them nearby. We rode just behind Artaxerxes, who sat propped up on his largest warhorse before a cantle as tall he was. A dozen of the empire's best physicians had argued for days about whether the crown prince would survive the journey, at his precarious point of recovery. And yet the busiest hive of activity surrounded Mordecai, who during this time of transition represented the very glue of dynastic continuity.

I remember little of the month-long ride itself, except plodding on my mount for what seemed like forever through a scorching desert sun to the very outskirts of Persepolis, symbolic seat of the Achaemenids. Someone had offered me a litter, but given the circumstances of the journey, I knew it would prove a near-death sentence for the carriers. Which, for many in the Persian court, would have been of little consequence. *Let the slaves perish,* they would have said, for this is an important trip. As you know, Mordecai did not raise me to even contemplate such an idea.

If it sounds as though I'm complaining about the severity of the trip and the bleakness of its surroundings, I am not—really. For you see, in my grieving silence I actually found that the featurelessness of the desert and the harshness of its conditions matched my inner climate exactly. The desert's vastness and spareness soothed me, somehow. Not only that, but the sound of so many people riding together in complete silence was both comforting and highly odd. I recall the sound of hooves striking the brittle sand, the creaking of saddle leather. I remember the blinding glare shining from the solid gold sarcophagus of my dead husband. And the tragic stateliness of my old friend Hegai, standing his ceremonial final sentinel, symbolically guarding a body that no longer required watch care.

What I remember best, however, is the overwhelming sense of loss and disorientation that swept through me time after time during those hours. In a way, even with my twin anchors Mordecai and Jesse beside me, I was glad for the enforced silence of the convoy; for I would have been at a loss for anything to say. What remains most vivid now is the almost physical sensation of being utterly and completely bereft of direction. *Lost entirely.* Had I found myself in a desert, thinking myself within range of an oasis but unable to find it, unable even to ascertain its direction, the feeling would have exactly matched my emotions of those days.

At last we reached the Husain Kuh Mountains and the soaring cliffs of Naqshi-i-Rustam, where Darius already lay buried and where Xerxes' tomb awaited. I remember glancing up at the great stone ramparts and wishing they would seal me in, too—simply leave me there to die alongside him. But the ritual of the observances kept me distracted, I suppose, from falling back into complete despair. We entered the darkness, with torches blazing and the heat still radiating from Xerxes' coffin, and we bade him good-bye. I did not weep until the final moments, whether from fear of showing weakness to the co-conspirators most assuredly in our midst, or perhaps my well of tears had gone dry from overuse in the previous days. Then Mordecai looked over and caught my eye, and the devastation in his gaze brought me right back to my old bed in the royal chamber, and the sight of my beloved struggling for his life.

I looked down and let my tears fall through the darkness onto the sand beneath my feet. Then I walked forward for one final caress of the sarcophagus. I bent down, kissed it—*him*—and whispered a faint farewell in Hebrew.

And then I inched my way back through the dark tunnel, and once more into the harsh brilliance of the desert sun.

Of the ride home, I remember two things. One was that it proved much more disheartening than even the ride up. Not really knowing what awaited me back in Susa now burdened my heart like a physical weight. And, two, I recall once turning to Jesse, quite purposely, and letting him glimpse, for an instant, deep into my own misery.

I found myself thinking, strangely out of step with the occasion, *Jesse, what has become of us?* What became of that vigorous, attractive pair of youthful companions who ran so fearlessly through the King's Gate market on that day so long ago? Where did the blissful promise of our first kiss disappear? Or the innocence of a girl who did not even know such things could be shared between a man and a woman? Or that love could even feel like that?

And I was pondering, *You are no longer even Jesse; why do I continue to refer to you as that?* I willed myself to say it. *It's Hathach.* But voicing his Persian name only compounded my feelings.

And I was thinking this . . .

. . . *it should have been you, Jesse. Had I been given my choice, you surely would have been my husband.*

Instead, here we were—famous and prominent perhaps, but nevertheless, two adults approaching middle age, moving toward a very uncertain and unpromising future.

PÂTHRAGÂDA (PASARGADAE), CITADEL OF CYRUS THE GREAT—TWENTY DAYS LATER

Obviously, the astonishing outcome of the coronation ceremony hardly helped matters, as you might imagine. It certainly wasn't the treatment I was accorded, for in fact I moved about very much as a Queen Mother, or at least a Queen Regent. At least until—well, you know what I speak of, as does any well-informed Persian subject. Nor did it surprise me for Artaxerxes to treat me kindly, in the absence of a mother he had never really known.

I remember standing beside Mordecai on the top level of Pâthra-gâda's *Tall-i-Takht,* the "throne hill," awaiting the arrival of the prince, and looking out over the crowd of Persians assembled to watch their new sovereign be crowned. And taking deep, long breaths to keep myself from weeping out loud.

Despite the respectful manner with which I was dealt, the whole celebration seemed at that moment to be little more than a pointed and grandiose way to drive home the fact that another king was about to take the throne. And that I was only part of the past. A relic of history—an honored part of it, to be sure, and a virtual heroine among my fellow Jews of the Quarter. But still, a remnant. And, despite the ever-abiding kindness of Jesse and Mordecai, very much alone.

It was all I could do to keep my mind on the present—too often and too quickly my memories galloped back to the glorious day when my beloved had announced me as his Queen. Indeed, Mordecai and I, and Jesse too, had witnessed some enormous gatherings during our long-past time in the sun. I never thought I would see their like—so huge and sprawling and enthusiastic were these crowds. But clearly, nothing in the life of a kingdom matches the coronation of a fresh young king. Even with Persia's waning fortunes, her Greek and Egyptian enemies gaining the better of her more often than not, her far-flung boundaries shrinking by the year, her satraps complaining of staggering taxation and imperial excess—all troubles of the sort were forgotten on a day like that.

I remember looking out over that sea of heads that filled the plain of Cyrus' old palace, then past it to the ring of stunning mountain peaks surrounding us on every side. And I wondered if anything more momentous could be happening anywhere on the whole earth on that particular morning.

It was a cloud-strewn, tumultuous day. It seemed as though the elements had absorbed some of the crowd's seething anticipation and were tossing all forms of turbulence into the heavens. A restless wind blew into our faces omens of a coming winter. It all seemed fitting, as if the whole world was in transition.

I felt as though I was attending my own execution.

Then at once, in one of the most exquisitely timed and executed entrances I have ever seen, Artaxerxes was walking through us, arrayed in splendor. I shook my head in disbelief, for he seemed to have grown so much in authority that he appeared significantly older than the last time I had seen him. He had recovered amazingly from his wounds. He stood so straight and tall, and strode forward with such a glow upon his face that I could not tell if it was the daylight or the warmth of the people's cheers. Just then a gust of wind billowed up his robe, great flames leaped up on the fire altars to either side, Artaxerxes threw up his arms in the classic posture of Persian adoration, looking every bit like the Persian god Zarathustra in the Gathas, and a great roar from the crowd blew through us like a whirlwind.

Mordecai turned to me, shook his head, and smiled, and I understood. It was hard not to grin before such blinding beauty and adulation.

And do you know what I was feeling, at this sublime moment? I was feeling that all the glories of Xerxes had been forgotten, that by comparison the reign of my beloved husband and his contemporaries had just been relegated to little more than a shabby, dreary cast-off. Everything about that moment was so perfect, so pure, so ordained, that my own days on the throne seemed dreadful in contrast. I wanted nothing more than a dark place to hide.

Writing this, I know of course how self-centered and self-pitying it all must seem. But then again, that's why I am taking the time to describe it to you—so you will fully understand the bitter inner journey I have undertaken.

You're probably chuckling, thinking, *My goodness, if she's feeling a bit lost right now, I can't wait to read how she feels after the next ten minutes of the ceremony. . . .*

You're perfectly right, of course, as usual. Even though you were not present, I know you've heard time and time again what took place next.

Chapter Thirty-six

CORONATION DAY

To begin with, the feelings certainly did not abate while I watched Artaxerxes flawlessly perform the rituals of coronation. He knelt, removed his own velvet robe, and tossed it aside like an extravagance unworthy of him. And then he remained there, looking downward in a solemn expression, while the high priest walked over and draped the very robe of Cyrus the Great, removed from Cyrus' nearby tomb just for the occasion, across his shoulders. There came another ovation from the crowd—deep and lasting, though not as exuberant as the first because of the gravity of this moment and its symbolism. Everything about the rite was supposed to evoke the humility and simplicity of his great-great-grandfather Cyrus, first and greatest of the Achaemenids.

After a moment, Artaxerxes stood to his feet, and being given a tassel of figs, he raised the humble fruit high for everyone to see and devoured every one. The priest handed him a wooden handle dripping with the boiled sap of a pine tree. Artaxerxes unswervingly placed it into his mouth, sucking the wood dry and forming not even the first twinge of a grimace. Then he was handed a goblet filled with sour milk, raised that high, and drank it. He hesitated, as though savoring the bitter taste, then handed back the cup and fell abruptly to his knees. He had successfully ingested the Persian symbols for humility and austere modesty.

The ovation this time was even more powerful than the first. It seemed that a god had stepped down to embody the essence of the ceremony rather than a sixteen-year-old palace lad caught up in the gravity of the moment.

And then, just as suddenly, the vast crowd stopped cheering and a strange disturbance, like a rustling of ghostly wind, swept through the midst.

Leah, I wish you could have seen the full effect of this moment for yourself.

It started, of course, with the Immortals, as everyone now knows. These royal palace guards should have been in place along the ceremony's perimeter, but they suddenly appeared, carving a swath through the crowd. The warriors' procession was such an ominous and awesome sight, blazing their dense path through the crush of bodies, perhaps a dozen men on each side forcing the adoring mob to step aside through the mere weight of their presence. I remember that one or two people, unsure what the sight meant, began to clap senselessly.

But the overwhelming majority of the crowd remained silent, reserving judgment. Clearly this was not part of the ritual. Coronations were notoriously fraught with danger and consequence, so no one knew quite what would come next.

The columns lined up ramrod straight before the new King. The crowd itself moved ever so slightly behind it.

Then they seemed to open a bit, to widen the path their bodies had created.

And I saw someone walking through the ranks. I saw the bottom of a robe and realized it was a woman. One dressed as beautifully as any Queen in the history of the palace, I must say.

She stepped away from the columns' protection, and in the moment she did, each Immortal drew his sword and held it flat side upward in a gesture of supreme allegiance and warning. *Do not harm this woman. We will trade our lives for hers.* I focused on the lead Immortal and recognized their commander, Otanes. I noticed that his lip was quivering, that tears were flowing freely down his tanned and timeworn face. Now he alone had left the ranks and was closely following the woman up the steps, ready to catch her at any awkward moment.

And then I saw her clearly. The truth struck me, and I almost fell down at the mere realization.

But it couldn't be. It was impossible.

I stepped out, not caring now who saw my advance toward the inner circle of ceremony leaders, and steadied myself against Mordecai's arm. For his part, he was watching with a deep frown upon his face, still having not realized the answer to the great mystery approaching us all.

She reached the top dais, and I saw again that she still had her beauty, although with age it had definitely acquired a most ferocious gleam. Immediately upon her arrival she knelt with an exaggerated flourish, and behind her Otanes did the same.

Artaxerxes stood there, staring, narrowing his eyelids, his fingers reflexively grasping and releasing his sword handle.

Otanes spoke first, his deep, usually authoritative voice now filled with fear.

"Your Majesty, may I introduce one who has waited long for this day, to proclaim her adoration and gratitude for your royal grace."

The next voice I heard made me nearly jump with surprise, for it was Mordecai's.

"Commander," he said in a tone of both shock and anger. "This is a coronation. It is no time for introductions, no matter how . . ."

Whether foolishly or not, I became overwhelmed with a belief that while he was ceremonially correct, Mordecai was committing a grave, strategic misstep. I gripped his forearm and whispered into his ear, "Please, Poppa. You are making a mistake."

Without turning to face me, Mordecai relented; he took a deep breath and stepped backward.

A long pause followed. The next move was up to the King.

"Who is this?" Artaxerxes finally asked in an impatient voice that betrayed his first attempt at royal imperiousness.

She answered for herself. "I am Amestris, O great King. The widow of your father, the dearly beloved Xerxes, and Queen Mother of the Empire of Persia. I am your mother!"

Artaxerxes sank onto a seat. Not abjectly, out of some sort of surrender or subservience, but so abruptly and swiftly that it seemed his lower limbs had simply lost their ability to bear him up. Like a puppet whose string is snipped without warning.

Coming near to him in his role as Prime Minister, Mordecai struggled to help the young king to his feet—yet he himself seemed to sway in utter shock.

It was a surprise worthy of true astonishment. The woman who had done this, climbed the stairs toward Artaxerxes and shown the audacity to interrupt his coronation for this display of revelation and allegiance, was his long-grieved, supposedly murdered mother, Vashti.

Chapter Thirty-seven

I could not catch my breath—Mordecai, beside me, was in even worse condition; his cheeks went ashen, he stumbled backward as though struck in the face, and I seriously believed he was about to suffer some kind of fatal spell. Whereas he had been holding my hand and giving me support throughout the day, now I, despite my own severe shock, was compelled to seek a small stool and help him sit.

Vashti's coronation appearance was remarkable. As I now approach my fourth decade, having availed myself of all the beauty secrets taught me by Hegai over the years, I have few complaints about the harshness of age upon my countenance. But time had been far kinder to Vashti—she would have been at least a decade older than I but looked a decade younger. Her only concession to time was a distant hardness in her eyes, which it seemed she could soften at will with a faint smile.

As you might imagine, I went all at once from feeling like the forgotten stepparent to someone with a very keen stake in what was taking place. It had been almost sixteen years since Vashti had been Queen of Persia, lauded the greatest beauty in all womanhood, and had boldly refused Xerxes' order to parade that beauty before his war banquet. Drunk and provoked, Xerxes had promptly banished her as Queen and exiled her from the palace. Mordecai and I had stood in the audience as those events took place; it was actually my very first official trip outside of the house, which had sequestered me every day of my youth.

That event was the reason why Xerxes first sought a new Queen and ordered young virgins from throughout the empire brought to the palace. A group which would come to include a frightened young Jewish girl from Susa named Hadassah.

My point? Not to recount well-known history. But to say that all of a sudden I realized how my own place in the world had begun with this woman's demise. I had never given it much thought, for reliable rumor had it that Vashti had been murdered by a squad of assassins shortly after leaving the palace.

I had reason to believe the rumor was true, for shortly after that time a new addition had been quietly carried by the great general Otanes into the royal nursery—a newborn baby prince, presumably orphaned like myself, who would turn out to be Otanes' grandson. An infant we would call Artaxerxes. Surely no living mother, I reasoned, would simply give up her son like that, especially to the custody of the same ruler who had ordered her banished.

So was I unreasonable to fear that a former queen who had sat in some sort of hiding place all these years, watching me assume her place at the palace and raising her son nearly as my own, would harbor ill feelings toward me?

As I pondered these things, I felt a pair of eyes upon me and looked back toward the center of the terrace.

And as I feared, the eyes in question belonged to Vashti. Her hand on her son's shoulder, she glanced at me with a dark, piercing stare.

My mind thrashed under a storm of realizations and calculations. As much as my status had changed in the days leading up to this moment, now I knew it had been turned on its head. In fact, it struck me that my very survival could depend upon what I did in the next few seconds. No matter how beloved I might have once been to him, this woman was the mother of the King and would naturally assume the title of Queen Mother—a role I had been gradually acquiring by default. Furthermore, she was likely to be quite angry after all these years of exile. I might well prove the very first political purge of such a woman, if I gave her the provocation.

"O YHWH," I whispered. "Give me wisdom. Guide my steps...."

And as soon as I said those words, they became my solution. *Steps.*

I stepped forward, toward her. Again, then again.

Mordecai breathed inward with a sound of shock. Courtiers on every side of me gasped. The sound emboldened me and I continued walking, concentrating on breathing, on not fainting, and on maintaining the warm smile upon my face—the countenance of one who was encountering an old friend for the first time after a long absence.

Finally, I reached her. Out of the side of my vision I could see Artaxerxes standing beside her with an expression of shock and wary anticipation.

I stood before her, straight and silent and matching her gaze for gaze for the briefest of moments, to show that I was not coming to her in a state of weakness.

Then I sank to my knees, just as Artaxerxes had, and held out my hand to hers.

"My Queen," I said in my most reverential tone.

I had no idea what would happen next, but even my wildest imagining would not have shown me what actually took place.

First, a sound that was actually a strangled sob tore from Vashti's throat, and she stumbled forward. Any distant spectator might have been forgiven for assuming that she had thought I was falling and had reached out to break my fall. But the truth was, my downward motion had caught her totally by surprise. She was expecting nothing less than a confrontation and was steeling herself for some sort of insult when I had knelt.

Vashti's startled motion actually provoked Artaxerxes to reach out and keep her from toppling into me. Others in attendance would later tell me that the new King had reacted even more emotionally than his mother, that his eyes had filled with tears at the unexpected conciliation of the moment.

But at the same instant the entire terrace, and even the foremost rows of spectators outside, murmured their own surprised responses. It seemed my impulsive gesture had defied the expectations of even the most jaded and self-important courtiers.

Vashti then did something almost as shocking.

She gave me her hand and suffered me to bring it against my lips. I looked up, and despite my calculated role in what was happening, I felt a surge of sincere emotion flood through me.

"My Queen Mother, let me add my welcome to your return. And please call me Hadassah, for upon the passing of our beloved sovereign, I am Queen Esther no more."

I will never forget Vashti's gaze down toward me in that moment. For one thing, she was incapable of speech. Her eyes were moistened to the point that her elaborate face-paint seemed in peril of melting away. Her thin, almost bony hands jerked in mine with some involuntary contraction, as though she was having trouble maintaining control over her muscles. But it was her eyes that seared an image into my memory forever. They were brimming with a shocked sort of gratitude and even love—but also tinged with an edge of surprise that told me she was hardly acquainted with these emotions, nor knew how to manage them. It was as though she was experiencing unreserved goodwill for the first time in her life. The awareness pierced me with a sense of how impoverished the woman's inner world must be.

I looked over at Artaxerxes again. He was weeping quietly but openly. And when I think of it now—how overwhelming this must have been for him, to have a mother he had believed dead suddenly appear at the most pivotal and sublime moment of his life, then make a dramatic show of conciliation toward the woman who had played such a maternal role in his childhood.

I rose on shaky knees, and Vashti, unaware of how to further acknowledge my gesture, simply clasped my hands in hers.

Only when I stood did I become aware of how the crowds around us had reacted. Had I been asleep I would have been dreaming of summer storms, for the people's acclaim echoed throughout the building like thunder!

And then she spoke directly to me for the first time.

"Thank you," and I knew that she meant it deeply. "And I mean to be called Queen Mother Amestris from this day on. Queen Vashti died on the day my King sent me from his sight. And Amestris is the name of my birth."

I hope no one heard the sigh I unleashed at that moment. Inwardly, I thanked G-d for His favor. It would become clear to me over time that I had without doubt saved my own life with the impulsive course I had taken.

Then Queen Mother Amestris turned back to the crowd, and the acclaim, and the upheld arms of her son, the new King of the World.

And Hadassah of Susa, royal member of the harem, untitled citizen of Persia, stepped back to take her place behind them.

―――――――――   ⇌   ―――――――――

Chapter Thirty-eight

"Mordecai, what comes next for us?"

I asked this as we were returning from Pâthragâda the next day in a vast royal procession, of which I recall very little except this meaningful conversation with Mordecai.

"I don't know," he said with a warm smile. "I truly do not. But I know that G-d is faithful, and He has never ceased giving me tasks of great consequence to carry out."

"Are you speaking of raising *me*?" I asked with a small laugh.

Now, writing this, I recognize how self-centered it was for me to assume that his "task of great consequence" necessarily involved me. For some reason, I seemed to continually forget that Mordecai had become an even more famous and greater figure in the Persian Empire than I ever was as Queen. As Xerxes' Master of the Audiences, he was the sovereign's closest advisor and most trusted set of eyes, even though during those first few days of Artaxerxes' reign, his own continued role at the palace lay very much in doubt.

Perhaps it is because I still think of him as my Poppa, my adoptive father, in fact my cousin who cared for me after the sudden murders of both our families. It is difficult for me to picture him as a national figure, a beloved grandfatherly type whose name and face are known to nearly every child in all of Persia.

"Hadassah, raising you has been the most rewarding thing I have ever done," he continued. "But yes, it is a task which consumed a great part of my adult years."

"Hah! There are easier ways of getting a child out of the house than sending her off to the royal harem. . . ." I regretted my thoughtless quip as soon as the words were out of my mouth and I saw his expression.

"I hardly sent you off, my dear," he chided gently. "If you knew the grief Jesse's grandmother Rachel and I endured after you were taken. I wept for days, thinking the light had gone out of my life. I begged G-d to make some sense of it for me."

"And He did, didn't He? Sometimes I need to be reminded of that."

"Sometimes we all do. Especially at times like this."

"Yes," I said, suddenly brought back to the situation at hand. "Especially today."

"I made an agreement with G-d back then—did you know that? I made a solemn vow that if He would redeem the cruel abduction of you and Jesse to the palace, I would devote my days to His service, and to yours."

I peered curiously at him, for I had never heard of this agreement before.

"Is that why you never married and had children of your own?"

"Yes, I suppose," he answered, fixing me with the strangest look of exasperation and disgruntlement I have ever received from him. "But the important part is, He has been completely faithful to that vow. And I do not expect Him to start failing me now. Or *you*."

"But surely my own fate and Jesse's has been resolved. Could you not now find some comfort and companionship in your old age? Why not find someone now whom you could love for your very own?"

He chuckled at this and looked around him, as though a suitable mate was hiding out amidst the rocks and crags of the Persian desert. "Have you looked at me lately, my dear? I am an old man. My face is more contorted by wrinkles than this desert has rocks and mountains! Who knows how many years the Lord has left for me? And besides—I spend my days among preening politicians, courtiers, and concubines. How will I find a suitable woman in those surroundings?"

"I don't know, Poppa," I said. Then a stroke of wisdom. "Are you starting to suddenly underestimate G-d's creativity?"

He laughed again, so fiercely it sent him into a spasm of coughs that nearly doubled him over in the saddle. "Excellent point, my dear. I suppose I believed this sort of matter was beyond His interest, that's all."

"No more than the fate of three palace discards like you, me and Jesse," I said.

"I suppose we had both better remember that. No matter what *does* come next."

It was his astute way of changing the subject. And it succeeded; we would not bring up this question again until the banks of the Ahava, years later, in the conversation I have already told you about.

On that day, we both fell silent and spoke of it no more, for the faint, bristling shadow of Susa's citadel had just come into sight upon the horizon, and something inside of me sank with a great foreboding. . . .

◆ ◆ ◆ ◆ ◆ ◆ ◆ ◆ ◆ ◆ ◆ ◆ ◆ ◆

Chapter Thirty-nine

PRIME MINISTER'S RESIDENCE—THE NEXT MORNING

H*adassah ben Yuda awoke* with the motion of a strong hand shaking her about one shoulder. She opened her eyes and started at Jacob's face looming large, leaning forward in concern as he crouched down.

"Honey, what are you doing here?"

She looked about her. *Carpet and wall.* An angle of the room she had never seen before. She had fallen asleep sitting with Esther's memoir in her lap, leaning against her makeup table.

"I don't know, Jacob. I woke up last night with the most restless feeling, and the best distraction I could think of was a few pages from this. . . ."

She saw his eyes dart down to the cover page in her lap, register the title, and look back again without a reaction.

"Queen Esther." He said the name flatly. "She doesn't seem to leave us alone, does she?"

"Whether the document helps your crisis or not—her account is just fascinating. There's something about her troubles that seems to . . ." She didn't want to seem cloying or simplistic, so she did not finish her sentence. And then she realized what she'd said . . .

Whether the document helps you or not. . . .

"Honey, I don't mean that I don't *care*," she hurried to explain. "I just mean that even beyond its usefulness to the crisis at hand, the memoir has a lot to say. A lot to offer."

He nodded slowly, and she knew he was assessing her words in light of the difficult times she was living through. The thought galled her somehow. She wanted her observations weighed on their own merit, not the demeaning standard of someone "not quite herself."

"Listen, sweetheart," he said with a brush of her cheek, "I have to go. I'd be glad to stay this morning, but it's another meeting with the Gaza folks." *Gaza folks* was his usual, wry pseudonym for the revolving door of diplomats he saw from the Palestinian Authority. As much as he confessed to her his disdain for the petulant and self-important suits who filed through his door, he was obliged to give them his utmost attention. Especially now.

"I'm sorry," she found herself saying to him as he rose. Her hand clawed helplessly around the back of his neck in a vain attempt at affection.

"Sorry for what, sweetheart?"

"For . . . for bringing all this down on you. For being such a distraction just when you're about to win the prize."

The prize, of course, meant the same thing to every Israeli politician or politician's wife since the early days of 1948. It meant *peace*. A solution to the quagmire that had agitated their nation's life from day one. More than any of his predecessors, Jacob had reached the brink of this seemingly impossible goal. Then she and her Byzantine family secrets had ruined everything.

"Don't be silly, sweetheart," he said, interrupting her gloom. "*You* are the prize. You're more important to me than any of this."

She closed her eyes against the tears, for she could not bring herself to believe his kind words just then.

When she felt bold enough to open them again, he was gone. And once more, the only thing that held any life for her was the document lying in her lap.

Thank you, Esther, she whispered silently. *Thank you for a few hours' sleep.*

And for being a companion whose life seems to mirror everything I'm going through. . . .

———————— ⤳ ————————

. . . Leah, the following day was the worst of my life.

Following our return from the coronation, I spent the night on a pallet in a corner of Mordecai's apartment. I cannot say that I *slept* there, for what I actually endured was a sort of prolonged good-bye, a restless floating in an ocean of loss and melancholy.

Dawn mercifully rescued me, and at midmorning I allowed in a team of royal slaves to pack up everything I owned and place it on a litter. When they were ready, I glanced at the load, which they easily picked up with a team of four, and realized that despite the mind-numbing opulence in which I had lived for so long, remarkably little actually belonged to me. Most of what I cared to keep were small, highly valuable gifts from Xerxes himself and some other ornamental keepsakes of my life as Queen.

The item I cherished most, however, was one I bore with me into my royal life. A treasure I wore upon my person: the beautiful Star of David I have already written about to you. The one which my parents gave me upon my seventh birthday, on the night of their deaths. I slipped it around my neck, took a deep breath, and inwardly said my good-byes.

And then, accompanied by little more than a few crates of bundled trinkets, I walked out into the hallway of Susa's Great Palace. As so many years before, I watched the great crowds that filled the marble floors fall silent and part to make way for me. I turned back to the great doors of Xerxes' living quarters and remembered how desperately my heart had pounded on that day fifteen years before, when a young virginal member of the harem had arrived accompanied by Hegai and greeted furtively by Memucan at the front door. It seemed it had taken place in another lifetime, with a wholly different person—some pale and frightened young woman posing as myself.

Then I also remembered how close G-d had felt to me then. I had spent the entire trip between the harem and palace in pitiful prayer, and at the moment of reaching these fateful doors I had felt Him as closely as I felt my own damp skin.

The thought gave me a twinge of regret, for over the years I have not maintained the same closeness to Him as I did in those days. Perhaps, I wondered, this was the reason why I harkened back to those times as the highlights of my life, and my latter years as a sort of slow, dismal descent from their luminous perch.

The difference? Maybe it had something to do with how fervently I had once sought Him, with a hunger and a passion borne maybe of youth, but maybe . . . maybe simply a purer heart.

I turned back to my path through the hallway. And just ahead, where the dividing of courtiers ended and watchers still barred my path, the crowd ahead parted with a startling suddenness.

One person stepped forward, her eyes firmly planted on me. This fierce, aging beauty wrapped in a breathtaking pearl-hued robe inlaid with gold threads and fine jewels. A woman with a carriage and manner that bespoke both anger and supreme control. It took my eyes a moment to recognize the new arrival at the palace.

Vashti. Or should I say, Amestris.

"I wondered if you might not grant me a few minutes of your time, Lady Hadassah," she said with a calculating smile.

"I would love the chance," I answered, "but as you see the litter bearers have to come to bear me away to the harem."

"All the more reason," she said. "I would have my words with you before your departure from our halls. Besides, the slaves will wait. Put down your load," she proclaimed to no one in particular, unwilling to grace the men even with her eyes.

With a solid *thunk*, the litter was lowered to the floor, and the slaves slowly raised themselves back to full height.

Amestris had already turned and was leading the way to her own apartments. I dutifully followed, surprised at this interruption and apprehensive about its meaning. After several turns, we walked through a pair of open doors into the same quarters previously reserved for the once-prince Artaxerxes. Already, though, they were unrecognizable. Whereas her son had been contented with a basic abode in which to sleep and change clothes, Amestris had in less than a day re-covered every inch of the walls with velvet, gold damask, and rich lamé, even replacing his modest bed with a gilded construction akin to a small sailing vessel.

It doesn't matter, I forced myself to say, for it did not. Who knows how much modest living she had endured in her days of shadow?

She swept onto a low cushion with the grand confidence of one who had never left the palace, and bade me sit beside her with a wave of her fingers. It had not taken her long to reacclimate herself, I realized.

"So, Hadassah," she began. "I had never seen you until yesterday, although your name was a constant presence on my tongue during my time away."

"I am most pleased to see you return," I replied, determined to maintain my approach of the previous day.

"Yes, you were most gracious in expressing that to me the last time we spoke. I thought perhaps more time to talk in private might be called for. It seems I owe you my thanks."

"I hardly see for what cause."

"Oh, surely you do. I am thankful for your gracious welcome, but I speak of something far more dear to both of us. I speak of my son."

"Yes. He has been a blessing to my life from the very day he appeared."

"As you can imagine, nothing pained me more than giving him up. But I knew that if he were to have a future at court, I had to insert him into its everyday life as soon as possible."

"I understand. And he made that transition remarkably smoothly."

"In no small part to you, Hadassah. You treated him like your own child. Again, I owe you my thanks."

"You are most welcome. But if I may ask, starting at the beginning, how is it you survived those days? I had it on very good authority that you were killed in your bed, soon after leaving the palace. We all thought you were murdered, even your own son."

"And it is because of my son that I was not, my dear Hadassah," she answered with a sly smile. "You see, I was great with child in those days. In fact, my impending delivery of a baby is the most important one of the reasons why I refused our husband's order to appear before his accursed banquet. I was in no condition to parade my naked form before any man, let alone a leering group of drunken soldiers."

"And the baby was Artaxerxes?"

"Yes. Artaxerxes' arrival was the cause of my disposition, of which, to their eternal curse, his chamberlains did not see fit to inform the King. And on the night of which you spoke—yes, my bedroom was indeed attacked. In fact, you had no way of knowing this, but in the years that followed I did some prying of my own into their background. And it seems the killers were followers of one Haman the Agagite, a man who gave you and your people a bit of trouble at the palace, from what I heard."

"You mean—the riders bearing the twisted cross?"

"The same. Twisted crosses were painted in blood across my sleeping chamber. In the blood of my youngest sister. For you see, that night I was occupied by the actual delivery of my son. Zoriana asked if she could use my bed that night, as several of my sisters were at our house for the occasion and sleeping space was scarce."

"So a beautiful woman was indeed murdered, but it wasn't you."

"Exactly. And as Haman was at the height of his influence with the King during those days, I can only surmise that it was your dear Xerxes, our beloved King as you put it, who ordered me killed."

"I find such cruelty hard to imagine," I murmured, casting about for something I could say in his defense.

"Cruelty? Oh, you have no idea, my dear. You see, there was another reason why I refused my husband's demeaning demand. One of which, I hear, you have remained blissfully unaware during your time on the throne. It also concerns our husband."

"I am still grieving his loss, my Queen Mother. Must I hear unsettling news?"

She laughed bitterly. "Still closing your eyes to the truth, I see. So your reputation as a naïf was well earned. Well, I am sorry, but I will not spare you the whole picture of your husband's depravity. Perhaps it will even ease your pain. Nothing like a little rage to lighten the load of grief. You see, your husband has spent the years of his life not only . . ."

"Your Highness, I really do not wish to hear this," I said, attempting to rise from my cushion on the floor.

"I am not asking you, Queen *Regent*," she said, fiercely twisting the last word to emphasize the subordinate status it conveyed and waving imperiously for me to remain seated. "You will listen, or you will die."

"I came within seconds of being murdered myself," I replied, quivering with intensity and fear, "on the night of his death. And I have asked myself every minute since if I should have perished with him. So do not think I won't avoid it now to keep my love for him alive." I finished far more bravely than I felt.

"You would die for a man who was unworthy of you? Who betrayed you at every turn?"

I was now close to tears, for despite the evil in her eyes, I feared she might be telling the truth. "Please, Queen Mother, I beg you, I have never done anything to harm you. You have my full loyalty. So why are you trying to torture me like this?"

"Because you had the audacity to proclaim such a precious, undying love with that very same man. You insulted the suffering of me and every woman he ever defiled with your pathetic fawning over him, your lovesick pretense of married bliss. As if he didn't have hundreds of spare bedmates waiting for him only yards away! As if he wasn't so twisted that he used sex as a way of establishing superiority over those around him, as if he was marking his territory!"

"I'm sorry," I whispered, navigating the conversation by sheer instinct.

"*What?*" My willingness to defer to her had once again defied her credulity.

"I'm so sorry that my husband treated you and so many other women so badly. I really am. I do not excuse his behavior, any more than I will dilute the wonderful reality of being married to him."

Upon hearing those words, Amestris fixed her eyes upon the floor and blew her breath out deeply, clearly in thought.

"Fine. Well, do you know why I am going to let you live?"

"Because I pose you no threat? Because I am utterly loyal both to you and to your son, the King?"

"No, but it does have something to do with Artaxerxes. It's because when I tore my own heart out and allowed my baby son to be taken from my breast and inserted into the royal nursery, I was told that the Queen of that day fell in love with him. And protected him from all harm. And showed him the love and caring that I could not, although I wanted to more than anything in the world—because I was deep in hiding and in fear of my life."

"It's true. I often thought of Artaxerxes as the son I never had. And he probably thought of me as his mother."

"Yes. And although it pained me to have another woman occupy a role which I longed to play, I know that you were good to him. And he loves you dearly. As I am a loving mother, despite what you may have heard of me, I have accrued these actions toward my son to your credit. So I promise you this. As long as you and your fellow Jews do not threaten the throne or the empire in any way, you will have my goodwill and protection. Do you understand me?"

I nodded. "Yes."

"But know this. If I ever have reason to suspect your allegiance or even tire of your presence on this earth, I will deal with you as I surely would have if you had not shown such kindness toward my son."

"And how is that?"

"*How is that?*" She seemed amused by the question. "How is that? Well, let me tell you a story. There was a woman I will not name, who rebuffed Xerxes' adulterous advances. Well, after he was crowned, he offered me a wedding present whose terms you might recognize. He said to me, 'Darling, I will you give anything you ask of me, even if it is half the kingdom.' So I thanked him and asked him for the custody of the woman in question, to do with as I wished. The color went out of his face, but he knew he could not refuse me, so he delivered the woman into my hands. And do you know what I did to her?"

"I dare not even begin—"

"I didn't think so. I watched the royal torturer cut off her breasts, her nose, her lips, her ears, and her tongue. Then I sent her home to her family, to live out her life."

She smiled as she said this, like someone remembering a cherished family trip.

I thought I was about to vomit right into her lap. I had never heard a person speak like this in all my days.

"Why did you do that?" I asked, my voice trembling. "I thought she resisted him. *She* did nothing wrong."

"Wrong? I'll tell you what she did wrong. She replaced me. For weeks people were saying, 'Vashti is no longer the world's most desirable woman. Xerxes wants another.' So I replaced her back. Besides— she spurned him. Who was she to consider herself too good for him, when so many others, including me, were forced to become his victim? She did plenty wrong." The venom in her voice turned my heart to ice.

She turned toward me, smiling slyly.

It was at that moment I realized the truly treacherous and bitter woman with whom I was dealing. She was not to be trusted—or even completely believed.

"Although that wasn't my supreme reason for doing it. I did it, most of all, to spite *him*. She was the one he'd really wanted. So I destroyed her because I was the Queen, and I could. I had the power, so I used it. Do we understand each other?"

I nodded, struggling with every ounce of strength to keep my composure. I felt as though the life had just been sucked right out from my marrow. I felt so diminished, so drained, by the encounter that I honestly wondered if I could stand when it came time to leave. So I decided to risk one last entreaty.

"As I said, Amestris, I love your son and I will devote myself to his fortunes as King. And I do not covet your position as Queen Mother. I am glad that Artaxerxes has regained the mother he thought he had lost."

She gave me the strangest smile then. It did not touch her eyes, which remained as cold as those of a corpse.

"Then we understand each other. Good day. . . ."

Chapter Forty

Indeed, I did find my legs to leave, but only because I was so eager to be rid of her presence. I struggled upright and, without further word, left the room. Walking out into the reassuring light and spaciousness of the hall, I realized that the conversation had been all the more unsettling because of the strange mixture of threat and gratitude Amestris had displayed. Perhaps that was her way, I pondered as I walked over to the slaves waiting beside my pallet. *Keeping people off-balance.*

"Let us away, my man," I told the lead carrier, but just then a loud cry interrupted me from behind.

"Esther! My Queen!" It was Mordecai, with Jesse, I believe, behind him, both of them running and out of breath. It seems I had taken my leave of the palace without warning them both, and neither looked happy with the manner of my departure.

"How dare you simply slip out of here like some discharged servant!" Mordecai demanded between pants of his breath. "You are Queen Regent, the past Queen of the Empire. You deserve a litter, at least, to carry you out."

"Please," I said. "I do not wish to call attention to this departure, in this fashion. Let me just walk out of here on my own strength, with my own dignity."

"I will not hear of it," huffed Mordecai. He was still Master of the Audiences, and so a small host of lesser aides and attendants had gathered at a respectful distance behind him. With a wave of his hand, he summoned over his chief assistant.

"Have the royal litter brought here with all due haste," he ordered. The aide nodded and disappeared.

"And what shall we do while it is being prepared?" I asked in a low voice. "Stand here and endure half of the palace staff standing there staring at us? You see, this is what I did *not* want."

"Let them stare." I believe it was Jesse who answered, in an intentionally loud voice. "Let them remember your beauty and grace, and that you were the beloved Queen in the history of Persia. Let them recall how you canceled the Queen's Tax, championed the lot of the concubines, the prisoners, and the slaves."

I lowered my head, remembering why I loved him so.

"Hadassah, do you remember," said Mordecai in a reflective whisper, "the two traitorous guards, Teresh and Bigthan, who were dragged through this very hallway on a veritable carpet of human fists intent on tearing them apart?"

"Yes, I do. Those were dangerous times. A conspiracy around every corner, it seemed."

"Well, those times are returning. Artaxerxes' ascension has not been met with universal pleasure. Aspamitres, our most brilliant young chamberlain, has just been tortured to death in the most horrific fashion for his part in the plot against Xerxes. There is rumor that more conspirators walk the palace unpunished. The Princes of the Face are fighting among themselves. The King's own brother Hystaspis has launched a revolt in Bactria. Egypt is restless."

"Are you trying to discourage me further?" I asked. "Please—do not bother. This day has been disheartening enough."

Mordecai held my hand, and his tone became the same one he had used so long ago, when I was but a girl. "No, my dear. I simply warn you to watch yourself, to keep your eyes open, and to stay close to our G-d. I worry about you—especially now that you are leaving the King's quarters, with my help now farther away from you."

"I will do all those things, Poppa," I said breathily. "I promise you."

"And you promise to ride in this—" he said, turning to the royal litter, which had just emerged over his shoulder. Fleetingly, I recalled the proper name for a four-man litter—a *palaquin*.

With a sigh and a fair measure of fatigue, for I had now been standing for quite a while, I accepted his thoughtful offer and stepped inside a semiprivate enclosure of velvet and overstuffed pillows, sheer draperies fluttering in between. At least, I remembered, it offered some parallel to the most exciting day of my life, that day so long ago when I had made this journey in the opposite direction—a painted and pampered young beauty on the final day of a year's preparation for one night of passion.

Well, I told myself with a chuckle as the litter rose in the air and began to move forward, *today I am a decade and a half older, no longer perfumed or fresh or even virginal.* Whether I was still to be considered beautiful, I seriously doubted. But I supposed I was wiser—at least if the old adages about age bringing wisdom bear any truth. So I attempted to reassure myself.

The great palace doors parted before us, and I shut my eyes against the flood of daylight and felt myself instantly transported, as if not an hour had passed, to that very day. The heat. The fear. The uncertainty—for I had not yet visited the innermost palace, and lacked even the knowledge of how vast and forbidding a place it was. As keenly as a spice on the tongue, I once again tasted every flavor of the experience: the heat about my face and head, the moisture upon my brow, the smell of spices warming across my body from the day's unexpected torpor, the swoon of my overexcited senses, even the metallic taste of my fear.

And then, as we now made our way out onto the great courtyard into that very sun, I recalled the most striking of all that day's sensations—the nearness of G-d. The feeling of a Father beside me, all around me, who loved me with a fervor I could never extinguish.

I sighed, for the return of so many feelings at once overwhelmed me, combined with all I had already lived through that day. So much had happened in between these twin, opposing journeys—losing my innocence, falling in love, my spectacular wedding, being named

Queen, the dizzying time of nearly dying in a plot against my own people, the Jews. And the Feast of Purim still celebrated every year on the anniversary of our deliverance from wicked Haman.

Yes, my life had now become a High Holiday, of all things, a feast of remembrance, named in honor of my actions. *Purim*—the day in which the tide had turned favor into our direction. How could I exceed that with anything to come? Surely, my day had passed. With every step I could feel the shadow of my own twilight approaching.

Such is life, I told myself. Few have experienced the victories and historic events I have lived. Yet all are called on to weather the passage of years—either that or die young, which I did not particularly desire. The time had come to face some of life's grim realities. At least I had the great memories of those days to warm me as the chill deepened.

Once again, thick crowds of people parted at my approach, for not only did I ride the King's litter, but in this day of uncertainty just following the coronation, interest in the royal family's doings were at a fever pitch. A scattering of folk, mistaking my retinue for the coming of the King, even fell to their knees. I waved and tried not to appear too haughty, for I knew that in a day's time I would be among them, ranked not far from their status in palace society.

At last we crossed the three successive royal courtyards and reached the harem, which despite its beauty awaited me like a haunted, lonelier version of the place I had left. All of Xerxes' concubines had been given a royal reprieve following his death—allowed to stay or leave as they wished, the women with child remaining to press their status as royal mothers, the women with living family members and some vestige of their youth departing at once, and most of the older women staying simply because they had forgotten how to live any other way.

Jesse stood awaiting me, of course, with Mordecai behind him—the both of them having walked behind the litter to grant me privacy during the passage. But theirs now was the only human presence in sight.

Within minutes, I was installed back in the same corner suite into which Hegai had moved me after granting me his special favor during my Days of Preparation. My pallet was untied and its component packages unloaded into various corners of the main retiring room. The whole unloading took less than half an hour.

Little did I know that before long one of the vacant rooms so near mine would house a young girl who would quickly catch my eye, confirm my instinct that her bearing and poise betrayed a Jewish lineage, then soon provoke me to embark on a series of endless missives to explain my life and its many lessons to a new "young sister."

I walked around that once-familiar space, touched the boxes, grazed the ribbons and items of clothing with my fingers as I sought to reconnect both what I had left behind and the once-familiar sensation of my new home.

I remember how Jesse and Mordecai both hovered around me, unsure how to help me through the moment, occasionally reaching out to me with tentative hands but inevitably letting me pass.

Finally, I felt a smothering sense of confinement crowd in around me, and their presence became too much. I remember saying, with the greatest reluctance in my voice, "Mordecai, Jesse, I am so grateful for your help on this day. I am not sure I would have endured without you. But now, I think the moment has come for me to be alone."

"Are you sure?" Mordecai asked, and I think Jesse voiced a similar doubt.

"No, but I think it. I believe it might be best. I will have many hours to myself in this place, no matter how often you come here. I need to start with a good one, in the glow of your visit."

Mordecai met Jesse's gaze, I recall, and a spark of agreement passed between the two of them. With lingering touches of my hand and forearm, they both took their leave.

And I breathed in deeply, looked out the window at a palace wall glowing distantly in the afternoon sun, curled up in a shadowy corner, and survived the first moment of my personal twilight.

That moment lingered into an hour. An hour became a day. Days and nights alike blended into each other, each one seemingly as empty and lifeless as the one before.

It is there, in the endless pauses and the eternal silences that followed, that I struck bottom. Or should say I, bottom struck me.

At first I found myself, of all things, weeping for my long-dead parents. Although I had not mourned them for years, now I whimpered like a lost child and called out their names—their absence as fresh and cruel as if it they had been wrenched from me only yesterday. I remembered with startling clarity the warm, bell-like ring of my mother's laughter as she played with me. The feel of my father's beard when he kissed me good night, and the sparkle in his eye when he scolded me with his usual gentleness. On several occasions, I even found that I was calling for them, *"Momma . . . Poppa . . ."* into the shadows, with the same lilting tone I had given my calls when I was a carefree youngster. As if I had every reason to expect their reappearance.

The next stage began with anger. Or rage, to be more honest, directed straight at G-d. I remember snarling into the emptiness, calling to Him out loud, "You—you did this! You spared your people through me—wonderful. You were my companion, a long time ago. Well, what about now? Is this my fate? Is this how your great figures wind up when you're done with them? Tossed away like old rags? Well, let me tell the people now about your vaunted faithfulness. Let me warn anyone who would listen—beware, watch out, do anything . . . except follow G-d's purposes. . . ."

Later, with a slowness that seemed to mimic the passing of seasons and the wearing down of mountains, I felt my anger wane and gradually melt into self-pity. For days, I wallowed in the frailty of my diminished station and my sagging limbs. Lamented my once-considerable personhood. My growing loneliness.

Then, on a bright morning only a few days after learning that Artaxerxes was going to imitate his father and scour the empire for a suitable queen candidate, I heard a knock on my door and opened it to Jesse and Mordecai, both wearing faint smiles.

"Come here; we want to show you something," Jesse said, for I remember it perfectly. Mordecai bent his index finger and waved the tip to beckon me forward.

The two of them escorted me out to the veranda, planted fists on hips, and smiled. I followed their gazes, squinted against the sunlight, and felt myself suddenly whisked back in time.

Chapter Forty-one

For there on the terrace, milling about with uncertain and even a few traumatized expressions, stood several dozen shockingly beautiful young girls in the attire of Persian satrapies near and far. I don't know if it was the effect of stepping outside so suddenly, but I felt the scene spin and became physically disoriented by how powerfully and vividly the sight plunged me into my past.

Observing the girls' utterly smooth skin, their unwrinkled eyes, the casual flawlessness of their figures, I remembered the few hours I had once spent in this strange waiting state. I recalled what it felt like to be so young, so naïve—only vaguely aware of how the flare of my bosom or the line of my thigh could inflame a man's desires beyond common sense. I felt once more the vague, unsettling awareness of people's eyes traveling up and down my body, appraising, comparing, coveting.

Yes, I had forgotten the image of girls like these—partly because when I had stood there as they did, I did not remain unaware or naïve or disoriented for very long. Nor would they, if my experience had any bearing. Likely, they would find themselves clothed in traditional concubine attire within the hour. Then they would quickly learn the ways of the harem and begin to parade about with the petulant swagger of some of the girls I had known long ago. Soon, most would transform into the petty, backbiting, unspeakably vain creatures who traditionally populated this place. Truly, the picture before me captured a most transitory and fleeting moment in their lives.

I felt a bitter rise of bile within me and turned away. The display of precarious innocence and unearned beauty suddenly felt like a wound in my soul.

"Are you all right, Hadassah?" Mordecai asked me, leaning toward me with concern.

I remember turning back to the group, of which you were a part, Leah, with the muscles of my face pulled tight from anger.

"Tell me, why did you show me this? Did you relish the prospect of torturing me?"

"No, my dear," Jesse stammered. "I merely thought the sight would bring back happier times."

"It has not done that."

"I am sorry," Mordecai interjected. "But what could this possibly provoke? Tell us, please."

I remember turning on him with utter incredulity. I could hardly believe a man would willingly request a rebuke, but then I had momentarily forgotten what longsuffering friends the two of them were.

"I don't want to say it."

"Please tell us."

I took such a deep breath that I recall craning my neck backward and catching sight of a piercing blue sky. I kept my gaze averted to deny them the sight of my tears and replied. "Seeing these girls, I want to say to myself, *Esther—or Hadassah, it matters little—you are no longer a queen. No longer a wife. No longer a lover. Long past a beauty. Mother to no one. Without family, but for one. Friend to few. A footnote of history. Forgotten. Discarded. A dweller in shadows. Counting down the dregs of my days with no other purpose than to endure them.*"

I wish you had seen how Mordecai spoke to me in that moment. How powerfully he turned to me, as he once did so often in his younger and more forceful days, grabbed my hands and spoke to me with tears in his own eyes and with the intensity of a prophet!

"Not in G-d's eyes," he said fiercely, "you are not. You *do* have a father, who loves you beyond all imagining. You *are* loved and desired and beautiful beyond measure. You *are* mother to countless generations saved by your courage. Your family may only now number the two of us, but it will one day number among the nations. Your story will be recounted among children a thousand years hence, a story which has far from ended. . . . Even now, your name is invoked every year on the Feast of Purim."

I could not help myself. The balm of his words unleashed a watery torrent down my face. I threw my arms around Poppa, buried my head in his shoulder, and wept with bittersweet relief.

After a few minutes, I pulled back, felt Jesse's hand search for mine, and grasped it warmly while the three of us stood together, regarding the arriving concubines like a trio of adoring parents.

But Mordecai was not through with me. He had more in mind than simply showing me the group's arrival.

"Look," he said, pointing discretely, keeping his finger close to his side.

Mordecai had indicated a particular girl standing off by herself. At first all I noticed was the dress, for she was clad in a striking robe of blue silk, which, besides its flattering form and elegant shade, reminded me greatly of the robe I had worn in to the King on my First Night. Then I noticed her face. She was a most composed young woman with dark hair, porcelain skin, and eyes that glimmered with a deep and mature-seeming beauty. Something stirred inside of me as I caught sight of them, and I found myself looking closer, staring harder.

It was *you*, of course—as if I need to tell you that.

"Isn't she beautiful?" Mordecai asked, with such a twinge of longing in his voice that I turned to him with a bemused curiosity. I had never heard him use that tone before.

"Yes, she is," I answered. "Obviously, you appear to think so."

"I believe she's Jewish," Mordecai said without shifting his gaze, his voice now husky with emotion.

As soon as he said it, I knew it was true.

"*Believe?* Wouldn't such a thing be known for certain?"

And I remember the odd, bemused look Jesse gave me. "You have a short memory, my Hadassah. Like another girl who came here not so long ago, she is likely under what is now called an Esther Edict."

"*Esther Edict?*"

"Strict orders to keep her Jewishness to herself."

"Why would her family have given such an order now, of all times?"

"Today more than *ever*, my dear. Precisely *because* Jews are so powerful in today's palace. You are still very much known and spoken of. Mordecai is the Master of Audiences, the man closest to the King. I am the King's chamberlain, Master of the Harem, and have been ever since the day of Hegai's death. And there's the whole host of other Jewish friends and allies we've nurtured through the ranks of royal service through the years. My friend Nehemiah, the cupbearer, Chaim the royal procurer—"

"Yes, I know them all," I interrupted. "But why does Jewish power translate into a need for secrecy?"

"Because, as you should know better than anyone," Mordecai answered, "power breeds resentment. There lingers a great unspoken dislike of the Jews in the palace, and the empire as well—provoked probably by fear of our influence over the King. A candidate like her would be most wise to withhold the fact that she is of the Jewish race."

"Do you mean for us to do anything about this? Seek her out? Help her in some way?"

"Perhaps. But it must be done in the most covert manner possible. She cannot become publicly known as your favorite. But surely you would have deep counsel to give her about her upcoming training in preparation for her night with the king."

"I suppose . . ." I said absently, lost in my thoughts. And then it struck me. *This is it. This is how it starts.*

I returned to my apartment and quickly fell into the deepest and most restful sleep I had experienced in recent memory.

When I opened my eyes again, the edge of sunlight was creeping toward me along the ceiling. And something remarkable happened, something I find difficult to describe. For the briefest flash of time, the glow transported me to a different place. I began to see myself from above, through different eyes. I saw my own body curled up and realized that it resembled the same heartrending pose in which baby Artaxerxes had lain in that basket, the very first time I had laid eyes on him. As a result, I viewed my body through the gaze of a parent watching his or her newborn offspring. For just a moment, truly seeing myself, I loved this baby Hadassah with the strength of an actual mother or father. Infinite worth and beauty radiated from the figure below like waves of heat. I found I loved that person with an almost frightening power, for it was so unrelenting I would gladly have given my life to save this precious creature who was Hadassah.

And then I heard the very words Mordecai had spoken just two days earlier. Words concerning an agreement with G-d. A solemn vow with the Almighty, the Ancient of Days.

A fresh notion struck me with the brilliance and suddenness of sunlight. Could there actually be a meaningful life ahead for me? Crisis? Peril? Ultimate victory? A need for *me*? I had refused to consider it, but now I thought: *Why not?* Could something that great happen twice in a lifetime? Or if not as great, something close to it?

Strange: I had asked myself the same question that night on the hour of Xerxes' death, when I awoke beneath a sword. Twice in a lifetime—it's not likely, but it happens. With G-d, anything can happen.

An agreement. A solemn vow.

I thought back to my education at Mordecai's knee. The history of my people.

A covenant.

Was it arrogant of me to think that I could make my very own covenant with G-d? It did not feel like it when the thought had first come my way. It felt natural. Inevitable, even. It felt like a first step back to that dependence I had experienced on the day of going to the palace to meet my future husband. A dependence so childlike and complete that it reminded me of my need for my next breath, and was just as faithfully rewarded.

And then I remembered—at that moment, the covenant He had made with my people lay in shambles. Here I was, living thousands of miles from the Land of Milk and Honey, having never seen Jerusalem, to say nothing of the Temple harboring His presence. What knowledge I had of G-d's Word was merely history, taught to me as a child.

Did I even *want* to enter into a covenant with this kind of god? A deity who would let this sort of thing happen to His people?

Then, almost like a dialogue, a reply to that thought came to me in the form of a question. *Who left whom?* Didn't He warn Israel of the consequences if she continued to abandon Him and chase after foreign gods and the pleasures of sin? And didn't she ignore Him, time after time after time—as all humans are prone to do?

And wasn't Jerusalem waiting for us to come back? A sob choked in my throat at the thought of it—at the mental image Mordecai had nurtured within me, that of a pile of stones in some forgotten desert, its dusty air thick with the longing of a distant, far-flung people. Weren't G-d's promises lying unclaimed, simply waiting for us to return?

In another lightning flash, I thought I caught a moment of G-d's heart on the matter. A stabbing twinge of profound sadness and regret—not for himself but for us. For His children's foolish and fatal choices through the centuries. For our—my—endless ability to forget all He had done for us.

Was I crazy? What about the incredible deeds He had wrought on His people's behalf during my very own lifetime? Miracles brought to life through me. Did I have no memory? Was I incapable of recalling even my own life?

Suddenly the thought of my own covenant with Him seemed like a greater priority than anything else I could think of.

Without forethought, I spoke out loud. "O YHWH, if you show me the way to a meaningful rest of my days, I will follow it in your strength—no matter what."

And, Leah, I have never meant anything more in my whole life.

———————— ⌒ ————————

Chapter Forty-two

PRIME MINISTER'S RESIDENCE—LATE EVENING

"Hadassah? *Would you* put down that old manuscript for just a second and look at this?"

Even more urgently than the volume of his exclamation, there was something in Jacob's voice—a thin edge of shock and fear—that compelled her to break away from her reading. She laid down the document on the bedspread and looked into the face of their opposition party leader, oversized in the florid colors of their bedroom's plasmascreen television. Even with the monitor's exaggerated hues, his cheeks seemed flushed. The Prime Minister held out a remote control, jabbed his finger down, and the volume rose. The man onscreen was angry.

"After learning of these matters, it is now clear that Jacob ben Yuda is not fit to lead the government of Israel. In fact, the question we should be asking ourselves is whether he should be allowed to walk the streets in freedom—or be arrested at once. These disclosures are absolutely scandalous."

"What disclosures?" Hadassah asked her husband.

Without turning aside, he put his fingers to his lips in an urgent bid for silence.

The broadcast had cut to a correspondent standing before the London Embassy's gates.

". . . the First Lady's presence in London. According to confidential embassy sources, Mrs. ben Yuda flew into Luton on a secret military flight and was rushed to the Israeli Embassy under armed cover. There she met Mr. al-Khalid and an unnamed relative."

"Oh, brother," Hadassah muttered, "I am going to kill somebody."

Jacob made no acknowledgment.

"Now here's where the various reports differ," the correspondent continued. "One embassy official stated unequivocally that Mrs. ben Yuda greeted Mr. al-Khalid as an old relative, although other reports indicate that the meeting was hardly cordial. In any event, all sources agree that shortly after the encounter, doctors were summoned to the embassy complex to treat an elderly gentleman in severe cardiac distress."

Hadassah jumped at the slap of her husband's hand on the headboard behind her.

"I knew I shouldn't have done this," Jacob fumed.

"Preliminary research does seem to support these accounts, as bizarre as they seem. According to British municipal documents, Mr. al-Khalid was married in the 1950s to a Rivke Kesselman, which is, of course, the maiden name of First Lady ben Yuda."

Jacob's lips were pressed tightly together, and he held up the remote as if to turn the program off, but his political adversary reappeared, and the Prime Minister stood as if cast in stone.

"Tomorrow morning, I will introduce a motion before the Knesset for a vote of no-confidence against Mr. ben Yuda's leadership. I am certain we will have a new government by week's end. One who will level honestly with the Israeli people."

A desk anchor now joined the fray.

"And what does the Prime Minister or his wife say on the matter? Government spokesmen only say that the couple are both in transit and remain unavailable for comment."

"*Enough!!*"

A balled-up sock flew from Jacob's hand across the room to strike the politician's televised face head-on. The screen went blank with a small click of the remote in his other hand.

Hadassah turned to her husband with an anguished expression. "I'm so sorry, honey. I never imagined this all would come out—at least this way, or that your enemies would go to such lengths about it."

"I should have known," Jacob said with a somber shake of his head. "It's nothing new—things that should remain secret being leaked for political purposes. And I won't be the worst victim."

He glanced at her, then looked down to the floor, his face reddening, jaw muscles clenching, and pounded his fist into his palm. "But it's our people back in Iraq who will pay the price. Complete innocents. Women and children." He sighed heavily, the entire burden for their fate clearly at his door.

The telephone on the night table beside him startled them both. He picked it up and made a small grunt in lieu of a greeting, then several more as he attempted to break in to the conversation.

"I know this is going to sound strange to you," he said at last, "but the most important security goal of this nation is to find an ancient scroll proving that the Mordecai of the *Tanach* married and fathered a son of the bloodline of David—three-thousand-some-odd years ago. Now, I don't care whether you're a cabinet secretary or a military general or dogcatcher, I need sleuths right now. I need literary and historical detectives. Unless we find, translate, and disseminate such a document today, dozens of our people will be murdered, the leadership of Iraq will likely be toppled, and our hopes for peace will be in shambles. Do you understand?"

He hung up the receiver with a bang and sat down heavily on the edge of the bed.

"We're in trouble, big trouble," he muttered, his voice muffled by his cupped hands over his mouth. "No one is willing to believe the truth. The truth is just too bizarre. Too unbelievable."

"What can I do?" Hadassah asked in a small voice.

"Well, first of all, I need you to take a break from that old journal and get your mind in the twenty-first century." His tone fell just short of sarcastic.

Hadassah breathed in deeply, attempting to quench her irritation, for she knew that the frustration behind it was richly justified.

"Jacob," she replied, "those old journals may not have contained the exact data we were looking for, but"—she exhaled carefully now, anxious to avoid the tears she could feel behind her eyes—"they've helped me. She may have lived three thousand years ago, but there's something uncanny about how closely her problems match everything I've been living through lately. Her plight, her words—they've been like a close friend I wish I had in real life. Like a sympathetic shoulder that can relate to every single one of my emotions. If nothing more, that has been her contribution to this crisis. She's rescued *me*."

Jacob reached across the bedspread and took Hadassah's hand into his own. The calm on his face made it clear that his anger had been soothed by his wife's poignant response.

"I'm sorry, my love," he said almost inaudibly. "I'm so sorry I haven't been wiser. Better able to . . . respond to you. I just haven't known how."

She smiled crookedly and squeezed his hand. "It's all right, Jacob. Sometimes a woman just needs another woman friend. And it seems like G-d sent me a kindred heart from across the centuries."

He glanced quickly at her for the first time in the conversation, looking surprised. They both knew he had never heard her mention G-d in such a positive way before.

"That's great. It really is, Hadassah. It's just that as a man, I tend to want hard-nosed solutions. So I wish He," he said, pointing heavenward, "would also send us more of the story, along with the outcome we need. Because I'm in trouble, as of tonight. Real trouble."

Jacob kissed her on the forehead and left the room for his traditional nightly document review in an adjacent office. As she picked up once more the now-infamous document, Hadassah forced a chuckle.

"Join the club. Ancient Esther and I are both at the lowest point in our lives. But I suspect she may be about to point the way for the two of us. . . ."

———————— ⚯ ————————

And so, my dear Leah, you ask—what happened? Did I receive a reply? How long did it take?

The first thing I experienced was a small awakening within. I find it hard to describe, especially without resorting to overly familiar and sentimental words. But a small nugget—I suppose of hope—somehow took shape deep within me. It started to grow, slowly and gradually. It was not much, yet it was everything—to know that it was even remotely possible for something great and good to lie in wait for me again.

Nor did this future's precise form come to me immediately, as some finished work. In fact, my writing to you is a large part of its culmination.

I suppose I look at its unfolding as a tapestry, woven of threads that curled my way one at a time.

The first thread arrived less than a week later in the form of a faint sound, carried on the wind.

That morning I awoke with a strong desire to venture out into the gardens as I had once done, and spend some time in prayer. Even the wish came to me as a blessing, for I had not even mustered the vigor to attempt this until that day. And so I took one of my finest woven tunics, wrapped it around my clothes, and walked out, playfully pretending to sneak as I had done so many years before—even though the need for secrecy was now long past. I breathed in deeply of fresh, cool wind, closed my eyes in bliss, and smiled into the dawn.

Then I looked around. It was that tender hour before the sun appears, when it has merely announced its coming through a deep reddish glow upon the mountains and a general lightening of the air. Its breeze bore the slightest hint of the coming autumn's chill.

And it bore something else, so faint that it took my ears several moments to even apprehend.

The gentle sound of sobbing.

Now is the time to sneak for real, I told myself. Knowing the palace grounds as well as I do, I realized that the noise had carried from somewhere near the Eastern Gate. With a knowing smile I remembered that this was the same place I had sneaked to on my first morning as a concubine to try and see Mordecai for what I had thought would be the final time.

I lightened my step and took care to tread silently upon the gardens' carpet of brittle leaves, marble squares, and earth. *Walk like a spy,* I reminded myself, grinning wryly at my old admonition. Gradually I approached, using the trunks of the lemon trees to shield my silhouette. Peering around the last one, I focused my gaze and finally caught sight of the one in tears.

She was no longer wearing an elegant wrap, but from the shining dark hair and lean figure I recognized the girl Jesse had pointed out to me. The one we had believed to be Jewish. And now from the bobbing torso, I knew it was true. The girl may have been weeping quietly, but it was also clear that she was at prayer. Stray syllables even revealed themselves as familiar strains of the *Midrash* Mordecai had taught me over the years.

A deep strain of emotion overtook me as I stood there, watching her from my hidden location. Clearly, I could identify with what had likely provoked those tears—homesickness, fear, resignation, resentment. But the sound struck me as something even more profound. As I stood there at a safe distance, you—for of course it was you, Leah—you seemed to embody the sadness and vulnerability of my lost people—along with the strange arms'-length relationship I had experienced with them for so many years.

Just then I was torn by two opposite compulsions. The first was to reach out and do my best to comfort you right away, in the very throes of your sorrow. And second, to respect the intimacy of your pain and spare you the embarrassment of being introduced to a strange, forbidding acquaintance at the moment of your anguish.

So I retreated, taking even more care to remain silent. I spent some quiet moments with G-d in an opposite corner of the orchards, praying for guidance and favor.

And then I began to take action.

I began by making myself known to you—whose name I soon learned was Leah, and who was most definitely Jewish—in the best way I knew possible: a letter. Or should I say, a missive. I intended for it to be a short introduction. But as you well know, I could not stop myself from writing. Perhaps I had nothing better to do, but, in any event, the words seem to gush out of me.

For the next weeks and months I threw myself into the writing of that long and impassioned document in which I described to you my life and my experience as a young concubine in the harem. In the most helpful words I could find, I took all I had learned from Mordecai, from Hegai, and most of all from G-d himself, about how best to win the favor of the King. I included the most intimate details of how I prepared my heart and soul to offer my whole being as a beautiful gift—first to G-d, and then to the King. To love Xerxes as no other woman had even thought to do. More than anything, however, it was an instruction manual in how best to become prepared for your one night with the King.

I also felt compelled to detail for you the events that now compose the Feast of Purim—the attempted elimination of our people from the face of the earth. As you must have heard the story from childhood, I did not do so merely to repeat the facts but to make them come alive. And perhaps alert you to the fact that you, too, might someday find yourself in the position of doing something heroic and vital for your people.

And do you know something? I believe the process of telling my tale enriched my own life every bit as much as it did yours.

And then came the night we became friends—the shattering event that brought us together.

It started as I sat beside the pool, reading over my words and contemplating these thoughts, and something odd on the horizon caught my attention.

A thin trail of pale smoke wandered high into the blue sky from the royal palace's highest point—the gleaming golden dome that housed the King's own living quarters. I strained my memory to recall any reason why a celebratory bonfire or ceremonial pyre would have caused smoke to rise from that spot. I could think of none.

I stood straight and took a few absurd, awkward steps—as though being a few cubits closer would have made such a distant sight any clearer. My gaze stayed so riveted and my posture so frozen that before long the young concubines around me began to stare as well. I think you must have joined them around that time. Within a minute, the air was filled with gasps and exclamations. By then the thin trail had become a thick, dark column. A bright red flame shot into the air, wrenching a single cry from our assembled group. Clumps of soldiers and royal aides were now running toward the first of the enormous courtyard gates. From where I stood I could see the fear in their eyes.

I stumbled into an abortive run but immediately felt Jesse's hands and torso block my way.

"Hadassah, you must stay here," he commanded. "You would not get within a *stadium* of the palace, and even then you would succeed only in imperiling your own person."

"But Mordecai is in there!" I cried. "I have to make certain he is safe!"

"I'll have someone go to the palace and learn of him. But you must stay here or we will have two of you in mortal danger. Please. Stay and pray."

He forcibly turned me around and faced me back toward the harem spectators. Reluctantly I walked back and took my place among them.

Strange—it felt as though my very life was going up in smoke. The familiar shape of those ramparts, those giant statues, those dizzying towers and mountainous columns, seemed to embody my whole adult existence. I found it even more ironic that while I had recently felt I was dying inside, now even the *outward* manifestations of my life were being wrenched away from me. Not to mention that they likely housed the person who meant so much to me, my Poppa, *Mordecai* . . .

I hardly moved twenty cubits the entire night, for the very worst outcome imaginable came to pass. The entire royal palace burned. I alternately sat and stood with the group, and Jesse came by for a few moments at a time while he wasn't ferrying refugees from the palace into spare harem quarters.

In spite of its inherent tragedy, and my growing panic over Mordecai's fate, the fire proved the most spectacular display I have ever witnessed. Flames the size of houses tossed huge glowing tongues of yellow and red, cascading sparks into the darkness. In the later hours, collapsing palace walls added their own eruptions of coals and cinders while against their radiant afterglow, tiny silhouettes could be seen scurrying about, apparently dragging out bodies and piles of precious objects. At times it seemed a war was being waged, for column after column of wide-eyed soldiers seemed to pour across the terrace from Susa and parts beyond, to disappear into the inner courtyards. I could not tell if they were there to wage some form of battle, restore civil order, or simply to assist the helpers. . . .

Chapter Forty-three

In the long hours following the fire, rumor after rumor swept through our ranks of spectators. Had the King been overthrown? Had some form of judgment of the gods befallen the empire? One odd whisper had it that Artaxerxes had gathered all those he suspected of conspiring against him—the Princes of the Face, the highest palace echelons—into one great banquet hall, locked the doors, and set the place aflame. As you might imagine, that particular report multiplied my panic about my beloved Mordecai.

If that terrifying night held any solace for me, it was that it afforded my first opportunity to meet you. Without fanfare I slipped beside you in the line of spectators, smiled, and we exchanged some of the oft-repeated phrases about the appalling crisis. Before too long I had introduced myself, and in the process confirmed our suspicion about the Esther Edict. When I told you my name was Hadassah, I remember your eyes widening and your saying in an awestruck voice, "You mean Queen *Esther*?"

Your gaze quickly fell, and I am sure you realized you had just betrayed yourself in recognizing my Hebrew name.

"So it's true—you've been placed under an edict. An edict named after me?" I encouraged you.

I'll never forget how you looked deeply into my eyes, even as you nodded, then burst into tears.

"Please do not think me a coward, Your Highness . . ."

"Call me Hadassah, please, my dear. Just Hadassah. No one but fellow Jews know of my maiden name. And few outside the court know I retook it when His Majesty was killed."

"Oh, Hadassah, you don't know what a relief it is to speak freely with someone about who I really am! I have felt like such a prisoner. As if my life was over. The day those soldiers brought me through the Royal Gate, I felt something wither inside me. And I told G-d, *Just take my soul, for I am dead from this day onward. My life is over, even if my body continues to mimic the pretenses of life.*"

"You know, Leah," I answered, "I have endured many days of emotions just like those. Some of them, as a Jewess, you already know about—the near extinction of our people at the hands of Haman, an enemy of our people who somehow acquired authority with my husband."

"Of course, your High—I mean, Hadassah . . ." she responded.

"But I've suffered through other occasions to feel that my life was over," I continued. "I know the emotion even now. The overwhelming certainty that everything is over for me. That the end has come. That things could not grow worse, and they will not recover. But do you know something? *It was never true and isn't even now.* As much as my inner tendencies prod me to believe otherwise, no state of affairs ever turns out to be as permanent as it feels at the time. Every time I thought my life had ended, G-d intervened—and it turned out to be just a beginning."

"Surely none of them rivaled the Haman crisis, which became a turning point in history," you noted quietly.

"Oh yes, they did," I answered. "For instance, did you know that my parents were murdered when I was just a child? It is the reason I was raised by my cousin Mordecai. And I thought my life had ended even then. Though I was too young to articulate it at the time, being adopted by an older cousin I hardly knew seemed to be just an aftermath—the beginning of my life's slow decline. It hardly seemed like the start of anything meaningful. Yet it was."

I remember that this recollection triggered another sad response in you. You lowered your face into your arms and sobbed, whispering of your parents, "Perhaps my father is the reason I consider myself dead," you confessed to me. "He tore his clothing and went into mourning when I was taken. And maybe he's right. Maybe I ceased being a human being when I entered the harem to become a royal plaything." You lowered your head, and I could barely hear your last words.

"You know, when I also was taken by force and removed to the palace harem," I said, lifting your face to mine, "I knew beyond a doubt that my life was over. After all, I had been stolen away from everything I knew, just at the dawn of my womanhood, to a life of depravity and luxurious imprisonment. I would never leave those walls. I would never know real love or fulfillment. I would be forever a disgrace to my people. *And, how wrong I was!*"

"Yes. It was the beginning of your journey to queenhood," you replied, looking a bit dreamy, I thought.

"But even when I became Queen, I assumed *that* was the culmination, although hardly an unfortunate one. It still seemed like nothing more could happen to possibly top that wondrous event. After all, I was Queen of the largest, most powerful empire in the world! Even better, the King was truly, genuinely in love with me. What more could a woman ask for?"

"Saving her people from extermination," you replied softly, thoughtfully. And that was when I knew you were indeed a remarkable, insightful young woman. And I knew—if I had any uncertainties before—the long missive I had been working on would indeed come into your possession when I had completed it.

"And you know what?" I asked you. "Here I am watching this ornate, overdone palace burn to pieces, once again feeling sorry for myself. Defying G-d to add another episode to my life! When will I learn? My only true concern right now, Leah, is about Mordecai. . . ."

At some time in the early morning, when you had fallen asleep and some fellow bystanders and I had fallen into a sort of numb stupor, I saw the figure of a good friend approaching, one of the many worthy, G-d-fearing young Jewish men Mordecai had sponsored into positions of influence throughout the palace. Nehemiah had already risen to royal cupbearer—a position far more exalted and close to the King than its mere title might suggest.

"Mordecai is safe," he said breathlessly. "Although he is very frightened and his body was badly taxed in his escape. He asked me to come give you news of his condition."

I embraced him out of sheer gratitude, found a place to recline outdoors, and promptly fell into a deep slumber. I felt safe surrounded by palace guards who, despite my demotion, watched over their former Queen with some respect and loyalty.

Soon afterward I awoke in a pile of cushions, with the glare of morning light beating down. I opened my eyes, coughed at the smoke in the air, stood, and then nearly fell again.

Our old horizon had been transformed. The stone outline that had for years framed my every morning sun was gone, leaving a void of almost palpable emptiness. In place of the palace's formidable profile lay a jagged, ungainly pile of rubble and a lingering mist of light brown smoke. The once-grand terraces that had framed it now lay cluttered with charred piles and rubbish.

Mordecai stumbled up to me an hour later, through a scattering of onlookers and rescued furnishings. He looked ragged, aged, and devastated. We fell into each other's arms.

"Oh, my sweetheart," he said, "it is so dreadful. Not only is it destroyed, but there are . . . dozens, hundreds dead."

"Artaxerxes?"

"He is well. Amestris and the royal family all survived. Most of the highest ranking got out alive."

"Where will they all go?"

"There are other palaces, you know. Susa will be rebuilt, but for now there is always Persepolis, Ecbatana, Pâthragâda. The empire will continue, even in a rather precarious state."

"But there are so many rumors, Poppa," I said, falling into my familiar habit of speaking to him like a young girl.

"Yes, and the worst one is that a Jew started the fire. That one of us began some sort of religious ceremony with festival candles in the living quarters, and one of them caught a drape aflame."

"But there are no Jews living in the royal living quarters. At least not since I left . . ."

Mordecai fixed me with the doleful stare that always warns me I'm being a bit dense, ignoring an important conclusion.

"Are you," I started, unwilling to even phrase the words, "are you saying that the rumor blames *me*?"

"Most Persians aren't aware that you've moved from the palace."

"Oh, my goodness!" It was inane, but it was the only statement I could think to voice my consternation. I took two steps backward and covered my mouth.

"It seems our own success has now grown to endanger us," Mordecai continued. "Many noble Persian households now resent the influence we've acquired. They consider Jews suspicious foreigners who've somehow developed a mysterious hold over their royal family."

"What am I going to do? What are *we* going to do?"

His eyes closed and he shook his head solemnly.

"I think you need to leave, Hadassah," he said, his voice low. "Not forever, but for several months—a year perhaps. Just to get you out of the palace."

"Are you joking with me? I'm not going anywhere!"

"I fear you must."

"You? How about *we*? Why wouldn't you come with me, if the danger is so dire?"

"For several reasons. One of them is another piece of news I haven't had time to tell you. You see, earlier yesterday, I received a visit from Ezra."

"A visit from the priest? What difference—?"

"Don't be impertinent, my dear," he interrupted. "You know that the priest of Babylon is also the head of the Exile. The Exilarch. Next Shabbat, Ezra will inform the synagogues of Babylon and Susa that he has named a new Exilarch. He has passed the title on to *me*."

I forgot all of my palace etiquette and royal decorum as my mouth dropped. "What? Why would he do such a thing?"

"Do you remember when I told you last month that our priest Ezra had made a special petition to the King?"

"Yes. Something about offering to beautify the Temple in Jerusalem."

"That's right. Well, two nights ago, the King ruled on Ezra's offer.

He accepted it! Ezra is leaving with fifteen hundred of our best men as soon as he can gather them."

"I was certain Artaxerxes would laugh Ezra out of the palace!"

"So was I. But I schemed, shall we say, with Nehemiah to smooth the way politically, as best I could. For instance, there is a prophet out there named Malachi, who persists in openly calling for rebellion against the King. Ezra, on the other hand, opposes him. Ezra believes in the Jewish people faithfully serving wherever we find ourselves. So it serves the King's interest to give Ezra the upper hand."

I threw my arms around him. "Oh, Mordecai. You have received such an honor! You'll bring such prestige and power to the office. It is a great day for our people."

"Well, not in the eyes of the rabbis. They will say I cannot lead our people because I am not of the line of David."

"But you are the Prime Minister of the Empire!"

"Not for long, if the sentiment against our people does not subside." Mordecai grabbed my hands in a show of sincerity. "Now, my dear, you know why I cannot leave with you."

"I'm not going anywhere, Poppa. I didn't escape when Haman tried to kill us all, and I won't now. It would be running away exactly when my people need me most!"

He smiled.

"Not if the place you run away to is Jerusalem."

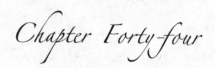

Chapter Forty-four

So twenty years after I first talked of a runaway pilgrimage with my beloved Jesse, my dream of returning to the land of my people was actually coming true! The thought of seeing Jerusalem blended a chill of reality with quivers of warm delight.

And yet I found the prospect bittersweet. I would be leaving behind so many people I greatly loved! Including, of course, my new friend—you, Leah. I was so glad I was able to leave the document with you—it would be some link, however tenuous, between us during the long time apart.

As you know, we said our tearful good-byes right outside the palace gates. I remember your arms around my neck, and wondering if either of us would ever let go. Then, weeping like a child, I glanced back from my horse to see you waving there, alongside Jesse in the shadow of the very gryphon statue where he and I had shared that first kiss!

It felt as though I was leaving my entire life behind. If Mordecai had not been beside me for that first leg of the trip, I am not sure I would have been able to follow through.

Mordecai escorted me as far as Babylon, outside which the travelers actually planned to assemble. So for the first time since he had rushed me out of the city of my birth as a traumatized youngster, painful wounds from my family's terrible attack and murder still under poultices, we now returned to our home city.

I harbored a few details that my battered memory had not banished from my mind, but when we passed under the Ishtar Gate, I looked up and felt a shudder of vague recognition wrack my body. I reached over in the seat of the carriage, which Mordecai had arranged for the trip, and grasped him tightly, overcome by a sudden paralyzing terror. I begged him not to take me into the area where our house had stood, and of course he emphatically agreed. Even as we left the gate behind and proceeded through the city's main thoroughfare, my mind's eye continued to hurl flashes of horror back into my consciousness. I clung to Poppa until we were safely past Babylon's far wall.

And yet now, with the fear behind me, I find a curious solace in the experience. In a way, despite the unpleasant emotions it unearthed, returning to my birthplace was the perfect way to begin this expedition. It was almost as though the impending voyage was a rebirth of sorts, a new beginning and renewal of my life.

G-d's hand seemed strong on our undertaking from that very first day we crested the banks of the Ahava Canal, on Babylon's far side, and gazed down on the sprawling crowd of people, vehicles, and animals gathered for the trip. I am not sure what I had expected, but the sight of such a large throng caught my breath. The whole enterprise had seemed like a half-baked affair to me until then.

When we approached the leader's circle, we found a caravan already in some disarray. As we drove up, Ezra, a lean, red-bearded man likely in his late thirties, came running over alongside our carriage.

"Master Mordecai!" he exclaimed, using the title when Poppa had been a palace scribe years before. Then, catching sight of me, he bowed respectfully. "Your Highness, welcome to our humble caravan."

We climbed out of the carriage, and Ezra stepped in close to Mordecai.

"We have encountered our first challenge, even within sight of Babylon, I fear," Ezra admitted. "We were close to embarking when I conducted a count of our people and discovered that there were no Levites at all among us."

This also surprised Mordecai. "Do you not intend to offer sacrifices in the Temple when you arrive?"

"Exactly, Master. This is why I have sent eleven of our men to Iddo in an attempt to correct this imbalance. Until they return, I must beg your indulgence. We will not be going anywhere until they return."

Mordecai fixed him with an appraising look. "And I am glad to hear it, my friend. I will remain here with Hadassah until you do."

Emotionally as taut as a bowstring in face of our departure, I was not as accepting when I heard that we would have to wait, camping here among smelly pack animals and turgid canal waters, with no knowledge of when we would leave.

But I did not have long to wait. On our very first morning, after a surprisingly restful night's sleep (for the trip from Susa had exhausted me), I awoke to Mordecai poking me in the ribs, as he had so frequently done to roust me from bed during my indolent teenage years.

"Come here! Look!" he said, pointing behind him, to the outside.

I scrambled out and followed the gazes of countless fellow bleary-eyed risers. There on the bank came a crowd of men. More than two hundred fifty, if I recall the count. All of them were either Levites or Temple servants—exactly the number David had once established as necessary to assist in the Temple worship.

Convinced that we would leave then, I promptly broke down our tent for an impending departure.

I definitely did not yet know Ezra. Soon his voice could be heard shouting over the noises of hurried preparations, asking everyone to gather before him once more. Mordecai and I walked back to the encampment's center.

"My friends, I proclaim a three-day fast," he called, "that we might humble ourselves before G-d and ask Him for a safe journey through perilous climes. I have been ashamed to ask the King for soldiers and horsemen to accompany us, although he is quite willing, for we have told him, 'the gracious hand of G-d is upon everyone who looks to him, but his great anger is against all who forsake him.' So let us cast our safety instead upon His mercy."

I glanced downward and exhaled impatiently. But Mordecai caught my eye and shook his head.

"This is a man who knows where his strengths lie," he whispered. "Heed his instincts and honor his commands, my dear. There is enormous earthly treasure among these people, intended for the Temple. But its existence places you all at risk. Listen to Ezra. I am convinced that G-d will honor his careful intercession."

And, of course, Mordecai was right.

The three days we spent in quiet prayer and meditation were among the most "magical"—if I may use that word in its most innocent sense—and healing, of my whole life. It was then, walking with my Poppa or by myself along the tranquil waters, that the absolute magnitude of the coming enterprise unfurled itself in all its majesty and historic proportions.

And now, even though I had no king upon which to cast my intentions, I began to recall the lessons of my "One Night" preparations. I prayed more intensely and earnestly than I had in many years, not as much for safety or success as for a clear understanding of the Covenant between our G-d and us. And I can honestly tell you that He answered, as He always does such prayers. He came alongside me and made himself my companion. Soon I found myself turning around and pausing at odd times, like someone with that strange sensation of being secretly watched.

It was as if I sensed the presence of the Almighty, abiding with me. I had felt the same awesome thrill years before while I prepared for my night with the King.

Finally the day of departure came. Mordecai helped me pack, a welcome diversion that allowed me to focus on a physical task rather than the pain of leaving him. Yet at last even that chore was accomplished, and I stood beside the camel he had chosen to carry me across the wilderness. I walked up to this man I love so much and saw his features twist with emotions that I had not seen since being carried off by Xerxes' soldiers on a Susa street.

I climbed onto the camel, hung on as it rose, and heard a cry from just up ahead. It was time to move. At once I was seized with an impulse to jump down and bury myself in Mordecai's arms.

Thankfully, the urge dissipated just as quickly. But I continued to weep and wave at Mordecai's dwindling figure, even as the camel stepped into the Ahava River's swirling waters and the unknown ahead rose to embrace my senses.

I must tell you—I have had few emotions more stirring than during those first few cubits of forward movement away from all I had known, toward my heritage, my past, and my literal future. I remember every aspect: the smell of the Ahava's mud as we treaded across, the fishy aroma of the water currents, the impatient whinnies of the horses, the cries of the children, the latent harshness of the sun just beginning to climb in the sky.

Yet most of all, what I remember was a familiar return of that sensation I had felt only once before: the feeling of being at the center of G-d's will for me, last truly felt on the day of my being escorted to the King's bedroom.

If there is one overarching observation I can make about the whole of our journey, it is that our world is so much more vast and forbidding and awesome than I had ever imagined. Remember, of course, that I am essentially a citizen of Susa, with only a residual memory of Babylon until now, mixed in with the occasional royal excursion to other palaces. My understanding of the Persian Empire was quite limited, and probably still is, in spite of its declining borders.

Soon we drew alongside the mighty Euphrates, swollen with its spring floods, and began to follow the familiar surface of the Royal Road, which would lead us over halfway home—I was surprised at how quickly I began to think of it as such—through the old Assyrian Empire to the edges of Asia Minor, before turning south onto the King's Road into the onetime Kingdom of David, where . . .

ROOFTOP OF THE PRIME MINISTER'S OFFICE, JERUSALEM

With a roar, the Prime Minister's landing pad plunged away beneath the plexiglass window and tilted sharply as the helicopter rocketed upward, blending into Jerusalem's patchwork of roads and roofs and treetops. The Old City's sand-colored maze sprawled into view—a ray of sunlight glinted off the Dome of the Rock and assaulted Hadassah's eyes, causing her to squint and turn away. Through the opposite window, the Israeli landmass had already blended into a gray sheet fringed by a mirrored strip of ocean.

It was Friday—Jacob and Hadassah couldn't wait to leave the capital's stresses for two days in the privacy of their family's weekend retreat in Eilat, a desert resort crowning the Red Sea tip of the Negev Desert.

When Jerusalem had faded from view, Jacob reached over to her helmet and touched four on her channel selector. Shin Beth had designed their headphones with scrambled and encrypted frequencies, accessible only to each other.

"I've been angry with you, Hadassah" came his voice.

"I'm aware of that."

"*Very* angry."

"Were you trying to hide this, honey?" She had noted his use of the past tense and decided that the door was open for a hint of levity. "Because if you were—if that was your best effort at hiding it—you'd be better off avoiding a career in anything requiring discretion and a poker face. Like politics."

He looked down and laughed abruptly, as if her quip was a welcome respite from the subject at hand.

"You're right," he said. "And if the whole affair proceeds the way it seems headed, your recommendation may come true. Politics may be the last option available to me."

"They wouldn't do that," she declared.

"Thank you, honey. But tell that to the head of the Labor Party. And the Israeli Supreme Court. And the editor of the *Post*. They're calling for my head. In case you haven't seen the news, half my cabinet submitted their resignations to me this morning. My poll numbers have dropped by half since before the attack. To make things worse, this whole scandal is undermining the peace talks in a major way. Falani has suddenly gotten a swagger in his step and a stiffer backbone, thanks to my problems. And that's not even the worst part of all."

"You're not through—?"

"My own party is turning against me," Jacob said, shaking his head. "It's not enough the other side has their knives sharpened, but my own colleagues are starting to read the tea leaves. I walked into a meeting expecting to forge a game plan to fight back, and I was asked to consider resigning. I'm on my own. On my own, sweetheart."

"No, you're not." She jerked off her headphones, then pried his off and cradled his face in her hands. "You're not alone," she said, exaggerating her diction to make herself understood. "You have me. And I think maybe you—we—have G-d."

He looked at her, and in that moment she saw an expression she had only seen him wear once before. The tiny muscles around his eyes began to constrict rhythmically. He twisted his lips into an unnatural line. His eyebrows flexed unusually close. He breathed in and gazed above her head.

"I need you, Hadassah. I'm probably still angry with you, but I can't, I won't, make it through this without you. And G-d . . ."

She rested her head against his chest. She felt no need to look up into his eyes and establish that they were filled with tears. He was a man and did not need to be reminded of his vulnerability at that moment. *Let him keep his dignity*, she thought, making sure he knew she was looking away.

"I know," she said softly, unaware whether or not she was being heard.

She was.

Chapter Forty-five

―――――――――――― ⌇ ――――――――――――

. . . There certainly was monotony on this journey back to the Jewish homeland—perched high atop a camel for the better part of every day with nothing but riverbank and sandstone bluffs for a view—but was there terror? Occasionally—such as when my camel stumbled in sand pockets a few times and nearly pitched me forward, or when bristling silhouettes on the horizon seemed to betray the watching eyes of marauding bandits. But truly, the Lord was with us. A sense of destiny, of eternal purpose, seemed to flow through my veins and animate every motion I made. Every breath seemed to fill my lungs with a fresh tide of hope.

Nor can I describe to you the liberating experience of those desert nights. They seemed almost like a reward for the day's privations. Fires waved in the cool breeze and crackled under the slow roasting of aromatic meats. Songs from long ago carried lustily through the night air, and old stories of our homeland were recited again and again. Better still, there reigned such a warm spirit of love and family, even of blissful optimism, among those traveling. It felt as if a large, extended family had been forced apart for a long period and finally reunited at last. Even the sleeping was often a thrill, as I would occasionally forego the sturdy canopy with which Mordecai had equipped me, to retire under the dazzling carpet of desert stars. With naught but a blanket or two and the softness of sand beneath me, I could feel the cool night winds tug at my hair. I am certain that a year or so fell from me within every passing night.

But do you know whom I thought of during those days of reawakening? Oh, the hour is late as I write this, and I fear my courage to say it will wane if I wait longer.

I thought of my dear Jesse.

I thought of how it felt for me to leave Mordecai's roof for the first time, to follow Jesse through the incredible sights and sounds and smells of that market outside the Royal Gate, to climb upon the gryphon statue and see him smile that engaging grin of his and feel the love of another person in a way I had never even imagined, let alone experienced.

Perhaps it all came back so vividly because of how strictly my life had been structured since that first adventure with him. But I also relived the terror that engulfed not only my heart but his dear grandmother Rachel's and Mordecai's when we realized Jesse had been one of those taken to the palace by the royal guards. And the horrible helplessness of learning exactly what would be done to him there. Being propelled back onto the streets by the despair and rage and defiance that seemed to fill my legs and force them to take me back to that royal gate, to the shadow of that now-empty gryphon.

I realized under the desert stars that I still love him. Yes, I gave myself to another man and deeply loved him after Jesse, but the deepest part of me never stopped loving that boy of my youth.

It is true that you never forget your first love—or your last.

I've thought about it. Oh, I spent so many hours of that journey thinking, trying to understand why the deepest gnawing of my stomach was my missing him above all else. I tried to fit my feelings for him into some kind of context, some framework that made sense to me and somehow fit with all that was to follow. After all, I have been a queen. I kindled and then spent a great passion upon a man who loved me in return, so much so that history was made in the process. Where does that leave Jesse—a cherished memory of my youth? What room does that leave for the untouched inner shrine where I had carefully hidden away my love all these years? Does G-d honor, let alone bless, long-delayed rebirths of love?

Then I realized: Jerusalem awaited me at the end of this exhausting though thrilling journey, patiently waiting for centuries as a pathetic and derided ruin, just as the embers of my love had waited, dim indeed compared to the glow of my grand royal marriage . . . but waiting. Oh, so patiently . . .

How agonizing it must have been for Jesse to see me muster my deepest youthful love and offer it so freely to a man whom, I know now, so humanly betrayed me. It must have eaten Jesse alive, for he had tasted the first flowering of that capacity for love before anyone else. And yet he not only endured it, but loyally and faithfully stood by me the whole time.

I had never thought of it in those terms. But in those silent moments in the desert—the long and plodding afternoons and peaceful, lonely evenings—I realized it all in a whole new way.

Yes, I believe G-d honors the dormant loves of nearly forgotten passions, for we have nearly forgotten Him more often than we can possibly confess. And yet no one welcomes us back into His arms with more unsullied, unreserved joy than He.

No, Jesse and I cannot enjoy the kind of physical union I had with Xerxes, not since Persia stole his manhood from him and changed his name from a proud Jewish one to that of a palace servant, Hathach. But that's one of the most remarkable things about the time I spend with him—I feel wrapped and warmed by Jesse's pure, unselfish affection every time I see him, even without physical touch. A flame still lights in his eyes every time he sees me. And his love and regard for me seem to glow from every word he says to me, with that smile on his face.

Therefore, this realization did not make me long to turn around right away and run back to leap into his arms—an act that might have caused us both great injury at this point in our lives! But it did make me realize that I am incomplete without him. And that even though a great purpose lay at hand in this return to Jerusalem, I would come back. I know it in my bones, now as I write. I will return.

So now, you ask, did my life-changing rediscovery of Jerusalem cause me to forget these thoughts? Did it confirm them? Alter them? Destroy them?

Let me tell you, my dear, for you will be amazed.

It was late in the morning of our forty-fourth day when we reached the outer approaches to Jerusalem. An early fog had cleared away under a warming wind and the sun brought out a dry smell of sap and pine. The bare hills grew steeper and began to sport outcroppings of crumbled limestone, crowned with tufts of olive, myrtle, and cypress trees. I could tell we had climbed and our environment had changed.

At first, our only signs of approaching the city were increased indications of population. The road grew wider and more deeply worn. We passed a small flock of sheep tended by a boy whose Jewish features sent a thrill down my spine. An old spice vendor leading a donkey passed us on the trail and gave our escorts such a frightened glance that it seemed he might turn and run for his life. I smiled at two young women gracefully balancing amphoras of water atop their heads.

We had been traveling long enough for me to recognize the signs of an approaching city, and my heart began to race. I wish I could tell you all the emotions that charged through my being. The truth is, I can hardly remember them all myself. I recall only a few: eagerness, trepidation, awe, and not a small measure of fear.

Then, almost before we could prepare our hearts for the sight, we crested a hilltop of sorts and looked across a broad, grassy valley. At first, I did not even know what I was looking at, so inauspicious was the sight. My eyes settled on a grove of trees, and a faint trail cutting diagonally across a path of bare earth several hundred cubits away.

And then I heard a murmur from one of the men.

"There it is. Jerusalem."

I squinted and peered forward.

All I could see, ringing the top of the hillside, was a pile of stones I had taken for mere outcroppings. Now, staring closely, I could see that some of them bore the sharp angles and smooth façades of masonry. Yet it was a ruin. A desolate hulk like a hundred we had passed along the journey here.

I looked ahead to Ezra's figure for support and direction. But he was staring also, looking as though someone had struck his head broadside.

I think I heard a moan wrench from my lungs before I voiced any other reaction. Had I been on my feet, I know I would have fallen to my knees—not out of awe or adoration but the impact of shock upon my body.

I remember reaching up and covering my eyes and feeling tears trickle through my fingers.

Chapter Forty-six

I am so relieved that Mordecai was not there to see this with me. *Oh, Leah—the shame, the disgrace, of our beloved home!* At that moment my mind raced back to all the hours he had once spent telling me of Jerusalem, his eyes shining with pride, voice bursting with joy and mirth, as he assured me that we were more than dispossessed exiles in an indifferent kingdom. We were the Chosen People, and one of the grandest outward proofs was the Temple of the very Creator himself, nestled amidst the most beautiful and ancient city on earth.

Even as a girl, I remember knowing from his very countenance that this was no fairy tale. It was so unlike all the other stories he had ever told me. I could be proud to be a Hebrew, I walked away reminding myself. I had a homeland, a capital city just waiting for me and my fellow Jews to return someday.

It was G-d's will.

Oh, Mordecai! I lamented. *Where was G-d?* I cried the moment I laid eyes on the hulk of His supposed city. Surely He had no abode amidst the carelessly tossed rocks and ruined battlements of this insulting mass. And yet I knew that a rebuilt temple had arisen some-where inside that clutter.

I felt as though every shred of pride had been ripped from me and tossed into the dust and dirt at my feet. For an awful moment I was a vagabond, a mere pawn, a human rolling die to be tossed onto the ground for sport.

My camel lurched as our band continued forward, but I hardly felt the motion, for now I was weeping openly, unable to stifle my sobs. We descended into the valley, then traversed the trail I had observed earlier, and emerged on the southern flank of a thin, rock-strewn strip once known as the Outer Wall.

But here is the part I am most eager to share with you. Again, I know I have told you some of this since my return, but never in this context. Never in the light of what I've been describing.

Only a few days after the delegation had rested from our journey and begun to return the treasures to their previous places in the Temple, word had leaked out among the city dwellers and pilgrims alike that Ezra had brought with him a book of the Law of Moses. Somehow, for a people who had lived for centuries with only the haziest notion of their spiritual heritage, the news sparked more interest than in all of the other treasures combined. An enormous groundswell of curiosity and anticipation began to gather. I encountered it myself, for as I strolled through the easternmost walls one afternoon shortly after arriving, an elderly woman shuffled out of a makeshift stone abode, eyed me up and down and asked me feverishly, "You're one of the newcomers, aren't you? Is it true they brought along the books of Moses?" I'll never forget the voracious fire in the woman's eyes. You might have thought I was offering roast mutton to one who was starving when I answered that yes, I believed so.

By that night, it was all anyone was talking about. I had been graciously offered lodging in one of the city's more inviting restored homes, and as I ventured out to where the Persian émigrés were gathered for a communal dinner, I overheard four snatches of conversation in which the words *Ezra* and *lawbook* drifted my way.

The following morning all work stopped, and everyone in the citadel gathered in the center of the ruined capital. I was one of the first spectators there, for I had spent most of the night walking through the city, spreading the word that something historic would take place in the morning, upon this very square. Without even sleep, I had approached in the cool before dawn and walked over to take my morning prayer at the spot. The only sign of what would soon take place was a small wooden scaffold apparently erected during the night. As soon as the sun had peeked its radiant sliver over the hills of Judea, people began to stream in from everywhere. *I had no idea so many even lived in such a ruined place,* I thought as I gazed around just before the readings began. And what a quiet, composed group it was, for its size! Even the small children seemed to sense something special, for instead of causing commotion, most of them stared about them with wide, fascinated expressions.

Then even the residual quiet faded into a dead silence, and I saw Ezra's ceremonial head wrap approaching above the heads of the crowd. Carrying a thick leather-bound scroll, Ezra stepped up, set down his heavy load with a wince at its weight, and looked expectantly around him. It was a perfect place in which to change history, and Ezra appeared to sense it. Two Levite priests climbed up behind him, their hands clasped before them in postures of respectful pause.

Now, having reigned as queen of the most bureaucratic empire in human history, and therefore having borne witness to the stupefying boredom that can ensue from a leader reading endlessly from thick bureaucratic volumes, I can tell you, Leah—I was shocked at what happened next.

You see, Ezra did not begin to speak in the Aramaic of the day. He read straight from the original text, in ancient Hebrew. As words began to pour from his lips, I saw a strapping, weathered man turn to his thickset wife with a perplexed expression. She rolled her eyes and shrugged. I turned; all over the square, people were exhibiting the same reactions.

Then Ezra stopped speaking.

There was a seemingly eternal pause, one like the hush before a storm. And then the Levites began to speak. To translate.

Now, you must remember that Mordecai taught me Hebrew, so I understood Ezra's first reading. But there was something powerful about hearing the words rephrased by the priests, followed by the crowd's palpable reactions as the words went forth and stirred a nearly visible swath across the square, like a strong downdraft sweeping into their faces.

In a strong, fervent voice, Ezra began to read the story of our people. How G-d had made an unbelievable promise to a man living in Ur of all places—a region we had passed through on our journey. And how Abraham's descendants multiplied until their numbers had fulfilled G-d's promise of uncountable progeny, and brought down a pharaoh. How G-d had promised them a land of their own and how they had spent decades in search of it, circling the whole time through endless cycles of rebellion and repentance, subjugation and liberation.

From the very first moment he opened his mouth, I knew something remarkable was indeed going to happen. This crowd, in this place, at this time, seemed incredibly attuned to the sadness of this saga of love and rejection between G-d and His people. I began to sense, and even hear, listeners respond audibly and recoil physically with each account of Israel's turning back to idols, turning her back on the G-d who had led her out of bondage and into the Promised Land.

Then I found I was doing the same myself.

It was strange, for you see, during the first few days there I had been too exhausted, then too busy trying to find my way in the new society of the freshly arrived, to fully appreciate where I had come to. Certainly the ruined state of the city contributed to my difficulty, for none of the landmarks or attributes Mordecai had spoken about were still standing—at least in the state he had described them. But I simply could not muster the inner response I had expected upon finally arriving at this sacred spot.

But now, through the words of Ezra, I began to look around me, and not only did I feel, deep down, that I was in the heart of my people's most beloved place, but I actually began to picture them living here, year by long-past year. I don't know if it was a result of the sun, the heat, my fatigue, the strain of standing for so long, my lack of water or breakfast, my overheated imagination, or just my own surging emotions.

But I began to picture and then seemingly see, like misty shadows upon the walls, the people Ezra was speaking about. I looked behind me at a façade of buildings in repair, and I saw the prophet Joshua walking up with his staff in hand. I gazed at prophet after prophet standing in Ezra's place exhorting the people back to holiness. I distantly glimpsed King David riding through a cheering throng, Queen Jezebel weaving crazily through the street, little King Josiah holding up a lawbook very much like the one before me in Ezra's hands. I saw the armies of destruction sweep through, with chariots and war steeds raining a judgment of arrows and swords upon the innocent.

I felt the sweep of time like a melancholy ache inside me, and the love of G-d for the people of Israel like a weary, unquenchable flame illuminating the entire tale. We had been living in a state of chaotic ignorance, and the whole G-d's-eye picture now seized us up in its grasp.

Even as this exalted state remained upon me, I heard a deep and powerful cry rise up from the crowd on every side, and something happened I will never forget.

Like an actual wave of stirred water, the crowd fell to its knees in a halo of reverence, beginning at the center, at Ezra's scaffold, and spreading through the remaining watchers like the rings of a stone thrown into still water. Strangely, I even remember the sound of it: the lingering echo of the people's cry, followed by a split second of silence, and then the slapping sounds of a thousand knees striking the earth. The suddenness and power of it ripped the breath from my lungs.

And then Ezra's voice rang out again, repeating the sentence that had just been interrupted.

"As Isaiah quoted our G-d, 'Speak tenderly to Jerusalem, and cry to her that her warfare is ended, that her iniquity is pardoned, that she has received from the Lord's hand double for all her sins!'"

Hearing that very phrase, I lost control of my emotions and felt my chest heave, my eyes flood with tears. In foolish pride I sought to fight them back, but then I began to hear the sound of weeping from all about me. It began faintly, at first in the voices of women, but then I heard one and then two deeper throats sobbing, and like a tide flowing in the opposite direction now, from the edges back in to Ezra's spot, it engulfed the crowd, man and woman, young and old alike.

I began to hear cries, voicing words I would scarcely have believed. "We repent!" "Forgive us, O G-d!" "Come back to us!"

Strangely, at that moment, I was transported again—only now to a moment in my childhood, when a priest of Jerusalem had visited Mordecai's home. And all my poppa wanted to know was, *Has the Shekinah returned? Has the presence of G-d been restored to the Holy of Holies?*

At that moment I thought, *This is what moves Him to return,* to bring His presence back to a place and a heart where He had once taken His abode.

Genuine repentance, humbled cries to Him, desperate pleas for His return.

And then, with my tears now flowing unchecked, I thought of my own covenant with Him. A thrill rushed through me, because I knew that I *had* in fact joined another moment of consequence, another front row seat at the move of history and stirring of G-d. I bowed my head further and allowed snatches, outbursts, even songs of gratitude, to flow freely from my lips.

When I raised my head again, I knew that everything had changed. Perhaps not outwardly—Jerusalem remained a wreck, its people still divided into various factions over issues both trivial and sublime. But invisibly, spiritually, I knew with a deep conviction that the people of Israel had just turned a great corner. And with a certainty just as embedded inside me, I knew that I had been intended to witness this. He had ordained my being there with a purpose I did not yet fully understand, yet whose existence was as sure as the sky above me.

Chapter Forty-seven

Leah, I cried out bitterly and desperately for such a moment to come, *and it did.* G-d heard my prayer and answered it in a spectacular fashion. He is not even through answering it, I am certain. As long as I live, I know now that He will use my powerlessness and surrender to accomplish His purposes through me. Even when I am not aware of it.

And I know He will for you.

I thought of you many times, you know, during my long hiatus in Jerusalem. Shortly after the day of Ezra's reading, I felt that my reason for being there was on the wane, and the next chapter in my covenant might well reveal itself back home in Susa. It seemed almost like some kind of war had been won in Jerusalem, or at least an inevitable triumph had been set in motion. But back home I sensed that matters were still very much in doubt. Danger persisted for you, Mordecai, Jesse, and indeed all the Jews of the exile.

So the months passed. Ezra continued to reform and reorganize Israel like a priestly whirlwind, aligning her ever closer to the image evoked in his readings, and I attempted to make myself useful, wondering how and when I would be able to make the journey eastward.

Then a letter came with the royal courier. It was written and addressed by you.

And I knew that my sojourn in Jerusalem truly was coming to an end.

Prime Minister's Residence—Rehavia, Jerusalem

"Hadassah?" said her husband's voice, small and tinny through the scrambled telephone.

"Yes?" She put down the Hadassah scroll, feeling somehow guilty that she was reading it again.

"I think you should see this. Channel eight."

"You mean there's something now coming on that's worse than the last thing you asked me to watch?"

"Yes, my dear. I believe so."

"You're joking."

"I'm afraid not."

This had better be good, she huffed inwardly as she reached for the remote and flicked on the television.

The bearded Arab anchor of Al-Jazeera TV was speaking into the camera, his face pale and drawn. Then it shrank to a corner of the screen and the same anchor returned. "According to Al-Jazeera, the footage of these executions is so grisly that even their own virulently Islamic affiliates refuse to air it. But according to the network's reports, this new video shows young Hana al-Feliz, the sister of the first girl killed on live TV and the very one shown recently begging the London Jewish activist Anek al-Khalid for her life, then being brutally executed—followed immediately by her mother and father. This would leave the family's two-year-old daughter as the only remaining hostage. Her name, we believe, is Hadassah. . . ."

The First Lady of Israel looked up from where she sat, saw the room go a murky monotone around her, and fell back against the headboard. . . .

NSA Headquarters, Fort
Meade, Maryland—later that day

At the center of the most secret and protected three hundred acres on earth, on the third floor of a structure so vast it could fit four Capitol buildings inside its mysterious mirrored walls, lay Room 3E099—hallowed nerve center of the National Security Operations Center, command post of the National Security Agency. The agency itself, with its acronym NSA, had once earned itself the nickname of "no such agency" because of the government's persistent denials that this employer of twenty-seven thousand people—largest in Maryland—even existed.

In one corner of a large room crammed with electronics equipment, a cluster of technicians leaning and standing before a vast high-definition monitor betrayed the fact that a major signals analysis was under way. "Signal intelligence," or SIGINT, was actually the agency's official mandate, although those parameters had stretched considerably over time.

Right now the Al-Jazeera video feed was the most tantalizing signal on earth.

Before them glowed the oversized face of a two-year-old girl, her cheeks tearstained, her eyes red and frightened beyond imagining— yet still beautiful in an unearthly way.

"Look!" came one sharp voice from the group along with a pointed finger. "Anyone else see that flicker? The way it distorted the scan lines—that wasn't in transmission. That happened during filming."

"Like a power spike?" asked the man in the chair at their center.

"Maybe. Usually they use power packs or even old-fashioned lithium batteries. But because they were using a kidnapped crew, they could have had a problem. They could have plugged into a wall socket."

"So is that a traceable spike?"

"Are you kidding? Remember where you are. Everything's traceable, if you throw enough bandwidth at it. Matter of fact, if we can get a decent degradation read, we ought to be able to calculate a distance from the source."

"Sweet. I want to get these scum, don't you guys? I want a report in five minutes about any event in Baghdad that could have caused power spikes."

A young woman at the back of the gathering swiftly walked away.

"The light on that al-Qaeda blanket is a little bit one-sided. Maybe a twenty-five-degree angle? You guys think they opened a window?"

"Why would they?"

"No power?"

"Don't say that."

"How about no air conditioning? It's hotter than Hades over there."

"Okay. Let's run with that. How about I jack up the brightness and we all stare at this thing really hard."

"For what?"

"Fluctuations, shadows, patterns. Anything. If I knew exactly, I wouldn't be asking for help."

Onscreen, the blanket bearing Arabic script shifted from black to an unnatural gray as the sensitivity of the signal's color palette was multiplied three hundred times. While the little girl's mouth moved in slow motion beneath it, the cotton surface seemed to shimmer with a million tiny luminous fluctuations. Digits galloped across time-counters at the bottom of the screen.

At minute four-point-sixteen, a discernible shadow roughly the shape of a cigar traveled across the fabric from left to right.

A shout arose so loud that four other NSA leaders in opposite corners of the room jumped to their feet, and an outside door clanged open against the foot of a pistol-brandishing NSA security officer on full alert.

The technicians at the screen hardly noticed—they were too busy grabbing for the rewind button. Voices called out speculations of the flying object that might have caused it. *Military chopper. Large bird. Commercial airliner. No way, you idiot—that thing's traveling below stall speed! Blackhawk. Apache. Huey . . .*

Then the young woman returned with her results. At 11:21 A.M. local Baghdad time, the Corps of Engineers reported that a car bomb had exploded only twenty yards away from a major electrical substation in the Khudra neighborhood. CIA estimates put the power spike at a six-kilowatt surge within an initial quarter-mile radius around the source.

"All right, who can tell me how bad six kilowatts looks to an ordinary household power plug?"

"There're too many variables. I could tell you in an American house, but see, Baghdad has four completely different, totally incompatible power supplies—depending on the neighborhood—originating from one of four European countries that have contracted with Iraq over the years. So your answer depends completely on whether we're dealing with the French grid, the German grid, the old British one, or the complete joke of a Russian excuse for a power plant. We don't even know whether they use sixty-nine- or one-thirty-eight-kilovolt lines."

The man in the chair slammed a large fast-food drink cup on the console. "I don't want to hear that! I know it's not exact—but give me a rough estimate. Your best educated guess."

"I'd rather work backward from what we saw onscreen," murmured a man leaning over his shoulder. "I'd say, if you're starting with a six-kilowatt spike, then that should be between two and five miles away."

Fingers punched on keys. A map of Baghdad splashed onscreen. "Okay. So that likely puts us within Khudra, which is one of the city's biggest neighborhoods." The map blew up by two levels of magnification, until individual buildings were visible. "Okay. We caught a break. Streets in Khudra run perfect north to south, so our angles are simple."

"Were any aircraft dispatched to the site of the car bombing? That would give us an easy ID on the blanket shape. . . ."

In fifteen minutes the site of the kidnappers' lair had been narrowed down to within a two-block area of central Baghdad.

Encrypted satcom messages flew out of Room 3E099 to military commanders in the Green Zone, less than two miles away from the site in question.

In the middle of an Iraqi night, thickly muscled men bolted from their cots and started pulling on black camouflage, then checking their weapons.

And not far from them, a frightened little girl with hauntingly beautiful eyes cried herself to sleep on a blanket crudely lettered with threatening Arabic words.

She was alone . . . in every sense of the word.

Chapter Forty-eight

The Independent Online Edition
17 April 2005

Thousands of previously illegible manuscripts containing work by some of the greats of classical literature are being read for the first time using technology which experts believe will unlock the secrets of the ancient world.

Among treasures already discovered by a team from Oxford University are previously unseen writings by classical giants including Sophocles, Euripides and Hesiod. Invisible under ordinary light, the faded ink comes clearly into view when placed under infrared light, using techniques developed from satellite imaging.

The Oxford documents form part of the great papyrus hoard salvaged from an ancient rubbish dump in the Graeco-Egyptian town of Oxyrhynchus more than a century ago. The thousands of remaining documents, which will be analyzed over the next decade, are expected to include works by Ovid and Aeschylus, plus a series of Christian gospels which have been lost for up to 2,000 years.

—DAVID KEYS AND NICHOLAS
PYKE, "EUREKA! EXTRAORDINARY
DISCOVERY UNLOCKS SECRETS OF
THE ANCIENTS"

MASADA, SOUTHERN
ISRAEL—THE FOLLOWING MORNING

Why do I have to go through with this?" exclaimed Prime Minister ben Yuda, repeating his wife's inane question. "You should know better than anyone why I have to do this. Because I have to keep up business as usual. Because I can't afford to have anyone think these charges are tying me to my office. Because Masada is one of Israel's most symbolically important places, and to cancel now would offend every voter who has ever lost a loved one in wartime. And maybe, above all, because I simply refuse to let the jackals take me down!"

"You're right," Hadassah answered in her most placating tone. "I do know those things. But in a national crisis, I'm just saying the people expect you to be in the capital, directing things."

"I will be directing things. I *am* directing things right now," he said, the veins bulging on his neck. "Now, admit it, Hadassah. You're just breaking my knuckles because you know the media is going to descend on you like vultures. And, my dear, I can't help that. I didn't exactly cause this, you know."

"You act as though I did," she said mournfully.

"It *feels* like you did, that's all," he answered, his voice softening. "I know you've done your best. I just feel so powerless. It's like some hoary old figure out of the distant past sat up out of his grave and grabbed me around the neck. I mean, think of it—my cabinet, my whole government, maybe the future of the Middle East, is now depending on whether Mordecai, a man who lived twenty-three hundred years ago, managed to produce offspring."

"You don't have to oversimplify it for my sake, Jacob. There are more logical steps than I can count between you and Mordecai."

"Well, count them if you want to. But the fact remains that if Mordecai did not marry Leah, then neither you or Ari have any claim to being the new Exilarch, and only a new Exilarch can negotiate with Iraq for the claims of the exiled Jews or persuade the hidden Jews to come out of hiding to save themselves. *Ergo*—my troubles have only just begun."

"I know. I love that a story so old and historical has such a hold on the present."

"Oh, Hadassah, please spare me the Oprah Book Club blather." But the bite was taken out of the words by his look of both pride in her and frustration with the current juxtaposition of events.

"Look, I just feel that her story spoke to me," she tried to explain. "That's all. I feel like we're sisters, almost."

Her cell phone rang with her personalized tones: the opening fanfare of the Beatles' "All You Need Is Love." She had the unit to her ear before her shoulders had even registered the motion.

"Hadassah?" It was Ari, with the buzz-saw noise of distance in the background.

"Where are you?"

"Paris, my dear cousin. I have honeycombed the world in my unceasing efforts to get you and your husband off the hook."

She raised her eyebrows—hopefully the banter meant there was good news. "Right. As if you had no self-interest in the matter."

"Listen. I'm at the Louvre. I know that sounds a little obvious, but that's where all the Persian antiquities are stored. I can't tell you more until it happens. But make sure you're reachable. Where are you?"

"We're leaving shortly for Masada. The three-thousandth anniversary or something."

"That sounds like a security nightmare. Be careful."

"Don't worry. I'll stay away from the edges."

"Well, just make sure you stay in cell range—either that or let Mossad know how to contact you. Because I think I'm on to something."

THE LOUVRE MUSEUM, PARIS—LATER THAT DAY

Ari Meyer descended the endless marble steps two at a time, mentally marking off the decades with each step. Mathematically, he estimated that it would take nearly sixty years per step to account for the journey back in time—from the twenty-first-century main floor, to the sheer ancientness of not only the museum's catacomb displays, but the very antiquity of the Louvre's bowels themselves.

Only a decade or so earlier, in the midst of renovations that had added the famous crystal pyramid and underground turnstiles, the French government had discovered battlements and buried structures that dated back to the time of Christ. To Ari, it only added to the Louvre's mystique—the difficulty of telling which represented the most stunning work of art: the pieces on display or the building itself.

Another fact Ari would pretend not to know: that the world's largest museum did not contain the world's most extensive collection of Persian artifacts merely because it was the biggest or best museum, or because it had become the famous setting for the fictional decoding of an ancient mystery. Rather, it contained nearly a whole floor of hidden Persian objects and archives deep within its foundations, somewhere between the floors tourists knew best and its prehistoric foundation layers, because the French had been for decades the colonial patrons of modern Iran. As a result, French archaeologists had an easy time negotiating unfettered access to the world's greatest ruins in exchange for coveted modern luxuries like running water and paid-off royal debts.

Indeed, what Alexander the Great did not cart off in those early years of the overthrown empire, the French had managed to ship away on large steamboats, all for the filling of the Louvre's nearly inexhaustible stacks.

Ari Meyer lost count of his decades somewhere around the last ten steps. Upon reaching the subterranean landing, he simply rounded off and gave himself an even thirty-five hundred. Then he turned into a barrel-vaulted, unlit doorway with the confidence of someone with an idea.

"The Marduk Love Letters," he said to the half-shadowed face of the after-hours Chief Archivist. "I would like to see them."

The archivist did not move but cocked his head with an air of suspicious curiosity. "We are most pleased, of course, to address the needs of a valued diplomatic friend. I only wonder why there is such a hurry that we need do this at such a late hour."

"Actually, *mon ami*, it is a matter of the gravest urgency," Ari responded. "And you will have the eternal gratitude of the government of Israel if you would please guide me hurriedly—no, swiftly—to the room where they are contained."

"All right, sir. Please come with me. . . ."

Ari could hardly contain his excitement. The sense of advancing history intensified with their descent through the rows of ancient racks. The idea had struck him like a long-delayed revelation. *The Letters*, one of the most cryptic and speculated-about cuneiform documents of all time, outlined an odd, unexplained love between a high palace official in the time of Artaxerxes and some kind of lowbrow woman within the palace. Over the decades, even centuries, these letters had acquired a dedicated following of scholars enamored with their secrecy, their eloquent, florid language, their oddly phrased and incomplete dialogue, and their abundance of references to palace staff, hidden beneath layers of encryption and misdirecting clues.

Today Ari had a secret weapon. The Mossad had acquired, through the most secretive of intelligence circles, the working prototype for a device developed for the CIA by scientists at Johns Hopkins and the Rochester Institute of Technology. It was a device roughly the size of a hand-held scanner that emitted a rare form of infrared light through a classified ultraviolet filter, all finely calibrated according to the parameters of the latest satellite imaging technology. Back in Jerusalem, the Mossad had already developed a full-scale laboratory model. But for his work, Ari had laid his hands on one of the few miniature-sized originals in existence.

They had arrived at the room in question: a vast square space fringed by wall-hung displays.

"Here," said the guide, pointing to a large unrolled scroll.

"Thank you, kind sir," Ari answered, smiling in anticipation. He waited till his escort had left, then pulled out his infrared wand and turned it on before the ancient scroll. New lines and phrases appeared, completely changing the letter's theme.

As he began to translate the illuminated text, his practiced eye discerned right away that the document was written not only in the proper ancient vocabulary but also in a bold, masculine hand. . . .

My lady, I love you.

I write these words so that I can say at the end of my life that I expressed the feelings which threaten to burst me apart. Even if I only express them to myself. You see, I am not sure I will ever show you this.

In fact, I am mortified to even imagine these words ever falling under your gaze.

However, I write it for you. I know that this is strange, illogical, and maybe even pathetic.

I know that this message may be dangerous, highly inappropriate, uncalled for, and perhaps even distressing to you. I know that it comes at perhaps the worst time of your life, therefore raising the prospect of my trying to take undue advantage of a woman in a vulnerable state. Yet I would disagree with that assessment of things. I must be truthful. First to myself and then, if my courage survives, to you.

Should I say it again? *I truly do love you.* Now, give me time, for it will be long—if ever—before I gain enough courage to say such things out loud. But here, in this place, I can.

I believe it's important that you know I didn't say these things out of trifling affection. The fact is, I do not love you merely as a friend, a colleague, a confidante, or even a maid of honor. I love you as a ravishing, desire-provoking, sweat-causing, stammer-inducing beautiful woman. A woman of G-d. A creation of the Almighty, who has infinite worth, value, and contribution to offer the living G-d and His people. And has found herself locked away due to circumstances far indeed from her control.

When did it start? My beloved daughter would tell me it was the first moment I saw you, although I must admit I was completely unaware. Or at least consciously. I am not even sure you noticed us that day. It was the day you first came to the harem, along with your fellow candidates. Probably one of the most confusing, bewildering moments of your life. Our mutual friend Hathach the chamberlain stood alongside, and he had already surmised that you were one of us.

I thought I was admiring your poise, your uniqueness from the others. But my daughter—whom I will not mention by name because of events we both know are taking place concerning the empire—is sure she noticed something else.

And then, of course, we met, in the passage of your time in the harem and my frequent trips to both my daughter's harem chambers and those of Hathach.

From the very first words that left your mouth, I realized you were a perceptive and well-spoken young woman, on whom I could rely for accurate observations of the Jewish community and their feelings toward the palace.

I had long conversations with your chamberlain about how much you reminded him of my own daughter at the same age, when she herself had entered the harem for her year of preparation.

I never harbored an un-innocent thought toward you. In fact, I pictured you so pure, so refined, that any untoward impulse would simply not have survived with you as its object.

Then, of course, there is the matter of your own night with the King.

And the morning after.

Even as you were being escorted back to the harem, I was being summoned back to the King's chambers. I had no idea what had taken place.

I walked in and noticed immediately that something was wrong. The King's expression toward me had changed; the slant of his eyes had narrowed, he suddenly would not meet my gaze, and he wore a perpetual scowl.

"Mordecai, I spent last night with a most remarkable woman. The most beautiful, the most refined, the most intoxicating creature I have ever met. Her name is Leah. From Susa, I believe. Do you happen to know her?"

"Leah," I repeated, trying desperately to buy myself some time— to decide whether or not I would be candid. "I believe I have. I am, as you know, sir, a close friend of Your Majesty's chamberlain."

"Yes, I do remember that, Mordecai," he answered. "In fact, the knowledge of it has troubled me much over the last few hours."

"Why is that, sire?"

"Well, as I indicated, last night was one of the most memorable in my whole life. Leah was most sensuous and, better still, intelligent and charming. She left me with memories I shall treasure the rest of my life."

"I am very glad to hear that, Your Majesty. . . ." but my voice held a question mark that didn't fit the statement.

"Yes, thank you—but there was one exception. Right in the middle of the evening, as we exchanged some quite candid and profound disclosures about ourselves and our lives, I began to speak of a most intimate and even secret matter. I spoke to her about . . . well, you know my relations with my brother Darius were rather . . . complicated."

"Indeed I remember."

"Yes, and the most amazing thing took place as I spoke with her. I began to think of the night of my father's murder. And all of the other secondary things that took place."

"Yes, Your Highness. I do remember—"

"You do, do you? Well, then, perhaps you remember that only you and the former Queen have any knowledge of how exactly my brother died. That I was tricked by my father's killers into ordering . . ."

His voice grew thick and husky, then faded away.

"Do you know what this amazing girl told me? She leaned forward and whispered into my ear, 'Don't feel guilty. It wasn't your fault. It wasn't your fault.'

"Now deep in the throes of grief, I did not fully appreciate what she had said for quite a long moment. But then, something about the tone of her voice stirred the deepest part of my brain. And I suddenly realized she was not merely referring to some general survivor's guilt over my brother's untimely murder.

"She knew it, Mordecai. She knew the truth. The minute I lifted myself up to look upon her with a questioning mien, I saw a flash of dread cross her face, the wilted demeanor of one who realizes she has disclosed something imprudent in an unguarded moment.

"So my question is, how well do you and the former Queen know this most well-informed young woman?"

And do you know, for the first time in all my years as a Master of the Audience, I found my words utterly lacking. I did *not* know how to answer. Never before has my own or my loved ones' self-interest placed itself at odds with my duty to the King.

Artaxerxes, though, did not seemed surprised at all by my sudden muteness. He looked away and shook his head, continuing his prepared speech.

"Yes, that is what I thought, my dear Mordecai. Trusted and beloved advisor to my father, revered figure to the world's largest empire, man of unaccusable, unquestionable integrity. And of course, human savior, along with his daughter, of his people . . ."

I worked very hard not to look his way or betray any reaction whatsoever to those words. But his tone now grew cloying and cunningly playful.

"*Jewish*—I was only a child at the time, but I was not misled, was I, Mordecai? Were not, in fact, your Jewish people the intended victims of a most vicious extermination plot in those days? A plot that forced you to risk your life to defy a nobleman and save your race from being wiped off the face of the earth?"

"It was G-d who saved my people, Your Majesty," I quickly blurted, thankful for something totally truthful I could say.

"You know what I mean," he said.

I was now trapped, for as you know I would never betray or deny my faith. If I would risk everything by refusing to bow down to a Haman, I surely would not turn my back on my heritage merely to deny the King a point in conversation.

So I answered him, "Yes, Your Majesty. Your memory indeed serves you correctly. I am Jewish. One of the exiles of Israel."

"And so . . . am I also correct in guessing that the young lady who has so enchanted me had knowledge of things only you know because she is . . . also of your people?"

I allowed a long pause to fall between us while I tried to think of any other way to answer him.

"I learned that quite recently myself, Your Majesty." My explanation sounded pathetic and contrived—even its sound echoed flatly across the marble of the vast room.

Artaxerxes made a small grimace when I uttered those words, as though despite considering them inevitable, he had nevertheless hoped they would never reach his ears.

"Oh, Mordecai," he said at last, in an almost plaintive tone of voice, "how I wish my acumen had not proven so correct. For you see, I truly fell in love with young Leah last night. And ever since I awoke this morning, I have been thinking of nothing else than the potential joy of making her my Queen. Until, that is, just when I recalled, out from the fog of last night's passion and healing, my memory of her statement."

Immediately I sensed one of those, quite literally, sword's-edge kind of moments. The kind of moment when silently, invisibly, unknowingly, you find that you have reached a most significant line in the sand, ahead of which lies instant destruction. So I knelt abruptly, grabbed his right hand, and began kissing it fervently.

"Your Majesty, please forgive your humble servant. I never meant to betray your sovereign word in disclosing of this matter to Leah. She, like all your queens-in-waiting, sits in the harem, gazes at the vast splendor of your palace day after day, and nearly goes insane wondering about all that goes on there. I only sought to give her sufficient knowledge to keep her wits about her should she ascend to the throne someday. I swore her to complete secrecy regarding any other disclosure of the information."

"You know something, Mordecai?" he answered almost flippantly. "I actually believe you." But his tone grew very serious as he went on. "Despite the fact that your betrayal is certainly punishable by death, not to mention the immediate end to a lifetime's worth of hard-won trust, I believe that your words are true. Of course, that does not make the choices before me any easier."

"I am sure you are right, Your Majesty. And that is why I cast myself at your mercy to await your gracious decision. I only ask that you not penalize young Leah for my lapse in judgment. She neither asked for nor repeated the inappropriate knowledge beyond what you heard last night. Leah is, as you so perceptively ascertained, a once-in-a-lifetime young woman of incredible beauty and astonishing personal qualities. She will make anyone the most wonderful wife and life-mate. . . ."

And, Leah, it was just when those words left my mouth that I knew how deeply and longingly I actually believed them. I would have given my life, had it been possible, for me to win you from him at that precise instant.

"Yes, I believe you again," he answered, deep in thought. "I most definitely agree, although not out of an abundance of trust in your judgment." Suddenly he wheeled around to stare at me. "Which is why I must, with the deepest regret, replace you as Master of the Audiences and Prime Minister. You have given my father and me invaluable and much appreciated service, Mordecai. But the time has come when, for this and various other reasons, I must seek a new voice and set of instincts at my side."

"I understand, Your Majesty," I said, trying not to betray my disappointment. "I only hope that whatever wisdom or understanding I may possess may still prove of service to Your Majesty somewhere in the future."

"Actually, they may," he answered, nodding. "I need you to perform one last act of extreme difficulty and delicacy for me."

"Anything, Your Majesty."

"I want you to go back to the harem and inform young Leah that she has been rejected as a candidate for Queen. She will remain in the harem as a concubine, although I will never seek her bed nor summon her to mine. No public reason will be given for this decision. Ever."

Chapter Forty-nine

I had felt these words coming, yet I dreaded them so profoundly that I decided to risk one last provocation to keep them at bay.

"Is Your Majesty certain? After all, a son of your father knows the value of finding a loyal and completely loving mate, even if her outward credentials may be somewhat lacking . . ."

The king turned on me and snarled, "Is the one-time Master of the Audiences making a veiled comparison between your daughter and my *mother*? Is that an inference you truly want to leave with me?"

I lowered my head again, feeling like someone who has raised a wild animal from birth and suddenly discovered that it has the fangs and the temperament of a fearsome beast. I shook my head abjectly, avoiding his gaze.

"No, no, of course not. I only sought to offer Your Majesty's wisdom a moment of reflection."

"I understand." His tone was now suddenly subdued and even warm again. "I am in a dilemma, my old friend. For I simply cannot name a Jewish girl as my Queen anytime in the future."

"Why not? For again, I am not remiss in believing that my own daughter served your father well."

"She served him admirably. Superbly," he said. "That is not the question. I have no doubt that Leah would make an equally astute and loyal servant. And my problem is keener still, my friend, for the bare truth is that I fear I have truly fallen in love with this girl. I desire nothing more than to spend every night I have left exactly as I spent the last one. And I have indeed considered whether such unlikely bliss is worth abdicating my throne in order to win it for my own. But I require more of that from a queen at this moment. As you know better than anyone, Mordecai, my court is afire with rumor, plotting, and counterplotting against my crown. Some of it is either from my own family—my dear mother Amestris included, and any number of my brothers—or the other noble families of the empire, most notably the members of the Seven Princes of the Face. These factions, as you also know, deeply resented the ascension of an exile girl to the throne beside my father. I feel I must tell you the truth in this matter, even though I am aware that she is your own daughter. Although they came to admire her other qualities and talents in time, they still never stopped chafing at the queenhood of an émigrée over one of their own. And they began to suspect, or at least spread rumors of suspicion, that the Jewish people had used some kind of underhanded ritual, or simply incredibly shrewd maneuvering, to obtain undue sway over my father."

"And I need not state, just now, that Your Majesty need place no credibility whatsoever in those claims. You can set your mind at ease."

"My mind is not at ease," he said with a dismissive wave of his hand, "and may never be again, after the decision I have just made. Yet it is not the result of any mistrust concerning you, your years of service, or the loyalty of your people. Yet you must be careful in the days to come. Word of this will certainly become known. Nor will I deprive the Queen Mother Amestris of the knowledge of this decision. She will no doubt react quite differently and more vindictively than I have. It will be in my interest to appear to side with her and acquiesce to her mistrust of the Jews. It is one of the reasons why I have relieved you of duty this day. Take great care, Mordecai. And use that vaunted wisdom of yours to spare yourself and your people from the fear and bloodthirst of those around them."

"I will pray for just that, Your Majesty," I answered with a bow.

"Then go now, Mordecai," he ordered sharply. "Go carry out my order. And then enter into your richly deserved retirement. I will see to it that you are well cared for and housed. You have served Persia well. Good-bye."

I did my best to turn on my heels like a young officer and depart the room crisply. However, my ankles ached and my leg muscles failed me, and I managed some sort of a pathetic turnabout, surely justifying his inferences about my age.

In some ways, the exit that followed was the most difficult hour of my life. I left through the room's large, ornate doors and plunged myself into the thick and fast-moving human traffic of the inner hall-way. As usual, everyone parted and bowed their heads in respect for me and my office. And I was forced to nod as always and walk past, knowing inside that very soon most of them would outrank me. The knowledge burned inside of me and caused me to feel like an utter hypocrite. However, I consoled myself in realizing that I could hardly walk through the crowd holding up a sign announcing the news.

And so, as discreetly and inauspiciously as I could, I kept my head up and made my way through the innermost palace out to the courtyard, through its front portico and out into the second, and the third, oblivious to the heat and the sun and its ill effects on unpro-tected faces.

All I could think of, you see, was your face awaiting me.

I will never forget the moment of telling you the news. In some ways I think you knew already, the moment you saw my countenance as I approached. Your eyes met mine and then fell immediately, and though I attempted a smile, I knew it was one of consolation, not glad tidings.

Yet you waited to hear the actual bad news from my lips. So I walked over to the side of the bed where you were sitting, knelt for the second time that day, grasped your hand as gently as I could and told you in the softest tone I possess of the King's decision.

You remained utterly silent and motionless for the longest, most cryptic pause imaginable. While it lasted I actually entertained the thought that you had somehow suffered a physical shock so devastat-ing that you would never move again.

Then you began to shake your head with a distant, wistful look in your eyes, focused somewhere out the window. And they began to fill with tears.

You reached forward at that moment and made a choice that in some ways changed my life forever. You leaned in to me and buried your face in my shoulder, grasping me about the torso. Desperate to console you, I squeezed your shoulder and did all I could to cradle you, whispering my best thoughts of solace into your ear.

Yet all I could think of to speak were words to reassure you that indeed, you are a woman of incredible beauty and substance, and that despite his verdict, the King had assured me he believed it equally.

And all I tell myself, with a painful mixture of guilt and ecstasy, was this: *So this is what it feels like to clasp a lovely young woman in your arms.* I am the worst friend and counselor in the world to even entertain such a thought. Yet I cannot escape it. I remain trustworthy, and sympathetic at my core to the pain you were living through. After years of being father to another beautiful woman, that day I found myself graced with another close relationship that other men might have envied. It was the most bittersweet of agonies, to be torn like this between the bliss of feeling the caress of your body against mine and your doelike personality—and the need to preserve complete trustworthiness and purity on the other hand.

It was the first time I knew that, despite their teasing, my daughter and the chamberlain had proven correct. I was not beyond the humanity of desiring human affection and touch.

"Then *why*, Mordecai?" you had then asked me with your lip trembling, bringing me mercifully back to the present reality. "Why *did* he?"

I sighed and decided not to give the truth any pause.

"Because he has learned that you are Jewish."

"How? I never told him. . . ."

"In a way, Leah, you did."

"Oh . . ." Her eyes went blank toward me while she recalled her disclosure. "That. He did not miss it after all."

"Not in the least, I am sorry to say."

And then you spoke the words that would haunt you, I know, and all of us for quite some time to come.

"My life is over."

Chapter Fifty

You indeed lived, if I may call it that, the next few days and weeks as though your earthly existence had ended. And I felt in return as though my own had ceased along with it.

For the first time in many years, I moved out of my palatial and opulent royal apartments right beside those of the king. I took up temporary residence not far from the harem, in the chamberlain's quarters, unwilling to quit the palace entirely until matters had calmed a bit throughout the royal family.

The last trappings of the offices of Prime Minister and Master of the Audiences were now gone. I no longer elicited bows or salutes or recognition from anyone, unless you counted the accidental bows and gestures of people who had forgotten the announcements.

If only my daughter, who was also my best friend and my finest confidante, had been there for both of us. Our despondency would likely not have been as deep. And I certainly would not have found myself drafting this letter—I would have been compelled to speak my feelings more directly and far sooner, I'm sure. But as you know, she was on a mission to Israel at the time.

I wrote her the most urgently worded letter I could, begging her to return. All courage had finally quit me, and despite all of my resolve and goodwill, I simply wanted my own little girl back to offer us all some comfort and stability during a difficult time.

And return she did, for great things had come to pass on her far-flung mission. She felt as though the good she had offered was now spent, and its usefulness completed. She also, thank G-d, had already felt a tug to return to us and attend to matters here. That is why she heeded our letters and returned to Susa at once.

As you know, she came back to a time of renewed peril for the Jews of Persia. The primacy of our homeland and our faith had just been restored, thank G-d, but for those in exile, matters deteriorated rapidly after my dismissal. I tried to remain a familiar face about the court, merely to keep abreast of the goings-on, and what I learned soon chilled me to the core.

Artaxerxes had been quite correct—in fact, his sobering warning proved only strong enough by half. Our people, as usual, were becoming the scapegoat of choice for the deteriorating condition of the Persian Empire. We had supposedly lulled the King into slumber by some stubborn insistence on preserving our own interests at the expense of Persian sovereignty, weakening his blood feud against the Greeks and his willingness to pursue it, turning him against the rightful heirs to his throne, and blinding him to dangers around him in an effort to restore behind his back a most dangerous potential adversary—our own renascent capital city.

Then we were blamed for another threat—this time the most dangerous and unexpected as any in the empire's history—the rebellion of Megabyzos and the King's failure to foresee it. Megabyzos, the same general who had quelled the Egyptian rebellion by sweeping through a pacified Middle East, was one of the most celebrated noblemen and generals in the entire history of Persia, a veteran of Xerxes' triumphant campaigns against the Greeks and even married to one of Xerxes' daughters, the lovely Amytis. He had returned from his latest triumph in Egypt with several prisoners, including the chief rebel Inarus, who had begun his rebellion by helping kill the local satrap Achaemenes, one of Amestris' other sons.

The Queen Mother, Xerxes' previous wife Amestris, was enraged because Megabyzos had not punished the Greeks to her liking. After all, they had been the collaborators of the man who had killed her boy. Initially, Artaxerxes did not allow her the revenge she sought, but after five years had permitted Amestris to crucify Inarus and kill several captive Athenians. Megabyzos, who had given his word that Inarus would not be killed, was unable to bear this humiliation and requested to be allowed to return from Artaxerxes' court to Syria. This permission was granted. He returned to his satrapy and promptly, angrily, launched a full-scale rebellion against Artaxerxes and the Persian rule.

As soon as he did, matters instantly grew far worse for the Jews. The fact that Megabyzos was Satrap of the Province Beyond the River—home to Jerusalem—gave rise to the rumor that my countrymen's malcontent had given the general's rebellious yearnings solace, and inspiration was an egregious charge. That, in turn, gave the Samaritan enemies of the city another pretext to bombard Artaxerxes with dire warnings of an impending revolt.

It would have been a perfect time for another of our people to take the throne beside Artaxerxes. I have no doubt that you would have proven as popular and as able when crisis came as my daughter did.

But when it of course did not happen, I felt—or even more exactly, I *knew*—deep in my heart that G-d had another plan this time. In His immense creativity, He would use the lessons of before—only use them in a manner utterly new and fresh.

He did just that by turning us away from your unfortunate outcome to the person of an unlikely friend, one of our last allies left with any degree of influence over the King.

But let me start at the beginning.

While I was now resigned from the Persian Royal Palace, the office of the Exilarchy brought its own pressures. As the new leader of my exiled people, I felt close to despair over my inability to champion their cause more directly. When I had been an official in the palace, addressing an issue had been as easy as whispering a few words into the King's ear, or even taking matters into my own hands and simply ordering that things be put aright.

Now in my new position, I had to carefully leverage my own waning influence and maneuver, rather than order, matters into their proper state.

It had been that way with the City of our Fathers. Behind the scenes, I worked feverishly to help champion the scribe's petition to the King. Then, when the expedition seemed imminent, I arranged for my daughter to increase chances for her own safety, not to mention fulfilling a lifelong dream, by accompanying the caravan. And for a time, it seemed things had worked perfectly. The scribe and his law-book revived the story of our ancient Scriptures and the godly fervor of the city's citizens, new and longstanding alike. At the same time, Ezra was a reasonable man, an opponent of radical partisanship who favored working faithfully within the existing empire rather than rebelling and fomenting some long-simmering nationalist fantasy. I knew how mighty Persia was. In fact, I was one of her leading and most illustrious citizens. So I had neither the desire nor the folly to defy her wrath. The Babylonian scribe was my flawless solution.

Then my daughter returned from her four-year sojourn in the City of our Fathers. You may not realize this, my dear, but you and your precarious state were the true reason she came back. Or at least the spoken reason she and I gave ourselves. I secretly suspect that despite its towering place in her prayers, the Eternal City and the primitive conditions had begun to wear on her. She seemed only too happy to return when she heard the awful news of your rejection by the King.

But when she first came back to us, I felt quite at ease that matters in Jerusalem were well in hand. Instead, I concerned myself only with the welfare of my people here in Persepolis.

That state of affairs soon traced a precipitous turnaround. Now in a very short time, the Eternal City had reemerged as the axis of all the risk and danger in the modern Hebrew world.

Now without hearing my constant counsel against it, Artaxerxes capitulated to our enemies both here and our ancestral homeland, and issued a halfhearted order to halt all work on the city's rebuilding.

To make matters worse, the emperor's official disapproval served to embolden the city's local enemies. The foes of my people and their regional allies promptly attacked the city again, killed many of her citizens, and reduced her re-emerging structure back into rubble once more. Oh, how glad I am that my daughter was no longer there to see the new devastation or to fall victim to such brutality!

The news struck my daughter and me as yet another reassertion of life's essentially bleak and ruthless nature. G-d, of course, being temporarily banished from the picture.

I remember our sitting together, watching the setting sun reduce the Atabana's columns to huge silhouettes, and wondering why I had tried so long and so foolishly to resist life's ultimate brutality. After all my efforts, my people's plight was no better or worse than before, and your own prospects had been dashed alongside ours.

"G-d, would you have mercy on us and lift your judgment from us?" I remember praying. "Will you please restore us to the glow of your sight? Return us to your favor?"

I felt weary. I felt like a foolish old man who had wasted away his years in the pursuit of idle, airy fantasies. Who had allowed his hopes to rise and fall on the winds like a sparrow before a hurricane. Beside me, my beloved daughter could only stare in the distance like a hollow-eyed survivor of some war, holding my hand tightly.

I turned at the sound of someone approaching from behind us.

It was our friend the royal cupbearer. He prepared to sit down with us, his face pallid and drawn.

"I just thought I would come and confirm for you the very worst of what you have heard," he began, his voice full of woe. "You see, my youngest brother just returned with several of his friends who had traveled to Jerusalem to deliver some construction supplies. He validated the most bloodcurdling of the descriptions you've heard. 'Our beloved city has indeed been laid waste,' he said in the voice of one with no hope. 'Those who survived the exile and are back in the province are in great trouble and disgrace. The wall of the city is broken down, and its gates have been burned with fire.'"

His voice broke and stopped altogether, replaced by the sound of gentle weeping. His was soon joined by our own, for it was an all-time low moment indeed for each of us. All the hopes, all the work, all the progress—apparently for naught.

I suppose this sounds pathetic, but we sat there for a time that stretched into seeming eternity. We neither spoke nor sang, nor even moved. Our harps were once again hung on the willow tree.

It was no symbolic gesture or even conscious decision. I will tell you the truth: we sat still because we were spent, and we hadn't the slightest idea what to try next.

After the pause had persisted through countless cycles of waiting with the length and finality of time itself, the cupbearer stood.

"I have no ideas. Merely duties at the palace," he said flatly.

"Go and perform them as well as you can," I responded, knowing the advice would likely fail to produce any difference. And then it came to me, like a dagger that flew midair and struck me somewhere right around my heart—

—*If this man were my own cupbearer, the sorry state of his face would have screamed to me that something was wrong.*

For a few moments at least each day, the one face in the kingdom that every king stares at most closely is that of his cupbearer—during that crucial time between the tasting of the wine and the nodded whisper that "All is clear, Your Majesty." During the next occurrence of those fleeting few seconds, our friend would have an opportunity to seize the King's interest like no other citizen on earth. It could be our chance—our only chance—to plead the case of the City of our Fathers.

I turned to the cupbearer and placed my hand on his shoulder.

"My friend," I said, "I am going to repeat some words I have not spoken for several decades, when I uttered them to my daughter at a similar moment of incredible risk and opportunity. My brother, perhaps G-d has brought you to the palace, to this place in your life, exactly for such a time as this. Perhaps history itself turns on what you, and you alone, do next."

He turned to me with an expression tinged with incredulity and even a note of defiance. I believe that for a moment he truly thought I was toying with him. Then he saw my face, he saw my daughter's reaction to hearing those words again, and he frowned more seriously.

"My life serves no purpose other than to intoxicate the King and his friends, and make sure they do not die in the process," he answered. "I fail to see the historical importance of such a thing."

Then I explained my idea to him, and he never spoke such nonsense again.

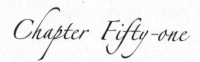

Chapter Fifty-one

And that is why the following New Year's festival, at the dawning of springtime nearly six months later, featured a Banquet of Wine—the premier Persian celebration of fine wines from across the world—as had not been seen in the palace for many a year.

At the center of it all, shouldering the burden of keeping full the cups of not only the King but several dozen of his most influential, and feared, invited guests, was our friend the cupbearer.

As many of the attendees would later take note, several pronounced characteristics marked the royal cupbearer's demeanor that night. One is that he carried out his duties with a swiftness and efficiency unmatched by any cupbearer in royal history. It was said the man was a veritable blur of motion across the vast dining chamber of the Persepolis palace, for he alone had the authority to pronounce a glass safe for imbibing. And given that Megabyzos' rebellion was at its height and that over half of the men reclining drunkenly in that great room and gazing out at an unmatched Persian sunset were whispered to be in league with the rebel, plotting in some manner and to some degree against the rule of the King, no one was taking any chances.

The other notable aspect of the cupbearer's state is that without speaking a word or consciously attempting to do so, he radiated an elegant sort of sadness so palpable and powerful that indeed it almost seemed as though he was about to burst into tears at any moment.

"Cheer up, my man!" shouted Otanes, one of the Princes of the Face. "After all, are you not drinking more wine than anyone tonight?"

"Yes, but no one is enjoying it less!" countered the King on his cupbearer's behalf. "What if you expected to die with every quaff?"

"I expect to die with every bite of my wife's cooking!" shouted back the great soldier, who also happened to be the king's grandfather. "It is why I stay afield in Your Majesty's service as much as possible!"

While a wave of masculine laughter swept across the room, the King rose up on one elbow, for he was reclining upon a bed of pillows, and summoned the cupbearer over to him with a delicate motion of his finger.

"What indeed is the matter tonight, my friend?" he asked.

The cupbearer was holding two flasks of fine Elamite wine for guests in the room's far corner, but he quickly made his decision. He knelt, set the two flasks on the floor beside him, and gazed at the King with two of the most forlorn eyes the sovereign had ever seen.

"Do you truly wish for me to tell you, my lord?" he asked.

"Yes. I have hardly witnessed such sorrow upon the visage of one who should be enjoying himself more."

Nehemiah allowed his peripheral vision to quickly gauge the state of the room, and what he sensed alarmed him. The King had spoken these words more loudly than he had intended, and a lull in the room's conversation had coincided with the speaking of them. As a result, many had heard the question, and he felt several dozen pairs of eyes trained intently upon him, anticipating his reply.

Like so many of his compatriots in the palace, he had never told anyone of his race. But he knew that some of its fiercest enemies that very moment surrounded him.

It quickly became clear to him that he had no choice. The evening was fluid, the King's mood mercurial, and he would not be asked this question again. This was the opportunity of a lifetime, not only for him, but for his people. So he swallowed hard, fixed the king with his most powerful look, and said, "Your Majesty, how can I pretend to enjoy my being here when the City of my Fathers, the beloved capital of my forefathers, lies in ruins, its ramparts destroyed, its proud buildings lying tossed and left to the elements?"

"What are you speaking of, my trusted friend?" the King replied.

The cupbearer of Artaxerxes revealed himself to the King that night, and of course we all know the historic events that followed. Our friend's incredible leadership was known to the rest of his people, and indeed to all of history, in the days after that, when the King allowed him to return to Jerusalem and rebuild the walls so essential to the future of the city and its people. Within months, the largest contingent of our people ever arrayed returned to their homeland, and a few short months after that, we began to receive reports of wonderful progress and overcoming of great odds.

So, my dear, you ask—how does this bear on the story of my love for you?

Because in the aftermath of this great concession on the part of the King, sentiment against our people, and fear of their influence, crested at a new and ever more virulent high. You likely remember how I looked when I came to you a few short days later with grave news, for your own face blanched merely at the sight of me. I had not tried to hide my deep distress. I had just been told that assassins had been dispatched that very night to murder you, my daughter, and me in our sleep. We three were thought to embody the pinnacle of Jewish influence in the palace, and therefore our doom was now deemed a priority by Megabyzos sympathizers, Greek allies, and other enemies of the King.

That was the night when Jesse, our dear chamberlain and master of the harem, took his greatest risk ever on our behalf. In the dead of night he spirited you, Hadassah and I down a back hallway of the harem to a dead-end wall I had never been able to understand. Smiling faintly, he gazed around him for onlookers, reached out his hands and pushed hard against a raised molding that framed a large statue of Ahuramazda. The statue rolled slowly along stone wheels and opened to a dark and narrow staircase leading downward. Picking up his torch, he led the way into the unknown place. At the bottom, cunningly lit by a series of cleverly disguised light holes, lay a secret buried apartment far below the harem floors. Its heart was a large open room lined with the most opulent silk-pillows, blankets, and rugs the harem had ever offered any guest.

"This place is known to nobody but the King and myself," he said into the near-darkness. "And certainly not to the Queen. It was built to hide and protect the King's favored circle of concubines in a time of war. You will be safe here. Please remain quiet, for the holes allowing in sunlight open to oddly situated parts of the harem, from which an unusual noise could be overheard by a passerby." He turned to a small alcove in the corner. "There is a water well, and in the far corner a privy. I will bring you each day's food at midnight. It is quite comfortable, but I am sure you will tire of it quickly. Let us pray that the crisis passes soon."

Without further instructions he smiled wanly at us, gave us each a small embrace, and marched back up the stairs.

This is when my last and deepest encounter with your true nature began. As I know you would agree, nothing reveals the contents of someone's character more quickly, more deeply, or more accurately than being shut with them in a confined space, however comfortable it may be.

You were quite fearful at first, anxious that no one hear our various coughs or sneezes through the grates or that the plotters would learn of Jesse's harboring us and kill him outright. I on the other hand, found myself enveloped in a strange sense of calm certainty. Maybe it is my advanced age, my lack of a fear of death. Maybe it was the additional presence of my beloved daughter, or even the chance to catch up on sleep for the first time in many a year of feverish palace duty.

But for whatever reason, I was soon in a position to calm your fears and converse with you at length about this stage of your life. For you were still in the throes of incredible disappointment over the outcome of your night with the King, convinced that unless he reversed his decision, you were doomed for a life of wasted opportunity. "Look, Mordecai," I recall you whispering to me one night—for nighttime with less likelihood of being overheard was when we indulged in most of our conversations, "I am surrounded by historic and vastly influential contributors to the history of my people. You,

Hadassah, Nehemiah. Yes, you are in this dark place with me, but
you have the satisfaction that comes with knowing you have already
had your time to count for something. Me—I had my night with the
King, and it changed nothing."

"Or so you think, my dear."

"How could it be otherwise?"

"With an infinitely creative G-d," I answered, "I would never be
reluctant to say, What if your contribution to history and the welfare
of your people did not lie with the King?"

You nearly laughed, so great was your surprise at the notion.

"I can hardly see how, especially as a queen's candidate, I would
have an important fate outside of being chosen by the King," you
argued. "Surely, this close to the throne of Persia, becoming queen
must be the only way I can triumph for my people."

I stopped speaking of it that night, for I was overwhelmed by a
desire to take you in my arms and declare that your destiny lay with
me. I hardly trusted myself. But I saw you fight with your misgivings
and fears, and I witnessed your laying them down, gently it seemed,
one by one.

Day by day, as the three of us lounged around in the darkness and
whispered to each other our confessions of fear, loneliness, anger, even
anger toward G-d, I sensed an unlikely bond grow between us. A
friendship, to be sure, but a certain and profound one. Hadassah and
I already enjoyed a kinship deeper than words, and we often rested in
each other's arms, enjoying our closeness in a way we had not been
allowed to for years. In fact, the confined nature of our hiding place
reminded me of the home in which I had restricted her for so much of
her childhood, fearful of her being caught by the murdering Agagites.

Hadassah soon took notice of my growing interest—for the wondrous surprise of this time has been you.

Chapter Fifty-two

Again, I am highly uncertain whether you will ever witness these words. But since my cowardice also grants me complete freedom, I will unburden myself even further.

I want to marry you, Leah. Will you grant an old man's folly? I know it seems laughable that you might share the depth of feeling I have toward you. No doubt you see me only as a trusted friend, a cherished confidant.

Receiving Artaxerxes' approval would be a fearsome matter, I know. Granting the marriage of a concubine is something no king has ever done, in my considerable memory. It would require spending not only the accumulated goodwill of a lifetime's service, but receiving G-d's warmest favor besides.

I know to some people, at some times, the very notion would seem beyond contempt. I am an old man, with my years of outward attractiveness largely behind me. So rather than appeal to the lust of the eye or the ravishing of the flesh, let me ponder one more appeal that might sway you.

You have told me that you are a granddaughter of Jehoiakim, of the very line of David. If you would only marry me, a child of our union would represent the juncture of the rabbinic and administrative Exilarch title with the royal pedigree of the Davidic bloodline.

Is this sufficient cause? Is a consideration so practical, so calculated, unworthy of earning a beautiful woman's favor? I certainly hope so, for I would accept any pretext, embrace any goal, in order to have you at my side for the years remaining to me and to feel you in my arms once again, as I comforted you after Artaxerxes' rejection.

Dear G-d, if I cannot muster the courage to show these words to my love, I beg you to impress the ideas within it into her mind. Lead her, dear Lord. Prod her from her narrow grasp on the notion of a throne, of the trappings of power and outward glory, as your only means of working miracles. Let her fall in love with the humble, the familiar, the G-d-fearing.

Would you bring her to me, my Father? I will love you even if you tell me no. In this part of my life, the lacking is far more familiar than the winning. . . .

MASADA NATIONAL
MONUMENT, ISRAEL—LATER THAT DAY

The text message rolled across Hadassah ben Yuda's cell phone display just as her husband began to speak on the windswept summit of Masada, majestically framed by thousand-foot drop-offs and the bleak vastness of Negev's desert.

"Tantalizingly close, but no cigar, my dear," the scrawled words read. "The infrared array worked—I can read the document. Mordecai does indeed love her. But she remains infatuated with the King, for some reason. Need more. Will consult Baghdad rabbi. *A.*"

Sitting behind Jacob on the dais, she winced, fought a crest of emotion fatigue, and hoped the assembled press would attribute it to blinding desert sun. Her husband was right, of course, although she relished the delicious irony of it—it was outrageous to have their fates determined by the outcome of an unrequited love affair so old that its participants had withered into dust over two thousand years ago.

Maybe our actions *do* matter, she told herself wistfully.

But until this crisis was over, she and her husband both faced a hostile, hellish existence. Right before her sat three times the usual press contingent, each just waiting eagerly for the speech's end so they could mercilessly pepper the two of them about what was now being called "The Exilarch Scandal."

Jacob had barely survived his no-confidence vote two nights before, but the narrow victory had seriously eroded the Israeli public's perception of his leadership. Members of his own party were defecting, publicly "outraged" over his failure to disclose a family connection to a Middle East hostage crisis. His government, and therefore his prime minister's title, was not predicted to last very long.

". . . therefore, I hope we can all learn the lessons Masada holds for us today. Namely, that we in Israel do not have to die as our ancestors did in order to make a simple point against aggression. We do not have to sacrifice our lives and those of our loved ones on a mountaintop merely to make ourselves heard. Today, a cell phone connection and a video camera are all that's necessary to flood the world . . ."

A sudden gust of wind blew back his hair, just as a flat *pop* floated over on the wind.

Above their heads, a flapping banner bearing the words *Masada: We Remember* now jerked back and forth with a hole in its vinyl surface, then ripped free, assaulting Jacob's head with violent snaps of its ends.

A wild clamor of panicked voices, then the crowd fell to the ground as one. Shin Beth bodyguards leaped on Jacob, wrestled him once more to his knees. Another tried to tackle Hadassah, but in a wriggling move whose fluidity surprised even her, she shrugged him off and stepped forward.

Something had snapped deep within her. Civility and political niceties had just flown from her mind. Rage united with a wild, soaring elation. She felt a perversely exhilarating wish to see her assassin, to confront him, to avenge her father. As on the night of his death, she heard a faint ringing in her ears and felt utterly disconnected from all that had once mattered to her. Even as the shooting sound had faded on the wind and everyone around her continued to huddle on the floor, she stood and took four steps forward into the wind, her hair whipping about her face and shoulders, her face tingling fiercely, her rage throbbing within her.

On the stony horizon, she saw glimpses of the man—buffeted black hair, twisting shoulders, a silhouette making an agile leap.

"Hey!" she shouted at the top of her lungs, the throb of her voice making her seem as though her feet had left the ground.

She felt a hand graze hers, one of the agents who held her husband clawing away at her. In a perverse instinct, she looked down and stepped away. Two feet away lay the agent's pistol. She reached down, swept up the weapon, held it straight before her, aiming at the spot where her assailant had just disappeared, and pulled the trigger with a reckless abandon. The recoil nearly sheared it from her hand, but the sense of consequence, of dead-level seriousness, enthralled her.

She began to run. Before the bombing she had been a frequent runner and a conditioned athlete—now her limbs roared back into their previous form, flooded by her adrenaline's fury.

There he is—

—leaping from one place of shelter to another.

She fired again and saw a large rock splinter and shear away into the air, not far from her target.

Voices were shouting behind her now, protesting, ordering her back. With new determination she waved them away with her pistol hand.

It was time to sprint. Shouting her rage and abandon, she began to run as fast as the rocky and pitted Masada surface would allow her. The cries only grew louder behind her now, and she was almost glad for the trouble she was causing, the video trail she would soon have to face. It felt wildly free, to jump from rocky bulb to stony fissure, the pistol waving wildly in her grip above her, screaming like a she-wolf at the coward running away.

Soon, she knew, he would reach Masada's edge. She felt as though she would pursue him over its precipice into death itself, if need be.

I'll do it, she told herself through gritted teeth. *I'm going to reach him first, and—*

—a grinning face wheeled crazily before her, gun expertly gripped in front of him. Aimed straight for her.

The vicious beast had ducked and hid. Used her wild sprint against her.

Hadassah saw the man's trigger finger begin to clench, knew her final moment had come.

She heard an explosion, a gunshot.

Nothing happened to her except what took place out in front of her eyes. The terrorist, a small, grimy brown man close enough to make out a woefully short Members Only tan jacket, jerked backward under a bloody cloud.

She looked back. Hariv, her own Shin Beth bodyguard, stood not twenty yards back, a wisp of smoke curling from the gun barrel in his grip.

She faced forward again. The man was still standing, smiling ferociously as a bright red spot spread over the leather vest protecting his chest.

Then, amazingly, he turned and began to run again.

She sprinted forward, guessing the man could not threaten her again.

And then, with astonishing suddenness, the edge was before her. Swaying to halt her momentum, she found herself staring down at five thousand feet of thin desert air and sunshine. Squinting against the light, she looked down.

The terrorist was a thin dot. Still flying. She could see the edges of his jacket ballooning around him.

Then stone outcroppings swallowed him whole.

Behind her, footsteps approached and multiplied. They had caught up with her. *The crazy wife.* She smiled shakily, turned around, dropped the gun and looked for one brave soul's video lens.

Boring into the camera with her eyes, she spoke.

"I have something to say," she said as loudly as she could through panting breaths. "My husband is not responsible for the failure to disclose my family link to the Exilarch. See, you people have it all backward. We were attacked because of a family relation we did not even know existed. I was merely investigating a faint clue when I met Mr. al-Khalid."

At once the grappling crowd stopped in their tracks and fixed its assembled gaze on her.

"That's right. The man who just died here has tried to assassinate me twice. And he was behind my father's murder. He did not deserve the privilege of dying in a historic place where Jews died so heroically."

Her cell phone rang.

She smiled, held up an index finger, then turned the phone away and spoke again.

"It's family. You all will have to wait."

She returned the receiver to her ear and winced. She did not try to cover her words from those nearby.

"Yes, I saw it, Ari. That really stinks. You have any more options?"

She listened, then grimaced, prompting a new round of buzzing camera lenses.

"*Where?*"

IDF COMMAND CENTER, JERUSALEM—THAT EVENING

"Mr. Prime Minister, they're approaching the border. We need your final authorization."

Jacob stepped away from her and swept his eyes across the four cabinet members clustered before him with somber faces and heaving chests.

"Gentlemen? Have I lost my mind?"

The group looked at each other before any of them replied.

"No, sir," replied his Defense Minister cautiously. "It is proportional. It's measured. It serves a vital national security purpose, if not a military one."

He nodded and turned back to Hadassah.

"Honey, Ari asked to go," he said. "I'm not making him. Or any of them. So I don't want to hear any blame if something should happen to him, understood?"

She nodded, dropping her eyes to the floor. It had not been their best day as a couple.

He turned back to the console.

"Authorization granted. Proceed across the Iranian border. But I want egress within another thirty minutes max, understood?"

"Roger!"

Chapter Fifty-three

U.S. ARMY BLACKHAWK,
SKIES OVER IRAN—FIVE MINUTES LATER

It was a cloudy, moonless night, so the Blackhawk rode *nap-of-the-earth*—using its advanced terrain-following radar to maintain a minimal thirty-foot altitude over the desert floor.

Exhausted following a five-hour flight from France, Ari al-Khalid glanced at his watch and bunched his camo-clad shoulders to keep them limber. Two other men, veterans of the Zagros Mountain rescue, stood behind him, motionless. It would be a small squad. He preferred it that way.

The floor pitched hard beneath them; they were banking sharply. City lights tilted ahead. *Hamadan, Iran*—population seven hundred thousand, known as "older than history," swept into view. One of the oldest populated places on earth, Hamadan lay cradled between the Abbassabad Valley and the rugged peak of Mount Alvand.

It was also the famous home of an unremarkable Islamic-shaped domed tower, reputed for centuries to hold the remains of Queen Esther of Persia, also known as Hadassah the Jewess. One Mardocai or Mardkhay, otherwise known to posterity as Mordecai the scribe and Esther's adoptive father, also rested there. In a bit of graveyard humor, Ari chuckled to himself at the irony that Muslims would be guarding the grave of a Jewish icon nearly three millennia after her death. His muted chuckle ratcheted up a notch when his mental image included Mordecai the Exilarch, leader of the Jews in exile, in the scene.

The legends had better be correct, Ari thought to himself grimly. The Rabbi of Baghdad had privately assured him, over satellite phone barely a half day before, that they were. He had further assured him that if there was any chance of securing a final record of what had taken place between Mordecai and a palace concubine named Leah, it would lay with Mordecai himself. In his tomb proper.

It felt wrong somehow not only to be violating hostile airspace but doing so for the purpose of desecrating an ostensibly Jewish archeological site. But then, he had to remind himself, there was a crisis at hand. The Americans flying him here were under instructions to fly him back to Baghdad and conduct no more flights on his behalf, no matter the outcome. The Americans' patience had run out, and their indulgence of Israeli interventionism had nearly run its course. Things were about to blow up, literally and figuratively, if the Exilarch matter did not go away before the next news cycle.

And worse yet, Jewish innocents would be murdered. He had seen the footage of the beautiful little girl with the knife blade against her throat, and her tormentors screaming his name, *his very own name*, as the cause of her impending murder. The very thought of it made his throat go dry and filled him with an anger he could scarcely contain.

They were circling. The Delta Force held up the fingers of one hand. *Five minutes.* He raised up the satellite phone to his ear.

"All right, Jerusalem, we're five minutes out. Is the Chief Rabbi ready to authenticate as soon as I'm back up?"

"Roger, pit viper. Everything is go."

The chopper nosed downward into a valley, forcing him to wedge his elbows and knees against the firewall, and began its dive.

Soon they were near and low enough to see the dome itself. Close enough to see, at a wildly cockeyed angle, the dust plumes and rivers of street clutter being swept away by their rotors.

With a flapping sound, the ropes were away, one knot in his fist, and it was time to jump.

It all unspooled in a blissful whirl of violent motion.

The rope falling between his boots and gloved hands, then hard dirt, then without a pause he was running hard and fast toward the gaping black door of the tower, already kicked in by his companions. He was the man on the spot—not even spared this jump because they needed a translator, an early, onsite authentication—and flashlight beams swirled around the circle of the ornate mausoleum.

He could hardly gain a physical sense of the place, he was moving so fast, breathing so hard. Fingers gripping his arm pulled him over. Light beckoned him downward to a sarcophagus that already had been yanked open. An old coffin of splintered wood, nearly smothered in sheets of disintegrating parchment, shards of old jewelry, Stars of David in wood and plaster . . .

Swiftly, before they might dissolve in thin air, he ripped a large plastic baggie from his chest pocket and began grabbing each piece of parchment one by one. Every sheet. Every word—a mere sentence could save him right now.

He held one up for a quick glance. Ancient Hebrew to be sure, the paper remarkably well-preserved, yet old, surely old enough—the ink degradation consistent with—

"Time to go, sir. Let's analyze on the helo."

"Roger."

Another quick glance to confirm the sarcophagus was empty; he nodded and followed the men out into the night.

A swift wind announced their Blackhawk's return, this time for a hover evacuation. Things were safe. He gripped his baggie tightly and began to run for the deck, flexing his leg muscles for the leap.

And *jump* . . .

Twenty minutes later, he was back over Iraqi airspace and on the phone to Jerusalem, announcing that a promising scan was imminent. As he sat piecing the jigsaw puzzle of parchment together, he could not help but read a few lines . . .

———— ⌇ ————

Benjamin, my dear,

This letter is from your mother. Not the mother you know and love and who takes care of you, but the one who brought you into this world, loved you dearly, and whose life was taken from her before you could form any memories of her.

My name was Leah.

I have written you this letter, which I trust you will find after I am gone, to unburden myself of something I have long held to my bosom. I wish to tell you the truth of someone whose love claimed my heart before yours did.

His name was Mordecai, and yes, he was the Mordecai of great renown across Persia and especially to our own people. The adoptive father of Queen Esther, rescuer of the Jewish race from destruction.

He was a man of justly deserved fame and adulation. But he was also a man capable of great depths of feeling and affection. In the days before I first looked into your eyes, I spent much time with this great man.

You see, in the long months of Megabyzos' failed rebellion, before the general was unsuccessful in his attempt to overthrow the King and found himself pardoned and back at the palace, thanks to the Queen Mother's unpredictable loyalties, I spent my days in hiding, deep in a secret apartment below the Persepolis harem. That is where this strange affection for an older man grew into a love I can hardly explain, I fail to understand, and I refuse to dismiss.

I knew that I loved him long before I realized the nature of my affection, for in the months and years previous I had grown to see him as a protector, a wise and loving palace father. However, during those weeks in hiding, those interminable hours with no one else but Hadassah to speak with, my emotions grew deeper still.

I wish I could tell you the countless small courtesies and signs of thoughtfulness Mordecai showed me during those times. As you can imagine, the conventions of personal privacy and hygiene quickly fall to the wayside in such an environment. Yet never once did he fail to suffer any privation or undergo any effort to spare my dignity.

But then, as anyone in a highly precarious confinement might, I began to grow irrational. One night something gave way inside of me. I entered a period of wild, reckless agitation—thrashing, muttering, threatening with increasing loudness to shout out until someone came to extricate us from that adequate but awful place.

In my irrational fury, I only caught the briefest flashes of how Mordecai did it, yet he somehow reached in and, with only the most fleeting display of his masculine power, caught me. How he did a thing like this with the utmost gentleness remains beyond me, but he did. His fingers closed over my mouth. His knees pressed behind mine and buckled them. I fell backward into his embracing grasp.

I surrendered at once.

Even today, I fail to adequately describe or understand the sensation, for his was such a bewildering blend of control and tenderness. I could hardly move a finger, yet I felt wrapped in a blanket. I felt wrapped in love. And just as quickly, the urge to scream and flail about left me.

How long we stayed like that, I cannot tell. I only remember that ever so gradually, my breathing slowed and my madness quenched itself against the firmness of his hold.

At one point I became aware that his arms around me were no longer necessary. And somehow, I also sensed that he knew this, too.

I pulled my right hand slowly, softly, from his. Then I used it to reach up and carefully peel his fingers from over my mouth.

Then I looked into his eyes.

Only then did I see the tears which had hovered there, trembling just above those he had already shed. I have never seen such a combination of empathy, grief, and overwhelming love in the face of another person. Not even Artaxerxes, for all his beguiling passion that long-ago night, had come even close.

I reached up and traced the closest tear, along its bright path from his eye.

"Was that for me?" I asked in a near-whisper.

"No," he answered, smiling faintly at the twist of his reply. "No, it's not. It's for me."

"Did I cause it?" I asked.

He nodded *yes,* and more tears came into view.

"I'm sorry for acting this way. I'm just not sure I can take any more. . . ."

"Shhh," he interrupted. "That's not why. That's not it—not at all."

"Then how did I cause it?"

He closed his eyes briefly, delicately. He breathed in deeply, then out again.

"I weep because only in your pain can I hold you like this. And I would give my remaining days—"

He stopped. Then a look of determination came over his face, and he leaned over sideways. From the bedding beside us he retrieved a tightly rolled-up parchment. The one he often wrote upon over in a corner when he thought I was sleeping.

Then he began to read to me an astonishing document. It was a love letter, written with no thought of ever being delivered. A statement of affection like none I have ever heard before, or certainly since. A resigned but genuine overflow of love from someone who harbored only the faintest hope of ever seeing it come to life.

Listening to his words, savoring the strong and confident tones of his voice, scrutinizing every twitch of the male pride he was relinquishing to me at great sacrifice, I felt something burst into life within me. In some ways, it was like the birth of something warm and thriving out of nothing. But in other ways, it was merely a transition. A deep shift from one kind of love to another far more delicate and overwhelming.

Strangely, I don't know where Hadassah went during this time. I suppose she made herself unobtrusive in a far corner of the room, forcing herself to feign sleep. Yet I completely forgot she was even there—or anyone else in all of Persia.

Yes, despite his being considerably older than myself, despite his one-time role as a father-figure of sorts toward me, I capitulated to the affection I had for so long denied. I fell in love with Mordecai, sometime between his starting to read and the end of that remarkable narrative.

I felt in awe of this emotion, dazzled by its preciousness and vulnerability. It felt to me like the tiniest of infants, barely hardy enough to survive even the light of day. Yet I cherished it more than life itself.

I peeled myself from his arms, for I wanted to reenter his hold on my own terms, on the terms of this love.

I crouched beside him and placed his hands, one at a time, about my shoulders and waist. Then I moved closer. He peered at me questioningly, almost fearfully.

I smiled and whispered, "Your love has healed me."

I don't know if he understood fully what I meant, but I was not about to explain. I could only pray that he knew how his written adoration, read to me in a trembling voice over the past hours had crept into my deepest heart, had invisibly healed every scar and crevice left by the King's rejection and my own despair.

I allowed my reentry into his arms and the warmth of my kiss to elaborate for me, for I could respond no other way. And yet I believe he understood everything.

Five days later, the hole to our self-imposed prison opened and a rather frightened man descended. He removed his covering robe with a reassuring smile and revealed the garments of a rabbi.

And there, with only Hadassah as our witness, the Jewish wedding ceremony was performed in whispers and motions to mimic the ornaments we lacked. It was most humble, and yet I would venture possibly the most heartfelt and romantic that has ever taken place. We had no scarves, no canopies. But we framed them with our hands, and our smiles.

A dark, locked subterranean lair will strike few people as an idyllic place for a honeymoon, but I will assure you that it proved exactly that. As her dearest gift, Hadassah even left our hiding place with the rabbi, just before our honeymoon began. Where she stole off to, she never said. But she did not return until a week later, glowing with satisfaction.

But there is more than even disclosure of love and romance which drives this letter to you now, my dear Ben. One of them is my learning of a lesson that I wish I had more time to live out. For many months before surrendering to this great love, I struggled with everything within me to maintain my grasp on a highly stubborn notion which had overtaken me. You see, I was convinced, for what seemed like a lifetime, that only through the obvious route of becoming queen, with all its attendant power and privilege, would my life ever gain purpose and lasting impact. It seemed so obvious to me for so long that I could not even picture myself relinquishing the idea. How could any other outcome, I reasoned, offer me a place in history, other than the most powerful throne in the world?

Now I find that while the ultimate answers remain beyond my sight, a far more sure and subtle truth has emerged. That is, that sometimes one finds greater purpose by surrendering what the world values most than from grasping the obvious.

You see, I relinquished that dream when I married Mordecai. In fact, I have sometimes wondered if that was not part of the reason for my decision—to shake myself free, to wrest myself loose from the idea's persistent hold. It was not that alone, I will tell you readily, for I truly loved the man. My man.

This decision turned out to carry a very high price tag, as I'm sure you now know. Not Mordecai's death, although that did come hardly two months after we exchanged our vows. I awoke in his arms one morning to find him still and cold, a faint smile glowing in the light of a sunbeam pouring in from the subterranean apartment's largest light grate.

I would probably frighten you if I tried to describe the wave of grief that fell upon me at that moment. I will only tell you that I felt as though my life had just leaked out of my body, as though everything good about life had just escaped forever. I wept and sobbed as freely, as loudly, as caution allowed.

But yet Mordecai's passing would not prove to be the defining event of this story. It would, however, help bring it about. Mordecai's body was smuggled out that very day in a highly dangerous and intricate rescue mission of sorts. But the word of his death, and its circumstances, began to circulate as a bizarre rumor through the empire's Jewish communities. And this gossip reached the ears of our enemies in the palace.

Exactly one week after the death of my beloved, the locked door of our hiding place was shattered by the boot of an Immortal guard, and Hadassah and I were seized, marched up into the blinding light of midmorning, and paraded before hushed crowds into the royal prison. Esther and I were separated, each of us kept in cells which, despite being far above the norm, were still cruelly spartan compared to our former abode.

Three days after our capture, I heard the sound of many footsteps outside and the creak of the door being opened from outside.

I turned and saw King Artaxerxes standing there, frowning sadly.

"Hello, Leah," he said.

"Your Majesty," I replied and swiftly fell to one knee, like any good Persian. I truly did not know how to respond. I searched inwardly for any of the old emotions, but I could not discern anything of note.

"I came here to tell you," he said in a soft, regretful tone, "that the sentence imposed on you was not my wish. My hands were tied by an item of strict Persian law. You see, a member of the harem, even though she is rejected as Queen, remains bound to the King's palace until explicitly released by royal decree. You were not at liberty to marry Mordecai, I am sorry to say. Had you come to me and cast yourself on my mercy, I would have surely agreed to the request, however strange I might have found it."

"Yes, but I would also have been killed by others within your palace."

"Perhaps. However, the outcome is the same."

"What do you mean?"

"Unfortunately, Leah, the stated penalty for violation of this law is death."

Strangely, the news did not reach the deepest core of my being. My body recoiled, as though I had been struck across the back. But my emotions remained untouched. And even more oddly, it was at that moment that I realized something was profoundly different in the innermost parts of my body.

"Would Your Majesty be willing to grant me pardon?" I was surprised at the absence of fear in my tone.

"Yes, I would. For I have never stopped caring about you, since the night we spent together. The greatest night of my life. However, I cannot. There are laws even the King himself cannot alter."

"Would you, then, grant me one other request?"

"Anything."

"I am with child."

I allowed the words to simply hang in the air between us. My head felt dizzy from just hearing them spoken. I remained otherwise silent, for their implication was too clear to require explanation.

He nodded sadly.

"I will postpone your execution until ten months from today."

"Thank you, Your Majesty. You grant me a great gift."

"It seems a bitter one to me, yet I am glad to give it."

"What about Hadassah and Jesse?"

"I have great compassion for them, you know. For all of you. Despite all the rumors, you have remained faithful to the throne, and loyal subjects of Persia."

"That is true, Your Majesty."

"That is why I have shown all the mercy my discretion affords me. Hadassah, the once-queen and the eunuch Jesse, my chamberlain, will be exiled from the palace forever. They will be banished with nothing but a royal grant of monies with which to provide for themselves."

"Thank you, Artaxerxes," I said, in the intimate tone we had both adopted during the early-morning hours of our last time together.

"It is all I can do. Farewell, my dear Leah."

He stepped forward, kissed me gently on the forehead, then turned and left the cell abruptly.

A numbness gripped me, as though the world had fallen behind a thick veil. And yet I also smiled with the strange happiness of a mother who knows she has saved her child's life, even at the expense of her own.

And so, my dear Ben, this ends—or perhaps begins—the solemn tale that preceded your coming into my life. Which you did precisely seven months later, in a back room of the royal palace, attended by the King's own physician and under armed guard.

Even as I write these words with one hand, I hold you in the other. You are the most beautiful and lovely baby boy I am sure I have ever seen. You are asleep at this moment, yet your tiny eyelids flutter ever so often as though animated by some strange, fitful awareness of what is about to take place.

I have no regrets, my dear Benjamin bar Mordecai, great-great-grandson of Jeconiah, King of Judah and, G-d willing, the next Exilarch. You embody the purpose and peace which G-d granted the last days of my life. I know that He will work great things through you. You will be raised by two wonderful, godly people. Hadassah and Jesse love you as they loved me, and each other. You will have a fascinating existence in the lands outside of Persia and her stifling palace hothouses.

This is a good day. I will be reunited with my beloved Mordecai and be back in his arms by nightfall. That is the most precious anniversary gift I could ever receive, for ironically, we were wed one year ago today.

The soldiers have come for me. Please know that I die happy, fulfilled, having beheld my purpose and cradled it in my arms, and eager to meet my Creator. Be happy, my son, and care for our precious people as your family has been blessed to do.

Your loving mother,
Leah

Chapter Fifty-four

KIRKUK, NORTHERN IRAQ, PROVINCE OF KURDISTAN

D*amineh Shavoz wrinkled* her face into a scowl, leaned on the balls of her hands, and glanced out from the perch she had occupied half of her sixty-eight years: a fabric stall wedged deep in the last row of the Karkuk Bazaar.

During pauses like these, when nobody was trying to haggle her out of her priceless silks and Egyptian cottons, Damineh would grow completely still, narrow her eyes, and read the flow of passersby like an old fisherman gauging a river current. In the decades she had stood there, the old shopkeeper had learned to interpret the tiniest aspects of the day by the pacing of footsteps, voices echoing from vaulted ceilings, even the expressions on the faces streaming past her day after day.

To be clear, she had acquired this skill for a deeper purpose than merely a shopkeeper's amassing of street smarts. Damineh had closely held motives for being wary, and these she harbored deep inside her to fuel an unrelenting, hair-trigger vigilance. Her hidden reasons had paid off. Even for a creature of the bazaar, her instincts were acute. In fact, during the short years since the Americans' coming, she had actually learned to anticipate the arrival of a coalition patrol, even the passage of an armed convoy, full minutes before it could be heard or seen.

And now she sensed one again.

It came as a faint disruption in the flow. A vague disturbance with a source somewhere behind her consciousness. She resented its elusiveness, for it gave her no time to nail down its nature—whether ordinary street punks, a suicide bomber in a bulging vest, or soldiers of some sort, like the Baathist thugs from Hussein's day known to punish the least wayward glance with a truncheon blow across the neck.

Within seconds, the thinning stream of people dried up to a trickle. An eerie quiet fell over the bazaar corridor; less than ten people now occupied her field of view. She tensed her muscles. This had never happened at noontime on a Friday or any other day.

Then the quiet dropped into utter silence. An unnatural lull, like the gap preceding the plunge of the executioner's blade. She wanted to freeze into invisibility, to stop breathing and just disappear.

A helmet peered over the edge of the bazaar's rooftop, flanked by the thin barrel of a rifle. Then another, just ten yards beside it.

Her insides wrenched with fear.

Then she saw him, walking alone toward her along the empty corridor. He was swathed in a typical Arab robe, yet she did not buy it for a moment—she spotted immediately its brand-new creases, its unwashed, just-out-of-the-box sheen, its broad, beige stripes that crudely mimicked, yet did not match, the region's tribal *kaffiyehs*. It was the sort of attempt a big-city intruder would make, not the garb of a bazaar regular.

Then his face: his cheeks were smooth-shaven and his skin glowed with the radiant health of a foreigner spared two decades of sanctions and rationed food. But most telling of all were his eyes, which did not sweep across the goods like those of a shopper, but bore into the faces of the shopkeepers like a man searching intently for a particular individual. *Someone.*

This was some kind of spy, she just knew.

He eventually looked her way and approached the stall with an unerring, purposeful gait. Her pulse launched into a gallop. Two American soldiers stepped into a watchful posture just ten yards behind him, keeping their gaze neutral in an obvious attempt to remain unobtrusive.

Her left hand crept under a square of damask quilting and

gripped her emergency cell phone. Hard. She tried to look around the oncomer and appear casual, but her senses were inflamed, and she feared she might faint. *It can happen that fast*, she had always told her younger relatives, trying to impress on them the precarious nature of their lives—despite the decades-long success of their hiding place. *A soldier swerves toward you. A mob turns your way. A tank cannon clacks past your head, then stops and turns back. And your life is over. . . .*

The man was now standing before her. She tried to avoid meeting his eye by feigning an interest in a fallen stack of swatches beside her right hand. But she could tell he was being deliberate, ducking and leaning forward to catch her gaze.

So she spoke first. It was her way.

"You looking for the finest silks anywhere?" It was her usual opening, and despite her alarm she saw no reason to abandon it.

"Maybe," the man answered in a voice that impressed her with a note of kindness and strength. "It depends on the quality, of course."

"None better, right here." She patted the now-straightened stack at hand.

"It's so hard to find good fabric," he said in a voice that seemed to quaver a bit. An instinct she hardly dared to trust told her that his speech contained deep emotion. He continued. "My father used to tell me about the beautiful fabrics that would abound in these parts, before the war. For instance, there was this company named al-Khalid. Did you ever hear of it?"

At the sound of that name she nodded faintly, felt her knees buckle, and the sides of the store launched into a slow spin. The very world before her began to narrow into a rotating gray cone, and she grabbed at the table in front of her.

"Are you all right?" His voice seemed to come from a hollow distance.

She swallowed hard, took the deepest breath of her life, and struggled to find words.

"What do you want?" she said in a weak hiss.

The man leaned forward.

"I am looking for my aunt. The sister of my father. Her maiden name—her childhood name—was Hana al-Khalid."

It was her turn to lean forward now, gripping the counter so hard that she feared the wood would break. "Whose sister? Whose sister did you speak of?"

"My father, Anek al-Khalid."

She gasped, and her breath now stuttered in short, raspy pants. The man turned back to his escorts and motioned anxiously with his head. The soldiers trotted over to her side just as the man squeezed by the front table and made his way over to her.

He held her up just as she slumped over, and the main thing she noticed with her first close look was that his own eyes shined with tears.

"I'm your nephew, Aunt Hana," he said in a cracking voice. "My father Anek sent me to find you and the family. I apologize for doing it this way. But we had to make sure. Now, I know that I've given you quite a fright. But I'm here to take you away. And I need you to bring me to the others."

Through a storm of panic at her body's rebellion, she tried to process his words. On one hand, it was a wondrous relief to hear him say what he'd said—but what if it wasn't true? A ruse? She felt her head swim even more furiously at the thought. Some man out of nowhere walked up to her at the market stall, and she was supposed to let him turn her life upside down?

"Why should I trust you? Why should I believe you're my nephew?"

He turned to her, and she saw his Adam's apple bob as he started to attempt a reply. The light caught his cheeks, and she saw that they were soaked with tears. Then he reached out and engulfed her in his arms.

That is how she realized her question had been unnecessary. Her next one was hardly audible.

"Is he alive? Is my brother still alive?"

GOLDA MEIR HOSPITAL, JERUSALEM—THE NEXT DAY

Anek al-Khalid awoke at last to the rose glow of dawn through an open window, the pine-scented kiss of a morning breeze and a twittering crescendo of sparrows. His eyes strained to see beyond—

to focus on a framed landscape of olive trees, an Arab minaret, and a distant slice of the Dome of the Mosque beneath a cobalt sky.

He closed his eyes again and struggled back to his last memory before the darkness, the black fog that had held him until this moment. He remembered and winced.

The little girl, with a knife to her throat, her face rendered even more formidable by the magnifying power of high-definition television. Shouts off-screen, then the sound of his name groaned from her small, tense lips.

He turned his head away in dismay, and only then did he notice his son Ari standing in the opposite corner, dressed in his customary black suit. A woman stood beside him, and even in his state he recognized her as well.

Hadassah. The public figure. His private niece.

Closest of all stood a nurse, fiddling with an IV-stand less than two feet from his sore shoulder. Exploiting his first sign of wakefulness, she pulled out an electronic thermometer, switched it on, and thrust it into his left ear.

"I was starting to doubt that I would ever see this city," he groaned softly in Ari's general direction after the instrument was withdrawn.

With a startled glance, they stepped to his bedside. Two pairs of hands reached out to soothe the old man as the fog continued to recede from his brain. Adrenaline kicked in to help lead him out of grogginess—he realized where he was.

A smile fought its way across the wrinkles of his face.

"Jerusalem," he said in a raspy whisper. "At last." Then a perplexed look crossed his face. "But what am I doing here? Who took me here?"

The last wakeful moment he could remember had elapsed in an underground control room in London, the city he had inhabited for half a century. Now . . . *Jerusalem.* A hospital room. And this incredible pain throbbing from a line down his chest . . .

"I know, Father," Ari replied. "But you made it. We succeeded."

"We did? *You* did?" His tone rose in plaintive hope.

"Yes, Father. It is all accomplished."

He gave a sigh so deep and prolonged that it seemed as though he had spent a decade storing it up inside him. "I am so, so very grateful," he said after it was over. "Did you finish the final tasks?"

In response, Ari pivoted cleanly on his heels with a smile of anticipation playing on his face. His father frowned with curiosity, tried to rise up on his bed, and Hadassah reached over to help. From his position leaning against the pillow, he peered under lowered brows at a group in the corner of the room.

Someone stepped aside and a woman was revealed, standing there. She was an old woman, and she wore an oddly stricken expression. She took one doubtful step forward, then a second, more confident. Anek cocked his head with a questioning look. The woman grew closer and extended her arms, her lower lip quivering violently. She reached out with a tender motion, caressed his arm, and seemed to nearly swoon at the touch of his skin.

"Hana?" he asked, peering at her.

She nodded, her lip clenched between remnants of her front teeth, clearly incapable of responding in words.

Decades of deprivation had taken a toll on her, rendering her almost unrecognizable—almost, but not quite. It was she, his sister Hana. Those compelling green eyes gave her away.

He slowly reached out and uttered a pathetic groan that seemed to contain a dozen emotions at once: *surprise, love, relief, regret, grief* . . .

The newcomer let out a faint sob, leaned forward, and took her brother's trembling form into her arms. A long moment passed while the two swayed slightly, their knuckles whitening as they grasped each other's shoulders. Over six decades had passed since they had seen each other, barely out of childhood.

There seemed no reason for their embrace to end. The others merely watched, wearing looks of faint embarrassment at the tears freely crisscrossing their own faces.

At last Hana pulled back, smiled, and touched a drop about to fall from his jaw.

"Papa always said you would find us someday. He'd say, 'Anek made it, I know it. He got through. He'll come for us someday.'"

"I am so sorry it took me such a long time . . ."

"Oh, Ani," she said, her face softening at the sound of the long-lost term of endearment, "I too was sure you had made it, but then the years went on. And then when things got so bad, Father made the decision to go into hiding. He wept for a week. He tried to hide it, but we all saw it in his face. It was a disgrace for him, the failure of every promise he had ever made about your return. We all knew it meant giving up on you—especially Momma. She never accepted it. And their relationship was never the same from that day forward."

"Where did you go?"

"We went to Karkuk, and back into the textiles, only on a modest level. I ran a stall in the bazaar. Gabriel sold wholesale around town."

"Father? Mother?"

"He went in 1954 with the influenza. She died in 1961. In her sleep."

Anek nodded slowly, absorbing the knowledge. He had known that his parents would have passed, for he was a very old man himself—yet hearing the actual facts struck him harder than he had ever imagined it would. Finally, he took a deep breath and looked up to face her again.

"And Gabriel? Sabina?"

"Your brother Gabe was the man of the house for thirty years. But he was picked up by Saddam's men early in the Iran war and accused of espionage. We . . . never saw him again."

"Sabina?"

"Sabina married a butcher, a Muslim, against our wishes. He joined the Baath Party three years later, and within six months he had learned the truth."

"What truth?"

"That she was Jewish, of course. We were in disguise. Our names were all changed."

"What did he do to her?"

Her face fell and everyone in the room saw plainly that the answer was still too raw and unhealed for Hana to put into words.

A hoarse panting noise started up, and the faces all turned to Anek. The nurse rushed over, looked into his face, and grasped his wrist.

"I'm afraid we're going to have to postpone any further reunion for a few hours," the nurse said in a loud, official voice. "Mr. al-Khalid is still very much recovering and needs his rest."

Ari and the others turned to leave, but Anek reached out toward his son.

"No. I cannot bear not knowing. Did you follow my instructions?"

Ari smiled. "All your wishes are now met. It is the right thing, your being here in Jerusalem."

"Tell me."

"It is done, Father. We have proven the bloodline. The Exilarchy is reborn."

"You found our proof?"

"We had to make the shortest invasion in the history of the American military. Or Israeli intelligence, for that matter. Iran."

"You mean their tombs. . . ?"

"Exactly. Although we found it necessary to disturb the dignity of the dead, it was worth it. Miraculously, Esther's tomb in Hamadan still contained Mordecai and Esther's intact remains. It seems an almost constant guardianship by the local authorities spared them the plague of tomb raiders. And in Mordecai's sarcophagus, we found a letter. One obviously written after his death, yet buried with him. Father, you and I feared he had never married, yet this was a letter clearly written by a wife he had wed in his old age. The letter's contents confirmed it all. Mordecai *did* marry Leah, the recipient of the Hadassah scrolls and great-great-granddaughter of King Jeconiah, the last king of Judah before the Captivity. The legends are true. Mordecai did marry into the lineage of David!"

Anek sighed loudly and reached out to shakily grasp his son's hand.

"It gets even better, Father. Leah had addressed this letter to a child she bore shortly after Mordecai's death, a son, Bejamin bar Mordecai, who would have been Jeconiah's grandson three times removed."

Anek's mouth fell open, whether in awe or some internal spasm, it was difficult to tell. Ari leaned in to finish his report.

"The tomb's document's last pages told us the final chapter. When the tide of political favor went against the Jews once again— the same tide that brought about Leah's death—Jesse and Esther were both exiled to the edges of the empire. There they lived at the fringes of Persian society, out of sight but never completely out of mind from the Jewish exile community and seemingly never far from the halls of power. And while Jesse's youthful castration meant that they never were able to live together as husband and wife, they lived together as a loving father and mother to baby Benjamin, just as Mordecai had once taken in Esther as a child.

"Years later, when Emperor Darius the Second realized that the Jews were best managed by one of their own, he recalled the now quite aged Esther to a place of prominence and favor. Jesse and Esther both died shortly after her restoration, but by this time Benjamin was a young man, and the favor on his adoptive mother's life was transferred onto him. He was named Exilarch by acclamation, and led his people to the praise of both Persians and Jews alike. He was indeed father of the great Exilarch bloodline."

The old man closed his thick eyelids slowly. He seemed relieved as much by the end of the long report as by the triumphant outcome of his life's work. "Praise be to YHWH," he whispered to himself. "After all these years. All this time."

Hana spoke after the word had finally faded from the room. "How did you find us? With every passing year I lost a little more hope of ever seeing you again."

"Your father didn't tell you," Ari interjected, "but it seems he left behind a record of your hiding place."

"That's impossible."

"Not considering who he left it with. The Rabbi of Baghdad. He probably meant it as a last-ditch lifeline, a dormant link. It was kept secret in a hiding place below the Battaween Synagogue. Unfortunately, the synagogue was broken into and the record was stolen, along with that of every hidden Jewish family in Iraq."

"So you see, Hana," said Anek, "I didn't succeed at anything. I did nothing. It was my son who is the hero."

"Thank you, Father, but we all know that is not true. You have been working toward this moment for a lifetime."

Anek smiled broadly and closed his eyes, as though he was savoring a sweet scent. "Yes. I have." His voice seemed to weaken audibly with every word he spoke.

Hadassah stepped forward and took his hand. "On behalf of my entire family, I want you to know that I am so sorry for all that took place between us. I ask your forgiveness."

"You are forgiven, although I am not sure you need to be, my dear," Anek said. "The events I spoke of happened many, many years ago."

"Yes, that is true," she answered. "But I am the only one left who can atone for them. I truly regret what my family put you through. I loved my father very much, and I miss him terribly. But he was just a man, capable of making mistakes. I would ask him why he treated you the way he did, if only I could. But he died saving my life. I am proud of being his daughter, although I apologize for his mistakes. And still, I am also proud to name you as my uncle."

Anek said nothing but reached a finely trembling hand up to hers. She took his and held it there, tightly, for a long moment. When she lowered it, the old man's eyes were damp and shining. He was so weak she felt it necessary to physically carry his hand over his midsection and gently lower it there.

The visitors stood, basking in long-overdue healing.

Anek's smile did not waver. The tears quivered there, on the verge of falling from his eyelids onto his cheeks, yet hung suspended from their wrinkled perch.

A long moment passed.

Anek did not move even a hundredth of an inch.

Jacob had been standing quietly in the corner, and he stood still as stone as Hadassah's eyes shifted over to meet his. He acknowledged her, yet did not alter his expression. Even more deliberately, he glanced over at Ari.

Ari had not moved, yet the instant Jacob saw his face, he knew that the man had not missed what was taking place. Just like his father's, Ari's eyes were filled with tears.

They coursed down his cheeks but did not diminish his smile. A smile that precisely matched the satisfied grin permanently gripping the face on the body now lying before him.

A high-pitched tone on the heart monitor replaced the beeping that had long ago faded into the background. The nurse rushed forward, pried open Anek's eyelid, grabbed his wrist with one hand, and punched a wall button with the other.

Her frantic call was hardly even heard by those standing around her, facing the bed in a deep, satisfied silence.

Chapter Fifty-five

BAGHDAD SQUARE—
LATER THAT AFTERNOON

Holding *high a worn* and weathered document in the harsh desert sun's glare, Ari al-Khalid stood before several dozen television cameras and a thick bundle of microphones in the very center of Baghdad.

"I hold in my hand," he shouted into a brisk desert wind, "definitive proof that the blood of David and the lineage of the Exilarch both flow through my veins as a result of my descent from Mordecai of Persia. Also a faxed affidavit from the Rabbi of Jerusalem attesting to the historical veracity of this assertion. That is why, on this day, I hereby declare that I am the new Exilarch, leader of the Jews of the Exile, a line which began in the early days of the Babylonian Diaspora and continued unbroken through Mordecai himself and on until the mid-eighteenth century."

A scattering of light applause and cheers broke out at those words, causing the media to turn as one toward its source. The supporters turned out to be an old man wearing a yarmulke, his elderly wife at his side, braving their Arab spectators to shout hurrahs like front-row fans at a soccer match.

"It is a mantle I wear with a great sense of honor," he continued, "and yet enormous responsibility. I do not grasp it for purposes of personal enrichment or aggrandizement, despite the assertions of some. And I am about to prove it."

He reached to his side and pulled up a third document. "This is a sworn statement, authenticated here in Iraq and just faxed to my attorneys in London. With the full support of my father, World Court plaintiff Anek al-Khalid, in the matter of Iraqi reparations for the holdings stolen from Jewish citizens over the last century, I declare a jubilee. As proscribed by Scripture, a jubilee is an amnesty of all debts owed. I only ask that the government of Iraq set aside an amount equal to our claims for the express purpose of caring for the child victims of this war. That means feeding orphans, treating the injured and maimed, paying caregivers and foster parents, and subsidizing the rebuilding of schools and the awarding of higher educations. To any and all, whatever national heritage or creed."

At these words, more applause broke out. This time it was the Iraqi watchers joining in—members of the nation's newly installed government.

PRIME MINISTER'S RESIDENCE—REHAVIA, JERUSALEM

Hand in hand, Jacob and Hadassah ben Yuda sat on their bed, watching the news unfold on the television above their dresser.

"I am not doing this as a public-relations gesture," they heard Ari continue onscreen, "and I am certainly not doing it to grant the demands of child-murdering terrorists."

At those words Jacob turned to Hadassah and nodded his relief. That was an essential declaration for his government's cooperation in unfolding events.

"I am doing this in the spirit of a heritage that persisted for centuries in this country—and this is the message I most urgently want to convey. If you study the history of Iraq and the former Persia, you'll discover that for long periods of time, there reigned a warm and mutually beneficial relationship between its people and the Jewish leadership. The Muslim population was glad for its Jewish brothers' large holdings and their managing of national institutions for the welfare of the entire nation. Economies thrived, in fact the glory days of Islam flowered while Muslim and Jew coexisted in this warm and tolerant manner. The large and powerful Iraqi Jewish population was happy to be considered a vital partner in the flourishing of the nation. In fact, there are records of years when every Thursday, the Caliph of Baghdad would entertain the Exilarch like a visiting prince. He would embrace his Jewish counterpart as he would his own brother, grant him a place of honor in his very own home, and the two would feast together while the sun remained in the sky. This tolerance and friendship continued for decades until a time when the next merchant of hate came along to try to shatter the peace.

"My message to the people of Iraq is this—those who tell you that hatred of your Jewish neighbors is an essential part of Islamic faith ignore their own history, and are grievously mistaken. Remember, one does not even need to be Zionist to be an observant Jew. Your neighbors can be both Jewish and strong nationalist Iraqis. So let us resume the old tradition of friendly coexistence. Let us put some reality behind the rhetoric of peaceful religion. Let us work together for a strong and proud Iraq. And let this forgiveness of billions of dollars contribute to the welfare of Iraq's children as a first step toward that end."

On the television screen, Ari bowed his head briefly, grabbed up his papers, and stepped away.

On his bed, the Prime Minister of Israel began to clap slowly, emphatically. His wife joined in.

He turned to her and kissed her lingeringly. "Congratulations, honey. You and Ari did it. You made the right choice. I was wrong. My fears were for nothing."

Hadassah gave him a rueful pat on the cheek, acknowledging his confession, as his cell phone began to ring and he turned away. She, however, returned her gaze to the television news.

"What an amazing turn of events," the commentator said to a talking head sitting beside him. "Did anyone anticipate that the Exilarch would step forward, only to relinquish the proceeds of his legal battle?"

"No, but keep in mind that he has not yet done what he pledged he would do," said the other with a thick accent—a man Hadassah knew as a strong Sunni supporter. "I would caution anyone against drawing favorable inferences from this announcement. After all, we do know that this man is a cousin of the First Lady of Israel, so we know . . ."

CLICK . . .

CENTRAL BAGHDAD—KHUDRA
NEIGHBORHOOD—FIVE MINUTES LATER

A thick silence was shattered by the thunderous voice of an American officer on his bullhorn.

"Holders of Hadassah al-Feliz! You have been shown that Mr. al-Khalid's speech was real, genuine. You asked for the cessation of all Exilarch legal claims against the Iraqi people, and exactly that has taken place. Now comes your turn to honor your pledges."

A dark shape appeared at the window. Its glass shattered loudly and a blast of machine-gun fire split the late afternoon air.

The terrorists' defiant response.

At that very second, a black-clad commando leaped over the roof-top's lip, dangled over the void from a thick rope, and from an upside-down position, fired his pistol straight into the terrorist's chest. Less than a half second later he was jerked back up just before a crane-mounted, remote-controlled machine gun swiveled into place and began to strafe the room one inch above the windowsill level—a full two feet above where infrared scopes had shown young Hadassah al-Feliz lying prone in a corner. A calculated, but necessarily swift risk.

She blinked through the smoke and once again began to cry, a sound covered by the loud noise.

Strange—her three tormentors were gone.

BEN GURION AIRPORT

The wide-eyed little girl passing through the Ben Gurion customs booth in the arms of an American soldier did not react at the sight of the woman striding toward her—for the simple reason that she did not recognize her face. Nor did she recognize the pale, blue-starred flags overhead, marking the country whose soil she had just entered.

What she did recognize, however, and recoiled violently against in the process, were the *Uzi* machine guns gripped by the large men on either side of the lady. Hadassah al-Feliz's eyes widened suddenly—she let out a plaintive whimper, then a piercing scream, and began to climb up the GI's shoulder to escape the shining black spitters of death.

The approaching woman with the shining eyes turned frantically to every side and realized at once the source of Hadassah's distress. She motioned swiftly to the men beside her and the terrifying reminders were immediately hidden away, out of sight. Then she stepped forward, just as the same soldier who had saved the tiny Hadassah lowered her little body to the floor.

To comfort her, the same commando squad which had rescued her was allowed to convey her to Israel.

As the lady grew near and crouched low, peering into her face, little Hadassah could see that she was very pretty, and that she was crying freely. Though it did not seem the same sort of weeping that had overtaken her mother and sister before their deaths, Hadassah's fear remained. The lady was actually smiling through her tears.

"Hello, Hadassah," the First Lady spoke, in surprisingly fluent Arabic. "I'm sorry you saw things that frightened you."

The little girl had no response. She merely bit her lip and glanced back at the men standing now a few paces behind the lady.

"They're not going to hurt you in any way," the woman soothed. "In fact, they're here to make sure no one ever hurts you again. Just like the brave soldier who brought you here. Do you understand?"

Hadassah thought about the word *brave* and decided that she did understand. She nodded slowly.

"I'm so glad to meet you, Hadassah," the lady said, and she extended her hand. Hadassah reached out and softly gripped it. The two clasped and shook tenderly. "I want to tell you my name, and you're going to laugh when you hear it. It's a very pretty name, I'd bet you'll agree."

"What is it?"

"My name is Hadassah, too."

The little girl cocked her head back in surprise. "My mommy told me there was no other Hadassah anywhere in the land."

"She was right. But you just came to *another* land. It's a place where lots of Hadassahs can live together and be *protected* by the men with the big guns instead of hurt by them."

"Men with big guns and knives hurt my family," Hadassah said, the fear flickering back into her face.

"I know they did, honey," the lady said, and more tears reappeared in her eyes. "I'm so sorry. So sorry."

Then the woman did something the little Hadassah had not expected. Something that would change the little girl's life forever. She reached out slowly, caressed her hand, and held out her arms. Without even meaning to, the tiny form stepped between them.

They stood that way for a very long time, not even worrying about all the people crowded around them now, both of them crying for inner reasons that must have been different and in some ways very much the same.

At some point the lady Hadassah drew back and took a deep breath.

"Hadassah, I have a house that's very big and very safe and very empty without any little girls to keep me company. I haven't been able to have any children out of my tummy, but I love kids very much. And I have a husband who couldn't be here today, but who very much wants to meet you. We'd love it if you'd come live with us for a while. Does that sound like something you'd want to do?"

Without answering, the little girl stared hard into this new woman's face. *Hadassah*. Another—who would have thought it? The lady was nice, and she definitely cared about her. And Hadassah cared about being safe.

That was important.

Little Hadassah nodded yes, and reached her finger toward the lady's eyes, pointing.

The woman peered into the little girl's eyes and her own grew wide with surprise.

"O dear G-d in heaven," Hadassah ben Yuda said, laughing and crying at the same time. "I can't believe this. And you saw it, too, didn't you, sweetheart? Mine are the same as yours. Just like yours— isn't that wonderful?"

The little girl nodded and smiled.

And that was enough.

JERUSALEM POST—FRONT PAGE,
BELOW THE FOLD—THREE WEEKS LATER

The Office of the Prime Minister of Israel has confirmed that Mr. ben Yuda and his wife Hadassah have in fact arranged to adopt the nearly four-year-old Jewish Iraqi girl who appeared on television screens worldwide during the hostage drama that brutally claimed the lives of her family.

The girl, whose name is also Hadassah, was taken into Israeli custody when Mossad operatives, working together with American Delta Force commandos, stormed the Baghdad apartment where she had been held at knifepoint before a global television audience. She was rescued and taken from there to the Baghdad Airport, where in an unusual transfer of custody, she was flown directly to Ben Gurion Airport in Israel and met at the terminal by First Lady Mrs. Hadassah ben Yuda in person.

"I dedicate my life now to soothing this precious one's wounds and giving her a warm new family where fear no longer reigns," she told reporters. "The fact that she bears my name is only the smallest, although amusing, of coincidences. So is the completely unexpected discovery we made upon our first face-to-face meeting. That she shares with me an infrequent family genetic anomaly: a pair of green eyes."

Our reporter concurs—a double set of the most unusually luminous green eyes.

Tommy Tenney often prays for the peace of Jerusalem and Baghdad.
While writing fiction, one can wish for reality.

◆

Though this is a work of fiction, many aspects are based on fact
and chronological possibility. For more clues on how to decode historical fact from fiction in this novel, please visit:
www.hadassahcovenant.com.